BLACK CONCEIT

BLACK CONCEIT

by
John Leonard

doubleday & company, inc.
garden city · new york
1973

ISBN: 0-385-06776-3
Library of Congress Catalog Card Number 73–80732
Copyright © 1973 by JOHN LEONARD
All Rights Reserved
PRINTED IN THE UNITED STATES OF AMERICA
First Edition

Acknowledgment is gratefully made
for permission to reprint the following:
From *Ariel* by Sylvia Plath:
(Three lines) "Morning Song"—Copyright © 1961 by Ted Hughes
(Seven lines) "Lesbos"—Copyright © 1966 by Ted Hughes
(Nine lines) "Death & Co."—Copyright © 1963 by Ted Hughes
(Five lines) "Kindness"—Copyright © 1963 by Ted Hughes
(Three lines) "Lady Lazarus"—Copyright © 1963 by Ted Hughes
By permission of Harper & Row, Publishers, Inc.

FOR ROB AND BENY

With gratitude for their counsel and their daughter

"Faith!" shouted Goodman Brown, in a voice of agony
and desperation; and the echoes of the forest mocked
him, crying, "Faith! Faith!" as if bewildered
wretches were seeking her all through the wilderness.

NATHANIEL HAWTHORNE

For, in certain moods, no man can weigh this world
without throwing in something, somehow like Original
Sin, to strike the uneven balance . . . this black
conceit pervades him through and through.

HERMAN MELVILLE

BLACK CONCEIT

Prologue

MORNING. MAINTAIN ANONYMITY. It should be easier in a cold and empty house, a house colder because it is emptier. There are no other bodies in this house, pumping and pulsing. Amazing how just a baby can heat up a room. Fierce little furnace. Maybe heat waves come out of the hole in the top of the head, where the sections of skull haven't grown together yet.

A beating of wings in the apple trees: rain. He slides carefully out from between the sheets, from under the quilt to which an apologetic dragon has been stitched. He sits, embracing himself. Next to the alarm clock are his horn-rimmed glasses. Is it a mistake to put on the glasses? They will confer a harmless raccoon look. He hangs them on his ears. It *is* a mistake. You convince yourself that horn-rimmed glasses do not improve the insight, but that which focuses is inadvertently insightful. He stands, and must with bare feet on a cold pine floor transport himself to the bathroom, where the light comes on green at its edges, manifesting sink and diaper pail. The diaper pail is blue and plastic. Beware . . . there is a piece of definition in the diaper pail. Ignore it. Ignore, too, the image in the medicine cabinet mirror. No: unnecessary. Even with the glasses, the image is sleep-bloated, unrecognizable.

Question: Why postslumber puffiness? Answer: Probably edema, water in the face tissues. It will drain off now that you are standing. What a comfort to be so well informed.

Tools are at hand: to scrape him recognizable, pat him on his head, tamp down the waltzing dream shapes, make ready the teeth to bite into the day. Grin. Many gleaming tools for paring and defining. Scales to ascertain one's weight, and register it. A hook on which to hang one's pajamas. He stands naked, except for his glasses, not exactly a god of the young morning, but flabless. Affectingly austere. He tests his spring. However, there is no one on whom to pounce.

Out, now, of the bathroom. Stabbing one's way through sleeves, lowering one's feet into boots, winding the stem of one's pocket watch, acquiring purpose as the water drains out of the face tissues. The stairs, and no smell of coffee coming up as he goes down. Possibly he is wrong: an empty house hates anonymity. Unmoored, the denied self thrashes, seeks clues into which it might sink its fangs and cling. For example, the puppet with the glass eyes and rag dress, lying in the hall; the wagonload of Lincoln logs; the green, empty cider bottles in the wooden crate . . . Definitions!

A bent cigarette is extracted from a crumpled package in the pocket of the creaseless trousers. He takes pleasure in the fact that the cigarette is bent. He was once the sort of person who purchased filter cigarettes in crush-proof boxes. Now, like Rinsler, no condoms on his death. Feeble dawn light through broad living room windows. Fog in the valley like porridge in a bowl. And, clamped to the outside window frame, a thermometer, like the bathroom scale, weighing the weather. Thirty-two: not so cold. The match makes a little bulb of light, first blue, then orange, like an idea occurring to a cartoon character. Stop it, please . . . unlike. On the coffee table is last night's glass. Revise: rather, *a* glass. And *a* plate, with *a* fork on it. For objects: articles. For being: pronouns. Articles and pronouns are thin, are knives. Is there something about the angle of the fork on the plate? The stopped clock of last night's dinner. There you go again, writing press releases.

In the kitchen he resists those manipulations necessary to achieve a decent cup of coffee. He opts for Instant, which is more anonymous. Still, the water wants boiling. How to occupy the time it takes? By filling in the yellow cards? No. The will is induced by these manipulations. They are sneaky. He stands and waits, marveling, for patience is elastic, anonymity is flexible. The water boils. The coffee is fit for a Turk.

From the hall closet remove the green fatigue jacket. An embarrassment of pockets. Extra pack of cigarettes, matches, stub of red crayon, yellow cards, paper punch. Forgetting? Yes: the bottle of sweet white wine confiscated from Butterfly in the orchard yesterday. Brown paper bag. Stuff bag into pocket. Bulges. Now—open the door. Look out. See the rain. Step out. Close the door. And start to trudge.

Kenneth Mackenzie Coffin gets wet because he isn't wearing a hat. John F. Kennedy never wore a hat.

The road through the woods to the farm is mud; the rain writes a water-slang on it. Weak light through birches shifts, making puddle-glyphs to say: too early—6:30!—and because it rains, you might have stayed in bed. But why? He is acquiring purpose.

Exit out of birches onto farm. Right is the pit, where rain-slick tractors crouch. Beyond it are mud-colored storage sheds. Left is the pickers' camp. One building is a log cabin, once used for keeping chickens, now containing a kitchen and the rented television set. The other is a stone house that slopes below ground, where they used to smoke ham, then to batch maple syrup. The camp lavatory is subterranean.

He is no longer anonymous, for they may be watching him. From the barracks. Leroy clanging on the bottom of a pan with a long-handled spoon. Mummified bodies rising from their bunks, black silk-turbanned heads, empty beer cans standing on the long table that will be used for breakfast, the sound of the TV set. No, they will not see him from the cabin. The black turbanned heads will sit on low benches and flick cigarette ashes into the empty beer cans while watching children's programs on TV, waiting for bacon. But in the stone house, from the narrow lavatory stall, they might look up through the high, small, smoked-blue windows and see . . . his feet. His rubber-soled boots. Full of purpose now, he pauses and lights another cigarette. He intends to communicate an impression: it may be early, and it may be raining, but Honky is here with his weed, fatigue jacket, and crayon stub. Without a hat. Obviously, he *cares*.

Moving on. Past the storage sheds, to the packing room. The

3

dogs make noises. They are obliged to. It is the purpose of farm dogs to make noises. But they are without conviction. He has intimidated them with his superior purposefulness. Skulk, and you are suspect. Rightly. He opens the packing room door, to suffer a cloud of apple ripeness. Schiller used to write beside a bowl of rotten apples; the smell of their decaying was a stimulant, to Schiller. Goethe found the smell depressing. On visiting Schiller, Goethe almost fainted. You see: well informed. And relentlessly informative. How is it that someone so well informed is picking apples, after such an expensive education? But then, his father had also received an expensive education, and his father made rope for a living. Now: Mention Schiller to Rinsler and Rinsler would pull on an earlobe and out of his mouth would pop the aesthetic state. Walk into a grave of apples.

There's Dennison, fiddling with the tubes, valves, and petcocks that control the atmosphere in the storage sheds.

"Mornin', Ken."

"Good morning. Fine picking weather."

"Shore is."

"All day?"

"Don Kent says, should commence to clear up 'bout midday."

"Hope so."

Pause. "New hat?"

"Ayuuhp," says Dennison; "wife made me buy it. Said the old un was diseased."

Dennison's eyes have always been bluer than his cap; now his cap is bluer than his eyes, and Dennison is diminished. Ken says, "Well," and looks around for inspiration: at hand carts, picking buckets, half-filled bushel boxes. Presently they will discuss the mice, for every night the mice creep into the packing room and gnaw on the apples, and every morning the men discuss it. Why do the mice gnaw only on hand-picked apples? Why do drops not tempt them? To such early morning word rites Ken customarily brings a sort of dogged pluckiness, but that has been injured by Dennison's new hat.

Murdock comes to the rescue. Wool cap with ear flaps; hands thrust deep into mackinaw pockets; wet cigar. Murdock says: "Nice mornin', ain't it?" Dennison and Ken agree. Murdock, however, thinks it over, feels compelled to add: "Apples still want pickin'."

"Shore they do," says Dennison.

4

"Don Kent says mebbe midday," says Murdock.

Ken offers cigarettes, which are refused. "Any trouble last night?"

"Ah," says Murdock, "they was stompin' about. Broke them a window." He shakes his head. They all shake their heads, disturbing the odor-order of the apple grave, manifesting Short, as the green-edged light in the bathroom had manifested the diaper pail.

Thwacking his boots: "Wet 'nuff for ya?"

"Misty," says Dennison.

"Misty," agrees Murdock.

"Misty," repeats Short, listening to the rain come down harder. Short says, "Twenty-nine at my house."

They deliberate. "Thirty-two at mine," says Murdock.

"And mine," says Ken.

"Twenty-nine at mine," repeats Short. It is always colder at Short's house. Short is made proud by the indomitability of his thermometer.

Murdock says, "Short, that Ford tractor wants some work."

"Allus does," says Short, grinning. "Ah . . . boys act up agin last night?"

"Broke them a window," says Murdock. They shake their heads. Murdock adds, "Freeze their ass."

"Damn the rain," says Ken. They stare at him. He repents. "I mean, I just feel I'm going to spend the rest of my life in the West Orchard." And fall off a ladder into the irrigation ditch, and lie there under a mound of Macs, while helicopters sweep over him, spraying stop-drop.

Short says, "Them . . . those boys bitchin' 'bout the ditch?"

The mice gorged on apple pulp are watching Short from the rafters, through the walls. The mice are aware of what Short would say were not Ken a Coffin cousin of the Mackenzies, were not Coffin a child of the Enlightenment. Short avoids darkie, smoke, and nigger the way the mice avoid the drops.

"Yes," says Ken. "They're bitching about it. It's a lousy place to pick. And they're scared of snakes."

"Water snakes," says Dennison. "Harmless when you see un, and you don't hardly see un. Haven't seen un for two, three years. Used to put 'em in girls' desks at school."

"They've been picking oranges in Florida," says the child of the Enlightenment. "The snakes aren't harmless in Florida."

Murdock says, "They'da been out of that ditch a week ago if all of 'em 'ud come out to work in the mornin'."

Short says, "They booze all night, and try to get a piece of James T. Worthy's wife. They don't feel like workin' in the mornin'."

The child of the Enlightenment waves his arms around, making retreating motions. "Well. I guess I'll go home and stare at the rain till it stops."

"Should commence to clear up 'bout midday," says Murdock.

Dennison says, "Ayuuhp." They all nod. Ken backs out of the packing room. They are still nodding, up and down, a dream of slyly polite Orientals, nodding you to death.

There, in the rain, on the trailer, sits Albany Jackson.

"Good morning, Albany."

"Mornins, Kenneth."

"I heard you had some more trouble last night."

Albany Jackson nods: absurdly well fitted for the elements, in yellow nylon storm suit, hood and cape; yet assuming his usual fakir crouch, long legs spread to make a box, long arms hooked at the elbows under the knees, around, then over the shinbones to a bowl of hands. His head beneath the hood comes up surprised from out of the box. His face is also long, made longer by its goatee. His teeth leap out. He is very self-contained, Albany Jackson, and seeks by his fakir crouch to improve on that self-containment.

"Them mens is wild, Kenneth. Them Florida mens is crazy." Jackson comes from Virginia. "They was all likkered up and went wif dice. Peace, he took forty dollar from Bird-man."

"Peace was gambling? I told Peace—"

"Shua. You loaned Peace the moneys. I know that, Kenneth. I knowed it right off."

"I also asked Peace not to tell anybody about it. He promised he wouldn't."

"Peace, he piss promises. I told him . . . Kenneth give you them moneys 'cause you got took on the board. Stay 'way from the dice wif Kenneth's moneys. But Peace, he a young man and kinda wild hisself. He been drinkin'. Don't tell me, he says. And he win forty dollar from Bird-man. And ol' Bird-man, he pull a knife. He say he gonna carve up Peace. Peace say he gonna kill Bird-man wif his bare hands. So them Florida mens, they pull knives. Kenneth,

6

you knows Peace . . . Peace a big fighter wif his mouf. Them Florida mens gets Peace in the corner. And Otis DeKalb was sleepin'. I woke up Otis. You know, Otis got him a gun."

"I know he's got a gun. Goddammit, Albany, somebody's going to get killed if Otis keeps hauling out that gun."

"Now, Kenneth, Otis he use that gun to stop the fights. Otis he don't like fightin' and hollerin' and cuttin' up. If he don't have no gun, ol' Peace woulda been messed up bad. Them mens say they gonna carve a map of Florida on Peace. Otis he don't jive. That gun is his mouf. Loud. Otis allus movin' while he looks like standin' still. So Otis he got Peace out of camp."

"How did the window get broken?"

Jackson grins. "Well, ol' Peace he still makin' wif the mouf when they go out the door. And he still got this can of beer. And he throwed the can of beer at ol' Bird-man. Bird-man he duck down and the can go right out the window. Pow. You know."

"If Otis got Peace out of the camp, where did they sleep?"

"In your car," says Jackson, crafty now, looking at the rain fall into his hands.

"In my car?"

"Well, you said if the mens get wild up there, we ought come and sleep at your house to avoid the troubles. But your house was dark. Figured you was in bed. So Otis he made Peace sleep in the back of your car. Otis up front." He looks up from under his hood. He is selecting an extenuation. "Them Florida mens they took the forty dollar when Peace was gone."

"Not just that, right, Albany? Also the money I loaned him?"

Jackson nods. And Coffin could roll right now into the cabin and see the paper money make a flower on the table, see the money-flower spread and spin beneath the TV bubble eye. See Foy stretch and pop the elbow hollows; and Cindy Lou, clicking like a camera, polish her knees; and Bird-man cut out pockets from the air; and Butterfly, goatish grin, white stubble on sunken cheeks and cloven chin, blue paratroop beret, from under which curl matted tails of hair, wheezing; and Otis DeKalb—"Hey, hey, Dudley Do-Right, no-talk Dude-man DeeKalb, mouf for grits, hey?"—silently consuming breakfast. And nobody would know how the window got powed. What crap game? What gun? Who's Peace? And Coffin would roll not, knowing what he knew only

7

because Jackson told him; Jackson telling him only because Jackson knew he would not use what was told.

Jackson lets him think about it. Then: "Kenneth, we was wonderin'. You know your car? Well, if me and Richmond and Otis gonna stay up here, like you say, we need warm clothes. We was wonderin' if we could borra your car this evenins, to go down and buy us some warm clothes."

"It isn't my car, Albany. The station wagon belongs to the family that owns the farm."

"Richmond, he got him a license to drive cars."

"It's not my car. And it's not very reliable, either."

"We wanted some warm clothes."

Annoyed, Ken fishes for a cigarette, offering one to Jackson. Jackson, a Von Clauswitz in the strategy of credit, declines: refuse the small favor while the larger one is still on the table.

Murdock emerges from the packing room. Jackson nods at him, but Murdock has nodded himself out. Jackson says, "No pickin' this mornin', I bet."

"Not likely," says Murdock, giving nothing away.

Jackson says, "Even them Canadiands ain't out this mornin'."

The nine Nova Scotians usually come out of their hut behind the storage shed before seven o'clock, stamping their feet, blowing air, flexing like Olympic athletes anxious for the start of their event. Jackson and Company do not approve of New Hampshire in the fall, and have to be coaxed from the stove and the television set.

Murdock says, "One of them Canadians picked a hundred sixty bushel yesterday."

"Not in the West Orchard," says Ken.

But Jackson is bland. He is teaching guile to a Yankee. Yankee guile is as overrated as Jacqueline Kennedy. Jackson says, "Anythin' you needs done?"

The direct approach catches Murdock with his guile around his knees. Carefully, he thinks about it. "Well, there's some bins what want movin' in the Hall Orchard. Need to put 'em under the Cortland trees, for whenever and *if* ever you get out of the West Orchard."

Jackson grins. "Them Canadiands is already pickin' Cortlands, ain't they? Big mother-apples, Cortlands. I might be able to pick a hunnerd sixty bushel of Cortland apples. May-be." Then he strikes: "All right. I'll move them bins."

Yankee guile strikes back: "Takes two."

Jackson still grins: "I'll get Otis DeKalb to help me."

Murdock would prefer to award such work to the older pickers, the already-beaten and too-obliging Stepin No-Sass Fetchits. Jackson knows this; knows, too, that were Leroy consulted at the camp, the work would go to a couple of Alabama bullyboys. Jackson is here, has waited in the rain, to assume his priority. And succeeds, Murdock being trapped. Murdock attempts a nod and retires to chew his cigar.

Jackson lets Ken admire him, exerting silent pressure. Behind them, Murdock starts the fork lift. Ken admits defeat. "When do you need the car, Albany?"

"Well, if me and Otis is workin', it 'ud be past five anyways."

The little red fork lift trundles toward them, Murdock at the controls. Murdock wheels it smartly in front of a tower of bushel boxes, ignoring Ken and Jackson. With each turn, Murdock reduces the radius of his circle, the area of the humiliation of Yankee guile.

"All right," says Ken. "But Albany—stores in town close at six. That's not much time to buy clothes."

Click goes Jackson's face. Full stop; no more funny business today. As might have been expected: tentative advance of pincer questions on an exposed and duplicitous nerve . . . *click*. Eyes die, face shuts like a cash register, mask hung over it reading Out to Lunch. Inside his silent switched-offness, discontinued for a duration of his own choosing, Jackson waits.

"All right, Albany."

Jackson resumes speed. "Thank you, Kenneth." Dignified in triumph, he now accepts the proffered cigarette. "We 'preciates it." And, drawing on the cigarette, he rises, and in his nylon storm suit goes shuffling off toward camp. *Shuffling*. A man of many mocks.

Murdock, pronging the bushel boxes, dips his head at Ken, having reacquired at the controls his nod-knack. Which way? Back to the cottage and the typewriter? No. His glasses are rain-fogged; he removes and wipes them, then stands indecisive, rather liking the blurred edges of the things he sees. To put the glasses back on is to fog them up again. They go instead into a flap pocket of the fatigue jacket, next to the yellow cards. He walks, somewhat less purposeful, toward Thomas Hill.

Alone on a dirt road in an expiring overextension of orchard, passing then into a stately picketing, a tall double row of sugar maples, crowns conferring above his head, uppermost branches clasped, forming a tunnel to Thomas Hill, an avenue of yellow leaves onto which he ventures, feeling small. Left, lawn falls almost lavalike, a smooth obsidian, to flower beds and scrub oak. Right, yew hedge. Beyond, a pasture where sheep munch, then the valley, then the town. Rain and weak eyes achieve a mist-mixing of colors and contours. Have you seen *Last Year at Marienbad?* Perhaps.

The avenue of sugar maples opens on an asphalt prospect. The driveway loops around an old white elm, forty feet of buttressed shaft discharging a bell of branches. Gigantic, diseased, cement-packed, it stood here more than two centuries ago when the first American Mackenzie, glowering, raised his cabin of rude pine logs and ploughed his forty-acre parcel. Who said that farming was an Oedipal reduplication—incest with Mother Earth, the plough a symbolic phallus? Not a Mackenzie. Certainly not Rinsler. At the foot of the elm, a garden. Set in the garden, facing the elm, a cornerstone on which is chipped MACKENZIE BRIDGE, rescued from rubble by some zealot when the bridge was torn down three decades ago. There are as many Mackenzie bridges as there are Mackenzie books of sermons, because in the nineteenth century there was a Mackenzie engineer for every Mackenzie clergyman, as though the physical and spiritual worlds, being in equal need of repair, had been assigned like farm chores to alternate sons. This, however, had been the first bridge, and the only one so lacking in ambition as to be satisfied with spanning the Contoocook. No raging torrent, the Contoocook.

But over this bridge Mackenzies on horseback had galloped to Wyke Regis for Sunday services and town meetings. Over it, with shoes in their hands, traipsed sons of Mackenzies, sprung from farm drudgery, to Exeter for an education into conic sections and moral fiber. Over it, from Wyke Regis, Mad Tom Mackenzie fled, fearing a reclamation of New England by Old England in 1812. To direct the manufacture of Thomas Hill.

Here we are.

Thomas Hill had been something of a monstrosity in the

nineteenth century, much painted and sketched: reedy towers at either end of irresolute spurs, overdeveloped breastwork, a Corinthian kiosk on top, from which Mad Tom eyed the valley for approaching Redcoats. The twentieth-century Mackenzies did it over properly square. Now it is huge, but sensible, except for the kiosk from which succeeding Mackenzie patriarchs have eyed the valley to measure the malign intent of the weather and reported it to Boston and Don Kent. But for the kiosk, it might even be turned upside down, and still look likely.

Mounting the porch steps, addressing the door and lock, Ken Coffin disavows old styles of stealth. Once he had been unable to call it Horrors, a prerogative vouchsafed only the more authentic Mackenzie children. But now he has a key.

Which admits him into a hallway of oriental carpets, iron storks, umbrella stands. A penitents' bench, a grandfather clock, a bust of probity. Mirrors counterfacing portraits, multiplying the consanguine gloom, that smogged countenance of Puritans who pushed through their four-score, and now will hang forevermore, shades in frames, trying to intimidate the vestibule. Watching Coffin, as though he were malarial. He is not intimidated. He entertains a powerful brief against them: You can sniff out sloth, all right; but you forgot about evil.

Stamina. Virility. Fortitude. Each landing on the stairs seems a demonstration of the Mackenzie virtues as they have been scrubbed down for secular service. The water buckets of the fire brigade, the Indian tapestries, the black shaggy buffalo heads brought back from the Great Plains by Uncle Horace . . . Marcy hadn't been convinced, not by the buffalo heads, and certainly not by the portraits: that flush of port about the jowls; the paunch of too many meals enjoyed. Marcy thought they should hang up portraits of buffalo, and stuff the severed heads of patriarchs. That would have been convincing.

He is tempted by the library, for it contains brown-bound meditations suggesting soul-struggles seriously in doubt, epistemological quibbles not easily subsumed under, nor postponed for, mere process—the business of getting on with the quotidian. But he keeps climbing. The fourth floor is a honeycomb of cramped cubicles, the tool room, the trunk room, small cells for visiting children, meteorological instruments, blueprints, broken furniture. At the end of the corridor, though, is one large chamber,

11

intended as both den of games and family museum. A billiard table, pocketless, shrouded, and a rack of cue sticks. A settee confronting a television set. Ping-Pong. A Franklin stove. Glass-doored cabinets full of memorabilia: a Sioux peace pipe of polished stone, a mechanical flower, a collection of birds' eggs, marble games, jigsaw puzzles, report cards, grammar books, and the tennis racket that won the Dublin summer singles tournament.

Windows open on three sides. One bank looks down past the old elm and the avenue of sugar maples, to the orchards and the farm. Another oversees the brick walk, the herb garden, and, beyond, woods which in warmer weather are thick with laurel and blueberry bushes. The third bank of windows is reserved for contemplating Mount Monadnock. Above the windows, along the seam of wall and ceiling, pictorial panels depict in sequence the 105-day Siege of Londonderry, from the locking of the gates to relief by the British fleet. Between the windows, on the walls, are photographs and framed certificates. Mackenzies at affairs of state; Mackenzies commissioned for diplomatic missions; teachers and doctors and seminarians; on ponies, or playing croquet, or at weddings. The Old Man, Wallace Mackenzie, and his three sons scowling round a table at a contract about to go down during the last bridge game they ever played together. Letters from the presidents of nations and railroads. Snapshots of Harvard reunions.

And one particular photograph. A young woman standing on a lawn. She wears country tweeds: a long jacket with padded shoulders, a long skirt with mid-calf hemline. Pumps and a wide-brimmed hat. Under the hat, her hair would be cut pageboy style, though that is obscured. Most of her face is obscured, too. But it was a thin face, like the slender, narrow-hipped body of the girl, with large dark eyes, a straight nose, a bow-lipped but unlipsticked mouth. Scribbled across the upper left-hand corner of the photograph is "Hannah—1936."

Well, Mother.

He sticks kindling into the Franklin stove and ignites it. Then he rolls back the shroud on the billiard table, removes three balls from their box, selects and chalks a cue. Stamina, he says, attempting the tricky sort of bank shot he has always missed. And misses now. Fortitude. Three cushions, too much English. Virility . . . He thinks of Marcy, gaunt, wet-haired, death-white among pillow mounds, a disemboweled bird . . . This is insufficient. It is not—*complicated* enough. He crosses the room and flicks on the television set. A man is answering phone calls. He switches channels. A woman with a ferocious grin leads three-year-olds in dispirited song. Switches again. Captain Kangaroo, enduring his hour of humiliation at the hands of bunny-rabbit, Mr. Moose, Mr. Greenjeans. What would Foy and Worthy and Butterfly and Bird-man most likely be watching at the camp? Deciding on Captain Kangaroo, he leaves the screen absorbed in that man's benign bafflement; removes his fatigue jacket; opens Butterfly's bottle of sweet white wine; sets it in the middle of the billiard table; and proceeds to bank shots around it. The besieged look down from their Londonderry panels disapproving. After each shot, he hoists the bottle, toasts Captain Kangaroo, grins at the besieged, and swigs. I can drink anything but tequila. Thirteen apprentice boys seize the key to the city, to Thomas Hill, and shut the gate against the Irish Catholic hordes. There should have been a Mackenzie among those boys, but the only recorded Mackenzie had contented himself with taking notes and writing a historical pamphlet: A *Narrative of the Siege of Londonderry: or, the Late Memorable Transactions of that City, Faithfully Represented to Rectifie the Mistakes, and supply the Omissions, of Mr. Walker's Account.* Rev. John Mackenzie, London, 1690. Down comes the portcullis. The walls are weed-grown, the drawbridges have been neglected, the parapets are badly made, there is no moat before the gate, but still the cry is: No Surrender. Mr. Greenjeans is experimenting with the mandible of some frightened quasi-rodent. It is not hot enough. At camp it will be ninety degrees around the stove. It has probably never been ninety degrees in any room at Thomas Hill. He puts more wood into the Franklin stove.

MACAULAY OBSERVES: "The defenses were weak, provisions were scanty, and an incensed tyrant and a great army were at the gates. But within was that which has often in desperate extremities revived the fallen fortunes of nations. Betrayed, deserted, disorganized, unprovided with resources, begirt with enemies, the noble city was no easy conquest."

Rose of Londonderry, a privately printed, pseudonymous, black historical romance which has been attributed to Mad Tom, took a different view: "There were no maypoles in the city, no music, dancing, games, sports, holidays. No fun. Cohabitation with the Irish and adultery with anyone were capital crimes. But oh yes! There was our Rose, Rose the cinder-maker; dainty-footed, impudent, quick-witted Rose, full nether-lipped, outmouthed, blubcheeked, and bedimpled Rose! No maypole, but Rose was game; no music, but she hummed; no holiday, but she was sport. And the maypoles came to Rose!"

Captain Kangaroo is trying to feed a slice of apple to the quasi-rodent. The quasi-rodent will have none of it. The Earl of Tyrconnel, on learning of Londonderry's defiance, burns his wig in a fit of pique.

MACAULAY: "The number of men capable of bearing arms within the walls was seven thousand, and the whole world could not have furnished seven thousand men better qualified to meet the terrible emergency with clear judgment, dauntless vigor, and stubborn patience. They were all zealous Protestants and the Protestantism of the majority was tinged with Puritanism." Fortitude! But what about the women?

MAD TOM: "A singular Rose, whom the years did wilt. But many would remember, were they pressed—a brace of Bishops, a deputy mayor, a majority of the Corporation—her tresses in their disarray, stays asunder, the neat silk leg and pair of holland thighs."

Captain Kangaroo is pelted by Ping-Pong balls. The heat conspires with the wine.

MACAULAY: "Preaching and praying occupied a large part of every day, eighteen clergymen of the established church and seven or eight nonconformist ministers were within the walls. They all exerted themselves indefatigably to rouse and sustain the spirits of the people."

MAD TOM: "Her years were her flower, and she was skilled in the arts of gallantry. They brought her gloves, and fans, and lewd garters, and shoes trimmed with ribbons and rosettes, neckerchiefs and collars and petticoats. She was a buxom bona-roba, but singular, too singular, our Rose . . ."

Bunny-rabbit tricks Captain Kangaroo out of a clutch of carrots. The Captain appeals for justice. Mr. Moose hustles products. Ken Coffin knocks over the wine bottle but is quick enough to set it upright before much has spilled on the green felt. Lundy escapes the city, disguised as a soldier, bearing a load of match.

MACAULAY: "On the nineteenth of June, General Baron de

Rosen arrived at the headquarters of the besieging army. . . . His fury rose to a strange pitch. He, an old soldier, a marshal of France, trained in the school of the greatest generals, accustomed after many years to scientific war, to be baffled by a mob of country gentlemen, farmers, and shopkeepers. . . . In his rage he ordered a shell to be flung into the town with a letter containing a horrible menace. He would, he said, gather into one body all the Protestants who had remained at their homes between Charlemont and the sea, old men, women, children, many of them near in blood and affection to the defendants of Londonderry. . . . The multitude thus brought together should be driven under the walls of Londonderry and should there be starved to death in the sight of their countrymen, their friends, their kinsmen."

MAD TOM: "For Rose grew fat in her garret above the millinery shop on Bishop Street . . . fat on gossip and sour beer and quart bottles of brandy, a vast bulk, a mighty hulk, consoling herself with drink and that evil-smelling pipe of licorice clouds. No more the quarter yard of velvet, the four yards of bastard scarlet cloth for Rose, nor all her panther graces, the barmaid's bold and merry bawdy. As much put petticoats upon a whale! Poor Rose, her unreadiness no longer a delight."

It is still not complicated enough. He stations at the four corners of the billiard table ashtrays, lights up, and, in his circuit, adorns each tray with flicks of droppings. Sweat makes the cue stick slippery in his hands. Two worms mime along to a song about the sea. Bombs fired into the churchyard raise the dead from their graves, toss about bodies.

MACAULAY: "Dogs, fattened on the blood of the slain, who lay unburied about the town, were luxuries which few could afford to purchase. The price of a whelp's paw was five shillings and sixpence. . . . Such were the extremities of distress that the rats who came to feast in the hideous dens where the unburied corpses were, were eagerly hunted and greedily devoured. . . . The whole city was poisoned by the stench exhaled from the bodies of the dead and the half dead. . . . Even in that extremity, the general cry was 'No Surrender,' and there were not wanting voices which, in low tones, added, 'First the horses and hides, then the prisoners and then each other.' It was afterward related half in jest yet not without a horrible mixture of earnest that a corpulent citizen whose bulk presented a strange contrast to the skeletons which surrounded him, thought it expedient to conceal himself from the numerous eyes that followed him with cannibal looks whenever he appeared."

He smokes to keep his hands from scratching his face. Although he does, admittedly, take pleasure in the idea of his smoking, seeing himself, his palms cupped about a match, forks of shadow on his face, exhaling, thoughtful, turning, full of purpose, perhaps a predatory look behind the horn-rimmed glasses. Governor Baker and the apprentice boys throw the last loaf of bread to the enemy.

MAD TOM: "They've come again to me, thought Rose, clutching her smock, her spirits soaring. They have not forgotten that I am fun. Thus coyly she received the dark delegation, among them, regrettably, established and nonconformist ministers, hard-eyed, and not coming unto Rose on a mission of delight. Nor gallant, but with a flash of cold steel and the glint of a pike. Had she not once entertained the treacherous Lundy himself? Oh, Rose was too fat! The Siege was in its fourth month, and even the ministers were hungry. Poor Rose was to rouse and sustain the spirits of some of the people. Poor Rose went down under the rain of stout-shafted scythe-blades."

The grandfather clock makes fun of Captain Kangaroo. He remembers the smell of French cigarettes. They left a carton of them with the concierge: a care package containing, as well, a bottle of champagne and a map of the Métro system and a *Le Figaro* key fob and an invitation to a reception at the offices of Time-Life International. He compared stained fingertips with Marcy, over onion soup as thick as stew; their great greed seemed at the time hilarious.

MACAULAY: "Five generations have since passed away, and still the wall of Londonderry is to the Protestants of Ulster what the trophy of the Marathon was to the Athenians. The anniversary of the day on which the gates were closed, and the anniversary of the day on which the siege was raised, have down to our time been celebrated by salutes, processions, banquets, and sermons. It is impossible not to respect the sentiment which indicates itself by these tokens. It is a sentiment which belongs to the higher and purer part of human nature and which adds not a little to the strength of states. A people which takes no pride in the noble achievements of remote ancestors will never achieve anything worthy to be remembered with pride by remote descendants."

MAD TOM: "Rose, she added not a little to their strength. Rose, the men of Ulster do you honor. No fowl upon the plate can e'er compare with the dainty little foot of Rose. A part of you will always be with us!"

There is, at the pond, a Mackenzie family picnic every summer on the weekend closest to August 1, marking the relief of the Siege, where, in a puddle of light among pine trees, three-inch steaks are charred on an open fire, stone fences drunk, acquaintances renewed: with, to be sure, a self-consciousness deemed ironical. But the men wear jackets, and the women skirts, fashioned from Scots tartan; and a toast is raised to Ulster; and the beef bleeds into paper plates; and . . . Marcy, when she still found the Mackenzies charming, had called it "a gathering of hobbits."

Captain Kangaroo is signing off. "Remember, do what your mommy asks you to, and try to make her happy."

Captain, I am commencing to identify with you. Ayuuhp.

He opens the windows. The rain has not yet signed off. I would have done what my mommy asked me to, Captain. Really, I would. He looks up, expecting a deluge of derisive Ping-Pong balls. Back goes the cue stick into its rack and the billiard balls into their box. The shroud is replaced and the fire is extinguished. Down again, then, from the Vatican of the Mackenzies, descending through street stalls of generational detritus, his mood the color of their tartan. Locking the door, pausing on the porch, telling the elm that it hadn't worked, it wasn't complicated enough.

Whatever happened to my greed?

He takes the short route to his mailbox, across the pasture, avoiding the farm and the camp. In the box is a bulletin from the New Hampshire Apple Growers' Association, a solicitation from Resist, a postcard from Australia—Bates is trying to prove that the extermination of the aborigines was a Chartist plot—and the latest issue of *I. F. Stone's Weekly*.

Butterfly, the men of Ulcer salute you for your taste in wine.

Clutching these messages, he plods up the dirt road to his house, to find, waiting for him, like something cardboard crumpling in the rain, drab, slack, strange, abiding, inevitable (why?):

Rinsler.

Is it possible to ignore Rinsler, to pretend he is the rain?

"How did you get here?"

"By bus from Boston," says Rinsler.

"And from town?"

"I walked."

"Can the revolution get along without you?"

"I'm tired, Ken. I need a place to think."

But surely Rinsler has always been tired. Around the tribal drum of the mimeograph machine, under heroic posters of Che; or whispering on the WATS line to a project in East St. Louis; or conferring the night away with communards in a liberated college building; or bringing his "I" to an Indian reservation, in search of a "we" as spurious as body counts. Carpetbagger of the millennium, toad with ember eye at the traffic jam of money, psychology, power, he has from the beginning been burned out. The ash on his lapel is brain-cinder.

"Come inside. I'll make coffee." Letting Rinsler follow, not wanting to regard again and brood about the distinctive Rinsler waddle, the displaced center of gravity that tries to pitch him portside, headlong: what Marcy called the clubfoot of his integrity. Leaving Rinsler the living room, while Coffin in the kitchen drips. And adds to the coffee tray a bottle of Bacardi, to wash away the taste of Butterfly's sweet white wine, sour black whine, Butterfly himself.

In the valley the fog frays at its edges; maybe, like a ball of cotton, it can only absorb so much water before disintegrating. Rinsler isn't looking at the valley. His back to it, he slumps in a straight-back chair, staring into a box of hands where a cigarette is burning. He has, naturally, selected the only uncomfortable chair in the room. Odd: more than his waddle renders Rinsler asymmetric. A purposeful misshapenness, one ear grafted higher than the other on the head; one eye deeper in its cavity, nearer the cinders; off-center nose, shoulders freeze-dried in a shrug; tie askew; pants creases at cross-purposes, twisting to avoid the knees. Well, not so odd, really: Rinsler is truly, physically, a man of the Left.

The man of the Left interrogates the Bacardi bottle. A rum business, midmorning snorts. But what's Rinsler's business? He isn't ready to say. Nor will he comment on the rum. An enigma. He is fond of explaining that he has no time for enigmas. Finally:

"Why did you quit on me, Ken, just when we needed you the most?"

"Why are you tired, Rinsler, just when the revolution needs you most? Renegadism?"

"You know me better than that."

"Wrong. The state will wither away, and I still won't know you."

"How long are we going to play games, Ken?"

"What makes you think I run a motel for tired thinkers?"

"You told me once that I'd be welcome here."

"Yes. Do you remember the time I wanted a peace fair on the lawns of Thomas Hill? But you felt it would be too far away from the TV cameras."

Rinsler sighs, and shifts. Through the window, behind him now, an apple tree seems to have grown out of his head, like antlers. "We've gotten off on the wrong foot."

"When your foot is in your mouth, you might as well eat it. Rouses and sustains."

"All this hostility. That's one of the things I'm tired of." He uses his cigarette as a pencil, writing graffiti in smoke on a wall between them. "Shall I amuse you? Then listen. Just for a moment. No remarks. I wrote a pamphlet on draft resistance. I gave it to the steno pool. The steno pool refused to type it. They told me they thought it was a poor pamphlet, confused, unconvincing, gracelessly expressed. I explained to them that I had been a draft counselor on and off for ten years, had written a number of pamphlets, and that it was my job to write the pamphlets and their job to type them, not to be literary critics. That was a tactical error on my part. They caucused. They prepared an angry memorandum. The memorandum pointed out that the stenographers were, after all, volunteers, not office lackeys. They were, moreover, well-educated volunteers, Radcliffe graduates. The Movement claimed to be a true community of equals, but men did all the political work and women did all the typing, and the spirit of community had been hopelessly compromised by bureaucratic elitism and male chauvinism and Rinsler's leadership trip. Not only would they refuse to type pamphlets of which they disapproved, but they demanded greater representation on the planning committee. Rinsler could type his own pamphlets if he so desired." A full smile, now; his cigarette has burned down to the knuckles; ash in the coffee cup. "Of course, I can't type. Nor cook, sew, swim, dance, carry a tune, nurse a child, play bridge, or watch football on television. *Speckled Egg* published the stenographers' memorandum. Sapphics Anonymous picketed the institute—making a kind of pavane out of the practice of karate chopping. I had to do three different drafts of my pamphlet before the steno pool consented to type it. Ken, do you suppose I'm too old for participatory democracy?"

"I am giggling, Rinsler."

"Not for long. Your wife led the revolting stenographers. Marcy is a liberated woman."

"Good for Marcy. How many times have you told this story?"

"Of course, if you hadn't run off to New Hampshire, you would have written the pamphlet, and it would not have been gracelessly expressed."

Ken is beginning to like him again. "You didn't come all this way to sulk about your prose style."

"No. I haven't time for that much vanity." In the deep cavity, a pattern is discerned. "I keep losing people to drugs or jail or the army or New Hampshire. Every meeting turns into an argument about ecology as a cop-out or a debate on the proper attitude to take toward the Red Guards. The Red Guards! The Catholic Left moons about all day long bearing witness. The Panthers and the Freaks hate each other. People are talking about bombs."

"Machismo rubbish. A violence trip. You promised me that we were better than that. What happened?"

"Play it on your sitar," says Rinsler, impatient. "We learned something about the country we live in, that's what happened. What were we supposed to do? Throw flowers at helicopters? The only thing wrong with violence is that they've got more of it than we do. I've got to think it out. But it still boils down to whether you're one of the cowboys or one of the Indians. We're the Indians."

"Media apaches! The Molotov cocktail hour!"

"If," says Rinsler, "you can't petition the government for redress of grievances, who else is there to petition except the media?" He tugs his earlobe: watch out now, here it comes, the high hard one. "Shall I amuse you some more? A parlay. You'll remember that I was subpoenaed." Ignoring Ken's nod. "Of course you'll remember. The House of Representatives wanted to know just how I went about plotting insurrection, whether I was on the payroll of Castro or Albania, if I approved of arson, sniping, interracial sex, buggery, and the First and Fourth Amendments. Well, now, last week my testimony was released. I have my avid readers. One is an assistant district attorney for Suffolk County. He has sought, and he has received, an indictment. I'm to be tried, Ken, for conspiring to aid and abet the resisting of the draft. What wasn't good enough for the stenographers was more than all right for Suffolk County. That's amusing, isn't it?"

"No." But it does in some way dignify their activities, even their bickering. Just as, when Marcy discovered their home telephone was tapped, they felt important. Someone cared; therefore, they weren't merely ridiculous. Rinsler is owed something: either an apology or congratulations. "Have you jumped bail?"

Rinsler shakes his head, and then from his asymmetry throws the usual curve. "And you? Just what do you think you are going to accomplish up here?"

"Oh. Well. Would you believe I'm trying to find my head?"

"Certainly not."

"That I am bearing witness?"

"Self-aggrandizement."

Kenneth Mackenzie Coffin grins. "That I have a dream? Of black ice hockey players?"

Rinsler lunges for the Bacardi bottle.

One

RINSLER WAS A PRACTICED LISTENER, although one began to wonder after months of talking to him whether he wasn't at the same time riding a private toboggan slide, a blurred, lashed face leaning into a white curve, plunging toward rent strikes, coffeehouses, bond money, welfare clients, nuances of the Inauthentic. Whether his motion wasn't away from one's words, even as his eyes intersected at an angle somewhere near one's neck. . . .

He liked it that way, because he did not consider himself to be a complicated person, and yet there were advantages in being perceived as complicated. He was merely thorough, with the usual component of aggressive impulses and bad feelings. He hoarded his energy, like a saint. Saints were ordinary people, with an excess of discipline. He was waiting for, conspiring at, a situation appropriate to his energies, a confusion congenial to a new category of ordinariness, a reallocation of impulses. It was important to keep the fact of his ordinariness hidden from those who depended on him. Otherwise they would imagine themselves less splendid.

When Rinsler bothered to think about the *kind* of mind he had, he was prepared to believe that it was much like his workroom, in the lighthouse, with the sheets of Homosote suspended from the ceiling. He had pinned his materials—telephone numbers, newspaper clippings, projections, flow charts—to the sheets of Homosote. He was in the process of converting from Homosote sheets to IBM cards. He had twenty trays of IBM cards, liberated from the sociologists at the institute. Each tray contained hundreds of cards. On each card he would record a connection, an insight, such as the number of retired military officers who became executives in the aerospace industry, or the relationship between capitalism and anality. Eventually, all the cards would be cross-referenced, by means of notching them according to category along their edges in the numbered slots obligingly provided by IBM. If Rinsler then wanted to find out what he knew or had heard about a given subject, he would only have to insert a long needle into a tray of cards, and lift. The connections, having been notched, would fall out, rain down. The needle would not hold them. He would have converted his workroom into an information-retrieval system, like his mind, without having to depend on his memory. He didn't have time to do a lot of random remembering. Every time he did so, this graduate student of the apocalypse became angry.

It was possible, for instance, to become angry while remembering last night, in the lighthouse. Overt ordinariness was definitely a mistake. He had invited Marcy to the lighthouse on the pretense of discussing why her husband had deserted them both. It was advantageous in conversations with Marcy to descant on art, language, sensibility. She was a graduate student of herself. Rinsler obliged:

Would individual genius and passion still express themselves in the solidarity of a socialist society? (What I experience in the privacy of my emotional closet guarantees that there will always be closets.)

Did it matter what a writer used to focus his or her talent—the Greek idea of tragedy, the Christian idea of eternal salvation, the Marxist idea that consciousness was determined by being? (Beatrice must have resented it when she grew up and found out Dante had only used her for a poem.)

Do those literary experiments that screw up our verbal world and our linguistic perceptions delineate the social struggle at any discrete moment, and does such screwing-up clarify or activate the social passions that historically parallel it? (Revolution was a turning of the screw. Marcy was one of the objects of a revolution.)

Boring, but advantageous. At least she listened.

Rinsler suggested that literature attacks the established language of the moment; is a process in which language is the medium of whatever new consciousness slouches toward us. (Me!)

Marcy hooted: Artaud, Brecht, the Surrealists tried to smash the bourgeoisie by alarming its sensibility. Fat chance. Thin thinking.

Rinsler pointed out that reflective, autonomous language has an organic and suprahistorical relation with things as they are, *and* as they should be: the counterweight and energizer of everyday speech. (Not *all* passions were social, nor all relations suprahistorical. One's counterweight should be energized.)

Marcy shook her head. Rinsler felt bad. These tribal propitiations taxed his ordinariness, hunched as he was around the eye of her sex, into which he wished to stick his fingers. Language was foreplay. Sixties chitchat had been elaborated unto systems and categories as pregnant with ennui as the quibbles of Dark Age monks. Illuminate *me*, not my manuscripts. The reallocation of a Marcy . . .

He explained what he hoped to achieve with his IBM cards. He asked her to suggest a topic. She suggested *Moby Dick*. With his needle he skewered irrelevancies. What was pertinent lay in the tray, a meat loaf: Melville's bourgeois psychodrama; character as the cult of the hero; a stereotypical class fantasy of the power figure with all the longed-for potency and oppressive doubts of those with enough leisure to read novels; false symbols of domination; Ahab as entrepreneur cum zealot, outraged Boy Scout, pimply with bad faith, Babbit redux; whale oil poured on troubled waters. (He did not read novels, but he had heard about them: nineteenth-century moral tracts, living bras for soured milk. Nipples were opinions.)

She asked: Do you have our names on cards? Ken's and mine? Do you needle us?

He lied, saying no. This is important: Coffin's card was notched, in the same slot as Rinsler had notched a card for his own brother. Rinsler's brother had also been ordinary, but he had sought ecstasy and revelation where Rinsler knew they could not be found, and was stranded on a moon of the mind, among the many moons that move on wobbly orbits through yellow rooms in sanitaria, somehow out of phase with a suspected magic, causing tides of bad vibrations, giggling at the disrelation between what is seen (beauty) and what is experienced (terror). To be only approximate to oneself was a condition Rinsler abhorred. And a mystery he refused. There were always consequences. Either Marcy or Coffin would have to face those consequences. Rinsler's brother was a hostage, because he had refused to wait for, conspire at, the situation in which energy is released. Action would then be an anodyne. He also serves who only sprawls and rapes. Waiting around for a purgative of the nervous system is cowardly, not to mention counterproductive.

She was not to be moved. A trophy already retired. Property by right of prior possession.

He told her about his brother. You score off your intimacies, understanding them without succumbing to them. This was a parenthesis that connived at a change of direction. Repenting of someone else's sins, I need to commit—to invent—my own.

She said that he talked about his brother the way Ken Coffin talked about his mother. Analogical horseshit! Hostages! Disappointing, because Rinsler's anecdotes were used primarily as flirtations, as proofs of sensitivity. He could not tell her that her husband was a substitute for his brother. Not now, because she had refused the flirtation. And yet that had been Rinsler's intention from the beginning, decided upon at their first meeting in the offices of *Scope*'s Boston bureau, in Coffin's crypt with the gray desk, the white three-quarter partitions, the frosted pane, the crumpled drafts of last week's lies. Decided upon because Coffin's features were so regular, as sincere as a slice of bread, a perfect replacement for the long-distance runner who had gotten lost somewhere in his own synpatic cleft. Among the several ways to depolarize yourself, ideology was safer than acid. Speed killed; the synthesis gaveth life. To be used, certainly, this sincere Coffin with his straight typewriter and his candlelike fingers, lighting the way with words. But perhaps to be cherished as well. My own radical, raised him from a pup, taught him to bark at every internal contradiction. When he tangled with the porcupine of bad faith, I was there, to pull quills from his muzzle with my precise (my dialectical) tweezers. Everybody wanted to be an American, even Rinsler, who read the backs of cereal boxes and had once owned a Lone Ranger atomic bomb ring, the first on his block. Talk about your cult of the hero! Coffin, naturally, had been occupied when Rinsler arrived, playing at journalism the way he played at squash, perfunctorily. But Rinsler had waited him out, waited out the telephone, the research girls on roller skates trundling down the corridor with manila folders pressed to their breasts like shields, the rain biting the window. Had waited, like a bundle of old clothes in that vault of lies, that hospital for injured myths, until he could say: "I wanted to tell you about some of the things we're doing in the South. There's a story there." Had wondered whether there wasn't some factory where they pressed Americans the way they pressed buttons and keys. . . .

Since he hadn't been able to tell Marcy about the substitution, he could not tell her about the Lone Ranger atomic bomb ring. She would have made fun of him. He hadn't time to be made fun of. Waiting, too, in the lighthouse, hoping that the wine and grass would befuddle her, probably even knowing that they wouldn't, making his move with a lack of conviction so profound that he actually, momentarily, disliked himself. A hand on the leg.

As she was leaving, Marcy had said: "Stereotypical ass fantasy. It isn't Moby's dick you're thinking about at all."

Random remembering was bad for the bile duct. He listened. He was furious.

Two

THE MARCYPIAL WOKE UP THAT MORNING AT SEVEN, with a headache, having slept in a box. Hannah was making little barking sounds, tuning up for a scream. The Marcypial lay on her back and asked questions: Am I wearing pajamas or a nightgown? Pajamas. Is Stephen moving around downstairs? Yes. Does he have the TV set on? No. Is it raining? Too much light leaking through the blinds; it is not raining. Am I lonely? I am lonely. Organisms can't live alone. Fish have schools; birds have flocks; bees have hives; ants have hills; graduate students have seminars; even the albatross gives up every once in a while, to breed or to inflict itself on luckless mariners.

She sat up and attempted to touch fingers to toes without bending knees. The Marcypial, for all her Singleness of Purpose, is less alone than many other organisms. With her remarkable capacity for borrowing and adapting the specialized systems of lower life-forms, she has also bought herself a crowd of company. One of the penalties of being complex is that everything is more complicated.

All right, Hannah: cool it. She stood, sought slippers, stretched. Like the snail and the aphid, the Marcypial must operate in an environment. There are organisms on which she feeds, such as undergraduates in Professor Boynton's course on the Sclerosis of Modernism. And organisms—parasites and predators—that feed on her, such as husbands, and children, and Rinslers. But the hermaphroditic snail and the parthenogenetic aphid can at least be alone while engaged in perpetuating their species. The reproductive system of the Marcypial is, alas, less elegant. And more crowded. Sometimes.

And she had slept badly because he wasn't there to weigh down the other side of the bed. Although she sometimes slept just as badly when he was there, because he slept so well. Sleep struck him down like an ax. Coming, Hannah, coming! In order to maintain relations with her teeming environment, the Marcypial must change when the environment changes. This is known as Behavior, or Irritability, the capacity to respond to stimuli. The Marcypial is characterized by hyperirritability. The only known cure is a long book by Thomas Mann, *Joseph in Egypt*, perhaps, or *The Black Swan*.

Stephen must have heard her getting up. He climbed the stairs, calling off names. He had named each of the steps for a classmate at nursery school. "Ricky," he cried. *Thump*. "Lydia." *Thump*. "Peter . . . Sean . . . Sally . . . Pamela." *Thump, thump, thump, thump*. Pause: on the other side of the door, planning strategy.

Successful response to environmental change—that is, *survival* —requires the development of an Irritability Co-ordinating Mechanism, or Nervousness, which detects change, conducts that information to the brain, integrates it, and initiates a response.

She opened the door. "Good morning, Mother," said Stephen. "I'm hungry and thirsty."

The study of Marcypial behavior becomes, necessarily, an analysis of the potentialities of her Irritability Co-ordinating Mechanism. How does it control the release of energy? The contractions of muscles? The secretions of glands? The politic suppression of such autonomic functions as the Tactless Organ (or Marcypial Death-Wish)?

"Hannah, I'm coming, for God's sake!"

"God is great," said Stephen. "God is good. We thank him for our daily food." Smirking. His nursery school's lunchtime larder blessing, which he knew annoyed her mightily. She reached out, thumbed his ear. "Ouch!" he said. Hannah was now screaming. She stopped screaming the instant Marcy opened the door. Obviously not a mortal wound. Hannah sat up in her crib with her blanket over her head like a mantilla. She thrust out one arm, wiggled her fingers, and grinned, showing all six teeth. "Good morning to *you*, White Fang." White Fang had wet through her Pampers, sleeper, and sheet.

"Mother," said Stephen, "I'm hungry and thirsty."

Hannah bird-trilled all the way down the stairs. "Pamela," said Stephen behind them. "Sally. Sean. Lydia. Peter. Ricky. Mark. Butterfly!"

"Butterfly?"

"The funny man on the farm."

"Yes." Hannah tried to grasp the cord on the bathroom light. Marcy gave her three tries, then intervened. How were African children initiated into cause and effect, without light switches, toilet flushes, water faucets? Did they have to get mauled by a lion? She turned on the bath, threw the sleeper in, ripped apart the Pamper package, dropped the contents into the toilet. The bathroom bowl, as the vidcots say.

"Hannah smells," said Stephen.

"You would, too, if you slept half the night in a bag of strained carrots and reconstituted chicken. Wouldn't you?"

"Would I?"

"You would." Cotton pad; baby oil; new diaper. What happened to the safety pins? Hannah clutched the safety pins. Go ahead: get tetanus. Blouse, jumper, booties. Into the living room, into the playpen, we go. Hannah agonized. "Tell it to Yogi Bear." Hannah tuned up the volume on her agony.

According to Sylvia Plath:

> . . . *And now you try*
> *Your handful of notes;*
> *The clear vowels rise like balloons.*

Like balloons? Like wounded Zeppelins, like harpooned whales. What did Sylvia Plath know?

"Hannah's crying, Mother."

"Yes, Stephen, but she must learn to defer her gratifications."

She returned to the bathroom. Stephen followed. "Now, will you please excuse me?"

"Why? What did you do?"

"Ho, ho, hum. Don't be cute. I mean, will you leave? I want to use the bathroom. Go stick out your tongue at Hannah." Marcy closed the door.

On the other side, Stephen complained: "You never let me close the door when I use the bathroom."

"I would," she said, "if you stuck to business, and didn't spend all your time flushing hairpins down the toilet and eating the toothpaste."

Stuck to business? Once on the potty, a king on a throne, Stephen had peered between his legs at his modest extrude and cried out: "Look, Mommy, *pennies!*" Marcy had been Norman O. Browned-off. Ablutions. She weighed 113 pounds. When you stopped nursing, all the weight went out of your breasts, which was unfair. Still too much stomach. She put on black tights, a guaranteed authentic Bulgarian peasant skirt, and one of her husband's French-cuffed dress shirts. Her husband hated cuff links. Lipstick is Out this Season. How would you describe your eyes, Mrs. Coffin? Mischievous? Exploited? Critical? Motherly? At the moment, red-rimmed. Not exactly the lustrous umber that had gotten her into trouble on two continents. Ready . . . or, rather, she had run out of excuses to stay in the bathroom.

For most living matter, the development from protoplasmic irritability to Cognition takes about a billion years. For the Marcypial, however, it occurs almost instantaneously, as a precipitate by-product, a spin-off, of the Discovery of Purpose. The Marcypial usually discovers Purpose at about age twenty-four, in a *le jazz* cellar among mushroom faces, fending off a couple of turtle-necked torpedoes from Despair, Incorporated, who want to *acte gratuit* and get blown in congratulation. (What's the matter, don't you have the guts? No, I'm worried about my teeth; I just had them sharpened.) Discovery begins with a dull throb in the vicinity of the pineal gland. Heretofore, irritability has been general and uniform. Excitation, if experienced, spread slowly in all directions, like a boil burst. So long as the whole Marcypial organism experienced that excitation uniformly, it was subsumed under an acellular conducting system known as Resignation. But with the

Discovery of Purpose, there is Localization, or Pain-in-the-Neck. Descartes before the horsing-around; I think, therefore I won't. (I see, you're afraid of being a woman, a *real* woman, I mean. Yes, you are very mean.) At this point, *cognitive irritability*, or Rage, is channeled in two directions. In one, it is elaborated at a subcellular level within the confines of a single plasma membrane known as Boredom. In the other, it is elaborated at a cellular level, and develops a multi-cellular structure known as Creative Ambition. It should be noted that the only Ambition Structure a Marcypial ever develops is a Creative Ambition Structure. *I want to go home and be smart.*

"I'm hungry and thirsty, Mother."

"All right." She opened the bathroom door. Hannah was sobbing into Yogi Bear. Stephen obstructed the route to the kitchen. He had propped up his blackboard for her to inspect. On it was a huge, vaguely symmetrical, Technicolored abstraction, an explosion of chalks. Marcy looked more closely at the blackboard. "Stephen, I know what that is! A TV pattern! You were looking at TV this morning. You drew the pattern!"

"I did not!" shouted Stephen. Struck cold with awe: another bolt of Mother-knowing; phatic prescience. Marcy knew that punishment was in order, but she couldn't commit it. Perhaps, after all, she was fixated in the representational stage. If *only* he didn't get up so early in the morning, even before Hannah, and creep like some spidery little refugee down the stairs, into the living room, to switch on the TV set and sit, on top of the coffee table, blowing his mind with air force documentaries, religious shorts, farm reports, and lessons in Portuguese. Just squatting there . . . But of course he hadn't been just squatting there. He had been painting the pattern. Mightn't they leave an ear on the stairs, attached by neural wire to an alarm circuit in the brain, so when at dawn he trod upon it . . . ? She had descended once to find Ken and Stephen together, listening to "The Star-Spangled Banner." Ken had said: "The first jingle of the day."

"Stephen, would you like a bagel?"

"Half a bagel."

She took one from the bread box and slit it sidewise. Stephen liked to return the hole to her after eating the reality. They were stringing a necklace of doughnut and bagel holes. Hannah was plucked from the playpen, deposited on the kitchen linoleum, and handed the other half of the bagel. Hannah held it up to the light, appraised it, and then began to gnaw.

According to Sylvia Plath:

> . . . . . .
> *I see your cute decor*
> *Close on you like the fist of a baby*
> *Or an anemone, that sea*
> *Sweetheart, that kleptomaniac.*
> *I am still raw.*
> *I say I may be back.*
> *You know what lies are for.*
> . . . .

No. The lies came afterward. Unless emotions are lies. Cheer up, Marcy. He isn't exactly hugging his ball and chain down by the gate.

"What's a pattern?" asked Stephen, looking at his blackboard.

"Patterns are Out this Season," said Marcy. From the refrigerator: butter and eggs. Into the pot: water to boil. Into the toaster: bread to burn. Onto the table: instruments for impaling and dismemberment. She stole a glance at the wall-clock. Seven-thirty.

The multicellular Creative Ambition Structure of the Marcypial is similar in organization to the organelle system of the ciliates. There are sensory bristles, which register dissatisfaction and ask, Can a college education have been for *this?* Photoreceptors, which take snapshots of the situation and conclude that it is very dark indeed. Trichocysts, microscopic harpoonlike appendages of the Tactless Organ, used for convincing others just *how* dark the situation is. Fused cilia, for quitting Paris, being married, going back to school, getting involved with Rinsler. And cross-striated contractile fibrils, tentacles of caress which, employed in conjunction with the trichocysts, are usually effective in courting behavior and domestic squabbles.

For Hannah: milk and rice cereal with apricots and small slices of hard-boiled egg. For Stephen: toast, scrambled eggs (don't make them *dirty!*), cranberry juice. For Marcy: tea. Not much her father's daughter, fleeing his gluttony, his fearless fodder—syrup and sausage, dough and yolks, muffins and heavy cream, swordplay of Texas sunlight in the long orange kitchen, over gleaming prongs, bottomless mugs, groaning plates . . . He ate Texas.

"Stephen, would you bring in Hannah's highchair?" Hannah, although lashed down, promptly capsized her cup of milk. "Wretch! Stephen, get your clothes." She dressed him. He was capable of dressing himself, under his father's eye, so long as his father congratulated him on each successful negotiation of a sleeve or shoe. Marcy, however, hadn't the trick of turning investiture into a puberty rite.

According to Sylvia Plath:

> . . . .
>
> *He tells me how badly I photograph.*
> *He tells me how sweet*
> *The babies look in their hospital*
> *Icebox, a simple*
>
> *Frill at the neck,*
> *Then the flutings of their Ionian*
> *Death-gowns,*
> *Then two little feet.*
> *He does not smile or smoke.*
>
> . . . .

But he smiled and he smoked and he was terrified. You had to say that for him: he never wanted me to be his mother.

Knowing what she would see if she looked at the newspaper, knowing what she would hear if she listened to the radio, she chose instead to read a story to Stephen while they ate. Accustomed in the morning to a story from his father, he frowned. Marcy was supposed to read to him at night.

"Have you finished? All right, now it's time for Captain Kangaroo." She followed Stephen into the living room, and put Hannah into the playpen with her unfinished bagel. Stephen prepared the couch, securing the canister of watercolor crayons, the tablet of paper, the battery-equipped Phaser Pistol he used to shoot at commercials. Marcy started toward the dining room.

Stephen said, "Mother, can I type on your typewriter?"

"Not *now*. Now I'm going to type on it, and you're going to watch Captain Kangaroo. This evening when you get home from school you can type on my typewriter. Stephen, if your sister cries, maybe she's dropped her bagel. Would you give it back to her?"

"Yes, Mother." Already turning crayons into missiles.

She closed both doors to the dining room, sat down, poured herself another cup of tea. Silence. And the pile of clippings, and the Xeroxed field reports. Cambridge-Somerville, over 60 per cent Irish and Italian Catholic, over 90 per cent working class, 95 per cent white: don't Martin me no Luther Kings . . . the war is my overtime check . . . women belong on their backs or bending over a kettle . . .

Hannah howled. Marcy banged down her cup, spilling tea. She waited. Hannah continued to howl. Marcy stood, trembling, and then charged through the door into the living room.

"She lost her bagel," said Stephen at the playpen. "I gave it back." There was a red mark on Hannah's forehead; her skin mussed like satin.

"You threw it at her."

"No, I just dropped it."

"You dropped it as hard as you could, right on top of her."

"I don't think she wants the bagel."

"Why don't you think she wants the bagel?"

"She eats the holes."

"How would you like me to drop your blackboard on top of you . . . hard?"

"It would hurt."

"It would hurt, indeed. Keep that in mind."

"A blackboard is bigger than a bagel."

"You are bigger than Hannah. Do you want to go outside and play?"

"No. All the children are gone to school."

"Then sit down and watch Captain Kangaroo. Or draw. Or build something with your blocks. But leave Hannah alone!"

"You said for me to find the bagel when Hannah lost it."

Had he been taking lessons from Rinsler? Marcy picked up Hannah and hauled her into the dining room. Finding nothing lethal-looking on the floor, she plopped her. "All right, let's see you crawl." Eight forty-five, and nothing accomplished. . . .

The Purpose Gland may be thought of as the transformer or generator that creates and maintains the electrical field between the Creative Ambition Structure and the subcellular Boredom

34

plasma membrane. Because this electrical activity is in a constant condition of depolarization, there is just no stopping a Marcypial once she has Discovered Purpose. The early Marcypial investigators, trying hard to explain the Urgency Phenomenon, posited the existence of subvisual charged particles, known as Anxiety Cells, in the electrical field. Each Anxiety Cell is conjectured to consist of three major parts: the cell-body proper, containing the angst nucleus; a long tubular extension from the angst, called the angst axle; and the dentists, a clutch of tiny drill stems sprouting from the other end of the angst axle. The angst nucleus depolarizes; the angst axle keeps it rolling across the electrical field; and the dentist drill stems vibrate with agitation. Of course, there are many, many anxiety cells, all of them rolling around on their angst axles. The excited dentists of one anxiety cell confer or vibrate with the excited dentists of many other anxiety cells, creating what is called a *snappy*. This tells the organism, over and over again, *Snap It Up*. Or: *Make It Snappy*.

According to Sylvia Plath:

> . . . .
> *And here you come, with a cup of tea*
> *Wreathed in steam.*
> *The blood jet is poetry,*
> *There is no stopping it.*
> *You hand me two children, two roses.*

With thorns on her dilemma, Marcy rose from the dining room table and returned to the living room. Stephen was watching television. She sat down beside him and raked his hair. He kept his hands to himself. "Do you want to write out your name for me?"

"All right," he said. "Shall I use a different color for each letter?" They forgave too easily.

"That's a good idea. Until you run out of colors."

He took up his tablet and began selecting watercolor crayons. Hannah, progressing from the dining room, poked her head around the corner, saw them, bird-trilled. Stephen in large block letters began to spell out his name. "Now the address?" he asked. Marcy nodded. He wrote the address, then the telephone number. Marcy was about to suggest another project when the school bus honked on the street. "My bus!" shouted Stephen. "I have to get my coat!" He leaped from the couch, then turned to Marcy:

35

"Mother, can I take my paper to school, and show Lydia how I wrote my name?"

"Certainly." She reached for and hugged him. "Stephen . . . I'm sorry."

"Why, Mother? What have you done?" Precisely. Wrong on!

"Get your coat." Hannah, looking up at them, began her moan-heaves. "Shut up, White Fang."

Hand in hand, Marcy and Stephen went out the door, down the porch steps, along the walk to where the Volkswagen bus was waiting. The new driver looked like Bela Lugosi. She kissed Stephen good-by; he climbed in, and turned immediately in his seat to exhibit the piece of paper on which he had recorded his name. Marcy, gripping herself by the elbows, walked slowly back up to the house.

Of course, she had forgotten to put Hannah in the playpen. And, of course, Hannah was sucking on an electrical plug. Marcy scooped her up. No smell. Americans don't raise their children; they try to survive them; the baby-sitter is a pawn shop; the nursery school is a jail. They went upstairs, to the room containing Stephen's bed and toy chest, most of Marcy's clothes, and the piano. Hannah, on being dropped, lunged at the toy chest. Marcy searched through the sheet music for something to practice.

The four principal auxiliary irritability systems of the Marcypial, under the centralized control of the Purpose Gland and modified by the Creative Ambition Structure, are the Wife, Mother, Cook, and Pianist membranes. Each of these auxiliary membranes appears to have been adapted from the jellyfish structure. Each consists of a nerve-net or radial excitation system, which is shaped like an umbrella or a bell. While each has its specialized function, each performs that function in a similar manner.

She found a Liszt étude, and exposed the keyboard. Hannah liked the sound of the piano. Stephen did not. Stephen would not, could not, sit and listen. He had either to be seated beside her on the bench, pounding the keys himself; or to be off in a corner, out of sight, dismantling the cosmos. (Would Hannah build towers with her blocks? If she asked for a Susy Homemaker Oven, Marcy would put detergent into her porringer.) She began to play. Hannah grinned. Hannah made bird trills à la Berg.

Like the other specialized auxiliary systems, the Pianist Membrane consists of two nerve rings. The first is made up of ocellireceptors, cup-shaped lenslike bodies which are always looking at the clock. The second ring is made up of statocyst-perceptors, which locate the organism in space, geographically. Both rings register alarm, whereupon the nerve umbrella collapses to form an exclamation mark, or Imperative. The organism then jumps into boots, thrusts arms through red cape, straps on book bag and Hike-a-Poose, rushes out the door and up the hill to catch the 10:36 bus.

According to Sylvia Plath:

> . . . .
> *Out of the ash*
> *I rise with my red hair*
> *And I eat men like air.*

Marcy rose from the piano bench, annoyed with herself, Sylvia Plath, and Liszt. Liszt was being difficult. (Difficult? said Dr. Johnson: Sir, I wish it had been impossible.) All right, red cape time! Hike-a-Poose harnessing time! It was only 9:45. . . .

Hannah had to be lashed into the Hike-a-Poose before Marcy put it on. Then rest the Hike-a-Poose on top of the dresser in the bathroom, crouch, slip her arms through the yoke, and rise. All secure. As she moved out of the bathroom, Hannah grabbed the light cord and switched on the light. Marcy had to reverse directions to turn it off again. Doing so, she swung Hannah into the door. Hannah began to scream, and didn't stop until they were walking up the hill. Hannah liked to bounce.

Ken, I am going to take an earlier bus. Is that all right with the Mackenzies? Do I blame my feeling bad on history, biology or you?

Three

OF COURSE, THERE WAS A PRECEDENT. There were precedents in the Mackenzie family for almost everything except Roman Catholicism and murder. Elizabeth Smythe Mackenzie was the precedent: indefatigable pamphleteer, patroness-saint of the Wyke Regis way station on the underground railroad. Imagine five feet of stringy woman, wrapped in Bengal cloth, shovel-jawed and poor at curtseying. When she died in 1858, Elizabeth left a sum of money to erect a monument over her grave, and a will stipulating the nature of that monument. It was to be a granite obelisk. On three respective sides were to be chiseled the names of her great-grandfather's children, her grandfather's children, and her father's children . . . with Elizabeth's name listed only among the latter. On the fourth side was inscribed:

> THIS SIDE OF THE PILLAR IS DEDICATED TO THE SACRED
> CAUSE OF EMANCIPATION.
> MAY GOD BLESS IT, AND ALL THE PEOPLE SAY AMEN!

Then there had been Elizabeth's nephew, Nathaniel Dodd Mackenzie. Born in 1834, Nathaniel was the only Wyke Regis Mackenzie to enlist in the Union cause at the time of the Rebellion—after flunking out of divinity school. He died during a collision of the steamers *West Point* and *George Peabody*, on the Potomac, August 13, 1862.

So it was not as though Mackenzies had never concerned themselves with the Black Question. While few in the family ever equaled Elizabeth's zeal or Nathaniel's sacrifice, there had been Mackenzie clergymen in the nineteenth century preaching abolition from the pulpit; and there would be Mackenzie educators in the twentieth, worrying about deprived environments.

Still, it was a joke: that the Mackenzies of the 1960s should have wondered why their farm was losing money, and should have conscripted the Coffin cousin to investigate the situation. Ex-enricher of the minds of ghetto children, yes. Specialist in egalitarian rhetoric, yes. Press agent for history, yes. But student of character?

Marcy would have none of it, and returned with the children to Cambridge after Labor Day. I stayed; it was a question of finding out whether I had any character, and what it was. One night at Thomas Hill my uncle, John Mackenzie, told me: "The tragedy of Daniel Webster was not a want of intelligence, but a want of character." With a twinkle and a sigh, while portraits nodded and white moths beat on dark windows and wet pine hissed in the fireplace and old Bourbon shrank ice lumps in heavy-bottomed glasses. It might have been that same night he told me about the bachelors' dinner for my father long ago in Boston, when Sam at 2 A.M. came down the stairs, emerged from the club, stared up the street, and asked: "Which way is New Hampshire?" No one had been able to tell him. I listened, as I listened to everything John Mackenzie said, with the idea of the wrong father in my head. It was not my fault that I had not been permitted to choose the right father in the beginning; it would have saved some time, and perhaps even a life. But we go on making choices, after the original helplessness, and ultimately it becomes our fault.

Student of character. Victim of it. Mothered by it. Married to it.

What *is* character, anyway? Define. The accumulation of painful experiences? The things we do when we think we are alone? In computer technology, character is a symbol representing information which, if coded, can be used by a machine. In Roman Catholic theology, character is the ineffaceable imprint on the soul by the sacraments. At Thomas Hill, it was the way one accommodated one's pessimism. Does Rinsler have character? Or hasn't he time for it, along with vanity and enigmas? Those of us who worry too much about our character probably don't have one.

First, there was the character of idleness. The migrant pickers had been brought north three weeks early (why?) and had nothing to do while waiting for the apples to ripen. They sat on benches, faces blank, limbs loose and useless, obsolescent machines, while the busyness went on, the Shorts strutted by, white men made confident motions. Needed: some form of recognition, for the quality of enforced idleness was so perfectly textured that their eyes like lizards were alive to every movement. They watched intently: there must be a sign. But the very intensity of their watching intimidated potential sign-givers. Work itself became guilty. We scurried past them, our little motors going *putt-putt*, giving no signs because, if signs had meaning, we would be taking the meaning away from us by giving it to them. They: black, obsolescent, waiting. We: marvelously prosthetic, limbs die-cast out of see-through plastic, making visible the color-coded transistor units, the stamped electrical circuitry, the gear box of finely calibrated purpose. Very white, and operating on solar energy, gleaming silver reflector-shields strapped to our elbows and knees. While they just waited for a sign.

Needed, as well, some make-work, for while waiting they went into debt at camp. There were the new fifteen-bushel bins to build, on an assembly line in the storage shed, cold and poorly lit, a cave of eyes, fingernails, tools, giggles, bending wire, and hammering nails, as though they were making a Moloch. But Murdock only needed three men, and Leroy always gave him the same three. Work that like scant rations should have been divided up and portioned out to everyone, went only to a few and always the same few. (Why?)

"Who likes rocks?" asked the student of character one morning at seven o'clock. I relate to people by being jovial. "There's a pasture near the pond, where we want to plant some more apple trees. The bulldozer's been over it. Now I need twelve men to go with me and pick up all the little rocks. A dollar-forty an hour." Rocks? Well, it wasn't exactly *interesting* work, was it? But it was more profitable than watching television; and Leroy was downtown buying food; and all I asked was a social security number;

and one by one they signed up, climbed onto the truck, and went forth to wrestle with the earth, the day, their debts.

Surely the Puritan God was a Great Rock Frog, Cromwellian, granite-eyed, white cousin to Rakahore, the Maori rock god, who must periodically have hopped across the Atlantic to dump his obdurate absolutes. Nice little valley. A few Algonquins, mindlessly paddling their canoes. Ah . . . that feels better. Centuries of passing boulders through the bowels. Geologically: facies of deposition. And the boulders, by a copulative process about whose mechanisms we can only fantasize, multiplied themselves: a heavy, resolute, endless self-spawning of death-exempt stones. And the Cromwellian Frog God, weary at last of wars and exegesis, was possessed by malice. To his excremental dumping ground he would lure a band of pilgrims especially qualified to farm it, men with as many rocks in their heads as there are in the ground. At least Sisyphus glimpsed summits; the New England farmer, crouching, digging, pulling, hauling, was a hole-maker, and every hole he made only diminished his stature, for he had to stand in it. He harvested rocks; under them were more rocks; and under those rocks, fathers and grandfathers of rocks.

My apostles, lacking an intuition into Original Sin to sustain them in their hole-making, had to make do with money and mud. The bulldozer had been but an insect, and left only insect scratches on the dome of the underground metropolis of rocks. There were strata, bedding planes, sills and laccoliths, saddle reefs and plutonic plugs of which the insect hadn't even dreamed. We crept along the insect trails. With bars and shovels and hands and oaths we wrenched ten thousand rocks a day from twenty acres. They ranged in size from a football to a diving bell, and were tossed up on the trailer pulled by Short, to be transported to gullies into which we heaved them to make grave mounds and monuments to Frog God. And, looking back across the field upon the many craters we had carved, we saw: Murdock. Murdock in his mackinaw, chewing his cigar; Murdock morosely inspecting every hole and crying after us over the scarred acres: "Here's one you missed." Missed! He only saw it because we had dismantled its ceiling, exposed its nest. Nest! At the bottom of each crater-basin lay no mere stone egg, but the rounded back of a rock hippopotamus. What we had done was strip the hippo of its parasol. A vision visited me: upon the death of a sense of sin in

New England, Cromwell burrowed into the earth, to confound all those who would till without faith, without dread. Not mere frog, not even hippopotamus, he was leviathanic: a whale of a frog, in fact, just dusty with the topsoil of New England. Moby-Marble! We wanted to plant apple trees on the back of a rock whale.

But I was Establishing Rapport. We sang chain-gang songs, stole apples not yet ripe from the fringe of the Indian Orchard, shared cigarettes and water. Short wouldn't drink from the tin communal cup. Sat on top of his great steel horse, under an evil sun, resenting me because I let them steal apples and there were only 60,000 bushels of apples. I called too many water breaks and drank from a tainted cup and—a sign!—dirtied my Cambridge fingernails in the fraternal hole.

"Man," said Richmond, "I bet that jockey up there got him a powerful thirst."

"No, man," said Foy, "ol' Short, he got him hid somewheres a great big bag of all-white water, cool and clear."

"Rollin," said Root-man, "you shittin' us on these rocks, ain't you? You sneaks out nights and sticks 'em all back in the ground, don't you?"

"She-it," said Peace, "I could've done this rock bit down in Georgia, all I had to do was rape a woman. Rape a woman and they lets you work on the rocks all you wants."

"She-it, Peace, you rape a *white* woman in Georgia and first thing they do, they cuts it off, and next thing they do, they let you work on the 'lectric chair. They gives you a chair all your own."

"Ol' Peace, he don't know *how* to rape no woman noways."

"That Short, Short sure do look *thirsty.*"

"No, man, Short ain't thirsty. Short drink that radiator water."

"Hey, Foy, see ol' Mud-duck over there. They's a big mother rock ol' Mud-duck's spotted. He got a rock-eye, Mud-duck do. I bet he dreams rocks."

"She-it, man, *I* dreams rocks too. I even eats rocks."

"Bet rocks taste better 'n ol' Leroy's grits."

"You's right, Bird-man. Bird-man, you take care out there you hear? Twicet I almost mistook that head of yourn for one of them mother rocks. I 'bout stuck that bar in your ear. Would've busted that bar."

"Lookit ol' Peace. Peace he so tired he can't even beat his meat at night. Just about all ol' Peace can do to stand pissin'.'"

"I'll piss in your ear, Bird-man."

"Promise?"

"Ol' Mud-duck wavin' his arms out there. Batman! Rise, ball-busters. Haul that black ass. Rock-eye he done found one we missed."

"Hey, Short, we saved you some water. Hey, Short, got a straw?"

And Short would find, when the trailer bogged down in a mud patch, that nobody wanted to help unload. And Short would look at me, mad, because I was supposed to supervise, and how could I supervise when I was down on my knees with them, scrabbling?

"Albany Jackson," said the student of character, "you're going to use up all your laziness while you're young, and then you'll have nothing to look forward to in your old age but hard work."

After a pause, Jackson decided to laugh. Otis DeKalb laughed: why not? Foy in his checkered shirt held the bar like a javelin and whooped his Tarzan cry: at Monadnock. Short just didn't know how to Establish Rapport.

Why, sure, I *know* you can't become a friend, but sometimes you can at least stop being an enemy. That is, if you don't want people to hate you. Or is their hating you a necessary part of the development of revolutionary consciousness? I'm not an expert on revolutionary consciousness because, of course, I've never been sufficiently brutalized. The only people who understand a society are its victims. This was explained to me one night in Roxbury by one-eyed Rajah Born, who had a line in Fanonized yard goods: everything comes back bloody. His brothers and sisters didn't need my English literature; they needed guns. Stuff tutorial. His brothers and sisters were students of the street, Ph.D.'s in hate. No Band-Aids on our blackness, said the Raj, who knew better and worse. She-it. It was the end of a year of gestures, and on leaving I found that the street students had broken off my aerial and slashed my tires. Hell hath no fury like a liberal scorned. My sulk was eloquent. I still see the Raj occasionally, on the six o'clock news, explaining creative violence to New England. His dashiki becomes him more than my fatigue jacket becomes me, but I've got more pockets.

Leroy, old frayed-gray grinner at white folks, spoon-banger, grits-eater, concave-faced taker-of-cuffs and small commissions, did not approve of my rapport. "Mr. Coffin," he said, looking away, hands in the pockets, "you wants mens, you asks me. Claudis Cantrell he made *me* camp boss, he goin' to be mad. I gives you the mens you want, just ask."

"And the men you give me will be the same men building those bins, right, Leroy? The same men who get the broom detail and the box-stacking and the trailer-riding, right?" Pulling from one of my many pockets the check I'd cashed for Peace: "Look at this, Leroy. A full-grown man worked a forty-hour week to get this check. Twelve dollars. Twelve dollars!"

"I got it all written down. I can show you what he took out."

"I believe you. You bring these men up here three weeks early. You don't provide them transportation down to town. You take out their board and you charge them fifty cents a pack of cigarettes, sixty cents a can of beer. You charge them for the cream in their coffee, don't you, Leroy? By picking time, those men are working for you, aren't they?"

"Claudis Cantrell, he goin' to be mad."

"Claudis Cantrell may be unemployed when this season's over. I'm learning, Leroy. I'm finding out how it's done."

In the beginning, Wyke Regis picked its own apples. It was, after all, healthy outdoors work, in crisp autumn weather, and whole families could participate: father at the top of the twelve-foot ladder, mother on the lower branches, children gathering the drops. The ball-bearing and basket factories changed all that. Shorter hours, better pay, overtime, and no responsibility. Oh, there were still Wyke Regis families which, as a Sunday substitute for going to the county fair, would play at picking; as there were church groups, hoping to build up a slush fund for Sunapee snow parties before the skiing season started. But they only showed up on weekends, and spent more time standing around the tailgates of their station wagons, drinking cyclamates, than down in the orchards where the apples were suffering from separation anxiety.

John Mackenzie most fondly remembers the 1940s, when our apples were picked by German prisoners of war, who had been shipped across the Atlantic in empty cargo holds and were trucked up each day from Fort Devins to the farm. They marched into the orchards and were very conscientious; they didn't bruise the apples. Of course, they didn't sing, as do black migrant workers and schools of whales. But they were reliable. As I have said, it's a question of character.

Unfortunately, we ran out of German prisoners of war, and so we had to use American prisoners of war. The citizens of Wyke Regis were undoubtedly startled by the sudden appearance of black faces among white clapboard, but those early faces usually belonged to a Stable Family Unit; nobody got gang-banged on the Common to a beat of bongo drums. However, just as the ball-bearing and basket factories took away our local pickers, the potassium mines down South took away our Stable Family Units. They stayed home on year-round jobs. Seasonal work was left to Unaffiliated Individuals, notoriously deficient in character. Because a small farm found it tedious to recruit individuals who lived a thousand miles away, we had to rely on deputies.

Like Claudis Cantrell. My grandfather, Wallace Mackenzie, considered Claudis Cantrell the embodiment of capitalist vitality, a forty-five-year-old, six-foot, anthracite slab of ex-Marine. An entrepreneur extraordinary. He supplied bodies from the unemployed labor pool down South to whoever wanted them. Each year he brought over two hundred men north in a fleet of retired yellow school buses to pick apples. Some of the men were from Florida, jobless at the end of the citrus-picking season. Some were from Virginia, laid off once the tobacco crop was in. And some, like Butterfly, were derelicts dug up in the slums of Baltimore and New Haven to provide the promised number of bodies and to collect the promised ten dollars a head.

Based in Alabama, Cantrell operated on a very simple organizing principle: Terror. Each thirty-man work gang assigned to each of seven New England farms had a camp boss like Leroy, an old blood-relation entirely dependent on Cantrell for his livelihood, and trusted to handle the money, haggle with the farm, buy and fry the food. But since the loyalty of a Leroy was a consequence of his age, his fear, and his dependency, he could not be trusted to command the respect of his crew. To bolster his authority, and to keep an eye on him, each work gang also had two or three young Alabama toughs to take care of camp discipline. A black Gestapo.

The black Gestapo got the make-work, while everybody else waited for apple-picking and went into debt. And so Cantrell was a successful entrepreneur, who took care of his own. He got an eight-cent commission on every bushel picked, and a two-cent bonus for quality. Of that commission, the Leroys got two pennies, the bullyboys a penny apiece, plus their markup on company-store consumer items. Barring frost, hail, scald, scab, and radioactive fallout, Mackenzie Farm produced about 60,000 bushels a year. With comparable crops at the other six farms, Cantrell cleared $20,000 in six weeks. His proletariat was less fortunate. A picker got only twenty-seven cents a bushel, plus a three-penny bonus for quality, payable in a lump sum at the end of the season.

And the sullen proletariat bruised the apples. And bruised apples were a drug on the market. And the farm was losing money. And the student of character was employed to find all this out, which he did with his little sensitivity groups around the water bucket, where each member of his crew borrowed two cigarettes a day, one in the morning, one in the afternoon, accepting more if they were offered, never asking though but twice, except Butterfly, who grabbed, and was therefore the only one refused because he threatened the dignity of our small, unspoken arrangements; while we talked, I learned.

When picking finally started, we butchered it because nobody had thought out the consequences of fifteen-bushel bins instead of single-bushel boxes. We were still assigning individual trees. The bins would get half-filled and the man would have to move on up the row to another tree. The tractor with the fork lift was twenty minutes behind him, late bringing up his bin. So he would start a second bin. Then that tree was done, and he had *two* partial bins. And he would just have to stand there, waiting for the tractor, losing time, getting surly, until we learned to give each man three or four trees at a time, across from and next to each other. Perils of technology, just like the missionaries handing out steel axes to Australian bushmen.

Because we couldn't wait for Short—insulted by the pickers, he did not exactly hurry, he was an apple easily bruised; and he did not improve his popularity by hauling first the bins of the biggest and strongest and loudest members of the crew—I learned to abuse a tractor. One of the troubles with the Left today is that nobody knows anything about manual labor. Maybe we'll all have to learn it in jail. And so I mounted the old A-C with the fork lift and faulty ignition. Under combat conditions I overgassed it and went Ping-Ponging up and down the rows, sprung from my pancake seat, rattling my teeth. I hit one brake instead of both of them, spun the tractor, tipped it on its malevolent ear. I roared between the trees, got my face flayed off by low-hanging branches, crushed boxes, impaled bins, was bombed on the head by falling apples.

"Rollin, get your ass over here with my bin!"

"I've got three other bins before yours."

"Goddammit, man, what 'm I s'posed to do with these mother-apples? Eat 'em off the trees?"

"Where's your ticket? The blue ticket you're supposed to leave on the bin?"

"Fuck that blue ticket, man. You know my number."

"But how the hell am I supposed to recognize your bin?"

"Man, I been waitin' half an hour for that bin. I come one thousan' miles to pick them mother-apples, and now I got to stand around coolin' my ass whiles you go ridin', ridin'."

"Find your bin and put the ticket on it."

Because I was behind, they moved up on their own, assigning themselves new trees, spreading out over four rows of the orchard, which put bin-moving that much further behind time. And half the bins hadn't been placed properly, at the right angle, on the flat. So the iron forks gouged out great clumps of earth, and on those clumps the bins swayed, and you hit a bump and the bitch fell off, pouring a river of apples down the row. Coffin on wheels . . . hands wet, jaw set, feet stamping blindly for the brakes, rear-end swinging around on me: up . . . *down!* Apple ballet behind me.

"Hey, boss-man, you punch up my bin back there? No, man, I got three! Three, not two!"

"She-it, man, ain't enough red apples on that mother-tree to make a pie with."

"You shittin' me on these bins, Rollin. Must be twenny bushel fit in one of them bins. You call it fifteen."

Trees in the morning great clouds of water. The mist is made of wire. Crayon won't mark on wet wood.

"You didn't pick up your drops under that tree."

"Up my ass, them drops. Ten cents a bushel for a box of drops. That ain't pissin' money."

"We've got to get the drops, too. If you picked up the drops, you'd be making half a dollar while you waited for the bins to get moved."

On a carom, lighting up three fingers on my left hand instead of the cigarette that fell out of my mouth. The sun gets high, hides and waits, then hits you in the eye through a tree, and you almost run down a man on a ladder. Checker a retired cardiac case, standing with one hand on his heart, the other groping for a bottle of pills. Murdock saying, "They're pulling off the spurs. That's next year's apple. Tell 'em not to pull off the spurs." Murdock saying, "Too green. Don't pick the green ones." Murdock saying, "A man up there is pickin' Cortlands. Did you assign that tree? Cortlands ain't ready. Just Macs."

Then the tractor doesn't start. "Battery connection," says Short, hitting it with a wrench. Now it's hot, and the boots and the sweater and the long underwear that made the morning bearable are on you like a rug. Your sweat makes your mind slippery.

"Butterfly, get back on that other tree. You've got to take those apples off the top of that tree. The top is where they're ripest. Butterfly, you've got to use your *ladder*." He is never going to fill that bin. "Albany Jackson, lower your bucket. All the way down. Drop an apple two inches, and it's bruised." Jackson mocks it, falling to his knees, releasing the apples individually from the canvas sleeve of the picking bucket. "Richmond, you want to empty your bucket in a different corner of the bin each time. Rotate."

"Rollin, I been pickin' apples six years. I knows how."

"You haven't been using bins before. If you pile up the apples on one side of the bin, then empty a bucket on top of them, the apples will roll all the way down and bounce. There goes your quality bonus."

"Three cents," says Richmond, "some bonus."

Noon. "Dinnertime!" Four men want to stay and pick; the others won't leave unless all go.

"That mother Bird-man, he'll go round swipin' all my little blue tickets and puttin' his own on *my* bins."

"She-it, man, I been workin' whiles you standin' there with your finger up your ass. I don't need none of your apples."

"Everybody goes in for dinner. There won't be any checkers out here, and no tractor to move the bins."

"Got us a whole half hour to eat in."

"That's a half hour too much of Leroy's grits."

"Be back at twelve-thirty." Which was just enough time for me to walk back to the house, wrap a washrag around my face, change shirts and drink a can of beer and gnaw on a hunk of bread and stretch legs coiled in a case of tractor-crouch. That left leg was commencing to cramp. Would they really steal each other's apples? One thing about the rocks, there was rhythm: load for a while, ride, unload, stop, smoke. But that tractor . . . You could tell the good pickers by the look of contempt on their faces, like Richmond. Here I come, with my bladder kicked in and my hands trembling. The spring has gone out of my paper punch, and I've lost the rubber band around my yellow cards, and I think I'll prong Murdock with the fork lift. Look at the sky; a high, hard blue, with baseball trails across it. Keep walking. That tractor wants to throw you again, and it will go on throwing you until late afternoon when it gets cold, and all the hollows of the body numb-up, the wind is over you like a sword, your nose leaks, and the leak turns icy on your chin.

Four

RINSLER WAS ALMOST BORED. Rinsler had never quite made it all the way to boredom. Annoyed, even exasperated, certainly: after an estimated 7,500 meetings, who wouldn't have occasionally lost patience? The hungry faces, the jelly-bean words bitten off and spat out and bouncing on and rolling over the conference tables, cafeteria tables, coffee tables. . . . *All power to the pee-pull.* He was not in the habit of making fists, except to grasp a needle and stick IBM. He neither rapped, nor did he trash, and hog-calling had never been his style. Off the rip. After Havana, Selma, Atlantic City, Helsinki, he had nothing more to prove or groove. He had burned his draft card before he knew he had a heart murmur. He was the ambulatory scar tissue of our brave New Left, and it had occurred to him that many of his peers suffered from an upside-down digestive tract: shove words up their asses, and when they open their mouths, shit comes out. Especially at rallies with loudspeakers. It was a consequence of taking everything personally: apples, racism, death, war. War, unlike Marcy, was not a personal insult. War was . . .

Rinsler had been agitating against it for so long that sometimes the war lit up his mind like one of those maps in Paris Métro stations, telling you where you are and where you want to go and how you must proceed to get there. Sometimes he perceived it whole, a blossoming and withering of neon flowers, a kind of cancer eating its way to the brain of the earth along mineral veins. Or a closed energy system, passably organic, with the leukocytes —body counts, kill ratios, free-fire zones, search-and-destroy missions, terminations with extreme prejudice—rushing to attack the bacterial (the ideological) infection. To take it personally was to trivialize the issues. The United Fruit Company is *my* fault because I put bananas in the refrigerator. Not to mention my mouth. He terminated his attention with extreme annoyance. He would have liked, at meetings and at rallies, to pour Drano down the clogged plumbing of their brains, to flush all the metaphor from the life-pipe. He had lived his life instead of approximating it. Like *not* wow.

Rinsler squinted through the smoke at Coffin. Rinsler's brother had also always taken everything personally, especially God, and had fiddled with the oxygen flow to his cortical compost heap. Mystagogical gas fills a vacuum of the will. Most trips were bad. If only his brother had managed to die a salutary death, by political poisoning perhaps, bamboo shoot through the instep (insight): Rinsler might then have been able to use him as an energizing principle, the way Coffin was trying to use blackness. If only Coffin hadn't decided to take the slave trade personally, to make a career out of feeling bad historically, three hundred years of *my fault*. Rinsler had needed a Coffin at *Scope*. Rinsler believed in publicity: it *should* have happened, and if we say it *did*, maybe it *will*. On the sheets of Homosote, in the tray of cards, a release presses. Bladdermouths. Man was bile. If only they didn't persist in confusing the self with God, or with the cotton gin. . . .

And so, listening to Coffin take things personally, Rinsler was almost bored, which annoyed him. But he had trained himself to pretend attention, to harmonize the grimace on his face with the strophe and stanza of another's stutter-step. You never knew when you might learn something. Watching Richard Nixon on television once, it had occurred to Rinsler that there was a meaning to the mad method, that the words and gestures slightly out of sync and the ofttimes spastic vertical hold signified something. Too many missions aborted. The eyes themselves were broken TV sets, and Rinsler suddenly saw that behind those eyes, inside the locked projection booth of the skull, a little six-inch Richard Nixon went on endlessly rerunning the late shows of the 1950s, in black and white. The locked projection booth was more than just another promiscuous metaphor, it was *all* of it, an instance of what happened when your yawning metaphors swallowed you whole and you became what you sought to approximate. Lacking imagination, sheets of Homosote, you were what you ate, your approximation of yourself, an irony-poor diet, the *like* and *as though*. Similistic-minded. Too many people at the institute had six-inch homunculi in their skulls, endlessly rerunning the Port Huron Statement. And, no doubt about it, there was a six-inch Rinsler in there somewhere playing home movies of his brother in a seedy boardinghouse, pinned down on a bedspread patterned like the zodiac and seeming more like a roulette wheel, as though the room were spinning toward a sacrifice. *Seeming . . . as though*. The sacrifice preceded the approximation of it; a fact, not an idea. There had been a beach not far from the boardinghouse, and gulls that ate the garbage of his brother's brain. I shall not go Leary into that dark desert. The dessert was garbage. All games were for keeps. The sleep of reason was death. Beach was desert. To sea was not be bereave. Everyone had been gulled. No. Garbage could be fashioned into political art by small craftsmen, as a warning. Rinsler rinsed principles which weren't approximations and therefore never shrank.

He specialized in the broad picture. He was aware that this specialty amused those who thought they knew him. He was also aware that specializing in the broad picture was a defense against the banality of the particular, without cross-reference. He was meta-against, sticking to the grammar of blood and money. All clauses were disqualified. He could—he did, now—remind Coffin of Etzioni's classifications of power. He pointed out the coercive nature of a piecework, weather-dependent, privacy-lacking, labor-camp situation. He explained the migrant tide in terms of the decline of the sharecrop system and the mechanization of cotton. He was a statement, not a synecdoche.

For instance: Coffin was talking about migrant workers. Thus Rinsler had to respond, needle the cards. Therefore he claimed to have met César Chávez. To get to Chávez, says Rinsler, he had to hack his way through a thicket of Plimptons. What a harvest for the farmworkers: maraschino cherries, slices of candied orange, pitted olives, lemon peel, and onions like marbles, like the jelly-bean words on the conference table. *Like*. Rinsler Van Goghs it alone, in livid color, the broad strokes . . . to see the Hampton sunset refracted in the curve of a Steinem of champagne . . . to hear the insolent mariachi band, and embossed checkbooks opening like the crack of vertebrae or the breaking of sparrow leftwings or the knife sliding under the flap of the envelope containing the engraved invitation, one's bleeding throat . . . *like* . . . All necessary lies. Because Chavez had never made it to the Hamptons, and Rinsler hadn't been invited anyway (too ordinary). But necessary, because Rinsler had it on the authority of a SNCC field secretary that Chavez himself took things personally, confused himself with the Virgin of Guadalupe. Rinsler's personal experience of farmwork had been limited to two weeks in the San Joaquin Valley one California summer, picking strawberries, all bloody fingers and a hunched back, sleep itself a cradle of aches, a stiffening into the fear of dawn. He wasn't strong; he hadn't been able to take it. He had a tract house to go home to, a tub in which to paddle, a lawn the size of a lap-rug, a stepfather (which one?) who held him in contempt, a brother who rode a bicycle into mindlessness, thinking that mindlessness was a shopping plaza. Random remembering. Still, he knew more than Coffin did about it. He *had* seen peasants cutting sugar cane.

If Coffin were serious, says Rinsler, he would propose grievance machinery, guaranteed hours of available work, incentives for picking poor acreage, a savings and credit plan. Fidel Castro . . . It wouldn't work, says Coffin. But meanwhile Rinsler knows that Coffin has gone to the Hamptons, his fantasies in Pucci-print and Gucci-shod, swimming pools stocked with liberated women, an idea consuming him of erotic greed behind tinted glasses, Marcy on Mars two-mooned and worrying about polar ice-caps. Nightcaps exploding, Coffin imploding. That is, if Coffin is as ordinary as Rinsler.

No, says Rinsler, perhaps it wouldn't work. But it would prepare the way for a strike, and during a strike the perishable produce would rot. Rinsler never cared very much for apples. After Eden, ambiguity.

Coffin, however, was only interested in himself. What a student of character! What a social engineer! Of ice (domination) and fire (unreason) he knew nothing. He played his compunctions like a harp, and was too pleased at accidental tunes. *Like*. Telling Rinsler:

ITEM: Learning that Leroy buys all his cigarettes at the new supermarket, aware that Mrs. Bassett resents the supermarket for taking away her long-time customers, Coffin persuaded Mrs. Bassett to have her delivery van stop twice a week at camp to peddle packs at their proper purchase price. (Knowing that Rinsler will not believe Mrs. Bassett embodies a classless decency; that the mound of her is innocent, and her energy grafted to her instincts self-purifying.)

ITEM: Learning that Leroy charges fifty cents a week for cream in bad coffee, Coffin ordered a gallon of excess milk drained from Mackenzie cows, to be left on the kitchen porch each morning. (Knowing that Gravel, who plays milkman, would prefer to deliver grenades; grasps his crotch each dawn, the nerve ends cross-wired, a cold fear electrifying all notions of manhood: will milk bleach them?)

ITEM: Learning that Donadio Ford in downtown Wyke Regis rids itself each autumn of overused clunkers to wheel-hungry migrants, unloading wheeze machines whose carburetors could barely gasp it up the hill before expiring, Coffin called Donadio. Coffin pointed out how much business Donadio did with the farm and the Mackenzies. Coffin suggested that Donadio provide Mr. Terence Spider-Man Lavalle with a new battery, or the Mackenzie business might go elsewhere, as elsewhere perhaps as Nashua. I heard, says Coffin, a great voice out of the telephone, saying to the Coffin cousin, Go your way, and pour out the vials of the wrath of Mackenzie on all Donadiodium. A key to Thomas Hill corrupts absolutely. (Knowing Rinsler wouldn't understand. Clout is property, hereditary. Donadio wants to be a selectman, and needs the approval of apple trees that have been around Wyke Regis longer than French-Canadians. French-Canadians vote for themselves. Donadio is our future.)

ITEM: Learning that bullyboy James T. Worthy, whose wife Cindy Lou is supposed to help with the cooking, won't go down to pick so long as Foy stays back in camp, because Foy has something going with Cindy Lou; and that if Worthy won't go, a half dozen others, already angry at their small checks and Leroy's food and the West Orchard ditch and the bitter morning weather and the lack of transportation to town, will also refuse to pick; and that then the dice will roll and the wine will run and the knives fandango . . . Coffin importuned. He might as well have importuned the apples to go pluck themselves. (Knowing that Cindy Lou is as available as the Eastern shuttle from Boston to New York; she puts on extra runs if too many customers are standing in line. For her, tumescence is a credit card.)

Rinsler did not comment. Rinsler could have quoted the statistics on prostitution in migrant labor camps. He had notched them. He did permit himself, though, to wonder whether Coffin's sex life was anything like his political life: all foreplay.

And he thought. He could no more stop thinking than a pinball machine could stop lighting up: what else were the circuits for? He thought about Coffin, who had abandoned first his job, then his wife, to fumble among tokens. By those tokens, what subway ride did Coffin buy? A trip to self-esteem. An amelioration. Congratulations from the Mackenzies, to whom he seemed more devoted than to his wife: a New England conglomerate that had monopolized the local conscience-money ever since they slaughtered all the Indians. Improved camp morale, perhaps: the Hawthorne Effect; any change in the situation increased production. Enough bushels of apples to pay the taxes on the land that allowed the family to maintain its pastoral dream, its idyll of privacy, its bucolic historical garden. Rinsler knew. Often enough, he had taken advantage of the desire of such people to be used; their past weighed so heavily on them that they pleaded to be used. They had turned guilt into duty. Too often, later on, they started quibbling about definitions of usefulness—it's *my* conscience-money and I can spend it as I please. Rinsler knew that, too. Even the Movement was turning into one gigantic encounter group, with elephantiasis of the rhetorical organs. Therap *me*. The *Movement* . . . as though war and racism were a kind of Ex-lax for constipated Hamlets. *As though*. Did violence loosen the bowels? Yes. Rinsler made a mental note: bring it up the next time he wanted to irritate a Maoist. The Maoists frothed at the mouth when you referred to either their psychology or their physiology. Lately, he had wanted to irritate the Maoists almost as much as he had wanted to lay Marcy. They came by the identical dozen, cartons of eggs, round, white, and hatching all over you, pecking through their thin shells to cheep about the Moscow Trials and the Long March and the Cultural Revolution. When all you wanted to do was use the goddamned mimeograph machine. The Maoists had accused Rinsler of selling out to institute elitism. The institute was about as elitist as a pimple. He thought of omelets.

"So," said Rinsler, "you intend to get them all jobs for the winter."

"Some," said Coffin. "New Hampshire is overemployed. There's more work than there are warm bodies. Factories are hiring the lame, deaf, dumb, blind, mentally retarded, and chronically delinquent. Something as incidental as skin color doesn't bother a man with more orders than he can fill unless he raises a third shift. A night shift, maybe, so nobody will notice."

"Transportation? Housing?"

"I'm working on it. There's always a Christian minister somewhere, with a room to let and a need to prove that he'd read the Bible."

"The Bible!" Rinsler remembered a southern California church, rather like a latrine. *Like.* They sat in stalls; they wiped their metaphysical asses with pages from a book of very common prayer. They went out afterward to screw their best friends' wives, and cut corners on construction projects. "And if you spend ten years on this thing and get, oh, being generous, let's say fifty black faces on the night shift, what have you accomplished?"

"Who knows? Maybe, with a little luck in the sex department, we can improve New Hampshire's gene pool. Maybe an Oscar Robertson of hockey on the Wyke Regis high school team. Maybe —I'm not quite so blasé about this as you seem to be—just a better job and better pay for a few people I happen to know who wouldn't otherwise have a job or get paid. Individuals, Rinsler. With names."

"Green stamps," said Rinsler. "What a guilty little soul you are. You want to redeem yourself. Missionary work in Coffin's Congo of feeling bad. I get it. Everything you do has got to be a mission."

"You don't get it." Coffin smiled. "We live in a post-Protestant era, Rinsler. No more missions. Only hobbies."

"And hobbyhorses."

"I'm not really interested in whether you understand. Go give General Motors a hot foot."

Rinsler was about to become angry, which he hadn't time for, having already been furious. But there was a banging at the door. Coffin rose, removing his glasses, trying to rub some alertness into his eyes. The banging continued, out of habit: the mind at one end of the arm had wandered, and the fist at the other end had forgotten, or never knew, why it knocked. Coffin made it to the door. "Leroy?"

Leroy holstered his fist. "Lonzo, he need a doctor, Mr. Coffin."

"Why does Lonzo need a doctor, Leroy?"

"His arm, Mr. Coffin. Lonzo burned his arm."

"Badly?"

"Don't sound good. An' Peace, he got a bad back. Can you take 'em down to see the doctor?"

"Why don't you take them down, Leroy?"

"I got dinner to tend to, Mr. Coffin. An' my car ain't workin' noways."

"Wait a minute." Coffin put on his fatigue jacket. To Rinsler, he said: "Leroy's got a car with a psychosomatic transmission, which is different from a hobbyhorse. Leroy's car never works when Leroy would feel bad if it did."

"St. Francis of Assisi rides again," said Rinsler.

Coffin looked back. "The first day of picking here, Marcy heard them singing in the orchard. *Singing*, Rinsler. She wanted to call up the N-double-A-C-P. They weren't supposed to be singing, it was against the new rules. Make yourself uncomfortable."

Rinsler turned to stare down in the valley. He was staring into an aquarium. Or, insisted the homunculus, into his brother's eyes: a drowned self. He had always made himself, when he couldn't make anybody else. There had been in the boardinghouse room a five-pound bag of stale pretzels; empty bottles of a carbonated wine; a water pipe along the ceiling, with two hangers holding a coat, a pair of pants, and a high school letterman's jacket; cigarette holes in the zodiac bedspread; a shirt in the sink; psychedelic posters stapled to the wall; roaches on the trimming; canned laughter —only a can would laugh. I have been thinking about the Yo-Yo, his brother said, licking his thumbs; I don't want to be a Yo-Yo. Cut the string! Fly now, die later! Rinsler remembered another thumb-licker, a teen-aged *barbudo* in a small Havana bar off Malecon Drive, sticking his thumbs into a face that resembled an armpit, wanting a seventh Cuba Libre, being refused, bringing up his toylike submachine gun as though he were pitching a soft-ball, underhand, and writing his name on the mirror with bullets. *As though.* Rinsler had wanted to talk to the *barbudo* about sugar production, as he had wanted to talk to his brother about R. D. Laing.

Well, health *wasn't* politics. Serpents strangled swords. The tranquillizer pilleth, spit is full of life. Up against the wall, archetypes! Rinsler was capable of being (and taking it) personal, too. He knew names. A hobby was not a home, even for the Republic. They felt bad, did they? They didn't know how bad you can feel. He counted his knowses: an odd number.

Five

"WELL?" DEMANDED MRS. DEVLIN, her skull leaking electrical wire. "Didja see her? Did she crawl? Didn't I tell you she could crawl?"

"You were right, Mrs. Devlin. Hannah crawls."

"Now Monday I'll be needing some more baby food. Especially the pears. Dear Hannah adores pears. And some more of them Pampers, too. Ah, look at her nose! Runnin' again, poor dear. You shud really put mittens on her dear little hands, Mrs. Coffin. It's colder and colder a day."

Her nose runs because you keep this apartment at eighty-five degrees all the time. Anyone who must regularly enter and exit is going to develop a runny nose, unless she wears a space suit. Now, Marcy, it's unfair to resent Mrs. Devlin. Mrs. Devlin is warm and loving, *interested* in babies. Mrs. Devlin advertises in the newspaper that, for "mothers who *have* to work," she will *care* about their children, for a price. Children like Hannah, too young for nursery school; mothers like Marcy, too young to quit the world . . . or like Mrs. Weiner, who reads for a Boston publishing house; or Mrs. Safire, who plays the flute; or Mrs. Reverdy, a graduate student in linguistics. Not women who *have* to work, but women who *want* to. Mrs. Devlin manages somehow to shape her many

little virtues into one large reproach, a smog-ball she hands over
to the mothers in exchange for their children. The mothers have
to walk away with that reproach in their arms, or strapped to their
backs like a Hike-a-Poose.

Marcy did resent Mrs. Devlin. She resented Mrs. Devlin's electrical hair, her color television set, her simper. Marcy accused Mrs.
Devlin of . . . what? At one end of the simulated marble mantel-
piece was a plastic Jesus, bleeding; at the other end, a portrait of
the martyred President, grinning; in between, a bowl of flowers,
probably artificial. Lying on the coffee table were copies of *Family
Circle* and *The Record-American*. Hanging in the hall was a cow-
like, udderly beatific Madonna. The bathroom was a riot of fleur-
de-lys, zebra skins, polka-dot tissues, jars of hair tint, cracked death
masks of hardened face-cream cold packs. Marcy accused Mrs.
Devlin of being lower middle class, just like Marcy's mother. The
trouble with this country is that the peasants have money. Marcy
accused Mrs. Devlin of shuffling through each morning in a flame-
colored mini-muu and fluffy orange Pekingese bedroom slippers;
of lounging away each afternoon eating mints and watching *Dark
Shadows*; of voting for Barry Goldwater because of crime in the
streets, grins in the cockpit. But, then, Marcy's armorial bearings
were a horned elitist rampant on a field of emerald envy. Mrs.
Devlin, after all, hadn't denied Her Role. Mrs. Devlin hadn't
farmed out *her* children to strangers, nor had Mrs. Devlin's three
daughters farmed out Mrs. Devlin's eleven grandchildren, a
plague of contemptuous freckles. Mrs. Devlin had always been
there. When a child cried, Mrs. Devlin gave it a cookie and
a squeeze. Mrs. Devlin was immune to Marcy's disapproval because Mrs. Devlin held Hannah as a hostage in the great sorority
house of her smug sex. Hannah hadn't put in a request for Mrs.
Devlin, had she?

The four Mothers-Who-Wanted-to-Work had gathered one
morning in the corner cafeteria for a cup of coffee, black, and
toasted shame. What had they talked about? Publishing? Music?
Linguistics? The Sclerosis of Modernism? The New Left? Day-
care centers? Sexism in the professions? The myth of the vaginal
orgasm? They had talked about formulas, diaper services, bedwet-
ting, Erector Sets vs. Lincoln Logs, eczema ointments and cod-
liver capsules. They were a small band of sinners against the
sorority, seeking absolution. They rubbed the collective smog-ball,

and there appeared the mini-muued and mint-devouring image of Mrs. Devlin, saying Hannah adores pears and needs mittens. They made themselves feel so guilty that afterward they had avoided one another. And then were ashamed of *that* furtiveness.

Not that Frank Discussions were much better, as Marcy, a veteran of Frank Discussions, knew to her dismay. Mrs. A: "It's not the *quantity* of time you spend with your children, but the *quality* of that time. . . ." Mrs. B: "If I stayed cooped up all day long with my children, I'd start hating them and my husband. But if I'm using my brain, when my children *do* see me I can at least communicate a sense of *personhood* that must be worth more to them than constant nagging, resentment, and bad temper. Then I *want* to see them. I am ready and eager to play with them, instead of being *sentenced* to do so. . . ." Mrs. A: "To use that time intelligently and creatively. To be attentive, encouraging, interested. To have the *willingness* and the *energy* to be these things. . . ." Mrs. B: "My husband would come home every night to a cyclone of complaints. . . ." Mrs. A: "Psychological studies indicate that multiple mothering has no adverse effects. More often the effects are positive. Children learn to stand confidently on their own two feet, to deal with new people and situations, to esteem themselves. Bruno Bettelheim is inconsistent. . . ." Mrs. B: "I have a *mind*. A lot of money was spent training it. Is the world so full of trained minds, doing such a wonderful job, that it can afford to waste half of the ones available? That it can say to half of its minds, Your duty is to be a combination of den mother, domestic beast, and soothe-machine, to mop floors, fill mouths, wipe noses, make smiles and leave your brain in the sugar canister? I'm not going to spend my life being a servant for my children. Neither is my daughter. She's going to have the example of a mother who is an *individual*, with feelings and *rights*, not a kitchen appliance. Who can *do* something besides wash dishes and tie shoelaces. Who can be *respected*, not just a piece of biological furniture. . . ." Mrs. A: "We know the problem of the dependent child, the child who is always looking for and clinging to his mother's skirts, afraid of the outside world. . . ." Mrs. B: "I didn't get pregnant by myself, and when you're in bed and you start thinking of your husband as a Roto-Rooter, something's very wrong. . . ." Mrs. A: "After all, the great English statesmen were raised by governesses. Separation-anxiety is important in a child's development. . . ." Mrs. B: "Dr. Spock eats Pablum!"

Growing all the while more querulous and desperate; listening to ourselves as we talk, disliking the tone; knowing, because we are intelligent, that Mrs. Devlin is not an English governess; knowing we are riveted to a pendulum going *tick-tock* back and forth from apology to self-assertion; hating the fact that we assert ourselves *because* we feel apologetic; exhausting ourselves in denying a role that we resent not only because we know the role is unfair but also because we use up so much energy insisting on its unfairness, and energy is precious; trapped, swinging, screaming, guilty, *tick-tock*. To end by secretly resolving on a binge of Mrs. Devlinism. To spend the next day smothering our children with attention and embraces: love by machine gun, in violent little spurt-bursts which ruin whatever order and harmony and hierarchy of expectations we had been able to fashion for or impose on our family lives.

And of course the Mrs. Devlin who appeared in the smog-ball was only a slovenly doppelganger of the Great Bitch-Witch: the bright, tidy, mint-new, E. B. White–reading, *Romper Room*–reproving, Creative Plaything Homemaker-Makee, as serious as she is efficient, glossed over by her own floor wax, a giant in her washer, a bouquet in her detergent, a tornado in her kitchen, a coinbox between her thighs, and a worm the size of a boa constrictor in her ever-so-sexy gut. I shave my legs and cream my face and spray my hair and my armpits and my vagina so that one day, when my husband comes home from a hard day of coffee breaks, I will be totally indistinguishable from my Tupperware and my electric mixer. Perfect. Enamelized, with a cord dangling down from my ass.

Listen, Mrs. Devlin: To separate the fact from the lean of the maternal matter, I can only take so many hours a day with so many children. Beyond that lies lunacy. See Sartre on torture brutalizing the oppressor along with the victim. After a sustained no-exit of servicing or rejecting demands, of modulating whines, of straightening messes, of *living* in a world defined by children, the parent turns into a child. She is brutalized. Then *she* starts whining. Thus the situation is reduced to its lowest common denominator: infantilism. Urge, rage, lament. Reason dies, and the living room becomes an id. I have seen that world, and it is

Romper Room. My husband almost understands this; why can't you, Mrs. Devlin? *I* deserve as much as my children; nobody consulted me, either, on whether or not I liked the idea of being born.

"I'll bring the baby food this evening," Marcy said, "when I come to pick up Hannah. And the Pampers Monday morning."

"Super," said Mrs. Devlin. And, as Marcy retreated from the sorority door, Mrs. Devlin cried after her: "Enjoy your day, Mrs. Coffin!"

"Oh," said a trembling Marcy, "I *will.* I *always* do." Hannah had begun to cry. Give her a cookie, Mrs. Devlin . . . *please,* Mrs. Devlin.

"Now hush, child," said Mrs. Devlin. "Don't you like your old Aunt Maud? Aunt Maud *loves* you."

Marcy arrived at Harvard Square on wheels of panic. It didn't help that she was early: a yawn of time, when she was used to having all her hours zippered up, all her minutes buttoned down. Time to *kill,* when her whole life was organized like a science lab, each category of it a chemical retort in which she tried to synthesize an extra day in the week, an extra month in the year. What to do? Buy baby food for Hannah and cart it to class, to the institute, to Mrs. Devlin's? Rummage through the print-bins? Find a book for Ken: *Toilet-Training in Old Plymouth: Witch Stool Was the Pigeon?*

"La Passionaria! Frozen music with green book bag! Marcy-not-in-motion!"

Speaking of yawns: they are always full of something. "Hello, Roger." To look at Roger Beckwith, you would think he was a commercial for the Now Generation. From his curly blond head, the White Rock maiden, to his steerhide motorcycle jacket with the snap-on lamb collar, Hell's Angel out of J. Press, to his tie-dyed bell-bottom dungarees and his calfskin Wellington boots, Roger was the image of amiable phoniness: a little bit of menace and a lot more sunlight, in the pale eyes, bouncing off the perfect teeth clenched in the perfect smile, like a bar of metal burning white. You knew he would try to sell you something noncaloric. What you wouldn't know, but Marcy knew, was that Roger Beckwith was The Enemy.

"You've been feeding fertilizer to your sideburns."

"Now that's the Marcy I know. On the attack! You're beautiful."

"You look fit, as always."

"Handball. I play handball every day instead of eating lunch. Feel that hand." He extended it; she took it; he gripped, grinning. "Can I buy a liberated woman a cup of coffee, or does the liberated woman have to buy me a cup of coffee?"

"You can have your hand back, Roger." All a liberated woman meant to Roger was an easy lay; so much for revolutions of consciousness—we become more vulnerable. If we say no, it's because we're prisoners of conventions. But there was the yawn: "All right, you can buy me a cup of coffee."

They forded traffic to the Bick. Roger deposited Marcy in a window seat. All Cambridge was Roger's business; he liked to see and be seen. Going away to place their order, he was all menace, like a dangerous toy wound up and sent to whir and spin. Returning, he was all sunlight, proud of the fact that he hadn't slopped the coffee.

"Ken still up in New Hampshire beating the slaves?"

"Getting the apples picked, yes."

"Good. Then you can come to my party tomorrow night."

"Is that what I've been waiting for all my life? To go to your party?"

"Could be. You haven't heard my electric autoharp. You haven't seen my sinusoidal prism."

"I'm culturally deprived." Was it open season on her? Did it somehow show? She didn't want to look at the blond curl on his forehead, or to be burned by his metal bar. She stared at the motorcycle jacket. There were zippers at the pockets and the wrists; there were snaps on the flaps, lapels, and epaulets. Just like her life. As a matter of fact, she could almost see herself in the steerhide, which had been polished to a black mirror. "What are you doing with yourself these days, Roger? Or to the rest of us? Besides playing handball?"

"I have given up my search for the definitive deviation hypothesis."

"I'm sorry to hear it." Was she? She tried to remember what Roger had been working on. Conformity and deviation . . . the "how" characteristics of a response style . . . acquiescence sets and evasiveness sets and criticalness sets . . . Resolved, dominated, and compromised composites . . . When Hull says "parameter K," doesn't he really mean the same thing as Lewin when Lewin says "valence"? It was word-garbage in her mind; but it smelled of manipulation. Roger helped some people to manipulate other people more effectively. One foot in the heur-house door, while the other wore a hobnailed boot. She had accused him of it once. He had replied that not all of us have a trust fund to finance our soul-searching; not all of us live off our dead mothers. Ken had hit him. Roger and Ken had avoided each other thereafter. That Roger Beckwith had actually bled somehow surprised her; perhaps she had supposed he was made out of nylon or plastic, like other dangerous toys.

"Too academic," said Roger. "I thought it was time I got beyond the propaedeutic."

"I should hope so. What are you into now? Riot control?"

"Ha, ho, ha, ho. No."

"Prophylactic Random Terror Bombing: Counterinsurgency in Game and Earnest?"

"Come on, Marcy. Insystec isn't that kind of operation, and you know it." Interfacing Systems Technology, specializing in macrohistorical leaps from maybe to now. Instant scenarios, synergistic or serendipitous to match your warroom wallpaper. Was this the same young man, the *boy*, who had pounded on her apartment door in Berkeley at 3 A.M. over a decade ago? To announce, drunk and weeping: Albert Camus died in a car crash! The conscience of the West is dead! He had thought then that his grief was a ticket entitling him to her body; she had poured hot coffee into him and, ultimately, all over him. "We're into R & D. You know, Research and Development. We tell industry what to do with its brains and money." He clung to his coffee cup with both hands, the White Rock maiden now waiting to be goosed. "The purpose of a semi-attached policy studies center is to penetrate the smog-screen of what we at Insystec call preemptive obfuscation. Every Standard World has its Canonical Variations. If your reality-pastiche is sophisticated enough, you should be able to predict the Canonical Variations. But what you really have to worry about are systems breaks. Systems breaks cause Disarray, and Disarray plays hell with the dynamics of legitimacy. Look at the American economy. Since World War II the American economy has jumped over so many nodes of transition that it doesn't even know it's *living* in a Canonical Variation, a sort of dichotomized state capitalism. Seventy per cent of all R & D is federally funded. Ninety per cent of federal R & D funds go to nongrowth areas, like defense, space, atomic energy, and the Hudson Institute. Oh, we've come up with some new products, but there aren't very many civilian applications for a rocket engine or a nuclear submarine. And we've come up with a few new scientific and managerial techniques, plus a couple of new industries, but data processing, solid propellants, systems engineering, and so on actually depend on the government contract market, where cost-plus financing insulates them against the old Standard World of cost competition. Don't tell me about by-products. If you want the by-product, go develop the by-product. You want high-powered radio tubes? Spend some time and money developing high-powered radio tubes; don't build accelerators that happen to need high-powered radio tubes. You see what's happened: with its cost-plus contracteeship and nongrowth exclusivity, our dichotomized state capitalism has ceased to be competitive, which significantly reduces its repertoire of Alternate Futures. Autoemasculation, followed by the usual self-hatred. So a Canonical Variation of *colonialism* comes about. The *exploited* country is the *mother* country. What the Vulgar Marxists refuse to understand is that we are *not* in Vietnam to exploit the tin mines, the rubber bushes, and the betel nuts; we're there to colonize *ourselves*, to exploit the *American* taxpayer for the benefit of the aerospace, automotive, and chemical industries that have lost their competitive knack. We're just *asking* for Disarramification, the ultimate systems break of Peace. Marcy, we have entered what Sorokin might have called a Fourth Cultural Phase: the Insensate. Not a very pretty scenario, is it? For, without a viable American capitalism, semiattached policy studies centers will have nothing to which they can semiattach themselves."

Whether Roger Beckwith was really saying much of this wasn't important. The Edsel of Marcy's mind, on cruising alien slanguage, shifted into overdrive; the words blurred together in her mocking motion. When is a coefficient a no-efficient? When it is dichotomized. The Psychopathology of Price-Fixing: Onan Is Occam After He Razored Hell. Socio's your old mandate—Punnilingus, Ken had called it, and they had often turned it into a game. You protect yourself by doing to *their* language what they have done to *yours*: make it nonsensical. Of Vietnam: Maxwell's Taylor lives in Saigon, making Napalm Beach suits to order for the Joint Cheats of Strafe. Of Marshall McLuhan: on the banks of the *Sewanee Review* he lay down with the Mechanical Bride and they performed all sorts of unnatural acts of Typography. Marcy won all the word games but one. Of De Chardin she had said: Teilhard grinds his Privileged Axis. Ken had cheated by quoting directly from Teilhard. Well, it was a reasonable substitute for thinking about what was actually being said.

"And so," Roger might have gone on, "we need an independent variable we can ride to viability. One of my colleagues thought he saw some possibilities in the Consciousness Distortion game, obviously a growth industry throughout the counter-culture. Why let the Mafia corner the market in manipulating perceptions, sensory experiences, levels and states of Being and Becoming? He thought that tetrahydrocannabinol, or Delta 1, was our big beyond-the-propaedeutic chance. You remember: that artificial marijuana an Israeli chemist synthesized a couple of years ago—colorless, odorless, available in liquid form. The narks at the Justice Department had a systems break just thinking about it. Add a little alcohol and some coloring, and you could smuggle it into the country as after-shave lotion. But why smuggle it in? Why not manufacture the stuff right here, before they passed a law against it? It took the Food and Drug Administration twenty years to catch up with cyclamates; in half that time Delta 1 could be America's favorite after-shave, and whoever pioneered in the marketing of it would have made a macrohistorical leap into the Alternate Future of programmed dreams."

Marcy lit her first cigarette of the morning. Brother, can you paradigm? Nomenclature was a dangerous kind of antipoetry, borrowing magic, concealing meaning, associative without being responsible, an insinuation. In Roger's mouth, the insinuation was sexual: *he* was available in liquid form. But it always had to do with domination, priests using words to cast spells, authority residing either in the impenetrability of what's said or in the binding force of the banality of the spoken. Marcy was dissatisfied with the words, even *her* words, that tried to describe her feelings: feeble, proximate, cheapened by overuse, whores after votes of usage-acceptance, prom queens who secretly farted. Resist the spell of a verbal code, the leakings of a Beckwith: the code wasn't worth deciphering, only a disguised aggression. A little thing like leaving the house early sure screwed up a girl's day.

"It was a good idea," said Roger, "because he put his finger on the ultimate variable: man. The fly in the matrix of successful social planning. Until we adapt man to his environment, instead of trying to do it the other way around, we're nowhere. But the Delta 1 syzygy leaked like a sieve. The Feds aren't going to let you get away with marketing artificial marijuana without some Supreme Court knee-jerk deciding you have to legalize *natural* grass. The trouble with natural grass is that you can grow it in a window box. Which means it can't be taxed. The government only permits us those pleasures that it can tax, except, of course, for sex. Even worse, the Being and Becoming racket is dangerous because it multiplies the Disarray factors you have to take into account. It's tough enough at Insystec worrying about the normal cathexes; expanding and diversifying their forms and expressions represents what we call a High Asterisk. You want to *reduce* the number of variables, not increase them. And Beckwith has found a way."

"What way has Beckwith found?"

"Beckwith was brooding about the crisis of our hospitals," said Beckwith. "Where's the profit? And Beckwith discovered biomedical engineering. Piezo-electric crystals, permanent artificial pacemakers for regulating your heartbeats by electrical impulse. Air-driven pumps to supplement the left ventricle! Silicone hearts with synthetic valve systems! Laser-welding of retinal tears! Cryosurgical destruction of diseased tissue! Ultrasonic crystal frequencies to create decongestant fogs! Isotopic clot locators! Nylon and Dacron blood vessels! Beckwith was impressed. Clearly our future will be full of artificial motors, pumps, limbs, and organs more efficient and longer lasting than their phylogenetic prototypes. The boon to American industry is self-evident; the boon to American foreign policy is a dividend.

"Next, Beckwith discovered genetic engineering. We are well on our way toward not only deciphering but *controlling* the structure and the 'code' of hereditary materials—the form our cells assume and the reasons why they assume it and the ways in which we can manipulate it. Tissue cultures can be grown in test tubes. Computers are already analyzing genetic structure. Viral spies have been detected carrying crucial information from one bacterium to another, on the payroll of whichever host promises the most satisfactory tumor. Laboratory preservation of exceptional genes is a distinct possibility. Galton's Alternate Future of sensible human breeding is well within the circumference of the prob-

68

able. Muller's sperm bank for the promotion of the super-fetus is entirely feasible. DNA cryptologists have isolated the hyper-significant chromosome. Human cells have been hybridized with mice cells. Enzymologically speaking, most proteins can be engineered to function in whatever way we decide is appropriate. We shall soon be able to program our progeny, transplanting whole nuclei with their baggage cars of DNA from one cell to another, sexlessly replicating whichever individual permits his nuclei to be co-opted. Think what that will do to your popular idyllistic formulations of the romantic response-style! We are playing a very serious game of chromosomatic roulette, with immense profits potential.

"Beckwith put these two forms of engineering together in his mind and synthesized an independent variable."

"Which is?"

"Little people."

"Ah, yes, little people." Pedestrians swam across the window like balloon fish. Little people . . .

"A variable in four scenarios," said Roger. "Take genetics. The somatotropin, or 'growth-hormone,' is one of the active principles of the anterior pituitary gland. Its formation depends on the eosinophilic cells. Identify the gene that controls the enzyme involved in somatotropin synthesis, and boost it or remove it or kill it. Snatch the egg from a proestrous woman, fiddle with the gene, plug the egg back into the woman, and you can alter the eventual size of the eventual adult by almost four feet each way.

"Take endocrinology. Excess amounts of the growth-hormone could be injected into an embryo or infant. Gland activity seems to be inversely proportional to the amount of hormone in the bloodstream. Negative feedback. The more hormone in the bloodstream, the less active the anterior pituitary gland.

"Take immunology. By developing vaccines to kill, or biotics to augment, the activity of the eosinophilic cells, you can manipulate size.

"Take diet. Obviously, protein development is affected by protein consumption. Ingesting proteins and vitamins makes for larger people; ingesting mostly sugars and starch makes for flabbier but *shorter* people. Remember that the occidental introduction of refined rice to the Orient was a stunningly successful experiment in controlled diminution.

"None of this has anything to do with the brain. Brain cells don't grow very much after birth. What growth there is depends on synaptic connections—learning and experience—whose formation is independent of somatotropin. The head is fully adult-sized by the age of five. There is not much wrong with dwarfs except that they are *small*—with eosinophilic defects! Now, then, all we have to decide is whether we want people to be bigger or smaller than they are right now."

All the elastic appeared to have gone out of Marcy's synapses. "Bigger?"

"Wrong. Why would you want bigger people, what with the population explosion and everything? Reducing the size of man means increasing the size of the earth. Look at our transportation systems. Smaller people would mean smaller vehicles, greater capacities for existing highways, more off-street parking. Look at housing. Smaller people would mean more floors per apartment house. Look at conservation. Smaller people would use up our natural resources over a longer period of time. Look at sewage systems. Smaller people would extrude less waste. Look at space exploration. Smaller people would leave more room for fuel in third-stage capsules. Look at leisure. Hunting rats would excite the same sporting instincts and competitive enthusiasms as hunting deer excites right now. Look at—"

"Toothpaste would last longer," said Marcy, plucking at her book bag.

"You miss the point," said Roger. "We would reduce the size of the tubes. That's the marvelous part of it. The entire American economy would have to be retooled. Cars, houses, credit cards, diaphragms, garbage disposals, buttons, keys, hamburgers, cigarettes, *Vogue* patterns, would all have to be reproduced on a smaller scale. The same technologies, of course, but we would be doing everything all over again! To repeat your mistakes is demonstrably a low-risk, high-profit business venture. Not to mention the important precedent we'd be setting for a more imaginative manipulation of the Ultimate Variable in the future."

"Roger, Roger—what makes you think anybody wants to be two feet tall?"

"We start by buying into the hospitals. Nobody else is interested in hospitals. We work with prisoners, with retarded children, with the mentally ill, just to get some data. It's not going to take very long for the government to see the possibilities, and give us contracts to take care of troublesome minority groups. Presidential candidates will be all for it: maintain your television image while reducing your target-area on the campaign trail. And then, well—the door to the pediatrics ward stands open; Lilliput will march in!"

Marcy stood up. "You're insane."

"Of course," said Roger. "These days, that's the operational definition of a sense of humor. Will I see you tomorrow night?"

"Do I have to bring my anterior pituitary gland?"

"It's not your anterior pituitary gland that I'm interested in." All sunlight now, cherub with blond forelock and black jacket. "Marcy, you'd better learn which Standard World you're living in. The preeminent philosophical question of the next two decades for American democracy is this: Is the semiattached policy studies center a more viable pluralistic alternative than the government intelligence agency? Rinsler is irrelevant."

On the street again, and troubled: had he meant that Insystec and the CIA considered the institute irrelevant, or was he being personal? La Passionaria as the prize for which Roger and Rinsler competed, the one figuring out which Apocalyptic scourge was most cost-effective, the other calculating systems breaks according to their turmoil coefficient? Was Ken, then, some Standard World belonging to a senile century, with Roger-Rinsler representing a postconnubial *fin de siècle*? All she needed now was a Navel Intelligence stud unzipping his fly to show her his Polaris. What fun and war-games it was to be an Earth Mother! An Earth Mother of two. An Earth Mother late to her section, after all that leisure. Time was crystallized guilt. Let them play their whore-games in someone else's bedroom. Oh, Yard, thou art not Variable: must every undergraduate look as though he'd dressed in a burning building, from a closet full of Hollywood's ideas about Guevara? The Earth Mother of two skidded on crystallized guilt. Nine out of ten computer print-outs agree: Suck my Polaris. The male invariable.

It was an overheated little room, one-sided with high windows, through which light fell like water over a dam; on which, like lily pads, the yellow desks were floating; at which, froglike on this pond of fluorescence, her students sat croaking their insouciance. In every analogical mirror, a motorcycle jacket; propaedeutic dudes to gang-bang my scenario. "How nice to see you again, Mr. Segal." He was committed to the *Crimson* executive competition, appearing at class only according to the phases of the Plimpton Street moon, on the way from a postponement of the midterm paper to an incomplete in the course, complacent in the guilefulness he was still young enough to think others found charming. "Good morning, Miss Richardson." Moving like a tank toward her *magna*, wearing on her living bra a neon "A," one character of the alphabet for every ambiguity, born with a stenographer's pad instead of a *tabula rasa*, Marcy before she became an Earth Mother, a Marcypial. "Mr. Galton, hello." Right tackle on a good Harvard football team, capable of pinching Marcy's head off, as gentle in class as a mollusk, needing approval like Stephen, like Hannah. For Laforgue, a nod, and one of those smiles you save up for bus drivers when all you have in your purse is a ten-dollar bill. My prep-school dandy, skull so thin the filament shone through, pivoting his arms to palm his wallet and check the pulse of his disdain, downright cancerous with affectations: blue shirt as soft as sleep, a steamrollered snake for a tie, orange cigarettes, the air-mail edition of last week's *Spectator* hanging out of his pocket like a kind of toilet paper for the mind. Laforgue disdained Marcy because there had been better teachers his senior year at Grottlesex than there were his freshman year at Harvard. Laforgue had read and forgotten everything; Segal hadn't had the time to read anything; Miss Richardson and Mr. Galton conspired solemnly to synopsize, thus reminding Laforgue of the problem and acquainting Segal with it, and so turning the last twenty minutes of each section into table tennis, Laforgue with wrist-action putting a spin on the argument, Segal smashing it, the rest of the class scribbling notes, and Marcy gnashing her teeth.

It would have been just like Berkeley, when Marcy was Miss Richardson and the Segals and Laforgues were full of wheat germ, except that now each class had to have its resident radical: a Trot to kill the discussion with a harangue, a Maoist to wave it away with her little red book. Endless ideological quibbling among the fiercely pampered who were convinced their orgasmic Rendezvous with Truth would come, their "perfect moment" of communal violence, the existential whoopee of nightsticks, paving stones, and tear gas. Marcy had read Sartre; she knew. Her personal radical was Royce, a gentle young man with yellow eyes, who said bloodthirsty things about Nathan Pusey and the Somoza brothers. Come Royce's rendezvous with a nightstick, and his brain would be mashed potato. Was it her fault that she had left Berkeley before the Sproul Hall slump-in, and Paris before Danny the Red turned everything into a shaggy Godard story? Didn't it count that she worked every afternoon at the institute? She thought of their essays, wrestling with color symbolism. Color symbolism had lost. Becalm yourself, dear. Did other teachers around here, inspecting their class, long every once in a while to assume the role of a bottle of Johnson's No-Roach with the spray applicator? Let's clean up these minds!

"Well." She withdrew their papers from her book bag. There was a sigh. "After reading these," she said, "I was reminded of an anecdote. Louis XIV once wrote a sonnet. He submitted it for judgment to Boileau, a highly regarded poet who happened at that time to be Court historiographer. Boileau, after reading it, told the King: 'Sire, nothing is impossible for Your Majesty. You set out to write some bad verses and you have succeeded.' " She waited for a ripple of appreciation, then waded into its wake. "You set out to miss the point of poor Mr. Joyce's color symbolism, and you have succeeded admirably."

Off they went. Laforgue confessed to being bored by everything Joyce wrote except one phrase in *Finnegans Wake*, "the hitherandthithering river." Segal waxed eloquent on color symbolism; Segal hadn't even turned in a paper. Royce wanted to know why Joyce alone among the modern giants hadn't entertained authoritarian political opinions.

Afterward, Segal lingered, putting on a clumsy sort of diffidence: let's pretend that I'm being self-effacing, although we both know I could never really efface all the self I've got going for me, right? "Mrs. Coffin—" Marcy was tempted to correct him. *Doctor* Coffin. We are *Doctor* and *Mister* Coffin. But of course she didn't. "What did Louis XIV do to . . . what's his name?"

"Boileau?"

"Yeah. What did Louis do to him when Boileau dumped on his sonnet?"

"Nothing."

"Nothing? You'd expect a guy like Louis to hand him his head."

"Yes, well." The pedagogue sprang to attention. "Those were the days when poets were taken seriously, even by kings. Louis

XIV would accept the judgment of a well-known poet on his own stab at poetry, because Louis granted a certain kind of authority to the opinion of an expert in *that* field. Democracy has changed things. Now we believe that one man's opinion is just as good as another's. Maybe not in nuclear physics or automobile repair. But in art . . . We vote on it." Read all about it in Irving Babbitt.

Segal effaced some more of himself. Why do they talk with their chins on their shoulders? "Mrs. Coffin, Gerry and I were wondering . . ."

"Gerry?"

"Gerard Laforgue." He waved a hand. "He's out in the hall. We were wondering if you might want to join us for lunch today. Just a chance to rap, you know, without all the zombies around."

Laforgue and Segal! She was invited to a private party. Strip table tennis? "I'm sorry. I really am. But I've got an appointment. Maybe you'll give me a rain check?"

"Sure," said Segal. "Well. See you Monday."

Marcy smiled. "Possibly, Mr. Segal. But sections are on Wednesday and Friday. The lecture is Monday."

"Yeah. You're right, Mrs. Coffin." He shook himself off, like a hound climbing out of the water, and was gone.

Leaving Marcy furious with herself. She didn't have an appointment. Why couldn't she have gone to lunch with them? Teachers were always going off to lunch with students. Ah, but those teachers were men. Being a woman made it different. No. Being a Marcy made it possible to make it different—complicated, tense. Maybe they actually *liked* her. She wasn't entirely sure teachers should be likable. The lust for the approval of the young had left too many of her colleagues looking ridiculous. Had she ever liked her teachers? She had liked her French instructor at Cal very much, even if his poetry seemed in retrospect a sort of *symbolist* Spam. And he had liked her. But then, if you laid all his female students end to end, you'd find he had, too. She fashioned a small pause for herself by carefully restocking the book bag. That achieved, she fed her mouth a cigarette it did not want. Then she couldn't find any matches. Simply splendid.

At last she left the empty room. Hello. Segal and Laforgue were still standing in the hall. She watched in amazement as Laforgue thumbed to life a silver lighter, as the flame leaped up like a blow torch and swept toward her—she had forgotten about the cigarette in her mouth. Was the flame attached to the filament in Laforgue's skull? She puffed nervously. Laforgue looked disdainful; Segal looked sympathetic. She had hopelessly compromised her relationship with both of them. By refusing lunch? By presenting Laforgue with an opportunity to light her cigarette? She nodded coolly at them, wondering how on earth they had discovered each other. The young always gave the impression of not yet knowing their powers, capable of harm. And Marcy would soon be celebrating her thirtieth birthday; moss on the haunches. So walk away. And worry while you're walking what their eyes will tell their minds. She tried to walk, well, efficiently. She could think of nowhere to put the hand that held the cigarette. Let it hang.

Royce sat on the steps reading a magazine. She wanted to tell him about Roger Beckwith, but Laforgue and Segal were close behind her. Insystec would survive another day. She slipped into a phone booth. See the hurrying of bodies on errands, to appointments, through the Yard: parkas and raincoats, flung forward, burrowing blindly into the noon hour. She wanted to cry *Stop!* Then all faces would turn on her quizzically, and she would be as some doomed astronaut, floating helpless in her booth within a ring of moons. Stop? Wise old cratered faces . . . Mrs. Coffin, there is no *stop*. Dr. Coffin, if you please. There was no one to telephone. There was no Alternate Future. She had been permanently disconnected. Laforgue and Segal had disappeared. Royce and Miss Richardson should really get together. He could tell her about the dialectic; she could tell him about ambiguity; their child would be two feet tall with programmed dreams of existential whoopee. *Stop.* There must be, growing behind the ear or at the base of the spine, a switch you can flick, a switch to turn off the organism while you are waiting in line to buy tickets, or in libraries to receive books, or in phone booths remembering French instructors who had complained along with Baudelaire that each poem meant one less erection for the poet: *This time doesn't count against me.* She would go to the institute. Even Rinsler was better than a phone booth.

At the trolley stop stood a trio of parole-breaking high school boys, spaghetti-headed, pinch-faced, hump-shouldered under the weight of the iron crosses hanging from their necks, broken at their hinges. Dribbling her smog-ball down the pavement toward them, Marcy knew—did she need any more evidence?—that this was not her day. They stared at her. Do nothing, say nothing: invite nothing. It never works. They bent their heads to ignite their cigarettes, contriving at once to make a sacrifice to the demiurge of Slouch and to give the impression of three clumps of seaweed needing a fourth for sex. Breaking from the match, they examined her again, whispering about her book bag, her red cape, her black tights. Finally, after a lot of practice, they were prepared to make an audible remark:

"Hey, Batmen," said the shaggiest to the other two, "there's Robin, the girl wonder."

She knew that if she turned away, pretending to ignore them, their taunts would grow bolder. They expected her to be frightened and ashamed. She stared back at them. They grinned. She continued to stare, thinking of ants, worms, bacilli, tumors, atomic fission. They conferred again, then took several steps forward, swinging their bodies from the hips and knees, hands in their back pockets, mouths half-open around the dangling cigarettes, eyes half-closed to keep the smoke from stinging the retina. Her stomach turned.

The shaggy one addressed her directly. "Hey, girl wonder, do you know what I think?"

"I don't even know that you *can* think."

"Pussy talks, men. Wind it up, and it talks."

"Look," said Marcy, "why don't you just go home and count your pimples? If you can count that high."

"Why don't you come with me, girl wonder?"

"What for? Can't your mommy change your diapers?"

"You've got a big mouth for such a small cunt."

"What are you going to do about it? Whip me to death with your hair?" She was, of course, breaking the rules. She was talking back. She had embarrassed him in front of his friends. He hated her. And she was terrified. Terrified, and loathing herself for letting them get away with it again. Then a man who had been standing in front of the drugstore, studying cures for hemorrhoids, steeled himself to responsible citizenship. First, he pushed his rimless glasses up on the bridge of his nose, winging it like a plastic bat; next, he allowed his cuffs to kiss each other; finally, he approached.

"What's going on here?" he demanded. There was something wishful about his truculence. Where *are* all the heroes? But the boys backed away, and the temperature of his courage climbed ten degrees. "You punks leave the little lady alone, you hear me?"

All right, she was supposed to be grateful. Responsible Citizen had done more than most would. But Responsible Citizen would spend the rest of the afternoon feeling proud of himself; *the little lady*, pussy, cunt, would spend the rest of the afternoon knotted up inside. Little lady smiled at him anyway. He stood around her, like a telephone booth, until the trolley rolled in.

She had to wait for change. The three boys pushed their way to the back. Receiving her change, Marcy decided that it wasn't over. Humiliation might as well be a two-way street. She, too, clawed her way to the rear of the trolley, found a seat across from the three of them. They pretended not to watch her, uneasy now with so many people around. She loosened her bag and took out a book. *Portrait of the Artist*, naturally. She opened it, reversed it, pointing the pages at them, and then suddenly thrust it into their faces. "*Zap!*" she cried. They blinked. Marcy smiled. "I'm surprised and impressed. I thought the mere sight of printed matter would make you faint dead away." Her voice got louder. Maintain control; don't be strident. "This, gentlemen, is a book. Magical. Very dangerous. Have you ever seen one?" She concentrated on the shaggiest. "I'm sorry there aren't any pictures of sports cars or naked women. But there are *words*. A word is made up of letters. Letters come from the alphabet. Do you know the alphabet? A is for ass. B is for brainless. C is for coward. A coward is a three-headed creature who hangs around bus stops insulting women. When cowards die, the oil is drained from their hair and used to grease the wheels of tricycles."

Several passengers, including the responsible citizen, had turned and were regarding her with curiosity. She smiled at them. "Excuse me, but I am a teacher of the mentally retarded. These poor boys were born with an extra bile duct where their brain is supposed to be. And if that weren't tragedy enough, they've also got chronic diarrhea. Of the nonbrain. D, gentlemen, is for diarrhea." She couldn't think of an E. Enema? Epidemic? Evil? She slapped the book shut. They blinked again, then looked sullenly out the window. They were very good at being sullen; it was probably the only thing they were good at, besides masturbating and stealing hubcaps.

Two stops later they got off. She was relieved. If she had gotten off first, would they have followed her? But she wasn't pleased with herself. It was a game she couldn't win. And, according to Rinsler, these were the very people they had to organize. Get into their minds, said Rinsler; show them that their fathers have been willing ever since Gompers to exchange the sons, in time of war, for overtime checks at the factory. Sure. Marcy should have talked to El Shaggo about working-class consciousness. Don't you see what SDS is up to? They're trying to prove to *you* that they have the guts to take on the power structure. Off the pigs! Machismo! The jails are the place to organize. Marcy, then, was an oppressor. What did Rinsler know about oppression, anyway?

"Excuse me." She emerged from her revery to find the responsible citizen peering at her with an embarrassing intensity, as though his eyes behind the rimless glasses were suction cups. "I was wondering . . . are you a *clear?*"

"Am I a what?"

"A *clear.* I am a clear. I'm working my way up the affinity tone scale." He sighed. "Someday I shall be an operating thetan. It's simply a matter of escaping from my MEST."

"I'm sorry. Escaping from your what?"

"MEST. My Matter-Energy-Space-Time body. Theta is Beingness. MEST is the body. You liberate your theta from its MEST by getting rid of the basic engram."

"Of course. The basic engram." She wanted to put her book bag over her head. The maniacs were restless today.

"I see that you're not familiar with Scientology," said the responsible citizen. "An engram is the sound impression a psychic trauma makes on our protoplasm. According to L. Ron Hubbard, the basic engram was received by the human race many, many centuries ago, a supersonic shot in the forehead, incapacitating and reducing the size and function of the pineal gland."

"The pineal gland? Is the pineal gland making a comeback?"

"Lots of people confuse engrams with goals. But goals came long before engrams. L. Ron Hubbard estimates that his *To Forget* Goal was implanted in him some thirty-eight trillion to forty-three trillion years ago on the planet Helatrobus."

"Yes. The planet Helatrobus."

"Yes. Of course, you have to understand that each of us has gone through many, many incarnations; many, many MESTs. It's simply a matter of getting rid of the engrams, of remembering where you got your goals—which implantation station on which planet how long ago."

"How do you do that?" Perhaps she attracted maniacs the way Ken attracted children; and if Ken attracted children because he was a little childish, did that mean Marcy was a little maniacal?

"Well, you begin with auditing. Then there are the E-meters. It's amazing really. Once I had a toothache. There was nothing wrong with my teeth, and I was thinking about why I should have a toothache. The image of a gorilla came into my mind, and I understood that the toothache was related to the Gorilla Goal planted in me seventeen trillion years ago. Suddenly, my pain was gone."

"It certainly does sound amazing. Tell me, what good does it do you to become, ah, an operating thetan? I mean, what happens?"

"Why," and he was surprised, "total freedom happens. No more anxiety. A theta body is capable of telepathy and psychokinesis. A theta body . . . you must excuse me, this is my stop. Let me give you a brochure. Every Monday night we have auditing sessions for beginners. I do hope you'll come."

And he got off, leaving her to slide over the glossy pages of his brochure. Eight Dynamics, 24 Logics, 58 Axioms. Black thetans spitting white energy. Aircraft Door Implants. Alice games, Havingness processes, gradient scale drills, capping beams, opposition terminals. She promptly developed a headache. But the image that came into her mind was fuzzy: it could have been Roger, it might have been Rinsler, it should have been Coffin, it looked like Mrs. Devlin.

At last the institute. I can clear up my own MEST, she thought while disembarking; it's all those operating thetans who try to get me down. Her headache would go away when she ate some cheese.

Six

LEROY GUARDS THE STATION WAGON. Leroy superintends the closing of the doors, the switching on of the radio. Leroy seems hardly able to contain suggestions for using the choke, for shifting gears.

Hey, there's the sun, all spokes whipping the clouds to a puffiness of batter. It is commencing to clear up right over Mackenzie Farm. Now why are all those white men standing around in a semicircle under the sun, in the pit, staring at the A-C, nodding their heads? White men cast no shadows. Not Dennison, not Short, not Staples, who seem to be trying like a bunch of mourners to define an attitude, form a face somewhere between greed and regret. And Murdock: well, Murdock already has his attitude. Blotched ferocity, in whose thrall he teeters, comical really, hands groping in mackinaw pockets, almost a kangaroo. Somebody picked my pouch.

The student of character leaves Leroy in the station wagon, descends into the pit, says hello, gets silence. "What's happened?"

"Stole them a tractor battery," says Dennison. "That old Ford weren't startin' last night, so they took 'em a battery."

"Where did they go?" Nobody knows. "How many of them?" "Leroy says six."

"Six? Which six?" Nobody knows that either, nobody having inconvenienced himself to learn any black names.

Short says, "We called the cops." Murdock is busy being furious.

The student of character arises from the pit, advances on the camp, pauses at the screen door, ignores Leroy's semaphoric seizure in the station wagon, wonders what cookie-shape to stamp on his reproach, hears James T. Worthy talking loud enough to carry over the TV blast:

"Listen, niggers. Now, a buck with the itch, he's from outa town, right? And he come messin' 'round my wife, and he make it with Cindy Lou, right? Well that buck he doan know me, do he? No. So he ain't done it to *me*, is he? No. He jes heppin hisself to what's for free. So I kills *her*, right? 'Cause she the one what done it to me. But now a stud he been messin' 'round with Cindy Lou, and that stud he been around awhile, that stud *knows* me, and I knows him, and he make it with Cindy Lou, now, then, *he* done that to *me*. Right? 'Cause he *knows* me. So I kills *him*. That's fair, ain't it? Now listen hard, niggers. I knows *all* of you. Right?"

Enter Coffin, stage left, upon a pond of black on which the body of Butterfly floats buglike, snoring; on which TV flicker plays with stove-glow, tag, and tic-tac, making a kind of moon out of all the available light in the room. Craps at one end of the groaning board, where Foy stands blind with the idea of money, dollar bills folded lengthwise and tucked at the knuckles between left-hand fingers while the right makes whipping motions to tame the spot he throws at: a black eagle. Root-man, hunched around his inward eye, whistling low, pretending to be bored, is probably losing. Albany Jackson watches.

"Mornin', Rollin."

At the other end of the table James T. Worthy, Porter, Mason, and Lonzo dabble in and lap at the shore of the pond. Cigarettes hang half-forgotten from their mouths. Their hands grasp empty beer cans as though they are stirrups on a day that has already thrown them and galloped away.

Ken says: "Well, Foy, winning yourself another semester?"

Foy grins. "I'm goin' to win me a whole college education from ol' Root-man all by hisself."

"Federal Pen A and M," says James T. Worthy. "They goin' teach you how to break up rocks, Foy-boy."

Foy keeps grinning. "James T. Worthless, ol' Rollin already

done showed me how to break up rocks. And I allus knowed how to break up heads."

Ken can think of nothing to do with his hands, not having a can to hang onto, and offers cigarettes, reminding them of the ones already in their mouths. They refuse. Well. No tangents in his quiver so he says: "I was wondering about the battery that disappeared last night."

They have nothing to say. They don't even bother to click.

"It was Terence Lavalle's car, wasn't it? So he must have been one of them." No she-it. "The problem is how many were on Dennison's crew, how many on mine. We may have to shift people." Whose problem? Not Foy-boy's; nor is James T. Worthless owning up to it. Ken stares at Albany Jackson: "I knew Lavalle's car was bum. He told me. I told him I'd do something about it. They were coming up here to fix it. But he couldn't wait a day. Now the cops will go after him. Not very smart." He has been injured in the rapport. "Six men." Turning to James T. Worthy: "The sun has decided to shine. I hope you intend to pick this afternoon."

Worthy cups his crotch to show he's thinking about it.

Let's try Foy: "The longer we put off picking that ditch, the longer we are going to stay in the West Orchard. And the Canadians will end up picking all the Cortlands, which is easy money."

To which Foy replies: "Hey, Rollin, think *I'll* work today."

To which Worthy adds: "Then we all goin' work today." In the kitchen, Cindy Lou rattles dishes.

"Well, I hope so. Lonzo, can I see your arm?"

Lonzo looms, one of the turban-heads, about as black as the best of imaginations, sits near Ken, looking away at the TV screen. His arm is offered, almost like a snapshot you secretly believe to be perfect in its way. Ken peels off the dirty towel. A crab-shape of pink flesh shows where the skin has come off, elongating itself from the elbow-hollow to the wrist. There are white open blisters.

"Jesus. Does it hurt much?" Lonzo nods. "When did it happen? How?"

"Las' night. I laid it down on the stove."

"Last night? We should have gotten something on it before now."

"I tole Leroy 'bout it." Lonzo is watching the television screen. "He tole Miz Abigail this mornin'."

"And what did she say?"

"She call the hospital. Got me a time to come down."

"When was that?"

"Ten o'clock."

"Ten o'clock? You missed the appointment?"

"Doan have no way to get down. Leroy wouldn't take me. Leroy he say he got thirty mens to fix the dinner for. Rice! Ol' mother-rice again. Son of a bitch tryin' to turn all of us into Chinese coolie-boys with that rice. Twice a day rice a day. Piss on Leroy's rice."

"Where's Peace?" Honkie sure does shuffle quick; a regular cam, that man, throwing all those motions around; see him get shafted.

"In the cave," says Foy. Meaning the below-ground smoking house. "Ol' Peace he fuck a lot of pillow."

"Well, somebody tell him if he wants to take his bad back down to the hospital, I'm driving Lonzo in about ten minutes. Lonzo, which doctor was it?"

"Dunno."

"Abigail didn't tell you the name of the doctor?"

Lonzo watches a soap opera.

"I'll be back." Ken leaves the cabin and heads for Murdock's house. Down at the pit all their heads have fallen off from nodding so much. Dogs strangle on their chains, longing to track down the fugitive battery-stealers. Abigail Murdock answers his knock, a great cloud of competence, wiping her hands on a psychedelic apron, heavy with bookkeeping the bushels. "Battery," she says.

"Yeah, I know. Did you make an appointment for Lonzo to see a doctor this morning?"

"The one with the burned arm? Ten o'clock. Did he go?"

"No. Leroy wouldn't take him down."

"Well, if their own kind won't take care of them, who will?"

"You, most likely. And me, sort of. What was the doctor's name?"

"Folger. Dr. Folger. Course, I don't know if he'd take him now."

"We'll have to try. It looks nasty."

"That boy burned his arm last night when they was all drunk and fighting," says Abigail. "The insurance company isn't going to pay for it."

This remark floats around for a while in Ken's mind, as though he has just completed a puzzle, only to find an extra piece. He decides it is irrelevant, and walks away.

Albany Jackson is waiting for him. "Kenneth, you should understand 'bout Spider-man and them others. Spider-man got hisself talked into it. Skinny Reid and his brother, and Jimmy Lee Allen and his brother, was the ones that wanted to go. Gerald Walker went with 'em, 'cause he go where Skinny Reid go. You know they's all Virginia boys. But they got theirself on ol' Cantrell's gang 'bout a year ago. And Kenneth, they couldn't get off. You know how it is down there. Ol' Cantrell he signs with some boss to do the pickin' of grapefruits. The boss got a lot of money, plus sheriffs and such. The mens do the pickin'. If they decides not to do no pickin', if they decides maybe to take off, why, them Alabama mens is rough. And the sheriff ain't innerested in stoppin' 'em from bein' rough. You know. They stays on that gang, and they does that work, and that's it. Doan go hollerin' to no cops down there, 'cause cops down there ain't innerested 'less the boss down there he innerested. And the boss down there jes want them grapefruits picked. See? Now, when Skinny Reid gets up here, well, the cops up here ain't goin' to let the Alabama mens beat him up, 'cept them Alabama mens do all they's lookin' at the apple trees through big iron bars. And the boss up here, well, you gets fightin' in the camp and ol' Mudduck he *calls* the cops to stop it. See? So Skinny Reid and Jimmy Lee Allen, they figger now's the time to split. They wants *out*, Kenneth. They's goin' back to Virginia whilst they got a chance. He's a good picker, Skinny is, but man, that shit with Cantrell. One long year."

"All right, Albany. But they won't make it." He can see Peace now, out of the cabin. Peace, Lonzo, two Reids, two Allens, Walker, and Lavalle. Eight pickers who won't be picking. He moves again, and stops at the pit. Dennison in rain-slicker and pith helmet, is backing out the big International. Ken waves at him. Dennison turns off the engine. "My God, you look like you're expecting a flood."

"Got to spray that Green Orchard 'gainst scald," says Dennison.

"Then you won't be handling your crew this afternoon?"

"Don't know if I got a crew this afternoon."

"James T. Worthy says they'll all be out, what's left of them."

"Apples want sprayin'," says Dennison. "Short can handle my crew."

"You know, they don't work too well for Short. They don't listen to him the way they do to you."

Dennison removes his pith helmet. His strong square face sags for a moment at the eyes and mouth. "Ken, what difference you think it's gonna make? They ain't workin' well for nobody. Oh, they pick—when they happen to feel like it. And when they don't happen to feel like it, why, they just set. Thirty men up there, and you tell me how many times you get your fifteen out in the mornin'? How many times I get my fifteen out? We're lucky if we get nine apiece, and we get that only four days a week. Now they don't like that West Orchard and that ditch. I don't neither. But there's some thirty-bushel trees in that ditch, big apples with good color. And Ken, I've been in that ditch myself. I was in that ditch last January, with two feet of snow on the ground. I was prunin' and I was graftin' and there weren't nobody there to talk to all day long, and nothing to see but snow, and you keep on workin' to keep from gettin' froze. That's what burns me, Ken. We was out there prunin' and graftin' all winter. And in the spring we was out there, plantin' them dwarf trees and burnin' them rubber tires to move the cold air out. And in the summer we was out there sprayin', and leavin' boxes, and waitin' to see if it'd hail on us. And the weather's been good, and the yield's been good, and the apples got color and this could be the best crop we ever had. All we got to do is pick the apples. And they won't pick 'em. When I see them darkies settin' up there in that cabin, lookin' at that TV, I get mad, 'cause we worked all year to get this, and they won't pick 'em."

"Well, it's your farm all year long, isn't it? You belong here. They don't. You can't expect them to feel about it the same way you do."

"Canadians don't belong here, neither. But we don't have to drag them Canadians into the orchard every mornin'. They come to work. And they get paid same as the darkies, twenty-seven cents a bushel. Some Canadians gettin' checks over two hundred a week. Seven Canadians picked more than thirty darkies. Don't the darkies want no money? What did they come up here for if they're not goin' to work?" He took off his gloves and examined his hands. "And that battery, Ken. I've been workin' on farms all my life. Ain't nobody never stole a battery from a tractor before. Now we're out one tractor 'til Staples gets back with another battery.

Is that what they come here for, to steal batteries? If they don't want to work, let 'em go home. And if they can't afford to go home, well, there's work here to get 'em some money. Them Canadians sure is makin' more money than *I* am."

This, too, seems irrelevant. Let Albany Jackson explain the battery. Let Rinsler come over and explain Etzioni's classifications of power. It's all so much piss in a leaky bucket. It won't get the apples off the trees, nor Lonzo to the hospital.

Ken returns to the station wagon. Lonzo and Peace are there. So is Leroy, who never got out. "Need to get some food," says Leroy. "Thought I'd ride down with you."

"But who's in there to handle those thirty hungry men, Leroy? Hadn't you better be seeing to dinner?"

"Dinner's set. Can't fix no supper without food."

"Lots of rice," says Lonzo. "Boxes and boxes of rice in the kitchen. Beer's what's gone, ain't it, Leroy? Got to buy you some more cases of beer. Sixty-cents a can, ain't that right, Leroy?" Peace hee-haws.

"Out, Leroy," says Ken.

"But I got—"

"I'm taking Lonzo and Peace to the hospital, Leroy. That's seven miles out of town, off 101. I'm not going into town."

"You could drop me. Then when they was done, you could—"

"Not this trip, Leroy. You'd better talk your own car into working."

Lonzo opens the door. Leroy gets out, then leans through the window into the grins of Lonzo and Peace. "Jes see what you git tonight, since I can't go buy nothin'."

"Shua," says Lonzo. "You goin' punish us. Give us twice the rice tonight, ain't you, Leroy? Twice the rice is twice as nice. Ain't it, Leroy? Grits galore! Oh, you's a cru-el one, Leroy."

Ken pulls away. Lonzo and Peace wave back at Leroy. "What's the matter with your back, Peace?"

"'Member that day I fell off the ladder? Think I hurt it then, that day."

"You said then it felt fine."

"Felt all right, then. Next mornin', felt bad some. Feelin' worse since, alla time. I fell off that damn ladder."

"You slept all night last night in a car, Peace. Maybe that's why your back hurts." He looks at Peace's permanently clicked-off face in the rear-view mirror. Features a sculptor might sacrifice three fingers to achieve; eyes that are dead. Built like a god, with the brain of a fruitfly. Were Peace city-bred, Ken would have explained it to Dennison in terms of lead poisoning, from eating paint chips. Since Peace had been country-bred, he would have to explain it in terms of protein deficiency. More piss in the bucket. Peace is dumb, like Butterfly, a stone flower almost inviting the mallet. Therefore, Peace is innocent. If we are men and women, and not just heads of cabbage, we have to take care of Peace. His prolonged dependency is an extension, a parody, of our own: the forever child with the dead eyes. Do we have to take care of Butterfly, as well? Perhaps not. He is already choosing. But we are not men and women; we are swingers of mallets. The forever children are an embarrassment. Such forever children he has known, and not only as a tourist—in the Algerian quarter of Paris—but in Roxbury, Massachusetts; in Winkham, South Carolina. Perhaps a tourist there, too . . . as Butterfly is a perhaps-not.

It started innocently enough, with a story for *Scope*. The poverty program put a little seed-money into Roxbury for after-school tutorial in reading, writing, and arithmetic. He heard about it at a dinner party in one of the white rooms in one of the white apartments of Cambridge, with the bookshelves on cinder blocks built low along the baseboard of the walls, and the inevitable bottle of Cointreau, and, probably, Scarlatti on the hi-fi harpsichord. There must have been cigars, too, not yet pot, except for the pot of cactus ringed around by wooden African figurines, black drummers and flute-toodlers, eyeless long-eared heads, bent stems of elbow and knee; and posters of Middle Earth on closet doors; and the middle earth of Marcy, ploughed, irrigated by Cointreau; and the blue smoke and the harpsichords drifting through the white rooms, bone-raftered vaults of gentility, the intestinal tract of the whale of the time they were having. . . . Anyway, the talk, put on like a record, turned to St. Thomas of Canterbury, a community in the making. Shouldn't they all send books—paperbacks, at least—to help build up the library?

Coffin sent himself, on assignment, to help build up a story. The program director was a grim young white man who held his head in his hands like a cup and poured out opinions: "For tutors, we want people with a low center of specific gravity. Professional people who know what it means to accept a responsibility. People who want to parade around with placards belong at CORE headquarters, not here. Tutors have got to *be here*, not tripping out or falling in love or taking exams or leaving for Israel. The children won't come back a second time. Really, you should sign on yourself."

It was inconsistent with Coffin's self-image, or at least that image of himself intended for Marcy, to refuse. And so, two hours a night, two nights a week, for almost a year, he became a light and diplomatic bird, lenient in their window tree—the attic of St. Thomas—where he volunteered to teach high school students literature and composition. Maybe it was a belfry, not an attic. He was not an expert on Episcopal churches, although he had seen their clock faces burning like coins on many a New England dawn and their steeples on many a picture postcard. (Almost two centuries before, Mackenzies had chucked the Mother out of their religion, along with inherited guilt and the idea of hell, their spiritual hides having been converted into leather by a process known as Channing, much approved of by the Harvard Divinity School.) There was, however, no bell in the belfry. Through the windows of his tree he heard only street sounds and the grinding of lathes and the hammering of metal in the craft shop next door. Eleven teen-aged girls, who wanted to go to college and needed tutoring to get there, sat around a conference table with their notebooks open and their mouths closed, while Mr. Coffin, wearing a tie and straight from *Scope*, if you don't count two scotches and four hot hors d'oeuvres at a bar on the way, showed them how to float on the muddy waters of the Metaphoric.

Good evening, Charity, Rosamund, Lavonia, Beatrice, Carol Sue, Martha Ann, Shirley, Sarah, Miriam, Ethel, and Aletha. He thought they were beautiful: a priestess, a panther, a witch, a lost angel, a muse of the hunt, a martyred orphan. From cream in your coffee to Ethiopian hauteur, the planes of their faces so various and yet so consanguine it seemed a perfectionist had kept on casting masks in the vain pursuit of essence. All that beauty should amount to more than giggles and mediocre SAT's. He wanted to open their mouths and close their notebooks. He allowed himself the highest hopes for Charity and Rosamund: perhaps because their giggling stopped when class started; perhaps because the school rings hung on chains around their necks, and the clarity of their penmanship, and the gum they wrapped in tissue paper on the threshold of his attic, and a sort of Christmas boxiness about their frowns (there is a gift inside me, but I can't untie the ribbons by myself), approximated his notion of what promising students should look like. Also perhaps because he was not yet prepared to deal with priestesses and panthers, and hadn't learned to read the eyes. He talked mostly to Charity and Rosamund.

About what? Oh, open that Coffin and all kinds of pedagogical preconceptions popped out and swarmed over innocent minds. Mimesis, not methexis. A poem, a story, or a novel was useless to him unless it was useful for them, articulating or confirming something they had seen or suspected. He grouped his materials around single ideas and passed them out each evening, bunches of Xeroxed bananas, without regard to chronology, without reference to Romantic or Classical periods, without respect for the autonomy of art, the honor of dead artists, the watermarks or thumbprints of genius. Let Marcy play Sontag with herself; in Coffin's attic, art was didactic: Connect! She complained that he was exploiting art. He explained that exploiting art was his way, the Mackenzie way, of taking it seriously—to discover in the artifact a glint of moral intelligence, a recognition. But, she said, among the things art isn't—self-congratulation, self-pity—it also isn't a Boy Scout manual for building ethical outhouses; it partakes of mystery, of otherness. I want, he said, to begin with one mystery at a time, the brotherhood of otherness—to show that other people have felt the same way we do, life happened to them in ways similar to how it happens to us; I don't think art is taken seriously by critics who seek in it a cure for their own ennui: pop goes the weasel! She reminded him of himself in Paris, at the Louvre, looking for a mother in Renaissance paintings, all that talk about curves and parabolas—seeking a cure, wasn't he? Yes, he said, but not for ennui: for a connection, the completion of a circle. Then assign them comic books, she said; you leave out all of the irony! He felt that irony was self-indulgent, and said so: if you were a *real* teacher, he said, you'd exploit art too, because your students would be more important than the writers you teach; they wouldn't be Harvard smarties who eat all the moral horror stories and smack their lips afterward. Better, she said, to dine on moral horror stories than to pretend you're living one; you haven't the *right* to feel so bad for both of us, you haven't *earned* it. Worse, he said, to have earned it, which we haven't and *they* have; *I don't feel sorry for Kafka.* It's reciprocal, I'm sure, she said. Notice, he said, that we're talking about moral categories. Only, she said, because you think in them, which means you can't really be described as a bundle of laughs, and I haven't yet seen any saintly stigmata on you, only neon, a fucking fever chart every time you stick the thermometer up somebody else's ass. The body politic, he said; I realize that you're bored. Three times a week, she said, especially on Saturdays; it's becoming a moral category. Maybe, he said, Kafka will feel sorry for you.

He would use poems and stories, then, about the death of a child, the anxieties of old age, the varieties of love, the vagaries of the imagination, the terrors of identity . . . James Baldwin versus William Faulkner, LeRoi Jones versus Norman Podhoretz. He would ask: Do you like it or not? Agree or not? Why? Why not? Nobody in the Boston public school system had ever bothered to ask Charity, Rosamund, Lavonia, Beatrice, Martha Ann, Shirley, Sarah, Miriam, Ethel, and Aletha whether they liked or agreed with a poem or a story, because nobody in the Boston public school system cared whether they did or didn't. Charity and Rosamund were considered to be machines for synopsizing *Silas Marner.* The pedagogue from *Scope* wanted his girls to ask that same arrogant American question the children of Scarsdale and Exeter automatically asked: "What did English literature ever do for me?" A healthy question, he felt, since he didn't have an answer to it. Marcy made a point, at every breakfast, of asking the tree outside their kitchen window: "What did you ever do for me? I mean, lately?" Neither lenient, nor diplomatic. More than bored.

Still, he had volunteered. How to understand the roots of poetry in the human voice and song? Listen to the Dylans (Bob and Thomas), Bessie Smith, Jacques Brel, Joe Williams, Leonard Cohen, Lady Day, the Beatles, and Anne Sylvestre on Mr. Coffin's portable tape recorder. How to understand the nature of the enemy? Watch Louise Day Hicks on Mr. Coffin's portable television set. See Louise Day Hicks, the chairman of our Board of Education, classify the Chinese children of Boston as "white" instead of "nonwhite." You, too, Charity and Rosamund, can grow up capable of making such marvelous distinctions. It isn't absolutely necessary to have a face like a cow-paddy to become Chairman of the Bored, although ugliness *is* a proof of grace. The drones downstairs taught ten-year-olds how to read, but in the burning attic the inventive pedagogue with his electric toys taught sixteen-year-olds how to manipulate. He knew what the world was all about. . . .

He knew, said his wife, how to curry favor. *Ad nauseum* and beat vigorously. This was before they were Rinsler-bright.

Until the first semester ended shortly before Christmas. His class was expected to turn in original short stories at the last meeting, full of connections and moral intelligence. Charity and Rosamund didn't show up; neither did their stories. After reminding the rest of his girls about the Christmas party at his house, the man from *Scope* took the stories home to ponder. Most of them were much as he had imagined they would be, anecdotes about their mothers, their boyfriends, loneliness. Three made unfavorable mention of the Jewish landlord or the Jewish merchant. (He had to work on that, make them wade through Malamud.) One was a funny, shaggy dog. But two . . .

"Read these, could you?" he asked Marcy. She seemed pinned to her pile of cushions, a nightgown of bandages, severe under the hanging wicker-cage of light, but careless of herself, flesh-lazy, a soft geometry surrounded by coffee cups and ashtrays and tomes of exegesis, plotting a scheme for *Death in Venice* on a legal-sized pad of yellow paper. Freudian ambivalence . . . the libidinal tiger? The pederast as Nazi? Art as fascistic? The Mediterranean as a bathtub, all of us strapped to rubber ducks and going down—"I want to know what you think of them."

After half an hour, Marcy said: "Well, this one girl has written what seems like straight autobiography. From being born in South Carolina all the way up to just about yesterday."

"Yes. Martha Ann. I recognize a lot of it from things she's said in class."

"But it's ghastly," said Marcy. "Was she really raped by her stepfather when she was ten years old?"

He wanted suddenly to talk to Marcy about rape. Did women imagine it happening to them as much as men imagined doing it to them? Questions that don't get asked by Coffins, answers belonging to an antimatter universe, black holes, dead stars, drains in the cosmic sink, invisible densities. He felt that his fantasies came secondhand, from a pawn shop. Going to bed with soft geometry was no surprise. Were there any surprises? He feared impossible comparisons, silent ridicule. He had always believed, wholly without evidence, that men fantasized precisely, women imprecisely—women were clouds of feelings, not trees, shrubs, worms, like men. Otherwise, it would be embarrassing: he considered the anatomy of men somehow silly, the anatomy of women somehow profound. "How do I know? She lives up here with foster parents. The awful part of it, the stupid part, is that I made them all read Ralph Ellison's novel. You remember the early chapter, the Boston banker or whatever he was, coming down South to put money into the Negro college? He wanted to meet the sharecropper who had gotten his own daughter pregnant. There were lots of hints that the banker wanted to meet the sharecropper because the banker had wanted to do the same thing to *his* daughter, but didn't have the guts. I had to *explain* those hints to everybody in class. Martha Ann said she was sick and left the room."

Marcy put aside her yellow pad and embraced her knees. She had a way of being serious that almost paralyzed him: he wanted to present her with a bone or a scalp. "The other girl's a real writer, Ken."

"Lavonia."

"She leaves out all the unnecessaries. It's like she was writing a telegram, only from very odd and different places. There's a lot of indirection, and a lot of irony, I think, although she keeps a good grip on it. Pencils turning into knives, fractions being—what was it?—'cut-up numbers.' It's an incredibly sophisticated story."

"Marcy, it's a story about prostitution. All that cruising on the South End. Black girls and white men in their big Buicks, the buying of black meat."

"So what?"

"What do you mean, so what? The thing is, do you think *her* story is also autobiography, like the other one?"

"As you say, how do I know? If it is, she's a whore who can write."

"She's only sixteen years old!"

"By which time Lolita would have been in menopause. You thought maybe she was the Little Match Girl? I've often wondered what the Little Match Girl was *really* selling."

What had Marcy been like, at age sixteen, in Texas? He preferred not to ask.

Nor did Charity and Rosamund show up at the church the afternoon he came to chauffeur them to his house for mulled wine and caroling. It was one of those perfect December afternoons when every edge is a dagger and all the buildings seem suspended from a scoured sky by wire and the world is wholly Arctic, awaiting polar bears and chiliasts. Lavonia was there, and four others, not including Martha Ann. Several, he knew, had gone South for the holidays, also not including Martha Ann. He was relieved not to see Martha Ann; he was distressed to see Lavonia. Navigating his huge yellow boat (not a Buick, thank you) across the Arctic toward the Charles, he heard from the back seat:

"Gee, this sure is a swell tour, Mr. Coffin. Exactly the way we get bussed to Brighton High every day."

Lavonia.

Inviting the Roxbury girls to his caroling party had seemed like a good idea on the drawing board. In practice, it limped along to inconclusiveness. The Cambridge people who always came to Coffin parties—do we rent them from a catering service?—wheeled themselves around the living room and the punch bowl as gravely as children on tricycles. Roxbury sat offshore, in its Sunday best, an island of blackness, politely accepting warm cups of cinnamon-flavored wine and leaving them untouched. The tricycles tried several times to approach the offshore island, without very much to talk about. What are you studying? Have you thought about a career? The unspeakable Beckwith was there, singing his curly head off, and looking as usual as though he were about to pounce on the nearest contingency, if it had breasts. Ken's cousin Susan and her husband Mike Culhane inspected the spines of books and the spines of each other. The Nigerian medical student, surely the least interesting man with the most oversubscribed social calendar on the eastern seaboard, threw away his grins like handfuls of dimes. An assortment of graduate students of indeterminate gender had emerged from their molely burrowings through the Widener stacks for a moment of blinding sunlight, the print still smudging their faces. An unknown girl spent all of the party in the bathroom with a nose bleed. Professor Boynton and his wife, serenely gray, agreeably supplied anecdotes about André Gide. Marcy stayed at the piano. Stephen and Hannah slept soundly upstairs. Once again, Ken's father failed to arrive. Rinsler did not yet exist. And the conversation, as it was destined, turned to MacGeorge Bundy, Lyndon Johnson, Vietnam. Darkness didn't so much fall as it sneaked up on them, like a ring around the bathtub, sloughed off in the wash of the party's prattle.

He went outside to stand on the porch with his collar turned up against the wind and a burning cigarette to warn off the evil eye, feeling guilty for having brought his students into an alien environment and feeling depressed because parties full of Cambridge people so often went this dreary way. They couldn't really exchange opinions because they had only one opinion, the same opinion formed by the same newspapers and magazines they all read, floating like pollen in the Cambridge air. They all sneezed the same sneeze. Being equally allergic, he believed it to be the appropriate sneeze, but it wanted novelty.

"Are these your friends?"

Lavonia, again. She had slipped out after him and sneaked up behind him, like the darkness. "For better or for worse," he said, "they are. You know, I don't think you choose your friends. They just happen to you, like the weather." A suspiciously Cantabrigian sort of remark; he was disappointed with himself.

She cuddled herself by her elbows. Not being able to decide on anything else to say, he counted the street lamps.

"Doesn't that seem a little vulgar?" said Lavonia.

"What?"

"That house." She pointed across the road to a house ablaze with lights. On the roof the Virgin and child were transfixed between blue and yellow beams from ground spots. Beneath them, Santa Claus and his reindeer operated on an alternating current. The wreathes in the windows had also been electrified, and the tree on the lawn was heavy with bubble-headed angels. It was a neon advertisement for the holidays. He tried to recall his neighbor's face. Images of Sunday came into his mind . . . a hardtop convertible in the driveway . . . a hose . . . every Sunday the Electric Christian washed his car.

"Well, yes, it's more than a little vulgar." Vulgarity didn't bother him much. A venial sin. Did Lavonia know what venial meant? "Nobody ever died from vulgarity," he said, "or killed anybody with it." More than disappointed, he was now disgusted with himself. The pedagogue as sausage machine.

"Aletha's mother called on the telephone," said Lavonia. "She wanted to know when Aletha's coming home."

"I guess I'd better drive you all home now."

They returned to an overpowering smell of cinnamon, and stepped carefully between the spokes of the conversational wheel to the coat closet. It seemed to him he was leading a small band of refugees across the border to the Free World. His girls thanked Marcy and they went down to the car.

Inevitably, Lavonia was the last to be let out, living the farthest away from his reference point, the church. She was silent beside him in the front seat. He struggled in his mind to accommodate the few fugitive things he knew about her: the irony ("Gee, this sure is a swell tour, Mr. Coffin"), the perception ("Are these your friends?"), the disdain ("Doesn't that seem a little vulgar?") and the short story (waiting for the white man in the Buick).

"Lavonia, what happened to Charity and Rosamund?"

"What do you mean, what happened?"

"Why didn't they come to class, or turn in their stories?"

"Oh, well, they haven't been at high school for two months."

"Why? I didn't know that."

"Why? Those girls are on the street, Mr. Coffin."

"On the street?"

"Selling. Tricks. You know."

"No, I don't know. What are you talking about?"

"Mr. Coffin, didn't you ever look at their eyes? They're smack-heads."

"Smack-heads," he repeated.

"Smack. Heroin. Strung-out. You know. They've got a habit to support."

"I don't believe it. Why on earth did they come to the church?"

"I guess they just liked it. But they don't have time to write any short stories. That Rosamund, they're going to find her some night in an alley. She's been mainlining two years, and she doesn't pay the man at the Royal."

"Jesus." What was she talking about now? Pimps? An organized vice ring? But they were sixteen years old! He had been hit in the stomach. He slumped over the steering wheel. They stopped in front of Lavonia's apartment house.

"May I please have a cigarette?"

"You're too young to smoke." This was his night for inanities. Even as he delivered the latest of them, he was offering her the pack. They stared at each other. "Then," said Ken, "that's where you got the material for *your* story. From Charity and Rosamund."

"Yeah." She stubbed the cigarette out immediately. "You thought it was all me, didn't you? All that South End cruising."

"Of course not." He had the sudden sensation that he was going to be sucked up through her flaring nostrils.

"Yes, you did, Mr. Coffin. That's what you thought." She opened the passenger door and was on the sidewalk before he could move.

Climbing back up from the bottom of his shame, surfacing in Cambridge, he experienced the bends; there were nitrogen bubbles in his brain.

From the street, the bedroom looked to be the only lighted place in his house. The guests had presumably sneezed themselves home. Unprepared at the moment for postmortems with Marcy, he sat on the porch in his overcoat, admiring Santa Claus and the Virgin.

Marcy appeared in the door, using a quilt as a shawl and bearing a bottle of brandy and two snifters. "I heard the car."

She placed the bottle between them. "You've got bare feet!" he said. She gathered herself into the wicker chair opposite, tucking in limbs and opinions. He poured brandy for both of them. She waited. He felt like an advertisement for something or other disreputable. At last he told her about Lavonia, from "swell tour" to "lovely party."

Marcy took her snifter in both hands, swirling the liquid. "She stared at you all afternoon," she said. "She followed you out to the porch. She obviously wrote that short story just to get your attention. She's after your ass, Mr. Coffin. I suppose it's a form of transference, like the patient and the analyst."

He found that he was confusing Marcy and her quilt with the Virgin on the roof; the Electric Christian rides again. "Marcy, are you so unhappy?"

It was a serious question. Marcy, being a serious young woman, took her time turning it over. Finally she said, "All my life I wanted to be an adult, and now at last I am one. That's funny. The trouble is . . . nothing happens *next*."

As much as he loved his wife, he couldn't help her there.

The following day they drove northwest to Wyke Regis for Christmas with the Mackenzies. It was John Mackenzie's first

Christmas as master of ceremonies at Thomas Hill, but the dream went on almost unchanged, a dream of ice, of blue motions in a winter palace in a ring of mountains. On the cloudless morning of Christmas Eve, they fixed the toboggan slide; a freezing rain had fallen after two feet of snow, and the crust was perfect. In the afternoon, they rode jeeps down into the forest to find totem firs for chopping down, hauling away, and trimming; their boots broke the perfect crust and it was like slogging through a swamp of glass. In the evening, after wrapping presents, they went to Thomas Hill, where Susan Mackenzie Culhane, wife of Mike and daughter of John, roasted a beef and lost her temper. Before supper there were martinis, which was a change; after supper, there were carols, which was not, with Marcy at the piano and Susan on the flute. The brothers Mackenzie, John, Sam, and James became Three Kings of Orient Are, Caspar, Melchior, and Balthazar. Mike Culhane applied his whiskey tenor to O Holy Night. Nicholas Coffin arrived at ten o'clock, all pinstriped deference, to shake the hand of his son, kiss the hand of his daughter-in-law, accept a highball, and sit down at the card table before the fire for a man's game of bridge with the brothers. Nicholas Coffin, who never overbid, played an excellent hand of bridge. Nicholas Coffin, who was always agreeable, agreed to transport Marcy, Stephen, and Hannah from Thomas Hill to the cottage in an hour. And so Nicholas Coffin's son strapped on his skis.

From Thomas Hill it was possible to ski to Sam's house, or to James's, or to the Coffin cottage, down the lawn, across the pasture, among the trees, from which hung icicles gleaming in the moonlight like frozen guitar chords the wind played. Under such a moon it was even possible to slalom through the apple orchards to the basin of the valley and Wyke Regis. Such a moon made alien scapes, as if with a scouring hand; upon them the trees formed a shadowy gridwork; down them the skier plunged, in black Russian bear-cap, blue jacket, green snow mittens, falling from a star through layers of brightness . . . to lay a fire in the Coffin cottage for his father, his wife, his son, and his daughter. To drowse upon the licking fingers of its light. To think long, historical thoughts. His people had been so indulging themselves for several centuries; the books built into the wall on each side of the hearth said so. Wallace Mackenzie, in his chronicles of the family and the town, said so. A few people, special people, not

Charitys, not Rosamunds, not Lavonias. Scots-Irish nonconformists, men of measured merriment, children of the long winter, good at governing, poor at art: revolutionaries with muttonchops.

Tomorrow he would present Marcy with *The Book of the Marcypial*, prepared in the offices of *Scope*, set in Gothic type, with original illustrations. She would present him with a heavy black ski sweater she had been secretly knitting. Stephen would scatter the contents of his stocking across the living room floor, and pull down ornaments from their tree. To their mutual confusion, Ken and his father would exchange identical cameras. Shortly before eleven, Ken in his ski sweater would walk to Thomas Hill with Stephen on his shoulders, admiring the diamond earrings on the sugar maples. Marcy and Nicholas Coffin would follow in a car full of gifts. John Mackenzie would be already absorbed in the memoirs of Prince Kropotkin, looking up slightly puzzled as each Panzer division of the family arrived in its appointed time slot with its tank of cheer. After the shredding of paper, the ululations, the snapshots, the dry sherry, the biscuits, cold cuts and beer; before the donning of tartans, the devouring of farm geese, the guzzling of champagne cider, the blue flames of plum pudding, and the reading aloud of St. Matthew's version of the Christmas story; during those three hours of the afternoon when, while the children tobogganed or napped, the adults sat in the library with gift books in their laps, listening to Handel's *Messiah* issue from stereo speakers on both sides of the fireplace, above which were crossed and mounted the swords the Mackenzie substitutes had brought back from the Civil War . . . Ken Coffin would take the opportunity to ask his uncle about his father. How had Nicholas Coffin happened to get involved with the Mackenzies in the first place? How come he was a member of the Kintail Artillery Society at Harvard? He hadn't been a roommate of any of the brothers, had he?

And John Mackenzie, not bothering to imagine the motive for such a question—they were careless in matters of personal feelings, these Mackenzies; fastidious in matters of public policy and state—would explain. No. It was Prohibition, you remember. The whole point of the Kintail Artillery Society was the Kintail Artillery Punch, a great favorite of the Harvard junior faculty. They bottled the hard cider in Wyke Regis, in the cellar of Thomas Hill. Sam was at medical school, and could get hold of lab alcohol. But

Artillery Punch needs rum. Where to find it? Boston harbor suggested itself. All those freighters from the Caribbean . . . Joe Kennedy moving in his so-called medical supplies of scotch and gin. Whom did they know with access to the harbor, besides Lucius Beebee, who had access to everything? Why, they knew Nick Coffin, whose family owned the Massachusetts Bay Cordage Company, with half a dozen sheds in the harbor area. The ropemakers had graduated to cables, as they would graduate to winches and other things during the war. Nick could arrange for a crate of Jamaican rum to be dropped whenever they needed it. When he proved to be able to play tennis and bridge as well, a summer in Wyke Regis was inevitable. So, one supposes, was Hannah. A rum-runner, even if he was an undergraduate, seemed glamorous compared to the instructor in history, the medical student, and the economics major who were her brothers. Five summers later, they were married.

Ken would take a picture of his father as his father was taking a picture of Ken, so that each of them had a snapshot of the other, showing and using the same new camera.

He returned alone to Boston two days after Christmas to finish an article for *Scope*, and to find Rinsler waiting for him with all that talk about the GI coffeehouses in the South. But he was not as yet prepared to take a Rinsler seriously. Roxbury and Wyke Regis were out of phase, and he sought somehow to synchronize them: hard cider in the attic . . . Lavonia on skis. The Boston public school system had slunk off for the holidays, to eat the body of Christ and, perhaps, practice its rattan whip hand. There were, however, files at the church on each child in the tutorial program. The files confirmed Lavonia. Charity and Rosamund *had* dropped out of high school. Lavonia's reading scores suggested that she was, ungratefully and to everyone's extreme annoyance, an Underachiever. Achieving Lavonia seemed more feasible than radicalizing the United States Army.

Still, he invited Rinsler to Wyke Regis for New Year's Eve. Although, in retrospect, Rinsler was obviously what happened *next*, at the time Ken thought of him as a sort of extra Christmas present for Marcy, somebody *different* for a change. And Ken thought of himself as a philanthropist, giving away tradition, sending an urban child to the Establishment camp. For the Mackenzies were definitely a part of the Establishment Rinsler reviled. John was the chairman of Berringer's Department of History and the author of dozens of articles for *Daedalus*. Sam taught at the Harvard Medical School and served part-time on the board of the National Science Foundation. James was a full-time foundation official, giving away millions of dollars a year to underdeveloped countries and underdeveloped symphony orchestras, to needy theatrical troupes and black capitalists, school demonstration districts and birth-control programs. See the Power Structure enjoy itself. Discover old portraits, authentic swords, real skis, dull axes, books of sermons, Artillery Punch, buffalo heads, apple trees, Stimsonian Republicanism, and the golden mean. Learn that the Left has neither monopolized the decencies nor, all too often, experienced—practiced, admitted—the civilities. "How," asked Yeats, "but in custom and ceremony/Are innocence and beauty born?" Yeats, of course, had several answers, but he had never been at Thomas Hill and he wasn't Rinsler.

Seven

TO RINSLER, WHEN HE FINALLY SOBERED UP that New Year's Eve, the Mackenzies were like Druids: quaint, prehistoric, unbelievable. Stonehenged supratribal chieftains with mallets and drinking cups. Judges and priests, perhaps. Architects of a blue ring to Apollo the Healer, maybe. But belonging to some mythic mist, a rain-cloud of superstitions. One cannot take seriously a world view that trifles with the transmigration of souls simply hoping to live forever, with no real notion of metempsychosis, and certainly not an inkling that it all depended on the class relations of a culture. The transmigration of property. (When your axis is skewed to the Left, you can't imagine a symmetry based on midsummer sunrise.) He could not find in Thomas Hill, which he prowled in borrowed moccasins, any altar stones or slaughter stones. There was not, among the portraits, a triple-headed and very horny Cernunnos. He rather doubted that they burned people alive in wicker cages. (They simply gave them too much rum.) Neither John, Sam, nor James had ever sacrificed anyone or anything that mattered to them except their weekends and vacations, which didn't actually constitute a sacrifice because work was their excuse for being. (He understood this: work was respiration; you did it all the time because there was nothing else you could do; stop and you suffocate. You must feel that you are *chosen* to work; otherwise, you will appear ridiculous, in your moccasins, Marcyless. Rinsler felt that he was chosen. Like the Mackenzies. Unlike Coffin, who volunteered everything but his wife.) Moreover, he had missed their culling of mistletoe.

Nevertheless, Druids. In that they played in their blue ring, to which he was alien. They distanced him, as their children had distanced him. Arriving in the late afternoon, he had found a cottage full of children, variously crawling, screaming, tugging, sobbing, upsetting porringers, tormenting dogs, scribbling on wallpaper, drowning in toilet bowls. Cambridge children, appallingly handsome. He hadn't seen so much blond hair since the California beach, but this hair was not sunned-upon, it simply grew out gold, chromosomatic threads, fingernails of trust funds. Tea without bags, in null-white cups, from a kettle under a cozy the color of sand. Albuminous eyes, full of firelight. And a greedy fire, around which the mothers and fathers of the scattering children had grouped themselves, standing, in ski pants, as though for a game or a message. And Marcy, of whom he approved.

"What do you *do?*"

"I'm a community organizer."

"What does that *mean?*"

"I make creative trouble."

"And you've enlisted Ken to help you make trouble?"

"Instead of making gestures, yes."

Outside, it snowed. Would they have extra mittens for him? Of course they would. Marcy seemed put together out of candles and green shoots; her hair wouldn't stay in its bun, despite the silver needle through the leather hasp. She made him feel like a centaur.

"We thought it would be better to have all the children in one place," she said. "That way there would only be one disaster."

"What is the drill?"

"We will presently dress for dinner, and drink rum. Then a woman from the farm will come to take care of the children. And we will go to Sam's for more rum and food. About ten o'clock, we'll leave Sam's for Thomas Hill. Do you dance?"

"No."

"Do you play bridge?"

"I'm afraid not."

"Do you play Ping-Pong?"

"There's never been a good reason for playing Ping-Pong."

"Well, then, you'll have to change the records, or help mix the punch. The others will be dancing, playing bridge, and playing Ping-Pong. Everyone's obliged to do something useful."

"Haven't the farm women anything more useful to do on New Year's Eve than take care of other people's children?"

"Perhaps you can organize them. Poor exploited slobs, they just *can't* think of anything more useful than making money. Abigail Murdock will bring the children over after dinner and put them to bed at Thomas Hill. If then she wants to dance, or play Ping-Pong, it's allowed. She has to get up at six in the morning, of course. Do you?"

"I'm sorry."

"For Abigail or for yourself? At midnight, there will be Artillery Punch and a ham. At two in the morning there will be three cars that won't work because the batteries are dead, and two cars that won't work because the radiators are frozen, and one car that won't work because the driver is drunk. None of these cars will belong to Mackenzies, who all drink antifreeze. All of these cars will belong to friends of mine whom I haven't seen since *last* New Year's Eve, so if you will excuse me—" And she deserted him.

Rinsler was no longer a centaur; he was a weeping bull. His teeth were cloven: foot-in-mouth disease. He poured rum into his teacup to wash out his mouth. She had cut him dead. He regarded the snowed-upon valley. The spines of two mountain chains curved toward Wyke Regis. Converged. The effect was amphitheatrical. *His* spine curved to the left, conned into thinking it might verge. Half an embrace is worse than none: he poured another cup of rum. Unknowable women annoyed him. He was used to carelessness in women; to involuntary spasms of rage; to guilt, chatter, and a willingness to be hurt; to lack of discrimination and a mute servicing; to avarice and panic. He wasn't used to being snubbed. He hadn't come to New Hampshire to be snubbed. Then why had he come? To drink 180-proof dark Jamaican rum, that's why. Which he did, muchly.

Everyone but Rinsler dressed for dinner. Extravagantly: the men in Scotchgard jackets and ruffled shirts, their cufflinks unwinking as lizards, their bowties like gun-slits in pillboxes; the women in long dresses, a clean sweep of themselves, a violent draping and impulsive swish, rings burning in their ears—*their* cufflinks, holding the face together while a wrist of thought stuck out of the mouth: watch it. *So prepared.* Heads inappropriate to the fabulous stilts on which they nodded, a clumping forward desperate enough to keep the innocence from spilling. In his rum, Rinsler wondered about his rumpledness. Aesthetics intestate. By not seeking to prove something, what was he trying to prove, what did he prove himself afraid to seek? The proof was in Jamaica. He wondered about Coffin, who had thrown himself into the role of the host and floundered there, like Rinsler unable to swim, except in rum. These seas of responsibility, they seethe; and lack of fins finishes us. He wondered about Marcy, perfect, correct to a fault whose lines were cracking (Rinsler knew): the seams of civility would split (Rinsler hoped): Quake me (Rinsler rumbled, sank).

The women in long dresses retreated from the Russian front door. They tried the snow. They tried, insanely, the road through the orchard to Sam's house. A tank would have stalled. Rinsler, in the back seat, got the drift of it: they sought to navigate a seethe of salt worms; they proved foolish; they foundered. Bootless Rinsler in a snowbank, his shoes collecting numbness, his control of himself foreclosed. *Push* this yellow boat. Gulled into shoveling, seizures of Sisyphus: we rock. The women, from behind, rearviewed in the light of the dashboard, seemed hooded fishermen's widows at Mass, communing with the demi-surge. The nature of wheels is to spin, flinging snow in our faces. Apple trees snatch at we's . . . Wheezy does it . . . Gastric attacks Rinsler; he hasn't the stomach for anything but faking . . . An accidental purchase; the snowbank extends some credit . . . I've been wetted, *but we move* . . . snow tires the soul, grips reality . . . a hiccough of the engine, and they fell into Sam's space, exhausted.

It looked in the snow to be a grand piano turned on its ear, tuned to warmth, eighty-eight keys of yellow light. It was in fact a barn, with more rum for Rinsler's tummy-quake. Rafters hopscotched above them. Lofts were implicit. Tables were strewn with chalices. Plastic refuse cans were heavy with ice and bottles of champagne cider. Small coal-stoves hotly exhaled. A rope from a beam waited to hang Rinsler. There was a goat named Pansy, harnessed to a wheelbarrow saddened with bricks. Marcy had brought her salad in a hubcap and used a wrench to mix it. Coffin played with the rope as though it were a dangling participle. *As though.* From somewhere, a guitar was affectingly inadequate.

They ate on cushions on the floor of the barn, although there was a couch or two. And occasional tree stumps for the plates, which were cardboard and came with preformed shallows, upon which gravy lapped. No one had the courage to claim a couch or stump; discomfiture had been elevated into a principle of fun. They ate turkey, stuffed with sausages. James Mackenzie did the slicing, asking Rinsler: "Tell me, are you one of those people who think that birth control is a genocidal plot against the Third World?" Rum was a genocidal plot against Rinsler; he switched to cider. Thirteen eunuchs sang madrigals from an amplified goat sty. The champagne cider evaporated. Marcy asked Rinsler to organize the coffee, just as a gesture. He complied. (Rinsler hadn't been as elevated since Bates took off for Australia and left his groupie behind. She had had the brain of an armadillo, the teeth of a comb, a tongue like an eel, and a belly button that reminded him of his Lone Ranger atomic bomb ring. Bates had told Rinsler about Coffin. Bates hadn't mentioned Mrs. Coffin. Mr. Coffin was not aware of Miss Groupie Bates. Quadrilateral. They were polygonists. Rinsler had been Miss Groupie's idea of unwept bull; she'd lacked desecration; her heresies had been feathers; nothing ever surprised her. Mrs. Coffin had never been surprised. To do it in a Coffin!) Coffee wanted Rinsler.

Adjoining the barn were stables, wherein there was horsing around. Sam Mackenzie told Rinsler about the three-quarter-mile track, even pointed it out, snowed under, Druidic, as they sat in a carriage complaining about the coffee, which had rum in it. Sheets of snow had been flung over the features of the countryside, as one throws dustcloths over one's furniture to protect it from one's absence. *As.* The apple trees seemed to be gasping, then drowning, in it. *Seemed.* Maintaining such an establishment taxed one's acres and caused one pain in the escrow.

Sam was worried about sickle-cell anemia, protein deficiency, and lead poisoning.

Rinsler talked about decentralization and pilot projects.

Marcy appeared, miraculously, stopping their conversation. Ten o'clock. Rinsler had spent so much time in the hammer-and-sickle cells of bohemia that he didn't know how to deal with non-groupies. Her carriage was excellent, his pleasantries were not.

Unstable, he left it, wishing she would lead him by the hand. He wagged. Like a puppy, all his emotions were in his tail. *Like.*

Sam said, We'll never make it up the hell to Thomas Hill.

Marcy said, Why rot? Hear, I mean.

Sam disappeared. Arctic whorls. Question marks scythed in the apple trees. The yellow boat again, with Coffin at the controls, under a bear-cap. Surely his wife wasn't perfect. She must have committed social disgraces. A moonly bleeding was unavoidable. She projected perfect expressions on the windshield, which were wiped off. In the back seat, Rinsler was learning to take her serially. They could not go up and so they went down, in reverse, to a loop in the highway and a fork forward on a lesser incline, susceptible to low approach.

All that he could perceive of Thomas Hill totaled up only to the admission that it was very big. Even the porch yawned, its pillars teeth, the throat of the house an amazing yellow vault. It swallowed Rinsler.

"Your shoes are ruined," said Marcy. "What are we going to do with you?" She found him a pair of moccasins. He could think of nothing to say to the buffalo heads. A rock group, Mama Sincere and the Sycophantic Three-point-Two, ruined the stereo. Already wounded and moaning bodies were to be seen on the dance floor, pretending not to know each other. Rinsler, humiliated in his moccasins, was introduced to the rest of the Mackenzies and their guests. They all had such *confident bones;* their faces behind steel-rimmed spectacles, fit their bones like gloves; they looked amiable. Trying to guess at the meaning of the tartan dinner jackets on the men, he assumed that his rummy eyes made plaid the world. His own face sagged from a nail in his brain. He was offered a liqueur and declined it in favor of ten tiny cups of coffee. He stood at the hearth, throwing pine cones into an enormous fire, while around him there was much efficient fluttering. Little black boxes appeared on silver salvers; they contained plastic playing cards. Tables with spring mechanisms were plucked from narrow recesses in the walls; their setting-up seemed to Rinsler the construction of some exotic flock of birds; their flat flapping and stiff legs would tilt the portraits and upset the lamps and bloody the faces of the women.

Perhaps an hour later, after having thrown up half of Jamaica in a water closet on the top floor, right next door to a Ping-Pong game four Prussians were conducting with cleated feet and oaths in Arabic, Rinsler rediscovered himself. His head had shrunk and his cerebellum had trouble breathing, but it functioned. He leaned over the stairwell and ascertained that the beat went on. Vic d'Azyr and the Seven Synaptic Clefts were raping an electric bathtub. He descended, looking for an empty room in which to plot his revenge.

He found the library. And when he in his turn was found by John Mackenzie, he was reading up on the clan's armorial bearings and wishing he hadn't left his Homosote sheets at home.

ARMS: azure, a stag's head cabossed or.

CREST: a mountain inflamed proper.

SUPPORTERS: two savages wreathed about the loins and head with laurel, each holding in his exterior hand a baton or club erect and inflamed, all proper.

MOTTO: *Luceo non uro* . . . I shine, not burn.

BADGES: variegated holly (or Deer's Grass).

SLOGAN: Tulach Ard (a mountain in Kintail).

PIPE MUSIC: Failte Thighearna Ghearloch. Or: Cumha Chailein Ruaidh Mhic Coinnich, no Cumha Mhic Coinnich . . . Lament for Colin Roy—

Rinsler had been born, naturally, in Washington, D.C. His arms were red, white, and blue, a Truman's head concussed. His crest was a Lone Ranger atomic bomb ring that made your finger turn green. His nonsupporters were three stepfathers wreathed about the loins with wet towels and about the head with gin-fumes, each holding in his exterior hand a razor strop, sometimes erect, always improper. His motto was *Fuck you, sheenie*. His badge was cabbage; his slogan was Rooms for Rent; and his pipe music was *Home on the Range*.

"We'll look it up in Frank Adam," said John Mackenzie, entering the library with his hands in his back pants pockets and his confident bones sticking out. He wasn't talking to Rinsler. Indeed, for a moment he looked at Rinsler as though Rinsler were a lamp that had inconveniently burned out. "Excuse me," he said. "I didn't know there was anyone here." Druidic chieftain turned to war party, the gaggle in his wake, and made seigneurial motions. Of the manor bored. "Mr. Rinsler, I believe you've met Polly . . . and Susan . . . and Dewey . . . Peter Swayze . . . Marcy Coffin, of course." Rinsler could not remember any of them except

Marcy. He rose and bobbed. "Mr. Rinsler," said John Mackenzie, "is a community organizer," and seemed genuinely puzzled, apparently realizing that he hadn't the faintest idea what the words meant. "A friend of Ken's." What did *that* mean, even if it were true? John Mackenzie gave it up. The blue ring of privilege permitted one to do so. Meaning resided in the familiar, the familial. "We've come to check on a prophecy, Mr. Rinsler."

John Mackenzie went to a wall, selected his shelf, and ordained the easy at-handness of the book he sought, a moss-covered volume that sat slablike and equable in his lap. He leafed, as his party plunged into chairs: *Clans, Septs, and Regiments of the Scottish Highlands*. Marcy snapped her fingers at Rinsler's ear. "How are you feeling?"

Try me, he might have said.

"Here it is," said John Mackenzie. "*Kenneth Mackenzie, 'The Brahan Seer,' Coinneach Odhar.*" He read aloud:

"I see into the far future, and I read the doom of the race of my oppressor. The long-descended line of Seaforth will, ere many generations have passed, end in extinction and sorrow. I see a chief, the last of his house, both deaf and dumb. He will be the father of four sons, all of whom he will follow to the tomb. He will live care-worn and die mourning, knowing that the honors of his line are to be extinguished forever, and that no future chief of the Mackenzies shall bear rule at Brahan or in Kintail. After lamenting over the last and most promising of his sons, he himself shall sink into the grave, and the remnant of his possessions shall be inherited by a white-coiffed lassie from the East, and she is to kill her sister. And as a sign by which it may be known that these things are coming to pass, there shall be four great lairds in the days of the last deaf and dumb Seaforth (Gairloch, Chisholm, Grant, and Raasay), of whom one shall be buck-toothed, another hare-lipped, another half-witted, and the fourth a stammerer. Chiefs distinguished by these personal marks shall be the allies and neighbors of the last Seaforth; and when he looks around and sees them, he may know that his sons are doomed to death, that his broad lands shall pass away to the stranger, and that his race shall come to an end."

Undeniably, John Mackenzie had a way of weaving on the gloom. He rose to fiddle a fire—Rinsler would learn that there are six chimneys at Thomas Hill, twelve hearths, cords of wood incalculable, the easy at-handness of a hurricane before the war having convenienced the cold members of the family by leveling a forest, trees to burn—and a fabric of silence obtained.

Finally, the woman identified as Polly said: "They knew how to write prophecies in those days."

Marcy said, to Rinsler: "Coinneach Odhar was stoned by fairies."

John Mackenzie said, to everyone: "Odhar was an early seventeenth-century prophet. He was born at Baile-na-Cille in the parish of Uig on the Island of Lewis. He is said to have exercised powers of divination and second-sight, derived from a magic stone conferred on him by fairies. He made himself unpopular in the Ross-shire neighborhood by predicting a nasty fate for several well-known families. The predictions are supposed to have been distressingly accurate, although some took several centuries to fulfill themselves, and others are still with us, waiting for us to get on with it."

Peter Swayze said: "What about *this* prediction?"

John Mackenzie was pleased to oblige. "Odhar uttered his malediction on the Mackenzies of Seaforth at a time when he was very annoyed with them, during the reign of the 3rd Earl of Seaforth. The Earl went off to Paris, and his Countess decided to execute Odhar. Odhar did his predicting just before she managed to do her executing. Sure enough, when Francis Humberston Mackenzie died in 1815, there were no more Earls of Seaforth. Francis is reported to have been born in good shape, but as a boy in school he was brought down by an attack of scarlet fever and became stone-deaf. He grew up with four Highland lairds— Mackenzie of Gairloch, Chisholm of Chisholm, Grant of Grant, and MacLeod of Raasay—who were variously afflicted with buck teeth, hare lips, missing wits, and a stammer. The Earl's four sons all died before he did; and on the death of the last one, he became dumb." John Mackenzie allowed himself a grim smile. "Whether because of his deaf-and-dumb condition, or because of his grief, or simply because of a poor aptitude for business, the Earl mismanaged his West Indian estates. When they got into serious trouble, he sold much of the ancestral properties to cover the loss. One of those properties was Kintail, the cradle of the Seaforth race." He quoted from Frank Adam again:

"To which it appears the prophecy was *actually* directed: the old idea being that the 'house' became 'extinct' if or when it lost its chief—and as 'Mackenzie of Kintail,' both land and *title* have vanished from the race. *Seaforth*, however, has remained along with the armorial bearings of Brahan."

Peter Swayze said: "What about that white-coiffed lassie?"

"That also worked out fairly well," said John Mackenzie. "A white-coiffed lassie, wearing widow's weeds and returning from the East Indies, took possession of the lands and was some years later inadvertently responsible for the death of her younger sister in a pony carriage accident. The important point is that, while Kintail remains on the Mackenzie armorial bearings, 'a mountain inflamed proper,' and in the family slogan, 'Tulach Ard,' the mountain and the lands are gone—sold to pay off a business debt."

"Let's see if we can work it out," said Polly. "Among the available lairds, James has a bad back, Sam's station wagon is a lemon, and John is always quoting from Ecclesiastes, which seems to me an affliction. Besides, my daughter is flunking French and Susan married an Irishman."

"This morning," said Marcy, "I burned the toast."

"You see!" said Polly. "Omens. Portents. If it hails on us again this summer, the apples will all have buck teeth and the farm will lose even more money, and John will have to sell Thomas Hill to pay off our debts, and Ogilvy will buy it and turn it into a motel for presidential candidates, and the cradle of the Wyke Regis Mackenzies will have been robbed."

"The white-coiffed lassie from the East," said Peter Swayze, "and the pony carriage accident?"

"There's more white in *my* coife than I'm terribly happy about," said Polly, "and last spring I returned from Bermuda, which *is* East, isn't it? We have a pony carriage accident every time we hook up a pony to a carriage. Not to mention the damned tractors. They ruined my herb garden."

"Herb today, gone tomorrow. Odhar, the horror of it," said Dewey Ross.

"Pun rampant on a crest of fallen," said Marcy. "But where *is* our Odhar?"

"The Old Man predicted extinction and sorrow for the family twice a week for the last twenty years of his life," said Polly. "I think it had to do with the fact that his breakfast blueberries kept getting smaller. Anyway, there are always prophets, except at the farm, where there are always losses. I'm sure we can find someone to maledict us frightfully. We wouldn't even have to kill him."

This did not appear to be John Mackenzie's sort of conversation, any more than it was Rinsler's. John Mackenzie played with the radio console in the far corner of the library, under a relief map of bridges spanning the Missouri and Mississippi rivers. (Rinsler would, of course, learn that a Mackenzie collateral had designed those bridges, and brought back the buffalo heads to prove it.) He tried to focus on the people who had interrupted his reading. Polly, clearly, and Susan, were family. Dewey Ross wrote novels, which Rinsler had never read because Rinsler did not read novels. Swayze, now—wasn't Swayze a Marxist economist? Yes. A member of the Old Left: Rinsler thought of sleeves of words hanging out of small gray magazines, statistical cufflinks on underdeveloped economies, fists of facts. (Rinsler had underlined and clipped them. You never know, enough.) Why was Swayze here, in the blue ring, playing family games? Proprieties are theft. A gray head among gross national products . . . He had to speak. He did so, creeping up on Swayze in his moccasins and startling him with expertise:

"I have admired your articles on Cuba. But everything is still sugar, and sugar isn't industrialization."

"I beg your pardon?"

And it was refused by Rinsler. "Loans," he said. "Credit arrangements. A colony of the Soviet Union is still a colony."

"Ah, what sort of communities do you organize, Mr., ah, Rinsler?"

John Mackenzie joined them. Marcy sat beside a lamp the size of a fire hydrant, on which elephants romped. Rinsler decided that her hostility was a form of socializing. "The white niggers of Quebec," he began.

"Guy Lombardo in twenty minutes," said John Mackenzie.

"The *fedayeen* are niggers, too," said Rinsler. "Sold on the oil market. Fanon—"

"Do you know," said John Mackenzie, "what we used to say about Peter at Harvard in the thirties? We used to say that Peter was the only one we knew who, come the revolution, would stand his friends up against the wall and shoot them. We were his friends. He was earnest. But, on the whole, Ecclesiastes could cope better with despair than Marx."

"John," said Swayze, "if you tell that story one more time—"

"Harvard lost a football game," said John Mackenzie, "and Peter was in despair. As well as being in his cups of Kintail Artillery Punch. He threatened to jump from the top row of the stadium. We reminded him that he might injure a proletarian. The ground, after all, was lower-class. One wouldn't want to lumpen them."

"Pete Seeger went to Harvard," said Marcy. "Not to mention T. S. Eliot."

"Fanon—" said Rinsler.

"Who organized *this* community?" said Swayze.

"Peter told us," said John Mackenzie, "that even though Roosevelt had recognized the Soviet Union, Peter didn't recognize Roosevelt. Who had also gone to Harvard. A blocked punt gathers no Marx. We grabbed Peter by his Hasty Pudding and explained that concussion among friends is not historically inevitable."

"Signet Society, John, not Hasty Pudding. You do it deliberately, every time. They gave me a rose."

"Mr. Swayze sent them back their rose," said Marcy, "pressed between the pages of a monograph on water capitalism among the *fedayeen* of French Quebec."

"Peter," said John Mackenzie, "owns a summer home in New Hampshire. Like all good Marxists, he raises sheep."

"Do not ask," said Marcy, "for whom the Red Guards, it guards for lamb chopsticks."

"Baaah!" said Swayze. To Rinsler, he added: "You will notice that among the upper classes, irony is a substitute for energy. The pun is a substitute for details of feeling."

Druids, thought Rinsler, waiting for Rome to happen to them. Stormbirds appeared on his mind's horizon, flying bridge tables.

"You all just have time to fetch a glass of punch," said John Mackenzie. "Ask everyone to join us in the library."

They trooped down the stairs. The dancers had achieved an advanced state of dilapidation. Their faces gleamed with sweat; the innocence had finally spilled; shirt tails had escaped cummerbunds; studs had popped, there was no dignity, only dishabille. At each end of a long table in the dining room sat huge punch bowls. Between them was a raft of glass cups, an exploded mirror. Rinsler accepted a cup of punch, not without trepidation.

"It's stronger than it tastes," said Marcy.

"What's in it?"

"A batch consists of Catawba white wine, brandy, rum, Bourbon, fruit in season, and an equal amount of champagne cider. It tastes like breakfast juice, but it's almost entirely alcohol."

He did not sip, but carried his cup with the others back up the stairs to the library. The lights had been dimmed. Thirty people stood in a circle. On the radio, the old year was being counted out in Times Square. As it expired, the Druids drank. And as Guy Lombardo and his Royal Canadians began to pump on their goats-bladders, the Druids joined hands in the library, a rough stitching, a ring of mouths, and sang along with "Auld Lang Syne." After which, they kissed. Ken Coffin and Marcy made a spectacle of themselves. Only Rinsler went unkissed, in a community he had not organized. Rinsler preferred to stare into the fire. He tried his cup of punch. He decided it could not possibly be as strong as Marcy had said. He wanted another, especially as they resumed singing. It was probably the lament for Colin Roy. . . .

Presently, he became aware of a commotion.

"Your wife," said Susan Culhane to John Mackenzie, "decided after midnight in the middle of a snowstorm to put feed in the bird-feeding station."

"That sounds just like your mother," said John Mackenzie. "She wanted them to have a happy new year."

"The wind blew her glasses off and they're lost in the snow."

"For God's sake," said John Mackenzie.

"Well?"

"Well, let's go find them."

And the Druids left the library. There was much slamming of doors and raising of voices. Rinsler stood at the window and watched, as gray bundles carrying lanterns moved clumsily through snow swirls, a heave of shadows and sudden white swords turning like the spokes of a water wheel on the impossible drift.

He was joined at the window by Peter Swayze. "Losing your glasses is no way to start the new year," said Swayze. Rinsler agreed. It was like watching some heavily enigmatic foreign movie, Japanese, perhaps, shot entirely by hand-held cameras underwater, in a metamorphical marineland that really wasn't worth trying to figure out. The lanterns were fish.

"Once, in New York," said Swayze, "I was at a cocktail party to honor a visiting French intellectual, some radical epistemologist whose name I can't remember. It turned into a brawl. I was arguing with August Sample and Bernard Goodman." Rinsler, who did not go to cocktail parties, tried to place the names: a middle-aged black novelist, a middle-aged Jewish literary critic. "We had all had too much to drink, especially Goodman's wife. I was telling Sample that he liked being a token more than he liked writing fiction. That as long as he belonged to the Century Club and kept getting invited to Washington for panel discussions about the arts, he was never going to write another book. Goodman was telling me that I was irrelevant because the young today want to make an existential revolution, not a Marxist revolution. Mrs. Goodman was telling herself that black sexuality is just as much a myth as the vaginal orgasm. August Sample was telling everyone that LeRoi Jones was a bad poet. The argument went with us into the elevator and spilled out on the sidewalk. Goodman said something about the raptures of the Zeitgeist. Mrs. Goodman said something about being sick. I said something about black middle-class arrivistes. Sample took a swing at me, missed, stumbled, and knocked down Mrs. Goodman. She lost her glasses. While Sample and I were down on our knees on the sidewalk looking for the glasses, Goodman stood in the street, his face full of Jewish suffering, trying to hail a cab. By the time we had found the glasses, he had flagged one down. We were all going to the West Side, but we started arguing about who should get into the taxi first, who was going to get out first. The driver finally got disgusted with the lot of us and drove off, leaving us in the middle of the street. Mr. Rinsler, do you know what that taxicab was? That taxicab was history."

Rinsler would have giggled, but Rinsler was not the giggling sort, and to start a new year giggling seemed dangerous.

They did not succeed in finding Mary Mackenzie's glasses. They did succeed in steaming up their steel-rimmed spectacles and chilling themselves to their confident bones, and so assaulted the punch bowl with renewed vigor. Rinsler went to bed in what was called the bachelor's bedroom, a well-appointed little cell on the third floor with paperback mystery stories left on its headboard. Before he fell asleep, he heard them downstairs, around the piano, singing Christmas carols.

When he woke up late in the morning, the sunlight was so brilliant that it bludgeoned him. Objects—a glass, a pewter pitcher, the mirror, the brass knobs at the end of the bed—were transfixed in this brilliance, full of tension, fragile as though the light had stretched them to an angry stress-point and their surfaces would shatter at his touch.

Thomas Hill was quiet, empty. He found that a note had been left for him in the kitchen: hot coffee in a percolator, fruit juice in the fridge, eggs if he knew how to scramble them, ski boots and long woolen socks on a bench in the hall if he chose to join the crowd on the bluff behind the house. Rinsler was nothing if not dogged. He found it preposterous that the house had not been scarred by the party, that something—the sunlight, probably— had scoured it; even the wood seemed knifelike at its gleaming edges, in its clarity. The ski boots fit tolerably well. There were even a sweater and scarf to swathe and strangle him. Mittens. Rinsler so wrapped rumbled out the door, rolled off the porch, into a perfect day, a day that had brushed its teeth with sandpaper, an electric cold, a sky from which clouds and birds had been flushed.

His experience of snow was minimal. He remembered a sled, belonging to his disordered childhood. But at the age of eight he had ended up in southern California, Rose Bowls and sport shirts every new year's day. The rest was cities, snow as something that gets dirty, the slush of inconvenience, a kind of cold garbage from a fat gray God. Rinsler walking into this *immense* whiteness felt needled, sucked-upon. His plod left holes. The trees were so many severed fingers. The mountains fell like hatchets on the valley. He had a sense of being so new that you squeak.

He found the crowd at the brow of the bluff. The children were tumbleweeds. They sank to their knees on polished shields, aluminum plates, plastic saucers, grasping straps that had been riveted on both sides of each shallow bowl, and pushed off heedlessly, plunging down the sheerness of the bluff with the speed of an eye-blink, receding to dark dots that were blotted out in dazzling emptiness.

Some of the adults still seemed to be dancing—a muffled minuet. Their faces were covered by woolen masks, their eyes unreadable. They greeted him, so much extravagant color, stripes and plaids that insulted the snow. He didn't know their names. He inspected the jet stream of trails the plates had written on the bluff. He was reminded of surfboards and their sand tracks, a snaking toward mindlessness on seas that combed themselves clean in the aftermath. At the bottom—there was a bottom, wasn't there?—were black fingers. Rinsler watched as a group disengaged itself from the trees, hauling what looked like a ladder, by its implausible reins. They were bringing back the toboggan. Their ascent was slow; they walked on each side of the jet stream. Tiny figures acquiring shape as they climbed, concealed in their snow-suits, sexless as donkeys, ink on the blotter. Rinsler tried to identify Marcy.

It must have taken a month for them to reach him. Marcy wore one of the masks, a phantom. Coffin was goggled. The nose of the toboggan curved upward in upon itself, like a shoe on which it had rained. The other donkeys collapsed on the brow, heehaw-ing.

"Good new year!" said Marcy.

Rinsler felt like a penguin. Absurd. He flapped.

"It's *your* turn!" said Marcy.

Those who had been minueting snatched at the toboggan reins.

"I've never done it before," said Rinsler. The bluff suddenly seemed to him a stomach pump, a basin with a drain. "I'm not exactly an athlete."

"None of us is more than approximate," said Marcy. "But the snow is perfect. Why don't you lead? Get in front."

"Marcy, you can't," said Coffin.

"Of course I can," she said. To Rinsler: "Just lean to the right when they shout behind you. Hold onto the rope, and *lean*. It pulls the wrong way at the bottom."

Coffin offered his goggles. Rinsler refused. He crunched him-self at the head of the toboggan, under the bent nose with his legs. Was it so uncomfortable in the womb? Others piled on be-hind him—five of them. Was it Susan—probably Susan—who scissored him? Ski boots in the manhood, electric lap. He seized the reins. This is the most idiotic thing I've ever done. Someone gave them a shove and they slipped into oblivion.

A parachute, the snow my sky. The arrow of me, air apparent only in its pure pushiness, a wall I pierce. Falling from a percep-tion, a cliff he consented to, down into a diamond cleft. Hands *off*. Then it began to sting. The wall slapped him. Finally he was whipped, the rush toward fingers and hatchets a lashing and shredding, flesh flayed from his face, bones bright with blood, a disclosure that made his teeth chew wire and his nerve ends snap: he was going to die. *Lean*, they cried. And there was no left and right. *Lean*, and his muscles were sponge, the sky was quartz, splinters stormed him, they rose blind into a wave of ice, teeth, wire, glass, bone, cold. They collided with a tree.

He couldn't move. What remained of him—a pile of undone ligature—was locked in Susan Culhane's legs and lay in the snow feeling puddly, knowing drain, wishing cancellation. She managed to push off of him and roll away. He was certain his kneecaps had shattered, his face was dog meat. Masks, gloved skulls, examined his disclosure, the spill and slivers of him, and then hooked up pullies to lift the leftovers from their bed of broken glass.

Susan Culhane said, "It always happens when you sit in front. When you lead. You should have worn Ken's goggles, or one of the face sleeves. Why didn't you *lean*? Poor thing! Your hair is *caked*. Well, I expect you'll survive. Let's pull the wretched toboggan back up to the top."

The bluff yawned at them. Beyond it, there was snow like dandruff on the shoulders of the yew hedge, and behind that Thomas Hill on castors seemed a tide of bricks; it would roll down and crush them. Glacial surcease. They pulled enough for two new years. His feet were marble blocks in the ski boots. The toboggan was a caisson or a casket. Marcy and Coffin were waiting on the bluff's brow.

Everyone giggled.

"Your eyebrows are icicles," said Marcy. "Frosty the Snowman!" Ken came forward with a handkerchief to wipe his face.

Rinsler had no choice but to hate these people.

Eight

THE INSTITUTE CONSISTED OF two old, gray, adjoining Cambridge houses off Brattle Street. The sociologists paid for it, because the sociologists had the government grants, plus a little seed money from MIT and Harvard. (Rent a liberal technologue, cheap.) Being sociologists, they naturally knew all about "domain assumptions," and so established themselves on the top floors, where they played with their computer terminal. (Each had a code name by which to claim his time from the IBM 7090 up the river.) They sought a theoretical convergence of academic and Marxist sociology—of, that is, Parsons and Marcuse—and so on any given afternoon you could hear them arguing about Goffman's dramaturgy, Garfinkel's ethnomethodology, Homan's social exchange. (Up against the wall, functionalists!) They were also very fond of seminars, to which everyone was invited and to which hardly anybody went: "If, in the realm of physics, there is no quality without some quantity, then, in the realm of society, can there be reality without value?" Or: "Is it fair that if you seduce my wife and betray me as a friend, all I can do is divorce her and feel sorry for myself, whereas if you steal my hat, I can have the state throw you in jail?" There were other, more popular seminars at the institute—on violence, abortion, radical school reform, the dangers of a Federal Data Bank, the practicability of an antiballistics missile system—but the sociologists tended to look down on them, the way a cosmologist would look down on a plumber: If you have a clogged drain, go find yourself a snake; meanwhile *I* am worrying about the *idea* of a drain and what relation it might have to the concept of entropy.

The sociologists were aware, however, of the various dysfunctions going on around them—war, racism, student turmoil, women's rights. Not exactly the equilibrium one would have desired. Nor did it seem likely that the dysfunctions could be wished away by agreeing with the political theorists that the notion of a social contract has more to recommend it than most utilitarians supposed. Moreover, no one wanted to see the institute "liberated" some spring night, the files destroyed, the plug pulled out of the computer terminal. And so the sociologists embarked on a controlled experiment. If the radical feminists, the black liberationists, the high school students mobilizing against Indo-Chinese adventurism, needed office space, the institute would provide it. That way, the sociologists could study subcultural behavior patterns without having to leave home, and who knew what the dividends might be for theory? In effect, the institute sought to legitimize itself in much the same manner as a modern industrial society legitimizes itself—not by invoking superior moral sanction (God, or something like that), but by distributing more gratifications (GNP, or something like that: in this case, office space).

It made for a zoo. For one thing, there were caucuses every day and emergency meetings at least twice a week. (An emergency meeting was defined as a meeting that interrupted the regular caucus.) One group would accuse another group of using its telephone lines to call long-distance to Bolivia or Nanterre. The sociologists objected to rock music while the computer was at work. The rules stipulated no marijuana-smoking on the premises, and the rules were broken. The radical feminists and the black liberationists didn't get along. (The radical feminists were white, middle-class, and absorbed in changing Massachusetts' abortion laws. The black liberationists were mostly male, mostly not middle-class, and considered abortion a pogrom.) The high school mobilization voted to give itself a share of IBM 7090's precious computing time, but no one in the high school mobilization knew how to make up a program. Refugees from various apocalyptic skirmishes tried to use the place as a crash pad. The coffee machine never worked, and the Coke machine was full of slugs. People liberated postage stamps.

For another thing, the trooping in and out of so many cadres, angry about so many causes, so many slogans weighing on their sandwich boards and so many betrayals sticking in their craws, prickly with doctrine and worried about VD, made getting any sustained work done almost an accident. (Those who are certain of their own perceptions, those who eat absolute truth, revisionist Rice Krispies, for breakfast, feel that interrupting is a moral right.) It was, often, like trying to think in a cloud of mosquitoes.

And yet, and yet . . . Marcy loved it. She had loved it from the beginning, when Ken—against Rinsler's advice—had quit his job at *Scope* to handle words for Rinsler. Pamphlets, press releases, the weekly newsletter, the organizers' handbook. Rinsler wanted to end the war. It was his idea that the war could be ended by adapting the techniques of Mississippi Summer to the nation at large: not a voter registration drive but a community consciousness-raising. Instead of going some place else, college volunteers would go home, to their own communities. They would ring doorbells and send out mailings. They would organize block by block, based on those whom they had identified as being sick of what went on in Vietnam. They would help set up neighborhood meetings. They would let those meetings determine what action, if any, was feasible in that community—the collecting of signatures on antiwar petitions, a community referendum on the war, a protest march, letter-writing to local newspapers, lobbying the local congressman, whatever. Such community action projects could, of course, go off in a variety of directions that had nothing to do with the war. All to the good, once they were established. But opposition to the war was to be the organizing principle. The target area was to be the middle-class families and communities of middle-class college students; and that target area most emphatically included places like Kansas, Oklahoma, Nebraska, Texas, Georgia, North Carolina, Ohio—not simply the New Yorks, Bostons, Chicagos, and San Franciscos of this country. The purpose of the national office would be to provide literature, money, and advice; to be a communications center and a sympathetic ear; to dispatch field representatives as shock troops in difficult situations. Rinsler had been able to convince several wealthy individuals, with a history of contributing to left-wing causes, and several private foundations, with a history of subsidizing social reform movements, that spending money on his idea was more useful than spending it on yet another full-page ad in the New York *Times*. No more committees of writers and film stars, wringing their hands and congratulating themselves on their capacity for outrage. But hard, grass-roots work. Rinsler intended singlehandedly to raise a generation of community organizers, tough and capable people who would know how to drum up money, establish an office, feed sympathetic reporters valuable scoops, talk clergymen into turning over church basements for political meetings, manage important primary campaigns, change the nation.

It was an umbrella concept. Under it, draft counselors, antiwar GIs, SDSers, old Quaker Fellows for Reconciliation, Southern Leadership Conferees, and unaffiliated drifters-in from what Michael Harrington called "the conscience constituency" could gather comfortably, helping out in communities where they were already street-wise, being helped on projects of their own that needed funds or adrenalin. Loose, flexible, promising, straight-forward. Four hundred community projects were at least in touch with Rinsler; 2,000 volunteers claimed to be working full-time; another 13,000 were said to contribute sporadically. Just maybe . . .

Ken had written a story for *Scope* about it, as he had written stories for *Scope* on the GI coffeehouses and the draft counseling centers. Marcy had known he was about to do something drastic: along with the other white tutors at St. Thomas, he had been asked to leave Roxbury and his energy had nothing to do with it-self on late spring evenings but write angry letters to the news-papers; his games with Stephen were too intense, as though something had to be proved; he disappeared for hours into their bedroom—she was certain that during this period he wrote *Rose of Londonderry*, the novel he attributed to a long-dead uncle—and was sometimes to be found there, sitting in the dark, reminding her of the mad preachers hanging from his family tree, the ones who had sunk into suicidal depressions on deciding that they hadn't gotten the call, the ones who destroyed their portraits.

In May, Ken and Rinsler went South, to Winkham, South

Carolina. Something to do with a strike in a furniture factory. Ken telephoned from a motel, considerably shaken. "It's a place that makes antiques," he told her. *"Brand-new* antiques, tables and chairs. Well, antiques need all sorts of pockmarks, don't they? So once they've finished making, say, a table, before they've stained it, they put it in this elevator and it goes down a floor, to a small, windowless room. There's a huge black man in the room, wearing nothing but shorts. He's got a three-foot length of chain in his hand. The chain is studded with nails and other bits of metal. The table comes down, and the black man *beats* it with his chain. He *whips* the table, making random marks all over it. Then they'll put some stain or lacquer on, and it's a genuine antique. We went down to watch him, whipping and sweating. I was told that Redford sure does like his job, beating up furniture. Redford said he sure did, true enough. I was also told that the previous 'nigger in the box' went crazy one day and almost killed the foreman with his chain. Antique foreman. Then we went off to the golf course, to a clubhouse that looked just like Howard Johnson's, for mint juleps. *Mint juleps,* for Christ's sake! A young lawyer wants to close the factory. He also wants to be governor of the state in ten years. *Scope* is supposed to help. Marcy, I think the whole country is insane."

He started going to the institute at nights. When she complained of not seeing him, he said it was just a substitute for Roxbury: he wasn't spending any more time away from home. And she could come with him. But what about the children? Bring them, he said. She refused.

In June, Rinsler invited him to a training conference for community organizers. He flew to a midwestern city and ended up running a seminar himself, on public relations and publicity. "You wouldn't have believed it," he said on his return. "Two hundred volunteers, and most of them aren't old enough to vote, and most of them have been doing something political for two or three *years.*" The training took place at a college. They slept in dormitories, and spent ten hours a day in sessions, including field trips to tough neighborhoods nearby to try out their canvassing techniques; staged psychodramas late at night, to teach them how to handle hostility; drank beer at a local pub known not to worry about the length of a boy's hair. "It was absurd," he said. "To get into the pub, you had to show identification. Most of these kids had told each other that they'd burned their draft cards. But their draft cards were usually their only identification to prove they were old enough to drink. We stood in a long line, with everybody deciding whether his boast was more important than his thirst. Furtive, it was, but thirst usually won. And inside, we'd all start chanting, *Hey, hey, LBJ, how many kids did you kill today?*, like a stupid fraternity party. But most of us had never been *together*, with so many other people who felt the way we did. It *was* a fraternity, the only one we'd ever had. And it made us feel good, powerful. And Rinsler took me to the door and pointed across the street. On the corner there was a big group of blacks, just standing there, staring at us and the pub. I thought there was going to be a fight or something. But Rinsler explained: This pub was the only place in town where the blacks could come down and stand around and watch the cops beat up white people. Long-haired white kids, with their bikes and pills. We were the *entertainment* for the blacks."

Already it was *we*. The quality of their commitment embarrassed and enthralled him; it was as though he had been tossing a Frisbee around while better human beings had endured a long march, and now they marched into his living room and he had to eat the Frisbee. In fact, they did march into his living room, at his invitation, Rinsler's janissaries, drop-outs, veterans of southern jails and a thousand cups of instant coffee, communards who worked part-time in Filene's basement and were otherwise on the barricades, bad-mouthers of Saul Alinsky, Illich-freaks who felt that school itself was a detention center, Marcy an oppressor, books an insult to the singularity of their experience. Their scars glowed in the dark. All they ever seemed to eat was ice cream, and if they read at all, it was Hermann Hesse, and the two were somehow synonymous with innocence, sexual neutrality, and even Marcy—whose skepticism was her armature—was troubled and moved. They took Stephen seriously, and he appreciated the gesture.

Marcy began accompanying Ken to the institute on those nights when Stephen stayed over with a friend, and she could sing Hannah to sleep in the Port-a-Crib under a desk on which petitions against apartheid had been piled. A shaggy environment: a bewildering clutter of papers and bodies, hortatory insignia, angels in winged sneakers swooping, the wet-towel slap of distempered typewriters, guitars among telephones, ideas burning out like light bulbs, ink smells, blue haze, the static and the chortle and the mimeo suction—*we*, stapled together like press releases. Marcy's *I*, a moth on the window of this warmth. Rinsler's *them*, a killer-smog. Ken's *who*, a disappointed bird in a bell-shaped sky, making question marks. The locker room of the revolution.

He quit *Scope*. Or, rather, *Scope*, like Harvard, granted him a leave of absence, that he might discover and acknowledge the error of his ways. He argued that his mother's trust fund, plus Marcy's salary, plus thirty-two dollars a week subsistence pay from Rinsler, would see them through. She didn't really need arguments; just action, another figure in the pattern, a new pattern, an input of anticipation after the perpetual-motion machine of the predictable. To be seized by possibilities. She would find herself at the institute after a class, typing. She would denounce the cream as sour and the coffee, weak. She would lick the flaps of envelopes until her tongue was bloody and her lips were glued. She would take messages, none of which had anything to do with her, or James Joyce, or Thomas Mann, or Ken Coffin. She was a switchboard and a mailbox, and perhaps she was going to help change the world after all. *We* against *them*.

And the radical feminists found her. They were, as they said with a laugh that would have shattered plastic, "beating the bushes" for victims of sexism. Marcy's armature was not made out of plastic, but how did one take seriously a woman who called herself Sergeant Pepper; who dressed like a gaucho; who spoke grimly of "penal servitude" and "clitoral clicks" and "the internalization of the conventional definition of a wife"; who proposed a sisterly group-grope based on the Maoist notion of "speaking bitterness"? Why was it that you always met the silly ones first?

"Why do you wear a bra?" asked Sergeant Pepper.

"Because," said Marcy, "I've been breast-feeding a baby. If I didn't wear a bra, I'd leak all over my blouse."

"How many children do you have?"

"Two."

"Did you want them?"

"The first was on purpose; the second was an accident."

"Did you consider an abortion on the second child?"

"No. We were the right age. We had enough money. A family of four seemed, well, symmetrical. Or *square*. Father, mother, son, daughter. Besides, I don't like knives in me, or the idea of killing *anything*."

Sergeant Pepper snorted. "Don't you feel that a fetus is like a work of art you're in the process of creating? You're the artist. You own it. You can discard it at any stage of the creative process, like throwing away sketches for a painting. No guilt. Your body is your property. You have sole ownership. Why allow yourself to be raped by an absentee landlord? Why sharecrop?"

"First of all," said Marcy, "if you're talking about children, there *is* a co-ownership. Second, if a child is like a work of art, when do the preliminary stages stop being preliminary? Can I burn him or drown him when he's six years old? Third, I don't like this whole idea of property and ownership. People, especially children, aren't *owned*."

"Doesn't your husband own you?"

"We've entered into what I suppose you could call a contract. I'd call it an intimacy. Agreed to by both parties. A creative process of trying to be adults."

"Does he ever force you to go down on him?"

"No! Besides, that's really none of your business."

Everything was evidently Sergeant Pepper's business. But she was so obviously disappointed by this datum that Marcy wanted to say something co-operative.

"I *am* for equal pay for equal work," was what she said, "and equal opportunity, and day-care centers. I'm also for diaphragms, just to reduce the number of times I have to think about an abortion."

Sergeant Pepper was not mollified. All women were members of an oppressed class, whether they admitted it or not. The oppression was not only social; it was historical and biological as well. The very organization of nature was unfair. When Marcy suggested that it was difficult to do much about the organization of nature, Sergeant Pepper disagreed. Technology was the answer: sperm banks; artificial wombs; a commissary full of seed packets; consenting adults with a shopping bag selecting frozen one-day-old embryos on their way to a meeting in the morning, dropping them off at the bottling works on their way home, picking them up when they were hatched, farming them out on two-year contracts to communes for a very extended family life. Rent-a-child, like leasing a TV set. No blood, no birth, no death.

125

Just Kleenex. And love? Sergeant Pepper doubted that men were capable of love. Marcy felt sorry for her.

Still, she found herself a regular visitor to this strange sorority. Not ever having been in the habit of divulging confidences, she mostly listened. Listening was what they desperately required, for there was much to be said: cries for help, horror stories, humiliating confessions, fury. They were trying to fashion new selves out of old wounds, and like small, blind kittens they explored the world of their own emotions. If there was something missing in what they said—men, after all, were unhappy, too; and why must the tenderness, the humor, the mystery, and even the breathtaking terror in the sexual experience be omitted from all the discussions?—there was also much that intersected with her own life, that started old memories throbbing in parts of her consciousness she thought she had long ago amputated. The families that conspired at the destruction of their children, especially their female children, unaware of what they were doing and had done (Texas) . . . the university departments that failed to promote their female graduate students (Berkeley) . . . the men who used you as a toy or a wastepaper basket or a crying towel, on their way with cleated feet to Olympus (Berkeley and Paris) . . . the sullen egos and unmade beds and the fear of being alone and the fear of being not alone (Texas, Berkeley, Paris) . . . revulsion, contempt, self-pity, paralysis (anywhere). . . . She was being told that she was not to blame, that none of them was to blame, that the *Other* was to blame, the fault was in the superstars of the boudoir and the underbush, the fault lines were cracking at their seams, tremors became quakes, phallic cities will fall into the victims' abyss.

And if she resented the way the same few always dominated the discussions—Sergeant Pepper with her technology, Karen Constable with her confessions, Justine Dershowitz with her post-analytic twaddle—Marcy had to admit that she refused to supply the qualifying detail, the personal secret that confirmed or denied the general assertion, the thumbprint of self. Such spilling seemed to her a violation of what she held most precious: her privacy. Were she to tell them that Stephen had been decided on, in the days before draft counseling and Canadian exile, as a means of Ken's avoiding the Army, they would bark at her. Were she to tell them that Stephen had been worth the joylessness of that nightly sawing, the ugliness of his ultimate issue, they might —with the exception of Sergeant Pepper—believe her; a qualm might be born. *Does he ever force you to go down on him?* No, but he wanted her to do so voluntarily, she knew that, and she was sometimes ashamed of her sexual passivity, of staring at the ceiling while he did what she wanted him to do to her, unable to imagine why he would even be willing to do it. They would conclude . . . well, they might even *admire* her. Shame was a sham. What *right* had they to know that her first experience had been with a boy who spent fifteen minutes putting on a rubber and then didn't know how or where to insert it, who had to be *helped*, who gave up in despair because she had been in spite of herself a clenched fist and he had *not* been a rapist; that she was innocent, after six men, of anal intercourse; that she had once dreamed of being gang-banged by the faces on Mount Rushmore; that she was convinced that men faked *their* coming almost as often as she faked hers, as scared as she was of being found inadequate; that she had declined her only invitation to go to bed with *two* men simultaneously—even suggesting to them that they really wanted to go to bed with each other and without her—and had morbidly regretted it ever since, because she wouldn't *consider* it now, she was astonishingly conventional, but what *if?* She thought of linked sausages, of grinders and cleavers, of quick-sand and garbage disposals, of mortar and bricks, the wedding wall, the wail of need, the sense of sanctuary, a belongingness eliding into boredom, Nazis who wept, Russians who combed the blond bush before poking their heads into it, everybody as a victim, the winners plastic, urea-derived, bionondegradable, a permanent erection, without temperature or compunction or guilt. Show and tell was not her game.

A *we*, then, that she refused. A sisterhood of sob, a sorority of execration. Among them, she discovered her own arrogance. *I* spent too much time becoming *me*, an enormous effort, at great cost, to fall now into the basket of *we*, to suck breasts instead of cocks. It was Justine one night who kissed her, Marcy permitting herself to be kissed, as a compromise which would confer dignity on what might otherwise have seemed merely ridiculous and therefore weak: a grab of need, an approximation of reassurance. Something else not to tell the other sisters: *snatch* is genderless; how vulnerable we were, how we conspired at the betrayals that gnawed us. You have *character*, Justine told her, and Marcy thought of a broken piece of alphabet impaled on a key of a typewriter, striking only after it had been struck, less than a thumbprint. She refused, as well, the *we* of thumbs and tongues, the substitution for the humor and the terror.

What, she had asked her husband once in bed, is the functional purpose of pubic hair? He hadn't been able to guess. It reduces the static electricity, she said. He had giggled his way to orgasm. She had been pleased with herself—and would not say so to moon-calves and commissars. Other nights it had been difficult to distinguish the hurting from the healing, which was at least interesting. Nights of galactic exploration, underwater marine maneuvers; nights of banality. Mornings, she was reluctant. Too much nakedness spoiled the psi. Nude in their attitudes—the day not having deposited its anecdotal grime, not having punched them drunk and sold them its excuses—they were absurd to one another, reckless accidents, children. Brushing one's teeth was more important.

All right, her consciousness was raised—up, up, to where she was alone again. There weren't enough options. Had there ever been? In their inchoate groping, the sisters seemed to imagine a perfect freedom *out there*, the new woman as a wind of change blowing through the temples of romance, over the realms of fun, a liberation into a childhood of manifold choices. They would chuck it all, this accumulation of mistakes and responsibilities and doubts and grudges, and rush off to Zanzibar—a revolution of sensibility that looked suspiciously like an advertisement for a Mediterranean luxury cruise. *But Marcy had done exactly that.* She had rushed off to Paris, brave child in a new Old World. A clean sheet between two dirty ones, waiting to be written on, erasable bond. The ball-point pens didn't differ that much, continent to incontinent. She had, unfortunately, taken along her head; the reality was inside it. New skies, old eyes. Only children supposed that tomorrow was going to be utterly different, a surprise box; and the only difference was suddenly, tomorrow, not being a child any more. What was needed was a different kind of adulthood, which meant going deeper, not dispersing on the surface like an oil slick.

She did, however, emerge from the sisterly huddles in late summer with a modest game-plan: there was no revolutionary reason why the women in Rinsler's operation had to cut all the stencils and lick all the envelopes, while the men played with the WATS line, talking up insurrection as they ate ice cream. Which was the more *authentic* revolutionary activity, establishing a day-care center or throwing rocks at a bank? If she was going to volunteer her labor, it ought properly to be in behalf of a cause that reflected her various concerns, and the way her time was used ought properly to reflect her various skills. As simple as that.

She broached the subject with Ken, on his return from Texas. She wanted to take over the weekly newsletter from him. How hard was it, anyway, to master the inverted pyramid? He was preoccupied: a boy had died in Texas, one of their volunteers. The boy worked part-time, alone on weekends, in a grocery store. Somebody had clubbed him unconscious and left him for eighteen hours in a meat locker. Apparently, no money had been stolen. Rinsler was certain it had been a political murder, and Ken had gone to Texas to bury a body and write a press release. They broke the AP national wire on it, and *Scope* ran a story, and Ken quoted Rinsler: after many a martyr, follows fund-raising. He wasn't happy. He didn't listen to her. She shouted at him: pay attention to *me*. If you want the newsletter, take the newsletter, he said; it's not important. It's important to *me*, she said. All right, all right, he said; you can't do a worse job than I've done.

And so she became so busy that she didn't really notice his disengagement. He would complain: in trying to prepare a fund-appeal letter, he had found that there were holes in their umbrella. The various divisions who had gathered under Rinsler's banner of community organization now refused to supply the names of their fat cats, their philanthropic sources. Come the fall, they would want to lean on those sources for their own purposes—the New Politics convention on the Labor Day weekend, assaulting the Pentagon in October. Mailing lists were private property. He had even begun to doubt the existence of some of Rinsler's projects. Oh, there were people out there who loved to talk on the telephone, but what *else* were they doing? The harassment was real enough in several communities—broken windows, splattered paint, a cross that failed to burn, pot busts—but being harassed didn't necessarily help end the war or organize a movement; it just increased the self-righteousness and paranoia of the people at the institute.

She heard, but didn't much credit, these rumors of discontent. Static, they seemed, late at night in the bedroom, part of the motion of the air made possible by the window fan; whispers. Stephen had gone to New Hampshire to be pampered by the Mackenzies; Marcy had begged off on the basis of a summer course, seeking to avoid the regimentation of leisure that went on in Wyke Regis. Preparing now to teach in the fall, she cared only that Ken let her run the newsletter in her own way, that at last she had a political dimension as well as an academic and family one. The fact that he disappeared more and more often with Hannah on his back, for long walks and visits to the aquarium, struck her only as exemplary thoughtfulness, like arranging for Mrs. Devlin in September: a father who cared and shared. She turned to him at night and found their congress peaceful, a sort of ceremony, when organs did actually make music, but of a courtly kind. And if, during the day, at the institute, she saw his pinched look, a shadow of anger like a vein beating at his temple, she attributed it to deadlines or policy disagreements or the war that wouldn't go away.

Then came the bad news: Their martyr in Texas proved to have been a dealer in drugs, and the drugs weren't soft, and the martyr had apparently specialized as much in unpaid debts as he had in bad trips, and the people to whom he owed money were probably the people who had martyred him. Rinsler didn't care, but *Scope* did, and so did Ken, who had arranged the *Scope* story. A question of trust, said Ken. One more lie in *Scope* magazine, said Rinsler, won't compromise any truth that matters. *Every* truth matters, said Ken, rather pompously, Marcy thought. We needed that meat locker, said Rinsler, to be taken seriously. Ken burned all the brochures they had prepared about their martyr, in wastepaper baskets at the institute, ridiculous incinerators that smogged the white walls, blackened the poster art. An overreaction, said Rinsler; why not burn *Scope*? *Scope*, said Ken, usually bothers to check its stories; they trusted me. Now, said Rinsler, you know something about the real world. I know the opposite, said Ken, and wrote a letter to his former editors, apologizing; and explained to Rinsler, I'm the sum of my compunctions. To which Rinsler replied: I can't count that high. To which Ken responded: stop counting, and there isn't any real world. Tell it to all the dead bodies in Vietnam, said Rinsler.

Still, Marcy was not prepared for what happened over the Labor Day weekend. She went to Wyke Regis with Hannah; Ken went to Chicago with Rinsler, for the New Politics convention. She could have gone with them and chose not to. She was waiting instead at the Keene airport when the tiny Beechcraft landed. Ken got out and immediately complained about the safety catch: "It was like flying in a teacup during a tornado. I read the instruction card, there was nothing else to read. In case of emergency, remove safety catch. There was only one door, I was next to it. I tried to find the safety catch. It hadn't even been connected. So I connected it, then forgot about it. We land, and the pilot comes down the aisle, and he tries to open the door, and he can't. I suddenly realize that he hasn't removed the safety catch. I remove it for him. He looks at me as though I was trying to hijack the plane to Albania. He's never even *heard* of a safety catch. Next time I'll go by pogo stick, if there is a next time."

In the car on the way to Wyke Regis, he only muttered to a babbling Stephen, very unlike his usual willingness to expand. Finally, Marcy asked him: "What *happened* in Chicago?"

"I'll tell you what happened. A bunch of black guys walked in off the street with a list of non-negotiable demands, about representation and so on. One of the demands was that we endorse all the resolutions of the Newark Conference on Black Power last May. Now, most of those Newark resolutions were secret, and the ones that weren't secret were mostly stupid. 'Sexual reparations' for black people—what does that mean? 'International Zionist-imperialist conspiracy'—lovely. Well, then, in the hotel I guess some of us learned what sexual reparations does mean. Your friend Justine Dershowitz certainly learned. She was coming out of her room when a couple of satraps from the Pig-Stickers of Islam took her right back into the room and reparated her for three or four hours. She cried a lot before we found her. She wasn't the only one. And the next day she wasn't the only one who voted to endorse all the non-negotiables, which of course we did as an act of good faith. Rinsler voted with her. Henry Adams should have been around. It was a wonderful example of the Virgin and the Dynamo. We were the virgins. Explain to me how I'm going to explain to Kansas and Nebraska what we did and why we did it. Explain to me how I'm going to explain it to *me*."

He said this in the same tone of voice he had used to talk about the safety catch on the airplane, as if he were leashed to a tree. He was in a controlled rage about everything: the static on the car radio, the truck they couldn't pass, Stephen's desire to stop and go pee-pee.

"It shouldn't have happened to Justine," Marcy said. What else could be said?

"It shouldn't have happened to anybody. That's not the sort of people we're supposed to be."

She couldn't think of anything but a furtive, compromising kiss and a young woman who had analyzed herself into grabbing at life. "What do you do now?" Surely something had to be done.

"I don't know." Because the cigarette lighter on the dashboard didn't work—it had never worked—he threw it out the window. "They did some experiments on temperature regulation. Did you read about it? You heat up part of the brain, the hypothalamus, I think. It doesn't matter how cold it is outside, whether you're on the North Pole. The brain tells the body it's too hot. A dog will start to pant, a man will start to sweat. Take off your clothes and maybe you'll freeze to death. That's the way I feel. Only I don't know if somebody's stuck an icicle or a red-hot poker into my brain. I don't know if I'm freezing or frying. I just know I feel rotten, and my brain and my body got a divorce."

"I never told you about the night that Justine—"

"I don't want to hear about it."

"You feel sorrier for yourself than you do for her."

"You have a remarkable capacity for understanding only what you want to understand, and then lecturing me about what you don't understand."

"Yes. The male mind, a mystery wrapped in a lot of baby fat."

"Are you arguing?" Stephen asked.

"No," Marcy replied, "we're fighting." Taking her eyes off the road long enough to see that he looked likely to throw up. "Ken, I'm sorry."

"Is it non-negotiable? Where's the safety catch? You've been unhappy for years. Now I'm unhappy. At last, we've achieved an equilibrium."

And that was that, because she had grown up in a household where, if you talked back to him, her father would slap her; and he had grown up in a house where nobody shouted at anybody else; and both of them had learned how to recognize bitterness, fear it, retire from it in silence, and hope that ulcers weren't the consequence. On reaching Wyke Regis, he vanished almost immediately into the orchards with his uncle John. He returned to announce that he would be staying for six weeks to supervise the migrant pickers. She reminded him that she had a class to teach: what was she supposed to do with the children? He suggested that she leave them with him; he would arrange for care during the day. She refused; Stephen was placed in a nursery school, Mrs. Devlin had been retained for Hannah. Better that they establish themselves in Boston, if he would be returning in six weeks. He didn't object. She promised to come up on weekends. He said that wouldn't be necessary. *Necessary.* She watched the pickers straggle down into the orchards, arranging the boxes for drops under each tree, singing the top ten instead of spirituals; she thought of them all as rapists, and dreamed her last night in Wyke Regis of being the pot at one of their crap games, a ladder of black limbs to the top bunk, their turbanned heads climbing up between her legs, Justine in a collar chained to an apple tree, the apples billiard balls, the lightning a cue stick, Sergeant Pepper naked on a tractor, Ken hanging frozen from a hook in the storage shed with the controlled atmosphere, her father's the last head between her legs on the top bunk, snakes.

It was your usual afternoon at the institute. In the corridors the ecologists talked about exponential curves, the fouling of spaceship earth. The economists replied by saying that men weren't fruit flies; curves flatten out into "takeoff plateaus"; social telesis will self-correct; chicken batteries are food sources; *Apollo* and *Sputnik* represent portable "earth environments," self-cycling, self-sustaining, waste-reprocessing "closed ecological systems." They fought about computer-time. *What about my marriage?* The name of Buckminster Fuller was taken in vain. *I want him back, giggling.* Had Christ "concretized" the Judaic conceptions of earthly utopia and individual ethical responsibility? *If the Mackenzies won't let him into their club, he can join mine, the dues are cheap.* J-curves of "relative deprivation" versus "cloning" as a substitute for sex. *I don't want a substitute.* Bastards! What have you done to my political dimension?

She couldn't decide whether she wanted to happen on Rinsler or not. Was he pathetic or bathetic? That heavy hand on her thigh last night: she hadn't moved, hadn't even gulped. If Justine, why not Rinsler? But the approximation had been misunderstood. Wretched lighthouse; his sheets of Homosote hung up like drying diapers; his needle, a noodle on eye-witness: what had made him think that he could walk away and with such dreamy nonchalance undress in front of her? Was she supposed to have been hypnotized? An unprepossessing sight at best, a mound of Silly-Putty, toad-shaped. And to this person, this organizer of communities, she had revealed secrets about Ken that she had withheld from the sisterhood. She had thus betrayed her husband, a small revenge, with words. But the larger revenge was beyond or beneath her, because it involved betraying herself as well. *And so I probably did invite it.* She had slammed the door on him, on her own mind, and driven off into a profound embarrassment.

Rinsler was among the missing, so perhaps the embarrassment had been mutual. She was momentarily cheered to see some men pecking away at the typewriters and slicing their tongues on the flaps of envelopes. They were incompetent, but it was just a matter of conditioning. Certainly if women could do it, it was not necessarily beyond the capabilities of men. She waved at them. The mail to the newsletter consisted primarily of requests for money, for rent and for bail. The small changes of emphasis she had introduced into the newsletter, particularly the articles on women's rights, had also excited some correspondence. What about forced sterilization for welfare mothers? Were the ZPG people basically racist? Voices out of the great land, confused and querulous, but speaking up at last. That's what they were establishing, a nationwide grid of information and opinion, a Diner's Club of the mind.

She was startled by the appearance of Rajah Born. Captain Black-Patch, Ken called him, the scourge of Roxbury, and not an institute regular. Nor toad-shaped, either; a king in his dashiki, surveying the desks, the in- and out-baskets, the rented Smith-Coronas, the poster art, the white bodies propped up variously by elbows and knees—and deciding that it was all so much flotsam on the African blood-tide. "Rinsler doesn't seem to be here this afternoon," Marcy said. She was rather in awe of Rajah Born.

"I wasn't looking for the duck, little lady," said Raj. "I was looking for your man."

The duck? Was that what he called Rinsler? She liked that. She didn't like "little lady." She was, however, certainly smaller than the Raj. Although she had always thought of herself as medium. "Which man?"

"*Your* man. The Coffin."

"What on earth for? You kicked him out of Roxbury six months ago. What's the matter, can't get along without him?"

Rajah Born had to make up his mind whether he was going to talk to a woman. He did not regard women, especially white women, as serious people. "Listen," he said, "the Coffin was all right. A pain in the ass with his honky folk singers, but mostly all right. It was the setup, little lady. Rinso-white at the top, niggers at the bottom. Poverty program shit. We got free schools now, with brothers and sisters at the top. The Coffin, he talked a couple of my baby-sisters into college. Maybe he can talk a couple more in, if he don't object to working *for* black folks instead of *on* them."

"College? But you told Ken you wanted guns, not bachelor degrees. Education on the streets, you said."

One of the reasons why the Raj disliked talking to women was that everything turned into a dumb argument. "I had me a lot of lazy niggers on my hands," he said. "Not black folks, *niggers*. Needed to whuppum into shape, put 'em together, straighten out all the shiftiness. That pilgrim shit—we used to strangle them mother-lions. We invented the wheel!"

"But not the axle, Mr. Born."

"That's a lie!" He folded his arms; he was restraining himself. "Little lady, I know we got to have lawyers, and tax people. Doctors. Shit, we got to have *teachers*. You know what the Man does. He goes down home to them little nigger colleges and he hires the top half of all the graduating classes and he spreads them around, one bright nigger for General Up Yours Motors, another bright nigger for IBMotherfucker. One each, he does, and puts them up front where everybody sees them. What happens to the bottom half? The not-so-brights? Why, they can't do nothing but teach at them little nigger colleges. So's that teaching that was piss-poor to begin gets poorer than piss. The dumb half is just too full of uppity shit to come down on *us*, right here. And the bright half, they's too busy sucking on the teat of white biggies, dreaming about split-level shithouses, they don't know where home is. The Coffin, he'd be all right 'til we got our own."

"And after you got your own, you'd kick him out again."

"After we got our own, he wouldn't need to be there no more. And then he wouldn't want to be. But black folks on top now, dig?"

Dug. The Raj had read Ken's character like a comic strip. Maybe if the Raj had a lighthouse of his own . . . "My husband, Mr. Born, isn't here, and won't be here for almost another month. His family has commissioned him to take care of the poor black trash that picks apples in New Hampshire every fall. Shall I tell him that you apologize for what you did?"

Pussy always talks too much, thought the Raj. It was a way of pretending you weren't pussy. "The Coffin's all right," he said again. "He's going to run out of places to go, though." He clasped his hands behind his neck; the flares of his dashiki winged him, charcoal archangel, horn a-plenty. "You like it here? You're so nervous you type with your eyes."

"I like it here. They aren't villains."

"The European frag," he said. She looked up; his cheekbones and his chin-jut made a slingshot; the elastic band was wrapped around her head, and he was going to fling her through his skull. Bull's eye. "You got away with it in the nineteenth century. None of that French shit here, no ma'am. Let all them little ideoloets run around acrost the Atlantic cutting up each other. You got your boo-jew-wah liberpimples to keep you warm. Bunch of Angle-saxophones, offing the Indos, trashing wigwams, ee-ternal vigilantes, let the micks and wops rumble for their shithouses, the state is quo is us. Suspended sentence for the U.S. of Ass. But Century Number Twenty comes along. Your con-sen-sus is con-cussed. By the *Aboriginal*—the Peru dude, Inca-dinca-doo! The bushman, we don't *waltz* our Matildas! The Afro, black trash-eater, voodooing it to you, groin and bare *it! I* am 1789, caught up with you at last."

"My Louis Hartz bleeds for you," said Marcy. "That *is* his theory, isn't it? In, ah, translation?"

"Yeah," said the Raj. "I took his course at Harvard. Does that surprise you?"

"Everything about you surprises me, Mr. Born."

"Good. Well, now, I look around this here institruit, and they's all European frags. They still think they can get away with it. No way."

"Including my husband."

"The Coffin, yes ma'am. He got the name for it." And the Raj did a little sidle, spun himself on his spine as though it were a sword, and swept out of the room, hearing a different drum.

Zero population growth, indeed. The Raj was going to clone himself. Then look out, frags! The Coffin would be a portable environment, self-cycling and waste-reprocessing. Buckminster was Fuller it. Marcy stared at the wall. *Are my curves exponential?* She spent the next two hours on the WATS line, trying to find out if what the Raj said about the graduating classes at black colleges was true, and planning a story on it for the newsletter. Then it was time to pick up Hannah.

"Where are the pears?" demanded Mrs. Devlin.

Marcy, of course, had forgotten all about the baby food. From the TV set inside: gunfire. Mrs. Devlin was watching a rerun of "77 Sunset Strip." "I'm sorry. I'll bring everything Monday morning."

Mrs. Devlin installed Hannah in the Hike-a-Poose. "I don't like to strap her in too tight," she said. "Cuts off the poor dear's circulation."

If you didn't strap her in tight, Mrs. Devlin, the poor dear would slump down, squash herself, and start screaming on the bus.

"Mrs. Coffin, aren't you forgetting—"

"What. Oh, yes." She paid Mrs. Devlin and turned to go.

"'By, 'by, sweetheart," said Mrs. Devlin to Hannah. "You tell your mother to be good to you over the weekend."

A sensible mind would have forgotten last night, Labor Day, Paris, Berkeley, and Texas; would have remembered to buy pears and pay Mrs. Devlin. A sensible mind would have ridden the quotidian like a cork.

On the bus, a woman who was content to sit while Marcy stood with her baby on her back, took one look at Hannah and said: "Isn't he enormous?"

"She," said Marcy. "And her weight is average. Fifty-second percentile." Buying silence for the rest of the trip.

She had time on reaching home to change Hannah, mix strained lamb and green beans, shovel it in, wash it down with milk, and unleash her daughter on the defenseless living room. Then the bus honked.

Stephen bounded out still clutching the sheet of paper with his name written on it. "Pamela can write her name," were his first words. "But she doesn't know her address. I'm hungry and thirsty."

"Yes, sir. Right away, sir. Would you like to see a menu?" He had strong views of food, and the views changed daily. One evening, peanut butter on graham crackers was absolutely the only alternative to starvation; the next evening, peanut butter on graham crackers might as well have been cat tongue on a slab of bathroom tile. They compromised on hot dogs with no mustard, one medium-sized carrot with the string tip chopped off, two rings of pineapple in a quarter inch of juice, thirteen chocolate chips, and seven ounces of Ocean Spray Cranberry Cocktail, all arranged *just so* on a tray, which Stephen bore into the living room, placed on the couch, sat down beside. Now he required silence. Nursery school, as usual, had been rugged. Fifteen minutes of Rocky and Bullwinkle would allow him to unwind. Only as the commercial came on and the last chocolate chip had been consumed did he look up, permit the TV set to be turned off, and agree to talk. "Ricky didn't take a nap. Sean fell down the stairs. Lydia had on *long* socks. Peter's mother came to school, with a big hat. Sally hit me."

"Why did Sally hit you?" Hannah hoisted herself up on the coffee table and tried to grab Stephen's tray.

"Because she wanted *my* truck," said Stephen. Furious that the tray eluded her, Hannah pulled all the magazines down on the floor.

"What did you have for lunch?" Had Marcy even eaten lunch?

"Spaghetti." He brooded. "Bread with butter. And applesauce! I hit Sally back."

"I don't doubt it. Did you draw anything?"

"No. We just played." Weary disgust. Blocks, trucks, soldiers, and singing were *play*; drawing, scissors, paste, and paints were *work*. Play was a "just"; work was serious, sanctified. Don't bother your father (mother); he (she) is *working*. When Stephen learned to read, he would have an immense tactical advantage over his mother: real *work*. Her reading as a child had always been interrupted.

Hannah, in a crouch, rocked back and forth, made bubbles. Suddenly she took off across the rug at top-crawl. Marcy was up from the sofa and ahead of her. There it was . . . a thumbtack. "Tough luck, White Fang. You gave yourself away by panting."

"Mother," said Stephen, "will you please buy me a rifle?"

"No."

"Why?"

"You already have a phaser gun." Guaranteed to rearrange the molecules of Martians.

"A phaser gun isn't a rifle," said Stephen. "When my father comes back, he will buy me a rifle."

"I wouldn't count on it. He didn't even want you to have the phaser gun."

"Why?"

"Because your father doesn't like guns." When he was twelve, he had killed a porcupine. The dogs had been having trouble with the porcupine. Ken had found the porcupine up a tree, and shot him. Looking at the corpse, he hadn't felt heroic. They had hoped to raise a gunless son, but had figured without the neighborhood, the nursery school, tinkertoys, pencils, brooms, spoons, toothbrushes, slices of bread with bites in them, a gun-chromosome. "What would you do with a rifle, anyway? Shoot Sally?"

"Not *Sally*. Birds."

"Birds? What did the birds do to you? I thought you liked birds. You put bread crumbs on the windowsill for them. We don't shoot birds in this house."

"But you told me we don't shoot *people* in this house, either. What *can* I shoot?"

"You can shoot trees."

"Then will you buy me a rifle to shoot trees?"

"No."

"Why?"

"You can use your phaser gun to shoot trees." Hannah had moved into a corner. This time it was a "Peace Now!" button. "We don't eat political buttons in this house," Marcy said.

"When *is* my father coming home?"

"Do you want to get the calendar?"

"No." He had started off X-ing out the days on the calendar. But when he learned he could X out a whole week in advance, and it didn't do any good, he decided that the calendar was *play*. It had no power.

She was suddenly at a loss what to do with Stephen next. His father wrestled with him. Stephen would not wrestle with his mother; he suspected her of lack of conviction. She picked up Hannah, who was making sounds that strangely resembled church plainsong, and dropped her in the playpen. "I'll start your bath," she told Stephen. "Tomorrow, do you want to make gingerbread men?"

"That's a good idea."

Hannah shook the bars of the playpen, sang, fell backward, grabbed her toes, thought about her feet. Marcy turned on the water in the tub, fixed herself a stiff drink, sat down, thought about Hannah's feet, Rinsler's feet, iambic feet. Hannah screamed.

"Hannah's hungry," said Stephen.

"Hannah is ready for bed." She took Hannah into the bathroom, disassembled and repackaged her, then held her up to the mirror. Hannah approved of her image. "Now," said her mother, "wave good night to your brother."

Hannah beat the air vigorously with her arms. Stephen threw a negligent hand in her direction. Up the stairs they went. Into the crib. Hannah sighed, seized her blanket, stuffed it into her mouth, and turned away. The way they flung themselves into sleep, like arrows or torpedoes . . . And she would later on lie down suspiciously or, like a dog, paw herself a spot. "Good night, Hannah."

Downstairs, Stephen was sniffing her untouched drink. "Would you like a sip?" He tried it, decided he preferred cranberry juice. "Now, can you get your clothes off? It's bath-time." He pulled his jersey over his head, then pranced about blindly, his arms foreshortened. "Batman!" he cried.

"And I am Robin, the girl wonder," said Marcy.

"No! Sally's Robin!"

He flapped around the living room for another five minutes, stomping Jokers and Penguins to death, before finishing his strip. Then he stood naked, perfectly formed, grinning, on the rug, his skin the color of clean sand, something feral about him, not in the least like Rinsler.

"Into the bathtub, buster." He loped off, and there was presently the sound of water being abused, friendly objects being hurled into his private pond. He would sing nursery school songs to them for about fifteen minutes. Then he would amuse himself by floating white worms of toothpaste around his kneecaps. Finally he would call for her, and protest while she washed his hair.

She lit a cigarette. It would be five days before she would once again be tickling the bare-footed minds of her section. On Monday, Professor Boynton would explain what modernism had done to conventional notions of tragedy. Tragedy was always good for a laugh. Mr. Galton, it has been said that the rhythm of tragedy is a movement from Purpose through Passion to Perception . . . do you agree? Miss Richardson, would you consider *repression*, in the psychoanalytic sense, tragic? Does it, or doesn't it, satisfy the Hegelian formulation of contradictory imperatives? Twenty minutes, class, on *Death in Venice*; twenty minutes on *The Judgment*; twenty minutes on *Waiting for Godot*. Mr. Segal, are Vladimir and Estragon tragic figures? Does their static waiting constitute a Purpose-Passion-Perception plexus? A meat-loafing of pity and terror? Where is the emotional emetic? Where is the vehemence? Mr. Laforgue, is the death of a child tragic? The raping of a lesbian? Why not? Are we saying that what is meaningless on one side of the dramatic equation is pathetic on the other side? And pathos is not tragedy? Compare, class . . . does the size of the flaw equal the size of the waste? Should it?

Mrs. Devlin, don't you think the Madonna should have a tragic flaw?

Mr. Beckwith, is handball an emotional emetic?

Mr. Born, was Hegel a frag?

Mr. Coffin—

"Mother, the worms are drowneded!"

She rose. Stephen got soap in his eyes because, while crying as his hair was washed, he rubbed his sudsy hands in his wet eyes; which made him cry more, rub more, cry more. She parted his hair surgically. The scalp shone like a pewter bowl.

"You're hurting me," he said.

"Get a story," she said.

They read a Babar book while his hair dried. Then she carried him off to bed on her back. "Dromedaries have only one hump. Camels have two humps. Right, Mother?"

Was that the difference? She didn't know. "I don't know."

"We better look it up," said Stephen. All children were natural Mackenzies. The meals that cooled while a disputed fact was tracked down in an encyclopedia . . . She went into the other room to look it up. Stephen was waiting.

"A dromedary is an Arabian camel," Marcy told him, "with only one hump. Bactrian camels have two humps."

"What's a Bactrian?"

"It refers to a part of Persia."

"What's Persia?"

"A place far away, on the other side of the ocean."

"Why do some camels only have one hump, and others two?"

"I have a feeling you've already gone through this conversation with your father."

"*He* told me the Arabs always cut one hump off their camels, to use as a footstool in the desert."

Zionist-imperialist propaganda. "Well, your father wouldn't lie to you, would he?"

"Sally lies."

"What does Sally lie about?"

"She told my teacher that I hit her."

"You told me that you did hit her."

"But she hit me first."

"Good night, Stephen."

"Tomorrow we're going to make gingerbread men?"

"Yes." He always became garrulous in bed, postponing darkness. "Good night, Stephen."

"You didn't kiss me."

"Yes, I did."

"No, you didn't." She kissed him again, on the ear. He said: "My father says grizzle bears eat belly buttons and earlopes."

"And camel humps, too," said Marcy. "That's why Arabs are so unfriendly. The grizzle bears ate up all their footstools. Good night for the last time, Stephen."

She rinsed the children's dishes, and then scrounged in the refrigerator for scraps to eat: cheese, and a cold chicken wing, and the remains of a mix of strained apricots and rice cereal which Hannah had wisely refused. We rush our children off to bed, in order to get to . . . what? To get to the drink that had only been sipped, to the mail that hadn't even been opened. A letter addressed to Mr. and Mrs. Kenneth Coffin in an unfamiliar script. She opened it. It was actually to Ken, from that crazy girl who wrote the short story in his class:

Dear Mr. Coffin,

Do you remember me? The above-named is a mostly *Negro* college in North Carolina. I have been a freshwoman for three weeks, and today I saw my advisor, and he showed me your letter of recommendation, for which I thank you very much. He said (my advisor) that he would like to see the short story you thought so highly of, and I told him I don't have a copy, you have the only copy. I wonder if you could send it to me?

I saw in the letter that you said I tended to be lazy, which is true. I haven't really had time to be lazy down here yet, I am too busy. But I think I will probably start being lazy when I have to take tests in natural science and in French. In high school, you may remember, I took Spanish, but Spanish is not recommended by my advisor. English isn't very hard, and do you know what we discussed in class last week? We discussed *The Invisible Man*. I explained to everybody how the old white man from Boston actually wanted incest with his own daughter and that's why he was so interested. They were all very impressed by how sophisticated I was in these matters, so I thank you for making me read the book and explaining it all.

The college has just gotten a lot of money from a Foundation, and the people in the town are nice to us. I think this is because they would like to see a *Negro* college become good, and that way they wouldn't have to integrate. Maybe that's just nasty.

I do not miss Boston very much. I was in a rut there, and also there are people I would just as soon not see for a long time.

You will be happy to know that I am not interested in taking any more pills. You may also be happy to know that I am so far away I will not be calling you at midnight for awhile to get bawled out. You will have to bawl me out in letters, if you want to write. But then, you won't know what to bawl me out for unless I tell you. I think my advisor here is too sympathetic. He always seems to be going to pat me on the head.

Well, so far so good. Please write if you feel like it.

Sincerely, your friend,
LAVONIA STRICKLAND

Surprise: there were people out there who weren't thinking about sex, or Rinsler, or color symbolism. There was a girl out there who had gotten into college because of *her* husband: a *fact*.

143

The world was altered. Well, Marcy had gotten a girl into college, too. Marcy had gotten Marcy into college, where she had taken French and learned a lot about natural science, especially the parasympathetic system. They should have called it Cherry Canyon. A loaf of bread, a thermos of Scotch, I-Thou beside ourselves on the army blanket, with the sports car tethered to a nearby tennis court. Not to mention frostbite. He had called her breasts snow-cones, which at the time they were.

What she wanted was not a series of muggings, but a relationship that had a history; like marriage. A novel, not of the absurd, but more Russian, to get to bed to beget children to get to bed. Hush, puppies.

And she was back in France. Back in a restaurant whose name she had never been able to remember, in Chantilly. One of twenty young women who had been bussed there from Paris that afternoon, along with a clutch of French architecture students wearing what looked like Confederate Army uniforms and purporting to be a brass band. Yvonne had given her the invitation. "You're supposed to be a model."

"How does one pretend to be a model?"

"One pouts a lot. Look, I'd go myself. After all, five hundred francs, a free meal, dancing and champagne. Only . . ."

"Only Jean-Luc."

"He'd kill me," said Yvonne. "Take it, please, Marcy." She did, without even the vaguest idea of whom they would be meeting or why. She needed the five hundred francs.

At six o'clock in the evening the restaurant was attacked by a fleet of Renaults, honking madly. The architecture students broke —never had the word been more appropriate—into song. "The Battle Hymn of the Republic," the "Marseillaise," and what she later learned was supposed to be the underground Australian national anthem. They continued blowing, wheezing, and flailing all during apéritifs. Emerging from the Renaults, stunned insensible by the commotion, was as spiffy a rack of summer suits as you'll see outside of an expensive department store. Inside the suits were thirty young men. The only thing rumpled was their faces. There was much yapping in high-speed French, low-gear English, unfathomable German. Hands became whiskbrooms, sweeping them in little pats and puffs into the anterooms of the restaurant. Crushed into corners, they were in danger of burning holes in each other's summer suits and the dresses of the women, from the Gaulloises everybody seemed to be smoking. Marcy was trapped by a perfectly appalling specimen of pudginess and bonhomie. "Hallo. My name's Andy. I'm from Australia. Who are you?" She identified herself as Yvonne, and rattled off several meaningless sentences in French as rapidly as she could manage. "You don't speak English?" said the Australian. She frowned, then shook her head, as though a stick of asparagus had spoken to her in asparagus language and she had miraculously guessed at what was meant. "Oh!" said Andy. Then, to her outrage, he grabbed her by the wrist and dragged her like a canoe through the crowd to the far wall, where a portrait of one of the less interesting French kings looked about to slaver on them. "Ken," said Asparagus, "this is Yvonne. Speak-ee no Anglais. Now I've got to find one who does." He patted Marcy on the rump and left her immediately, wading back into the confusion.

This one was at least not pudgy, and reasonably solemn, with light-colored hair a little long, tie a little askew, bones prominent enough to stamp an affecting shape on a face that seemed otherwise innocent of much mileage. Presentable, but not inspiring. He said something graceful to her in French, and she realized that his asparagus was as good as hers, perhaps better. She was stuck. "Actually," she said, "I speak-ee Anglais. In fact, I'm a wretched American."

"So am I."

"Wretched?"

"American. Wretched only by appointment."

"And my name *isn't* Yvonne."

"Well, mine *is* Ken. Ken Coffin." Gravely, he shook her hand. "Is your real name a secret?"

"There are kidnappers after me," said Marcy.

"Me, too," he said. "I think they've got me."

"My father invented a nonfattening bomb."

"Mine invented rope. Or was it the living girdle?"

"My name is Marcy Rutherford. I grew up in Stifled Hopes, east Texas. Why am I here?"

"Dumb luck, for me. You're our guest for the evening."

"Who are *you*? I mean, all of you?"

"We are journalists under the age of thirty," he said. "Some of us are electronic; I'm not. Each year the media moguls have an international congress in some place like Reykjavík or Stifled Hopes. They spend the morning in seminars talking about censorship, transistors, postal rates, syndication, four-color offset, and stock options. They spend the afternoons and evenings drinking. This year they decided to have a junior congress at the same time. Ambitious young men from various newspapers, magazines, radio and television stations were invited to write essays on how the media can help the underdeveloped countries do some developing." He indicated the crowd. "We are the winning essayists. We're here on scholarships. We've been meeting in the morning to shout at one another. In the afternoons and evenings we go sightseeing. This is the big wind-up. The media moguls and their wives are up the road apiece having dinner in the Stables."

"The Stables of Chantilly? I didn't know you could have dinner there."

"Media moguls can do anything they want to. I'm told there's even an orchestra, and dancing. Our French hosts wanted us to have someone to dance with, besides the wives of media moguls. I guess that's why you're here. You must like dancing very much."

"I like five hundred francs very much. That's what they paid each of us, plus a free bus-ride. Which magazine or newspaper or television station do you work for?"

"I'm the ambitious young man from *Scope*, America's leading thought weekly."

"Thought weekly?"

"That's what we call ourselves. Although we do have strong feelings. Look, so far no one has noticed that there's another room over there, and maybe even a bar. Are you spoken for? Do you want to come along?"

She allowed herself to be spoken for. Went along. Found a bar. And a bartender who pretended not to understand their perfectly respectable asparagus. "Armed goon of the oppressor," said Ken Coffin, and liberated a bottle of cassis for them. "Now, tell me about your Stifled Hopes."

She did so: the escape from the ranch in Texas; the disappointments in Berkeley; the retreat to the Sorbonne; the English lessons nobody seemed willing to pay for because everybody already knew English; the money and the time that had run out. He listened. Perhaps because he was a journalist—she visualized a disembodied ear, confessions nibbling at its lobe—he listened well, in no hurry to interrupt with his own stories. She hadn't talked to an American in a long time, having deliberately avoided them from her arrival in Paris, determined to swim in the sea of the people. This was a warm bath; the anecdotes were rubber ducks to cuff at. She told him about the *pension*, and her first few weeks of reluctance at padding down the hall to the communal toilet—of trying to take a bath in a bidet. She told him about bursting into tears on first seeing Notre Dame from a Bateau-Mouche on the Seine, a consequence of jet lag and culture shock. She told him about the Italian railroad conductor at dawn in Milan who refused to direct her to a hotel unless she gave him a kiss, and then showed her snapshots of his eight children, all of whom looked like raccoons.

"You want to go home," he said.

"Maybe, if I could find it. The glamour is insupportable."

He mentioned Boston. She thought of Paul Revere and picture postcards, Irish politicians full of baked beans: she had never been there. Andy the Australian found them; the fact that she spoke English injured him, but not mortally.

"You're not my type," said Andy; "you have a brain." He had latched on to someone else: "Half-Russian, half-Italian, living in Paris, with a British passport, and all mine."

"Andy thinks with his glands," said Ken Coffin.

"No," said Andy; "with my credit cards."

"What do you think with?" Marcy asked Ken.

"With my magazine, weakly, or my electric typewriter, which sounds like a giant mosquito. What do *you* think with?"

"I don't think," she said, "I qualm."

"The nonfattening qualm," he said.

"My mind's on a diet," she said; "nothing but cassis." All right, it was cute enough to make your teeth ache, but it was also comfortable. They bribed the brass band to stop playing and went in to sit down for dinner.

A *vin* so *ordinaire* that there was nothing to do but guzzle it; a *veau* so suspect they hushed it up with sauce; a salad full of sauerkraut and beets. ("The French," she said, "invented sauce to disguise the taste of bad meat." "And they invented perfume," he said, "to disguise the smell of bad women.") When she argued fiercely with an Irish TV producer—*Ulysses* was still banned in Ireland; tube-boobie hadn't read it; but tube-boobie was sure

Molly shouldn't have said yes—Ken Coffin maintained an almost avuncular silence. When, however, a Dutch newspaperman admired her décolletage and she automatically simpered back at him, Ken Coffin assumed a possessive interest, and talked her head around again: a question about California, about Proust, about music, about horses. She was pleased. She told him about the wine available in cans from a machine at the Sorbonne, like soda pop; he told her about the little flat packages of wine, with plastic lids, he had seen at the University of Paris, like Jell-O. They agreed that if the Americans had invented canned or plastic wine, Simone de Beauvoir would have written a bad novel about it. He had blue eyes and good table manners; she discovered herself holding his hand when he lit her cigarette, a trick she had silently promised never to use again.

They were interrupted briefly when a Nigerian introduced as Reginald Okpaku pounced on them from behind. "Mr. Coffin, I wish to grateful you profusely for your saying this morning. A very needed saying." Okpaku shook a finger at their French hosts two tables away; then he shook a finger at the Irish TV producer. "You people propose to lecture *us* on democracy, on basic freedoms! Be pleased to exterminate the vermin of illiberalism in your own homes, before so doing." Whereupon Mr. Okpaku gave Mr. Coffin a two-handed overlapping thrice-repeated pumping of appreciation and excused himself.

Marcy whispered: "What was that all about?"

Ken Coffin whispered back: "The French were going on this morning about radio and TV stations in the new Africa. They declared that it was important that the peoples of Africa have independent sources of information. Independent, that is, of the government, which controls everything else. Your Irish friend, Mr. Anti-Joyce, agreed with the French. Stable republics depend on blah, blah, and more blah. I just said French television was state-owned, and besides being stupefyingly boring, it was also unfair to all the parties out of power. The Irish, well, there's the Church, and censorship and guns, so what? Rhetoric causes acne. But Mr. Anti-Joyce is probably beginning to think we have a conspiracy organized against him."

"Anti-Joyce," she said. "I like that. It sounds like something you put in a car to keep it from punning."

He stared at her. "Have you ever considered writing for

America's leading thought weekly? I know a dozen associate editors whose reputations were established on the basis of lines worse than that one."

"Women don't become editors," she said. "They only associate with them."

"Now you're trying too hard."

"The second sex has to."

"Rent-a-Girl."

"That's how I got here."

At least the coffee was excellent, being Italian. Andy appeared with a twitch of mission. "Kenny, it's the consensus of the bushmen that you must speak. Say something jolly about the frogs, what? The junior congress promises to polish their pointy little shoes, their pointy little ears and noses. Not since Joan of Arc. The oceans that divide us are full of the milk of human kindness. Et cetera."

"Why me? You seem to have prepared a speech already."

"You wrote the Number One Essay. Logical choice."

"Was there a competition, then?" asked Marcy.

"There was, Yvonne," said Andy. "I must say Kenny's essay was *very* serious. Fraught with much, it was, alarm, I think. And appendices."

"Andy, no. I'm no good at it."

"There's no arguing with a consensus," said Andy. "I have raised some cognac"—he produced it—"and you must raise our spirits." He beat upon a wineglass with a sugar spoon. The brass band, which had been hitting the cassis bottle, took it as a signal to break into "Dixie." The band was hissed into retirement. Andy pulled Ken to his feet; he was applauded; he blinked.

"I am the man," he said, "who did *not* bring Jacqueline Kennedy to France." After that, it was a list of names unknown to Marcy, references to embarrassments and ecstasies she had been spared, general tittering, a guffaw or two, and much noisy self-congratulation. The French were moved. They had tears in their eyes. More cognac appeared. Toasts were proposed to President Kennedy, to Charles de Gaulle, to *Scope* magazine, to the Renault Motor Company, to Shakespeare, Racine, Goethe, Leopold Senghor, Dr. Livingstone, Brigitte Bardot, the Enlightenment.

It was Marcy's weakness to approve of men who were approved

of by other men; it had been her experience that men approved of by other women were louses.

At eleven o'clock, Ken, Andy, and Reginald Okpaku were summoned into conference with the French. Ten minutes later, Ken returned. "You aren't going to believe this," he told her. Once again, Andy beat the wineglass. He couldn't get everyone's attention until he shattered it. "Ladies and gentlemen," Andy said, "it is time for us to go to the Stables where, fittingly, the senior congress awaits us. Our hosts have planned a smashing ceremony. At short notice, I admit. But let's see if we can pull it off. We are to go now to our buses and our Renaults. I'm sure not all the young ladies will wish to go by bus, nor will all the young gentlemen give themselves up to the Renaults. We will gather outside the Stables. There, each of us will be presented with tickets. Each ticket is worth a drink; six tickets buys a bottle of champagne. Each of you will also be presented with a torch. Wait a minute, please! Mr. Coffin, Mr. Okpaku, and I—representing three continents, don't you see?—will be escorted through a side entrance, up many, many stone steps, to a balcony we are assured exists. There will be a microphone on the balcony, as well as the furled flags of our respective countries. We will unfurl the flags, permitting them to stream down the stone walls. We will step to the microphone, to deliver the greetings of the junior congress to the senior congress. While we are in the process of doing so, at a signal from M. Lamartine, you will ignite your torches. As we conclude, the Stables will be thrown into darkness. You will march in, with your flaming torches. Our, ahem, band will play something suitable. The effect should be spectacular. Are you game?"

They were, although unbelieving, game. Marcy said, "Is this a dream?"

Ken said, "A Fellini movie."

Andy bustled over to them. "Irma, this is Yvonne." Irma? "Follow me," said Andy. They went through the kitchen, into a back alley, where a Renault was waiting. "I paid Phillipe a little extra to save himself for us," said Andy. "Where's Reginald?" Reginald crept teeth first out of the shadows. He got into the Renault next to the driver, who was apparently Phillipe. The other four piled into the rear. On the far side of the restaurant there seemed to be fireworks.

"What are they doing?" asked Marcy.

"Taking flash photographs," said Ken. "The Renaults are brand-new models. They've been loaned to the junior congress, free of charge. All we have to do is allow our pictures to be taken twenty times a day, climbing in and out of the new models, looking beatified, for publicity. Phillipe, shouldn't you turn on the headlights? Turn them *on*, Phillipe!"

"How are you?" Marcy asked Irma.

"I have an English passport," Irma replied.

The night, like an enormous umbrella, collapsed on them. Phillipe took the night as a personal insult.

The night didn't care so very much for Phillipe, either. It struck Marcy as unfair that she was going to die just when she had started to enjoy herself: Phillipe sought to disembowel the Renault. "Stop the car, Phillippe!" shouted Ken. "Reginald, make him stop." There was a struggle in the front seat. The car heaved a whale of a hiccough, and halted. "Get the keys, Reginald."

"He is under much influences," said Reginald.

"He's drunk," said Ken, and got out. With Reginald pulling and Ken pushing, they managed to move Phillipe over. Ken took the wheel. "How do we find the Stables? Can we smell them from here?"

Marcy looked behind her. There were lights on the road. "Why don't we wait for the others to pass, and follow them?"

Ken turned from the wheel. "Consider it done. Are you one of those people who always know how to cope?"

"With details, yes. The universals mess me up."

They waited, and soon were a section of shield in the serpent track of lights that rose writhing toward the Stables. The Stables were a universal, details blotted out: an idea of size, steeped in cognac. They stretched Phillipe out on the front seat. "The internal combustion engine," said Ken, "and the Latin temperament are incompatible."

"Is that a racist remark?" said Reginald.

"That is an observation," said Ken. "Empirical datum."

"All right, then," said Reginald.

They groped around in the dark, grunting at one another, until the company was reassembled. Without analyzing the compatibility of it, Marcy found herself holding onto Ken's hand. Tickets and torches were passed out. Marcy's torch seemed to her the shank of some shaggy animal.

"I've got to go with Andy and Reginald," he said. "You won't get lost?"

She shook her head. He couldn't see it. "I won't get lost," she said. He went. She wondered if there was a ladies room in the Stables. She asked Irma.

"I am half-Russian," said Irma, "half-Italian, with an English passport."

They had to wait twenty minutes before M. Lamartine manifested himself with what looked like an acetylene flame, to turn on their torches and still their muttering. They looked like a bunch of molten lollipops, coins struck by lightning. M. Lamartine divided them into two columns, single file, before separate entrances, doors the size of basketball courts. She could swear he was sharpening his teeth. The doors creaked open like crypts. She should have gone with Ken to the balcony; they could have coped together. Well, well: someone had neglected to turn off the lights inside. Yellow doors rolled over them. M. Lamartine was doubled over in a snit; his whiplike hisses lashed out at unseen flunkies. A figure detached itself from their file and was sucked up by the yellow door. Moments later, night came suddenly to the Stables of Chantilly.

They marched in: a taper parade of ambitious young journalists, Parisian models, French architecture students in Confederate Army uniforms. Aztecs, for sure. They were going to rip out her heart and feed it to the King's horse. And, God help us all, the band played the "Internationale."

The screaming began immediately. It was reinforced by echoes as long as tunnels, falling glass, overturned tables, the thud of collisions in blackness, oaths of remarkable vehemence. What a fun house! Marcy stepped on a hand: *I am feeling slightly idiotic; could someone bring me a brain pill?* She held her torch above her head, with two hands, as if intending to dive into the dark. *"Merde!"* said M. Lamartine. "I live in Paris," said Irma, who then joined the screaming with gusto: *"An-*dee! *An-*dee!" How did one put out a torch? Bulky shapes hurled themselves at her, two-hundred-pound bats. One, perhaps, used one's torch as a club. *Didn't they include an instruction booklet with this farce?* She tried to remember the words to the "Internationale," until she remembered that she had never known the words to the "Internationale." Someone attempted to tackle her. Irma moaned momentously. "Watch out!" Marcy shouted to the unseen. "She's got an English passport!" "*Écrasez l'infame!*" remarked M. Lamartine. No wonder the French lost wars. Why was everybody crying out about an asylum?

The lights went on. Squashing them, really, like so many bugs. Marcy was flabbergasted. What kind of horses had they stabled here? Those of the Apocalypse? A horse this big could hold a regiment of Marines. "Maniacs!" said a man in front of her. He was her father's age. He wore a dinner jacket that must have been sewn together out of dead starfish and then laminated. His face was in the process of flushing itself; his indignation gurgled. He brandished a wine bottle, gripped at its neck. It was not empty; it was therefore doing terrible things to his sleeve and lapel. "There has been a misunderstanding!" observed M. Lamartine. "This is not the asylum! This is the junior congress!" A bed of lam, though. Those tables that had not been overturned during the invasion were covered with the bodies of sloshed media moguls, their dickies foaming. Middle-aged women in floor-length ballroom gowns hugged one another in twittering triplicate, their heads making tumbleweeds of blue rinse that bobbed on the sea of bodies, above which marble columns soared. Marcy tried to find the balcony—Ken, Andy, Reginald—and could not. You could have dropped a bomb from the ceiling. The floor looked as though someone had already done so. To her right, on a raised dais, an orchestra hid behind its instruments. Marcy slapped the laminated dinner jacket that was calling her a maniac, wrested the wine bottle from its flabby grip, and used what remained of the contents to douse her torch. To M. Lamartine, she said with sweet reasonableness: "Can you tell me the meaning of this? Shut up, Irma!"

"*C'est fiasco!*" explained M. Lamartine.

"Without a doubt. But why?"

He bowed to her. "The microphone did not work. They did not hear the greetings. They were surprised when the lights went out. We presented ourselves with the fire, and they naturally assumed that we had escaped from the asylum. There is a nearby asylum for the unfortunate deranged. A misunderstanding. It is nothing. I shall lose my job. I know the pain. Heartburns."

"Is there any way you can stop our band from playing the 'Internationale'?" The architecture students were storming the dais; the orchestra rose as one to repel them; a rumble seemed in the offing, bows against bugles. M. Lamartine emitted a whistle that must have punctured eardrums in the 23rd arrondisement.

Marcy noticed that the junior congress was sensibly extinguishing its torches in ice buckets. She turned to the laminated dinner jacket. "Do you know where I might find a ladies room?"

"I am an American citizen," he said. "This is an outrage."

"Splendid," she said. "You can hold Irma for me." She decided to stick to the walls and circle the building, seeking recesses. She walked the length of the Berkeley campus before bumping into Ken and Andy.

"The microphone didn't work," said Ken.

"Neither did anything else," said Marcy.

"There was a riot."

"Naturally. They thought we'd escaped from the local funny farm."

"Do you know," he said, "I feel like I've been tickled to death."

At last, she could laugh. She fell on him, giggling into his summer suit. She thought of mustard, pine needles, roller skates, Freud. She began to tickle him. He grabbed her by her ears and kissed her forehead. Finally, she said, "I need to go to the bathroom."

"You didn't say 'May I?' "

"I need to go to the bar," said Andy. "Give me your tickets."

Ken pointed: "There's a bathroom just down there. But I think it's co-educational."

"I don't care if it's a fire hydrant," said Marcy.

It was more like a Roman fountain, leaking from all orifices. She found an empty stall, and resolved to stop giggling. But it started over again a moment later, when in front of a mirror she tried to comb her hair with her fingers, while on each side of her men were solemnly relieving themselves, staring so hard at the ceiling that they bent their spines and peed on their shoes.

He was waiting for her when she returned. "The worst possible news," he said.

"We have to do it all over again, with candles," she said.

"No. They've run out of liquor."

She took his hand with total confidence, and looked around. "Couldn't we drain the bodies of these media moguls? Stick a tap in them or something? Drink their blood?"

"They haven't any blood. They consist of nothing but computer

tape. We have a plan. Follow me. I want us to find a place."
They staked out a deserted table, motioning to Andy. "All right,"
said Ken, "you'll be the bank. We need to collect about a hundred
fifty tickets, for a couple of cases of champagne. M. Lamartine
has promised to fetch it for us. He's mortified."

And so for a quarter of an hour she sat, while Ken, Andy, Mr.
Anti-Joyce, and two unknown others went table-hopping among
the bleary moguls, cajoling, coercing, stealing fistfuls of liquor
tickets, returning to her like retrievers with geese, while she kept a
running total. Mid-rounds, Andy brought back Irma instead
of tickets: "Watch her, love, would you? If she falls over, she'll
lose her passport." And Marcy was a traitor: she liked Andy. His
bonhomie was contagious; his pudge, forgivable.

Irma sagged: "I'm feeling Rotterdam."

Marcy shrugged: "Bombed, maybe?"

"Helsinki," agreed Irma.

When she had counted up to two hundred tickets, Marcy pro-
claimed it, and they brought M. Lamartine to her on a stretcher
of his own mortification. He scooped up the tickets in a hat and
departed.

"The orchestra threatens to quit," said Andy. "They were only
paid to play until midnight."

"The architecture students have disbanded?"

"*Mais, oui.*"

"Then promise the orchestra some champagne," said Ken.

"Right-o," said Andy. "Irma, are you awake?"

"I am not awake, Budapest," said Irma. "Venice we going
home?"

They danced until the champagne came. Slow boxes on the
great floor, a shuffle of the languidly wounded. He was an indifferent, although conscientious, dancer. That also pleased her,
being manly, a Stoic sidle. They were beyond chatter. She had
been washed up on an atoll of weariness where not thinking
was surpassingly pleasant. An amusing and effortless sloth, slow
motions and slow emotions, the time a kind of rain that washed
away numerals, Dali-high, slipping away from tick-tock to toccata,
I improvise myself. Champagne seemed lemonade. At one point
they had their heads on the table, facing each other on opposing
ears, in a contest to see who would crack the first smile. He won.
Your nose is off-center. That's because you can't see straight. Do

you brook crookedness? My rook was took by a queen. Knight falls. Comes the pawn.

And she was amazed to learn that just a dozen people were left in the Stables. The orchestra had laid itself away in a drawer, tails dragging. They sat at the bottom of a vast vault, the floor of an unplugged ocean. Outside, a startling and excessively Fragonard-ized dawn was seeping. They were miniature. Reginald had van-ished into the mists of illiberalism. Irma was comatose. Andy roused Phillipe from a slumber under the steering wheel of the Renault with wads of francs, applied like a poultice to the nose. "Can we trust him?" Marcy asked.

"Well," said Ken, "we can't trust me."

She slept to Paris on his shoulder.

She woke up when the car stopped, somewhere near the chapel of St. Sulpice. "Thank God there're no photographers," she said. "I'm not feeling beatific." Andy and Irma were disembarking. "We've got more champagne in our rooms," said Andy. "They gave each of us a magnum when we arrived. And cartons of Gaul-lois. Of course, the champagne is warm." He didn't want company *and* Irma. Marcy looked at Ken; his face was gray, a rained-upon newspaper. She couldn't read him at all. What did he expect from her? A double-decker in Andy's room? Parisian models, you know, they lay like hens. Whatever happened to the idea of a *date*?

"I don't think so, Andy," Ken said. To Marcy: "Where do you live?" She told him and he told Phillipe. Alertness was an alp she couldn't quite climb; someone had greased her spurs. He should say *something*. Ultimately, he did. "This will probably sound ridiculous, but I'm hungry. What about going to Les Halles for breakfast?" When she didn't reply—as a matter of fact, she couldn't think of anything to say—he apologized for himself. "That's not what I meant. See if this makes sense: I feel that ten or twenty years from now, *this* is what I'm supposed to remem-ber. To be lugubrious about. Only I'm still enjoying myself, and I resent the fact that it's going to stop. I mean, this is my *future*. There should be more of it, before there's nothing else to do but remember it. Flabby-minded, right? Let's get you home."

"Let's go to Les Halles," she said. She could read his face now. He was angry. At her? At his future? She took his elbow, and his elbow did not relax. Another thing she had promised not to do again was to reassure a man; it was a promise she was willing to break, but just now she didn't know how. Her brain cells and her blood cells seemed to be snoring. Don't be angry.

Phillipe left them at Les Halles, declining Ken's invitation to breakfast. There, among farmers and truck drivers and fiddlers of produce, squeezers of tomatoes, and chewers of beans, they had white wine and onion soup. A trio of middle-aged Frenchmen nearby made mean jokes about the Americans. Ken rose; there were threats exchanged; he was looking for a place to deposit his anger, and he actually succeeded in silencing them. Flabby-minded, he said again on rejoining her; he made fists. She decided not to be alert: the onion soup was a full day's meal, and how much approval, anyway, did one guy need? F. Scott Fitzgerald, he argued. Henry James, he admitted. The Talmud, she wanted to reply, and did not. Meaningless elaborations on a very simple situation. She could handle it.

Unfair, then, that he should have found a taxi so quickly. That they should have arrived at Yvonne's iron door before she had organized a perception, made a decision. That he should have asked the driver to wait, while he walked her to that door, while he seemed about to kiss her again on the forehead and shook her hand instead, while he plodded away into a slam of black limousine and slouched off. She was inside and he was gone and she had wanted to do something—play the piano for him, maybe—and she was annoyed. The pass she'd been dreading had not been thrown, and her annoyance meant she hadn't been dreading it, and what was there for her vanity to do in Yvonne's apartment, her charity hostel, but fall into a gift bed, bite at sleep, want to go home, not have one? *Merde.*

Maybe he was a homosexual.

She rose in time to catch the last train to Blois, where one of Jean-Luc's sons was waiting to take her to Montrechard. In a Renault, of course. And looking at her legs, of course. A fifteen-year-old who would grab a buttock ten times before it occurred to him once to shake a hand. A predator in the making, who wanted to make her because someone, his father probably, had told him that's what you did to anyone vaguely resembling a Marcy. French boys had motor scooters in their underwear. What a perfect afternoon she had picked to feel miserable and un-wanted: a sun that chose to shine, a river without craft, châteaux somnambulating, trees like spindles twisting threads of breeze, sleeves of cloud, an insulting blueness, scoured shame. *I would have liked to be a birthday cake.* Instead, as always, until her money ran out, which it was about to, she went down into the valley of the Loire to ride a horse.

Jean-Luc and Yvonne were waiting for her, along with what seemed like half the countryside. No wonder Jean-Luc's sons had the itch: Look what their father brought home while their mother was stashed away in a Swiss sanitarium, trying to get the pretzel of her brain straightened out—a beautiful Yvonne. And Yvonne *was* beautiful, specializing in long legs and bare-backed sunsuits, jet-black hair always ever-so-slightly mussed, huge eyes always ever-so-slightly clouded. Marcy supposed that Jean-Luc could be considered beautiful, too: the kind of head designed for the covers of magazines and the sides of coins; the kind of body that would be doing calisthenics on the day it died; the John Kennedy of France, if only someone would poison De Gaulle.

"Your friend is here," said Yvonne. She was amused.

"What friend? Who?"

"The young man from Boston. Marcy, dear, how did you do it? Go into the Stables of Chantilly one night, and come out the next morning with a love-sick American journalist?"

Dammit, of course she had to blush.

"Then," said Jean-Luc, looking at the blush, "this Mr. Coffin is not just a pest?"

"No. Not yet, at least." It was absurd: she wanted to put her head in a sack. "But how did he get here? I mean—"

"My dear," said Yvonne, "you apparently told him last night that you were going to the dedication of a lake in the Loire Valley. Not much to go on, is it? But American know-how, la, la! Since ten o'clock this morning, the entire Paris bureau of *Scope* magazine has been waking up people in their beds and asking, Who dedicates a lake?"

"And, of course," said Jean-Luc, "I dedicate the lake. It's *my* lake. Half of Paris knows. Perhaps that is an exaggeration. But it does seem that I have invited half of Paris to the dedication. They telephone me to, what, double-check the story? It is true. They do not know what to do, then. But on learning the details, *my* Marcy, *I* know what to do. I telephone Mr. Coffin personally, and invite him to come, too."

"But why?"

"For you, Marcy. And, naturally, for *Scope* magazine. They have been very sympathetic to me. Perhaps they will be even more sympathetic."

"Now that *le grand Charles* is anti-American, Jean-Luc must be pro-American," said Yvonne.

"Naturally," said Jean-Luc. "And your young man jumps immediately into a rented car and arrives. Early. And does not know what to do with himself. And so goes to advise the Algerians on how to roast the lamb. They have been roasting lamb on spits for thousands of years. But he goes to advise them, and is there now."

They both looked at her with broad grins. What was so damned funny about it? It was her life they were grinning at.

She walked around the side of the house. Jean-Luc's brother had inherited the family château. So Jean-Luc had built his own castle, modern, naturally, with a sloping roof, heavy beams, much glass. And a lawn fell from it through ancient trees to the lake Jean-Luc had ordained with bulldozers and dam equipment. He had probably selected each thistle on each tiny island personally, from a catalog. The only thing old about the place, aside from the trees, was a barn, which Jean-Luc had converted into a studio where he made massive objects out of clay. She considered hiding in the barn. But no. She crossed the lawn and walked down to where the Algerians were roasting the sides of lamb.

Indeed, he was there, very serious in a turtleneck sweater, and stood up.

"Well, hello," she said. A snappy one-liner.

He had the grace to blush, too. And gestured at the sides of lamb. "I've never seen it done this way before. Two beds of coals. Different temperatures. They keep moving the spits from one bed of coals to the other. I guess so that the sides of lamb won't get too charred or overcooked."

Come *on*. Was that all he had to say? After having loosed the entire resources of a big American magazine on the nation of France to track her down, after having found out where she was going, after having driven over a hundred miles to get there before she did, was he now at such a loss? Naked, without his magazine? Well, what could he say? I just happened to be driving by on my way to the Pyrenees, and stopped in for a lambchop? At least she was wanted.

"Would you like some wine?" she said.

"Yes, I would," he said.

Apparently, it was up to her. As they walked back toward the house, she said: "I thought you were flying to London with the rest of them."

"I canceled out."

"Couldn't you just have asked a girl for a date, like a normal person?"

"I haven't been feeling very normal lately."

That was funny. She had never felt more normal in her life. She took his hand. And that was more or less that.

There was white wine on ice, and red wine from a keg. It didn't make any difference. There was the black outside of the lamb, and the pink inside of the lamb. It was of no significance. There were the political and business friends of Jean-Luc, and there were the townspeople invited to the fête. They were not in a talking mood. The barn-studio had been rearranged, with haystacks turned into rows of benches, to accommodate the company for a recitation of several De Maupassant short stories by an actor from Paris who took all the parts himself; the style was so high they couldn't understand a sentence, and the night chill drove even Yvonne to an overcoat and the wine keg. Irrelevant. When everyone gathered at the lakefront to watch the charges of fireworks Jean-Luc had planted on the islands explode in perfect synchronization, a cold black sky full of giant spiders of color, it seemed part and parcel of a private showing, arranged for two people, including torches and champagne and onion soup. And afterward, when everybody went into the house for coffee and folk singing, there wasn't any particular need to sing.

"You'll spend the night here?" he said.

"Yes. Jean-Luc booked you a hotel room in Montrechard?"

"Yes. Tomorrow is your riding day?"

"Yes. You do want to see the château?"

"Yes. Can Yvonne or Jean-Luc drop you off at my hotel in the morning? We could drive there together."

"All right."

And, after a thousand thanks to Jean-Luc, he left at midnight. Yvonne was amazed. "Marcy, dear, I don't *believe* it. You're adults, after all. It doesn't make any sense."

"He didn't have any sleep at all last night," said Marcy. "And—

dammit, Yvonne, I'm being treated like a lady, whether I like it or not! And I happen to like it."

Sunday morning she found him in the garden of his hotel, overlooking the river, drinking coffee at a small iron table and scribbling on postcards. There seemed now to be no diffidence in either of them. And it seemed preposterous that this was the first time they had even kissed. He had already paid his bill. He put her bag and his into the rented car—a Citroën after much Renault, she noticed—and let her assume the driving. It was important that he like the château; it was the only part of France she still cared for deeply.

It was a *château de plaisance* that had been in the same family since the fifteenth century, and it was badly in need of repair. The present owner had been a hero in the Resistance. The library contained medals, and notes from Colonel Berger, as well as letters to his ancestors from people like Victor Hugo. Hélas. The owner was reluctant to sell the paintings to pay for the upkeep, and equally reluctant to close up shop after five centuries. And so there were three principal industries associated with the château: tourism (the library, the paintings, the furniture, the view); the stables, housing horses that were rented by young ladies like Marcy, along with their rooms in the east wing (a private riding academy); and the kennels, containing basset hounds (which were bred, raised, and sold there). "Do you remember the advertisements for Hush-Puppies?" Marcy asked him. "The picture of the basset hound? He was one of ours. That was the beginning of the kennels." She watched his face closely; others had decided the situation was comical, a great château reduced to raising puppies, renting horses, and enduring the indifferent hand on relics much revered. She didn't need another explanation of how absurd the economics of it were. But he did not appear to find anything comical about it; if anything, his reaction was gloom-riddled.

They admired the basset hounds, who had made a profession of looking gloomy. When they reached the stables, she was nervous. "It's not exactly Chantilly," she said. Their cross-references were so few, she could think of nothing else to engage him. He was, however, preoccupied, as he had been in the library, inspecting every nail and nostril. Albertine was her horse.

"You want to ride," he said. It wasn't a question. "Go on. I'll wait."

He helped her saddle and cinch.

"You won't get lost?" she said, smiling, hoping he would remember.

"I won't get lost," he said, not smiling. "And I don't expect there'll be a riot to contend with, either."

She was off. And she was remembering, too: what he had said on the way to Les Halles. This is my *future*, the mourning of it. She was certain she would not be riding here again. It was important to know that. It was obligatory to cry. And she did cry, feeling slightly phony, but genuine tears were available. She galloped to her crying, promising to remember, persuaded, prepared, already nostalgic, pretending against each bounce that every "maybe" had its *not*, a big girl.

He hadn't gotten lost. He helped her to rub down Albertine. They walked arm in arm back to the Citroën. "I want to tell you something," he said. "My family has land in New Hampshire. Not *this* much, but a thousand acres. I have a cottage there. And there's a big house on a hill. Not *this* big, but a Yankee idea of a château. An imitation of this, or of an English manor house. There are horses, and apple orchards, and a pond. Not a lake, but a pond people swim in, or skate on in the winter. It may be an imitation, but it matters to my family. Their people got there in the eighteenth century, not the fifteenth, and they started with a forty-acre farm, and while they aren't farmers any more, it still *is* a working farm. It won't last. It'll be turned into tract houses or parking lots or shopping plazas or industrial parks." He was angry again. "But for a while . . . I suppose the apples are our basset hounds. But during the summer we go horseback-riding. And during the winter there *is* a sleigh. It's serious, even though it's miniature. Do you understand what I'm saying?"

She understood what she wanted to understand. An offer was being made, a substitution proposed. She nodded. This time, when she took his elbow, he did relax.

They returned to the road. "To Paris?" he said. "To Paris," she agreed.

They stopped near Pithiviers for lunch at a small inn she had visited before, a place where people loved to eat. The wine, the bread, the mushrooms in butter sauce, were superb. She recalled, from last time, the strawberries, and extolled them. He inquired. Alas, the last of the fresh strawberries had gone for jam for tomorrow morning's toast. But the jam was not yet jammed. Should they be willing to *drink* strawberry essence before the final jamming, they would certainly know what the strawberries *had* been like. They were willing. They did drink.

"There's something I should have mentioned," he said, "knowing the state of your finances. There is, you know, a job in our Paris bureau, if you want it."

She was appalled. "I *don't* want it. I don't want a job in Paris. Or in Blois. Or in *Minsk* or *Hong Kong* or *Reykjavík!*"

He brooded over his essence of strawberry. "Then there's something else I should have mentioned." His face was lopsided. "I probably should have mentioned it over and over again. I've thought about it enough for the last two days."

"You're not exactly opaque," she said. "I doubt that I am, either."

He rose from the table and booked a room at the inn. There was much fumbling and some silliness: it always seems silly to stupid people with poor memories: it is never silly. They had strawberry jam for breakfast. They did not get back to Paris until Thursday. They museum-hopped. They said good-by to Notre Dame. They flew the following week to Boston. They were married six months later at Thomas Hill, in a Unitarian service that omitted "obey" from the promises, among people who might as well have been portraits, the way dust collected on them during this propulsion. They honored one another.

That was more than six years ago. Since then, Yvonne had committed suicide. Jean-Luc was in trouble because he had neglected to pay taxes for a decade. Andy had gone to work for the largest advertising agency in Melbourne. The château had become a real-estate development. Marcy had a job in Boston, and two children, one of whom was crying, as he tried the knob of his bedroom door. As Marcy was crying, all doors open.

"Stephen, what's the matter, honey? Did you have a bad dream?"

Stephen nodded. No wonder, she thought: guns, worms, elephants, camels, Arabs, bears . . .

Then he shook his head. "You *said* I could type on your typewriter when I came home from school. But I didn't."

"Well. Well, we both *forgot*. The typewriter isn't going to go away. It will be there tomorrow morning."

His hair stood up in horns; his face was blotched. "You *said*—"

"Sit with me awhile." They wrapped themselves up in a quilt on the couch.

"Can I watch TV?" Stephen asked.

"All right." She switched it on. A movie. Fortunately, it was not *An American in Paris*. Perhaps she should go up and get Hannah, too. No. Hannah slept in innocent fat, dreaming of thumbtacks and electrical plugs. And Marcy seldom saw Stephen alone, between her work and his. She tried to remember whether Pithiviers was the last time they had made love in the daylight. No: once in the snow at Wyke Regis, without getting out of their clothes; and once at the pond, helping each other out of bathing suits. She would drive to Wyke Regis in the morning; they had some catching up to do.

She held onto Stephen so tightly that he began to squirm. He hadn't ever liked excessive cuddling. And why was she clutching him like a life raft, anyway? They sat, and watched, and fell asleep, and if the tears on their cheeks weren't jewels, it was the fault of jewels. And they woke up to find the pattern staring back at them.

Nine

I CAN REMEMBER THE FIRST TIME. I was seventeen years old. The truck returning from Mexico stopped just after dawn for gas. Disembarking: young faces drawn, bodies unclenching from fists of sit-up sleep, jackets buttoned at the throat, boots, guitars. Flat and khaki as far as the eye could swing, and falling, it seemed, on knives of sky at every fanned extension. Bearing three thermoses to the diner. Behind me, the truck hood opening with an electric crack, smothered by all that space. Iron latch cold in my hand; white counter a trough of moons; waitress with her back to me, propped on elbows at the window, staring out. Asking for coffee and receiving a face as broad, bored, flat, and khaki as the land. Standing at her window while she filled the thermoses, trying to see what she saw: the Quaker project workers, summer servicemen who had paid for their right to serve, builders of lavatories and teachers of English, dysenterians homeward bound. I owed some explanation, was unable to decide which one. Watching her pour steam and stopper it, light-laundered, hair wisps on fire from window-washing. Witless witness, stiff in silence. Retreating . . . my element, like Hawthorne's, passivity.

I have been volunteering ever since. You name it, and I will have offered myself. I come cheap.

We climb out of the valley. There's a picket fence of pines behind a wall of stone, and little arrows directing the ill and injured to relief. At the end of a long gravel drive is a clump of plants, brown now, but they had been blooming the last time. Maybe the hospital's mistakes are used for fertilizer. The doctors have marked parking places. An ambulance sits slick in the drizzle. Do they snowmobile in the winter? Green bullyboys, with face masks and hypodermic needles, hide behind the shrubbery. There is a revolving door. A revolving door for a *hospital*. The churches will be the next American institution to discover how bad revolving doors make people feel, and take advantage of it.

"I'm afraid Dr. Folger isn't in the hospital," says the receptionist. She isn't afraid; she's pleased. "Friday is not one of his hospital days. I *am* sorry." She isn't sorry; she's triumphant.

"I know we missed the appointment," says the volunteer. "But I thought Dr. Folger might be able to see this man anyway. He had no transportation down from the farm this morning. And the arm looks nasty."

"An appointment was made?"

Would I lie to you? "Yes. For ten o'clock this morning. The name was Hudson. Lonzo Hudson."

"I'm sorry. I can't seem to find a card for a Lonzo Hudson. But you see, Friday isn't one of Dr. Folger's hospital days. He doesn't come into the hospital on Wednesdays and Fridays. He shouldn't have scheduled an appointment here."

Naughty Dr. Folger. "Where does he schedule appointments on Wednesdays and Fridays?"

"At his office in town. It is possible that he might have made a ten o'clock appointment for his office in town. But he wouldn't have made one for here at the hospital."

"I wonder, then, if you could call his office in town for us. After all, a badly burned arm . . ."

He is about to lose this skirmish: because he is unknown to the receptionist, and his fatigue jacket is not confidence-inspiring, and Lonzo and Peace look like people who get nailed to blue crosses instead of paid for by them, and perhaps the smell of funk is on him. My kind of funk, not Lonzo's. The receptionist is looking at the pay phone on the wall behind him; she will suggest that he call Dr. Folger himself; she hasn't a clue how much face he would lose if he did so. His face is saved by Dr. Kirkland.

166

"Ken Coffin! Good to see you! How's Marcy? How's Stephen?"
They are fine. Equally fine is wee Hannah, who came into the
world later on, without Dr. Kirkland's help.

"Glad to hear it. What brings you up here? Not another one?"
Dr. Kirkland does not mock; they hadn't taught him how to at
medical school. Maybe he doesn't even remember, such scenes
having happened so often, panic, death threats, the mind itself
a sewer. We were ordinary.

"There's been a mix-up," says Ken. "This man has a badly
burned arm. We thought he had a ten o'clock appointment with
Dr. Folger. He couldn't get here."

"But Friday is not Dr. Folger's hospital day," says the receptionist.

"The appointment was probably for his office in town," says
Kirkland. "Mrs. LeClerc, would you call Dr. Folger's office and
check on it?"

She does; Kirkland waits; Dr. Folger is in stitches for the rest
of the day.

"Let me see that arm," says Kirkland. Lonzo doesn't love the
idea, but complies. "All right," says Kirkland, "let's get something
on it. Come along." Lonzo wants to speak. However, he has faces
to save, too. He goes quietly.

Mrs. LeClerc is obliged to forgive Ken his fatigue jacket. "Has
the other boy been burned, too?"

"No. He's hurt his back. Mackenzie Farm will pay for treatment."

"Shall I try to arrange an appointment with Dr. Folger on that?
He will be in the hospital tomorrow morning. Saturday mornings
are one of his days."

"I'd appreciate that." She dials with the silver ball on the end
of her pen. The pen is strung from her neck on a chain. Peace is
deciding whether to shrug, and seems to have forgotten how.
"We'll sit down," Ken says, "and wait for Lonzo."

The place to wait is the waiting room, full of joke books, travel
books, and bad novels. He inspects the titles. They are probably
the same titles on the same shelves as four years ago, but how
would he know? After the twice-weekly Lamazing (Cambridge
couples, their wicks of individuality cased in ice, their anxieties so
many boxes of popcorn); the calisthenics and breathing exercises
on the living room rug ("Ken, are you sure I'm not *bending* the

baby?"); after every assurance had been assured ("It'll just pop out, like bread from an electric toaster") and alternative names agreed on (Stephen, Hannah)—the gestation was into pain, the thumbs inside were hooks, the fist was death. "If this is nature," said Marcy on the way to the hospital, "give me artifice." When they wheeled her into the delivery room, she started to scream. He was handcuffed to her, saying what all the piggy little books had told him to say. Dr. Kirkland conferred with the anesthesiologist. The anesthesiologist and Dr. Kirkland recommended a caudal injection. Ken told Marcy. But that would waste all those weeks, she said, it would be a humiliation. He said that a caudal was only local numbness, she would still be conscious. But her eyes had gone away; they saw bloody ceilings, basins of bone. She said— each word had teeth marks on it—you promised to protect me; I thought you would protect me. I hate you. Leave me *alone*, you son of a bitch! What do *you* know about it? Get *out!* They, he, Lamaze, the hospital, the baby, were conspiring to kill his wife. Two nurses forced him out of the delivery room. Into the waiting room. He could still hear her screams. Dr. Kirkland appeared to explain the injection . . . the baby's head . . . below the pelvis . . . sacral portion of the spinal column. This time, you bastards, you save the mother, do you hear me? Save the mother! Save my wife! Dr. Kirkland told him it was hardly more than routine. *Death isn't routine.* I don't give a shit about the baby: save my wife! John Mackenzie came, to observe his fury and impotence. You have a nine-pound baby boy. I want my wife! She's doing fine; she's only a little tired. Nicholas Coffin would not arrive from Boston until the following day. Marcy had left instructions not to notify her family of anything.

"I was born in this hospital," he tells Peace. And my mother died the same day. "So was my son." And something else might have died. The forceps marks disappeared from Stephen's head in five months. But not from mine. And not from Marcy's. Peace isn't interested. "Cigarette?" Peace refuses, paddling himself to some black moon. Ken will continue to offer cigarettes; Peace might as well accept one now. The longer he refuses, the larger the ultimate defeat. Peace accepts on the second offer. Ken resents it. You should have held out longer. Where's your pride?

"Mr. Coffin?" It is Mrs. LeClerc. "Dr. Folger can see your *friend* tomorrow morning at eleven. Is that all right?"

"That's splendid. Thank you."

She hangs for a moment by her hands from the pen chain. "Uh, what name do I give the doctor's secretary?"

"Peace. Leroy Peace. Spelled . . . the opposite of war. *Peace* time." Peace isn't even interested in the sound of his own name; it might be any name; it's never done him any good, anyway. Lonzo returns, with a very white bandage on his arm, a surgical burn.

"What did he say?"

"Put some stuff on the mother," says Lonzo. "Said I can take it off two days later. Then doan scratch. If it hurts bad, come back right now. Anyways, I s'posed to be 'roun' Wednesday."

Wednesdays and Fridays are apparently Dr. Kirkland's hospital appointments. Ken doesn't like hospitals. Not this one, not even Mass General, where they took Lavonia after she swallowed the pills, and after she called everybody in the Greater Boston Area to remind them that she'd swallowed the pills. Boyfriend trouble! "It's an attention-getting device," said the doctor at Mass General. Who on earth would want more attention from reality than we already get? Our little draft-dodger, Marcy had called Stephen. Hospitals are like motel swimming pools, only they add ether instead of chlorine, and the sharks are syringes. Lavonia felt rejected: what could he possibly do with a teen-aged girl who thought she wanted to go to bed with her teacher? Who unbuttoned herself instead of, like Marcy, waiting for him to unbutton her? What would Rajah Born have said? He did what he could possibly do, which was to refrain, a refraining that was a disemboweling. My father used to say, said Marcy, that a man ain't a man 'til he's split his first black rail. Black tail? Nicholas Coffin would not have said that, would not even have understood it. I have always wanted to be married, to have a wife and children, a sustaining circle: otherwise, none of it makes any sense. Stabs in the dark. He doesn't know about the baby, but he is certainly about to bend the steering wheel.

Neither Peace nor Lonzo speaks on the way back to camp. He has the feeling that his memories are live electrical wires, loose and crackling all over his scalp, creating a danger zone around him, a cone of static. After Stephen's difficult birth, Marcy began to resent Wyke Regis. He knows why. Unlike France, it was not a place you could leave, not if your husband was forever trying to prove himself worthy of the Mackenzies, a stand-in for his mother; not if your son was offered up to Thomas Hill in witness of good faith; not if your only child was also Wallace Mackenzie's first great-grandchild; not if the whole family perceived children as extensions of its self-esteem, excuses for sprucing up the feudal playpen, evidence of stamina and fortitude. Ken and Marcy had a healing to attend to. They were not allowed the necessary privacy to accomplish it. Their time went like coins into a Mackenzie machine which dispensed projects: their summers were committed, their holidays organized, their evenings oversubscribed, their hours and minutes allotted to croquet, bridge, tennis, tea, hiking, bottling the champagne cider, going to weddings, picking spinach, carrots, blueberries, and fights.

He thinks she arranged for Hannah to take some of the pressure off Stephen.

He explained: I gave you a family, to replace the one you hated. (Too much family, too many tartans, a glittering arc of silver spoons, peanut bowls, and gin bottles from the farm to Mount Monadnock, a valley of green talk.) I gave you a horse, to canter to your heart's content. (She sold it the summer after Stephen, saying she hadn't the time any more to care for it properly; perhaps, when Stephen was old enough, they could buy another.) I gave you the rest of my life, and you insult me by saying that it's not enough. (He was a bargain, wasn't he? Constant, devoted, with credit cards. He watched her thoughts escape him, whispers he couldn't hear, although his whole body was an ear.) He did not explain that the Mackenzies also gave her the section she taught at Harvard, with their letters and phone calls to friends. She deserved it, of course; they were loyal, but you had to be competent.

Roots, to get a grip on the earth, not to strangle it.

"Tell everybody I'll bring the truck around and take them down to the orchard, would you?" Lonzo and Peace get out.

He parks the station wagon. The only sound is far away, Dennison spraying, a banshee wail that had startled Marcy from bed many a summer morning at seven o'clock, right outside the cottage window.

The gear box of the truck is slush; he struggles with it.

Foy is first out of the cabin, explosive, flapping, jumping into the cab next to Ken. Porter, James T. Worthy, Root-man, Wornum, Fisher, Talley, and even Butterfly follow. "Butterfly, are you sure you want to go out there?"

"You bet, Rollin. Gotta buy me a Cadillac for them New Haven girls." The usual derision greets this. Butterfly has trouble climbing on the truck; no one helps him.

"Both crews!" shouts Ken, honking. "I'll take you all down." More emerged, a larger-than-usual number for Friday. Saturday's checks are computed only on work done through Thursday. Albany Jackson, Otis DeKalb, and Richmond bring up the rear: his experiment. Six men, of course, missing.

In the cab, Foy says, "Hey, Rollin . . . I was wonderin'." The pride of Foy is such that he will not look at you when asking for a favor. "When I get that check tomorra, if I was to bring it to you, you'd keep it for me?"

"Sure. You know, Mrs. Murdock keeps some checks. For Jackson and Fisher, I think."

"She-it, Rollin, I ain't gonna give my check to Mrs. Mud-duck. That woman, she allus make the mistakes on *her* side. I had me four bins punched up. She call it forty-five bushel. I showed my card, and she say she sorry, she musta been confused. Yeah, she been confused. But she doan be confused on my *side*. She doan call four bins sevenny-five bushel, do she now? No, man. You keep the check."

"How much more you figure you need, Foy?"

"I figger I take me back three hunnerd dollar, Rollin, and make me two hunnerd more spot-pickin' them mother-grapefruits, I got me one term startin' Feb-uary. Summer come, they's good tractor-drivin' jobs down home. I can make me one 'nother term."

"Hope it works. Have you got a high school diploma?"

"Yeah." He giggles. "You know how they does *that*, Rollin. You make trouble, and they switches you 'roun' from one school to t'nother, 'til they runs outa schools. Then they gives you the dee-ploma to be rid of you. I got me that sorta dee-ploma."

"What do you want to study?"

"'Lectrical engineerin'." And Foy retires inside himself, his thoughts in his pockets, where he can twist their heads off.

The rain has flushed the sky until it's squeaky clean. It is possible to believe that we are going to finish off the Macs in the West Orchard by sundown. Everything seems set for purposeful attack: the ladders at their angles in the trees, falling away from the eye,

ribwork on the vertebral row line . . . the yellow bins, their emptiness an incitement . . . the buckets hanging by their straps from
low limbs, cold to the touch.

Foy stoops to pluck up a small black branch and goes running
down the row, shaking it in faces, crying: "Snake! Snake!" The
checkers sit in their car with the heater running: plaid coats, deer-
slayer caps, pale green boots with yellow rubber soles, heart pills.
On the other side of the irrigation ditch, Short is standing,
pretending to be in charge of everything, hoping nobody will sass
him. Ken turns the truck around to head back to the cottage.

Rinsler is on the telephone. Ken has nothing to say to Rinsler;
nor does he want to hear what Rinsler has to say to anyone else.
He closes the kitchen door, sets water to boil, measures the coffee.
Later, milk, sugar, and gallon can secure, he returns to the truck,
and the truck returns to the orchard.

Smitty, the checker, is waiting. "You'll have to talk to Butterfly,"
he says. "He won't listen to us. You know, he's got four or five partial boxes—boxes!—of apples scattered around his tree. Nothing
in the bin."

Ken goes down the row, informing all of the availability of
coffee.

"Hey, Root-man!" Foy cries across the irrigation ditch.

"Yo!" returns Root-man.

"Hey, Root-man, ol' Rollin's brought out the coffee for us over
here again. Bet you'd like a cuppa coffee, Root-man."

"She-it," says Root-man, "all you do on that crew is drink coffee,
piss it off, and holler. I still sees me a lotta apples in your trees."

"I sing the apples offen the trees, Root-man," says Foy. "They
hears me and they dies of dee-light, plop, inta the bucket."

"If them mother-apples doan taste no better than you sound
singin', mighty ass, we gonna poison all the apple-eaters."

Butterfly gropes among his bushel boxes, leans on his ladder to
gasp, searches in his clothes for sticks of energy to lick: four-foot
garbage scarf knotted at the throat; gray sweatshirt over three
worn collars; rope belt; two pairs of trousers torn at four knees,
exposing oblongs of yellow woolens; broken-laced infantry boots
that go flapping at their splits. "Coffee? Coffee? Sounds sweet,
you bet, sure does, that coffee. Smells sweet, too. Lemme have a
cigarette, Rollin." There is the hand out, palm up, fingers stiffening. Butterfly is over sixty, claims a college education, may even

believe he has one. A Dagwood sandwich of yellow-leaved shirts, of dissimulations: the truth is as remote to him as the feel of his own flesh, as the memory of soap. "Gimme, Rollin?"

"Why, Butterfly? Why are you putting the apples into boxes when they're supposed to go in bins? When it's even *easier* to put them into bins?"

"Ah gonna put 'em in bins later on." His cunning is so low that only he could possibly believe in its utility, so transparent it's a form of self-betrayal.

"How, Butterfly?" But *how* is an ontological category; Butterfly belongs to material gone by, a proof of rot, beyond arguments. He leaves a few apples in a large number of boxes because he wants the world to believe that he's a quicker picker than he can be. The great bin-maw intimidates him. He himself might disappear into a bin. And his labor is so much smaller than himself—how could *it* ever possibly fill a bin? As in all death, *later on* is never. "Let me tell you how, Butterfly. You can take all the apples out of the boxes by hand, and put them in the bin. That will use up twice as much time as it would've taken you to do it right at the beginning. Or you can just dump the boxes into the bin, which will bruise every single apple you've picked. Was that what you were intending to do?" *Intending* implies free will, volition, an idea of the future, cognitive snap-crackle-and-pop. Butterfly cackles, in possession of the secret of rot. "Butterfly, don't you understand? One way, you're making twice as much work for yourself. The other way, you're going to bang hell out of all the apples, and when they see it up at the farm, you'll lose a day's picking." Butterfly articulates a desire for coffee, through his kerchief. *Desire,* now, is a condition, timeless, like gravity. "No," says Ken. "No coffee until you've consolidated those partial boxes; give me three full bushels, I'll give you credit. Then use the goddamn *bins*." I accuse you, Butterfly, of failing to be the least bit exemplary.

Back up the row, at the coffee stand, Smitty is telling dirty jokes to Wilson and Talley, who laugh obligingly. Wilson spills his third spoonful of sugar into the cardboard cup. Narrow of face, thin of moustache, with a snap-brim hat and a suit coat that long ago ran away from its pants, he indulges an attitude toward himself that can only be called avuncular. "Hey, Batman," he says to Talley, "know how I'm gonna make my first million?"

"C-c-c-counterfeit it," says Talley. They are both from Dixwell Avenue.

"No, man. I'm gonna build me a machine. Got two great big pairs of pliers. One come outa the hatch an' grabs that tree top an' shakes it like a cat 'til all them mother-apples fall down. The other come out wif a mother-net an' catch 'em. Apple-pickin' machine. I ree-tires countin' my money."

"Sh-sh-she-it, man, they already got them a apple-pickin' machine."

"They do?"

"Shua. *You*. You the apple-pickin' machine."

"Heh. Yeah, Batman. I forgot 'bout me." He grins at Ken. "Oh, oh, here come ol' Rollin, see what come of his machine. Needs oil, Rollin."

"It sure doesn't need gas," says Ken. "Actually, the final solution to the apple-picking problem will be the apple loaf. We'll run down the rows with clubs, beat all the apples off the trees, toss them into a masher, grind them to pulp, drain the juice, pat the pulp together, and bake it into bricks the size of bread loaves. Sell them pre-sliced, in wax paper. Call it apple bread."

"What you gonna do wif the seeds, Rollin?"

"Call them raisins."

"Heh. Yeah. Well, there goes my million, hey, Batman?"

"Your m-m-million was gone befo' you was b-b-born," says Talley.

"Yeah. I was born on the cuff, Batman. I jes' got started cryin' an' they said, Hush you mouf, black boy . . . you already owes us." With a two-handed grasp on his cup of coffee, Wilson goes back to his tree, swinging his sharp padded shoulders, knifing his way along. He isn't making any money, either.

"Acton," shouts Ken, "you keep that bucket in front of you. You're not picking oranges."

"Wisht I was pickin' oranges," says Acton. "Can't see no bruises on them oranges. Man, Rollin, I keep that bucket in front of me, an' it bounce on the ladder when I comes down. Then you say I bruised the mother-apples."

"Yes, but you keep it behind you like that, and you can't see it. Then you just reach behind yourself and drop the apples in instead of placing them down, and they bruise each other. Also you swing the bottom against the branches." A battle he will not win.

The experienced orange-pickers sling their buckets low, to the side, or on their backs. The weight feels unnatural any other way.

"Ken," says Smitty, "Wornum's going to kill himself with that ladder."

Another old man who should not be here, and cannot be taught how to move a twelve-foot ladder, place it. "Robert, you want to keep your hands a few rungs apart. Bend your elbows. Hold the ladder straight up and move it into the trees sideways. Like that. Not so much an angle, Robert. Get it straighter. You put it down that low, the branch will break under you."

"Rollin," says Wornum, "how'm I gonna get them top apples hangin' over the ditch? I put the ladder up this side, the branch breaks. I set it in the ditch, it doan come anywheres near the top."

"Pick everything you can reach. Then aim your ladder at the top. Then accidentally drop your ladder. Accidentally drop it a couple of times until those top apples get accidentally knocked down. Then you shake your head and put them into drop boxes." I hate this ditch.

"So thas how it's done," says Wornum. "Never woulda thought of that. Goes to show why I ain't no supervisor."

Ken moves. He is pointing out a new group of trees for Fisher when he hears a thrashing in the ditch. Out of the thrashing issues Short, madly mottled.

"That's it," says Short. He throws his yellow cards on the ground; then his paper punch. "I ain't gonna take it any more. That's just *it*."

"What's happened?"

What's happened seems to be thrombosis. Short's thrombi aren't circulating, he is shards, emotion doesn't flow, it clots. "Mason and Porter," he says. "Big mouths. That's it. I ain't gonna take any more of their fat lip. If they won't do what I tell 'em, then mebbe Murdock can tell 'em. But not me. First bad trees I give 'em in a week and they big bad-mouth me. Good for stealin' batteries, they are. Not so good for takin' orders or pickin' apples. Not me—no, *sir*."

"Short, where are you going?"

Short, running down the row, is a diminishing dot. Short is a little short this week. The pickers lean out of their trees. O, look at that man's lympics. "Hey, Short," shouts Foy, "you forgot to pick up my bay-ton! Hey, sport, the rabbit ran thataway!" The blot of him has had it; the sky sucks him up.

"Smitty!" says Ken, picking up the cards and punch. "I'm going across. You handle this side until I get back."

Sliding down into the ditch. On his side: black faces, grinning angels in the trees. On Short's side: nothing. He sinks to his ankles in soft mud. Coffin climbing, what a clot. There sits Short's checker, Partland, on his foam rubber cushion. "What on earth happened?" Partland shakes his head. Has anything ever happened? Not hardly likely.

"Mason!" says Ken. Short's whole crew stands in the middle of the row, waiting. Mason—shaved head, Islamic warrior?—regards pridefully his black fists. Mason is called Gov'mint-man because, when drunk, he claims he is a secret agent and flashes his draft card as credentials. "What's the matter with Short?"

"I'm gonna kill Short," says Mason. "I tole him I'm gonna kill him."

"You're not going to kill anybody."

"Oh yeah," says Mason. "You know, Rollin, I got me a mean temper. I killed a man oncet in Florida. He got me mad, an' I killed him. They sent me up."

"And you got out, did you? Were you ten years old when you killed him?"

"I got me a mean, mean temper, Rollin. Balls afire."

He is working hard to believe how mean he is. "Three drinks, Mason, and you love the world. I don't believe in your mean temper. What happened here?"

Mason claps Ken on the shoulder. "Now, Rollin, you see? *You* comes over here, and *you* don't say *boy*, does you? You says Mason. Thas my name, Mason. And you jes' look me in one eye. I doan mine you none, Rollin. But that Short, he doan look me in one eye, and he doan know my name. He jes' say get off yo' ass, boy. Thas why I'm gonna kill him."

"You've already killed a bottle. Am I right?"

"I ain't drunk, Rollin. Hones', ain't. Love the world."

"Short's a part of the world. A small part, but a part."

"Well, now, if I doan kill that Short, ol' Porter he gonna kill him. And I can't 'low ol' Porter have all the games."

"Porter? Porter, what's going on here?"

Porter is as huge as he is sullen. He wears an army jacket indicating he's been busted down to a single stripe. "That mother-fucking Short," says Porter, "he give me nothin' but shit-trees, man. Ain't nuff apples on that tree to fill two of them boxes."

"That's not the only tree he gave you, is it? He gave you the next two down, didn't he?"

"Man, I doan care what other ones that sons a bitch *gave* me. Lookit, I gotta spend me a whole hour puttin' that mother-ladder all 'roun' that ditch jes' to buy me one lousy bucket of apples. I ain't gonna do it."

They are gathering. Even James T. Worthless. "James T., you're supposed to be a crew leader. Will you explain that everybody gets a bad tree along this ditch?"

"This ditch is shit, man," says James T. James T. is scared of Porter. That, combined with trying to curry favor with the others by urging them on to do their worst, makes him about as useful as a cranberry. "An' ol' Short, he cussed us out. We doan gotta eat that shit, man."

Porter speaks again, words rolling like boulders down a moun-tain of black muscle. "I come up here to pick apples, not to take no shit from Short. Iffen Short-ass want them shit-trees picked, he can piss on 'em hisself. Or he can give 'em to one of them ol' men. I gotta make me some money. I ain't makin' no money offen shit-trees."

"Sure. Give all the bad trees to the old men. They've got a tough enough time making three bucks a day right now. So give them all the bad trees, and let them make two bucks a day. Right? No, not right. Everybody has to pick one of these lousy trees. No-body gets all good trees along this ditch."

They aren't impressed by the egalitarian approach to crap jobs. Ken turns to inspect the row. "All right. I'll assign you trees to pick." And he stabs at them, assigning groups of three trees to each man, a bad tree in each group.

Porter says no-sale. "I ain't gonna pick no shit-trees."

"Look, I know what happens over here when Short's alone. The guy who shouts the loudest and looks the toughest usually gets the easiest trees, because Short's scared. How long since you had to pick a bad tree, Porter? Well, everybody else has been picking bad trees. Those trees have got to be picked, like the others. If they aren't, they won't be *good* trees next year. Let's get *out* of this crumby orchard."

177

"I ain't gonna pick no shit-trees," Porter repeats. "You can shoot off your motherfuckin' mouf all you wants. An' when you gets done, you can stick that shit-tree up your tight little ass."

The silence now is prurient. Well, you calculate. Even when your jockey shorts have turned cold aluminum, your knees are sponge. Would he hit a man with glasses? I haven't hit anybody in years, except for Roger Beckwith, and Beckwith was nobody. "Porter, do I talk to you like that? Have I ever talked to you like that? Well? Have I?"

Porter clicks off. He's got a mouse in his brain, scrabbling behind the eyes. He listens to the mouse. Scrabble, scrabble. Shit-mouse.

"No, Porter, I don't talk to you like that. And nobody talks to me like that. You or anybody else."

"You can't make me pick that tree," says Porter.

Fuck you, Porter. Why don't you pinch my snotty head off? See the little white prick that cried. "No, I can't. I can't drag you up the ladder and operate your hands for you. So what do you do? Go back to camp? You come here to pick apples, make money. You aren't picking and you aren't making money back at camp."

"Them apples I doan pick," says Porter, "is apples you ain't sellin'."

"I can't sell any of this conversation, either. Go on back."

"Iffen I go back, there's mens here what go back wif me."

"Balls afire. You can all watch television, and catch the next bus back to Florida, and the apples don't get picked, and I lose money, and you lose money, and everybody loses everything, and what a tight-ass little world we end up with. Go on. Anybody who stays gets exactly the same deal, old and young, until *all* the trees get picked. If you want a better deal than the man next to you, you should have gone with Skinny Reid."

The mouse has gotten to Porter's nerve ends; they don't fire any more. But James T. has to stick his fingers in the shit-pie. "We knows how it works," says James T. "Jes' lookit them bins. Fifteen bushel, *you* say. Man, I knows how many apples my bucket hold. I get me one bushel ever' time I come down. I got to come down *twenny* times to fill that mother-bin. Twenny bushel in that bin. An' ol' Henry, he punch up fifteen."

"Tell it to the asparagus, James T. That bin can't even hold fifteen bushels, and you know it."

Porter has chewed some on his mouse; protein for the nerve ends. "She-it, man, I been pickin' apples ten years. You think I doan know?"

"You're right. I think you don't know." Mackenzies don't lie, do they? He turns back to James T. "You play a lot of craps, James T. How about a bet? Let's string out fifteen bushel boxes under your trees. You fill them up. Once they're filled, you take the apples out of those boxes by hand and put them into a bin. That costs time. But if those fifteen bushel boxes don't fill the bin, then I punch you up for thirty bushels. Double credit, fair? *Thirty.* But if they *do* fill up a bin, then you've lost the time it took to prove I'm right. A bet?"

James T. wastes a lot of craftiness looking around him. The others aren't giving anything away. James T.? Never heard of him. Bins? I bin a bushel of places, fifteen or twenty, don't matter. Even Porter hedges: "She-it, James T., you *knows* there's least ways twenny bushel."

Ken is unwilling to let all of them hedge. He needs a crew, not a scapegoat. "All right. Everybody up in his tree. Everybody fill up two bushel boxes. Then we'll all put the apples into the bin. Save time. And if fifteen boxes don't fill it, you all get credit for those two bushels, plus two extra ones. Plus, of course, extra credit for every bin you've picked this season. Well?"

They would prefer not to. A muttering of mothers . . . but they go at last, and pick in silence. Twenty minutes later, fifteen bushels are there, in a circle around an empty bin. Ken reminds himself that Mackenzies don't lie. "One by one," he says, helping: into the bin. It takes just a little more than fourteen bushel boxes to fill the bin. Of course, Mackenzies don't lie. He points at the remaining box. "First, the bins save time. You don't have to line up those little boxes and you don't have to level each one off. Second, it's gravy. Three quarters of a bushel credit for each bin picked. Not enough to make anybody rich, but nobody's cheating, either. Am I right?"

James T. is looking the other way. Mason says, "Rollin, ol' Porter, he doan mean to bad-mouf you. Only that Short, it's one fuckin' hassle."

"Forget it." Porter's forgotten it. I picked my crew on the rock pile, and that's why this one is all hassling. I took the smart ones, the ones I liked, except for Butterfly, who just wants cigarettes and coffee. "Let's work. Mason, you promise not to kill Short, at least until the picking's done?"

"Love the world," says Mason. "What'll do, Rollin, is sic ol' Butterfly on Short. Butterballs, he'd *breathe* on Short-shit. Death by breath."

He'd like a vine on which to swing, over the ditch. Maybe Foy could arrange it. But he mudrumps. Butterfly has winged. There is only one reason to check on Butterfly now. If Butterfly's gone on a wine sabbatical, fine. If he's gone on a bowel job, dandy. But if he's skipped a row, and off alone picking the easy apples, the ones reachable without ladders, bad. The real pickers won't even look at trees from which all the cheapies have been pulled. He finds Butterfly sleeping in a pile of apple boxes, struck down by the broadsword of incompetence, a puddle of dirty linen.

He remembers once having descended from the national city of *Scope*, airports, hotel rooms, credit cards, into the Under City, where they collect bundles of Butterflies in trucks and haul them away. Most of his experience has been with the national city: dour, attentive Coffin, being sent to Chicago or St. Louis, packing one suit, three shirts, two ties, a mound of underwear and socks rolled up into hand grenades, a book he will not read, his tools (safety razor, nail-clipper, brushes for teeth and hair) and his unguents (shaving cream, toothpaste, deodorant, shoe polish); phoning for a cab; standing gravely at his window with a raincoat draped over his shoulders like a police inspector's cape; being whisked through a depopulated Sunday city to Logan Airport, everything confirmed; ordering a Lowenbrau and smoking a cigarette on the Sky Deck; paying for his beer with a dollar bill as crisp as the crease in his trousers; knowing that his real power was plastic, to fly, buy, eat, and sleep anywhere in the world (or what he knew of the world, which was the national city); surrendering his ticket, boarding, fastening his seat belt, rising perfectly prepared into Sunday, a particle borne on the jet stream. . . .

There would be a chauffeur service at O'Hare to take him to his hotel, a bellboy to lead him to his room, an ice-water tap and an air-conditioner and carpeting to muffle his confident footfall and mirrors to record his dour, attentive image, and an elevator to the lobby toward fun and games. Fun and games means claw-collared conventioneers with plastic identification badges sitting like toads at tables the size of lily pads in go-go bars where topless black girls writhe in glass cages. It means dour, attentive Coffins buying weak drinks for lost young women in the skyscraper lounges of the national city, where a muted music is strained like baby food of all sinew, where muted people are strained like pronouns of excessive individuality (we are *less* than our badges), and there is only need. It means sex in a rented bed in a Winter Palace of credit, plastic instead of ice, its participants as odorless, weightless, and bloodless as plastic, silent pumps sucking up our mentholated smoke, our small spasms, licensed serfs, plastic people with perfunctory desires in every closet (every hotel, every airport) of the Winter Palace, eating electric light, passing it through our bladders, excreting it into vats from which new compounds of plastic will be synthesized, beyond (unaware of) good and evil, having rented our bodies in order to ice-skate on the lamination that is the floor of the national city.

And that is the ceiling of the Under City. To arrive bleak-of-eye at dawn in Grand Central Station off the Owl. To find the rotunda unlit and men sleeping in telephone booths. To descend to the cellar and rent a stall where one repairs oneself with tools and unguents, while in the stall to your right someone snores and in the stall to your left an aberrant act between two consenting males is noisily consummated. When in the coarse of human intents . . . To search for the superior bagel in a city made out of yesterday's newspapers. To discover, on turning a corner into a side street, a controlled apparition: a white truck, slowly, silently moving down the block. In the door of each shop and apartment house, Puerto Rican boys stand sentry-watch. As the truck approaches them, they dart forward with bags of laundry, commit their bundle to the truck, retreat, vanish. Not a word of greeting or complaint is spoken. A perfectly achieved ballet, damned angels issuing from doorways with dirty linen not their own, relinquishing it, extinguishing themselves; and the truck, a stomach, never surfeited, rolls on. It is followed by a grinding, a gray tank with jowls, a barge of sanitation, also hungry, but on treads, gangsterish, its attendants a Gestapo guard, a clattering of cans that shatters the panes of sleep. All that is not credit will be devoured. (This, you see, is the end of Butterfly: either as laundry or as garbage.) As the movie theaters in Times Square devour customers at quarter to eight in the morning. The promise of pornography: new uses for old organs. On the faces of those about to be gobbled are no stigmata, not of shame, not even of embarrassment: the faces of exploded paper bags. The Under City, for all its access to the elemental, has not thrown up representations of itself any more hopeful than those on the walls of the skyscraper lounges, than those exchanged in rented beds. Desperation is not vitality.

He is on his way to Paris. Isn't it about time to stop being a tourist?

Wed*lock.*

Here comes Dennison on the tractor, under his pukka sahib pith helmet, inside his yellow slicker, the man from Mars. With a tractor, you can stay in gear, any gear. What about the traction of the will? Can I select my gear, and stay in it, and get there eventually? Throttle myself? Dennison says, How are ya doin'? Ken replies, Jes' fine; did Short make it back to the farm? Dennison admits that Short made it back to the farm. Dennison is an advertisement for technology, but he will climb down and handle his crew. What will Short do: crouch in the controlled atmosphere shed, his funk at thirty-two degrees Fahrenheit? Commit prone self to rollers toward a resolution in the packing room? Short's face has been stolen, like the battery. No shops in Wyke Regis at which to buy new faces: firm jaws, steely eyes. Not even any bad mouths.

Butterfly returns, moves spavined among his boxes, counting them, climbs the ladder without hope, until only his broken boots are visible.

Acton insists he's owed a box of drops not punched up on his card. Wilson is pulling too many spurs. Image of Foy, at the top of his tree, motionless, inscrutable, staring at Monadnock. Black faces: Rorschach tests.

Advent of the apple-hungry trailers, tractor-drawn, a caravan of mutant ants. There, in charge of the heave-ho, is faceless Short, a flunked test. Staples on the fork lift. Bins, crayon-scrawled, rise and turn on the fork prongs, huge dice in a crap game between Mackenzies and the Frog God.

Missionaries should wear mittens, to keep from picking their eyes out. *I is out.* I am subtracting myself even as I try to extend and fill the empty afternoon. I am down now to nothing but the bone, which is a weapon; bedrock will; wedlock rusty; the key is a bone; alone at an intersection of sun and numbness, done with bloody sums, tourisms, entropisms, only a burning eye at the end of a walking bone . . . You won't get lost? Bone boomerang.

It is a terrible thing to try to make yourself more interesting to your own wife.

He climbs an apple tree. The ladders are stilts. He could walk across the valley to Monadnock. By the pocket watch that hangs from a twist of twine in his belt loop, he sees that it is time to go home.

They are all on the truck but Butterfly. He starts without Butterfly. Then, in the rear-view mirror, he sees Butterfly appear on the road and chase after them. Flap your wings, Butterfly, someone shouts. Butterfly is a scorpion. We got us some Nooo-Haven pussy on this truck, Butterball, sweet sixteen and spread like jam. Ken doesn't stop, but goes slow enough to give Butterfly an even chance at catching hold of the tailgate. Otis DeKalb hauls him in.

At camp, Cindy Lou is waiting on the porch, in halter and shorts, poised like a diver about to jackknife into the situation, testing it. It will certainly be found wanting.

He switches once again to the station wagon. He is not at all surprised, on the road to the cottage, to see a car tipped over in the culvert, blocking passage. An old, heavy Dodge, looking as though it wants to be tickled. He should have planted a red warning flag at the culvert. Rain tends to wash away at its foundations, and the inattentive driver ends up helplessly stuck, cursing everything that isn't a superhighway. He *is* surprised at Rinsler's being there. What does Rinsler know about cars or culverts? Rinsler is flanked on each side by young men, boys really; their whiteness and their acne remind him of soda crackers. Moreover, they are crumbling. Before his eyes, as he gets out, a blank panic unravels whatever definition their faces might have hoped to achieve. They've been trying to grow window boxes on their chins, under their noses, around their ears: a less than persuasive scraggle. What will happen when all the ears of America disappear, under hair? Earless, who will be able to hear the eternal verities? Why are they scared?

"Mark D'Allesandro," says Rinsler. "Toby Ransome. Ken Coffin." Rinsler is pretending he has some magic notion that will wish away the misadventure. A dodge, boys. Ken lets him pretend for a while. Finally, Rinsler says: "What do you suggest?"

"Well, if we cry a lot, we might float it down the culvert into

183

the irrigation ditch. Then we could pray for a monsoon. Wash it to Wyke Regis."

"I'm serious, Ken."

"I'm curious. Who are these people?"

"Friends of mine."

"An excellent cover story. Well, we could try the winch." He knows that the winch won't work. Maybe for a Volkswagen, but not on the excreta of Detroit. He has not, however, had a chance to try out his father's new winch. It still sleeps in its package on the back seat of the station wagon. He unleashes it. "Twenty-to-one gear ratio," he informs them. They don't know what he's talking about. He's pleased. He wraps one end of the cable line around a healthy tree, and the other end around the axle of the Dodge. Both are fastened. "Now," he says to Rinsler, "you can pump away. Just keep pushing down."

It is Rinsler's fault that he doesn't object, that he doesn't even know enough to realize that he should be objecting. He pumps. It's even-money whether he will collapse from a heart attack first, or the line will snap, whip him around the neck, and snuff him out just as he's learning something about the internal contradictions of tensile strength.

"Hold it," says Ken. "It won't work. I'll have to get a tractor." He enjoys their powerlessness to express a qualm, to fart forthrightly. We are raising a generation of mechanical morons; comes the revolution, and they won't know how to change a light bulb. Back into the station wagon. Backing off the road. Back unto the camp. I wonder if Cindy Lou uses the raffle system?

A hush obtains, the farm is stricken, our battery is gone, the dogs have been poisoned, to start the tractor is to blaspheme. Somewhere inside, Dennison is polishing his blue eyes, weeping on his cap; Foy fondles a buttock; Butterfly is dying.

Rinsler, D'Allesandro, and Ransome have not yet decided whether to hold hands or bite hubcaps. "A snake!" shouts Ken, throwing the chain at them, wondering what they'd look like with tread marks all over their Saltines. By these stings I thee bed; scorpions are in the ascendancy. Marcy has a mole inside her bathing suit; once I thought it was an insect; now I apply my ear to it and listen; it tells me that it is happier than I am, being where I'm not.

It proceeds dreamily: the fastening of the chain, the ox pull, the sliding of the Dodge along the embankment, a surfacing in slow motion. We are damaging the road. He will have to level it before it's ruined by another rain. He enjoys being inside the noise of the tractor, contained in the capsule of it; outside is a vacuum, the asteroid of Rinsler.

D'Allesandro seizes the wheel of the Dodge.

"See if it'll start," shouts Ken. "See if it moves." It does. "OK, follow me to the farm. We'll have to put it up on ramps and look at the bottom."

He leads the Dodge past the camp to the shed. Albany Jackson, Otis DeKalb, and Richmond are just coming out of the cabin. They are so carefully dressed as to appear faintly sinister. Jackson sports a Tyrolean hat. DeKalb and Richmond have unwound and discarded their black turbans. Their hair lies close and sleek on top, and at the temples; then extends straight back in wings with irregular edges. What might have been an elaborate pomade deteriorates at the back of the head. The wing tips are tufted or spiked, and a tension seems to be uncoiling: during the course of the evening the heads will fly away. Of course, they want the station wagon he has promised. *What are they going to do with it?*

"I just have to check this out," he tells them. He places the ramps before the front wheels of the Dodge. D'Allesandro is incapable of driving the car onto the ramps; he is going to run over them. Ken orders him out. Without being asked, Albany Jackson takes the wheel and smoothly achieves lift-up. I thought Richmond was the one with a license to drive cars. Now for the trouble-lamp. There is no difficulty in securing the trouble-lamp; there is much difficulty in finding an electrical outlet in the shed. Fine old Yankee electrical engineers: one outlet for a whole shed full of power machinery. Foy could do better. "You see that reel," he says to Rinsler. "It works like a fishing reel." Rinsler doesn't know how a fishing reel works. "Only it feeds out extension cord instead of line. Just turn it and I'll pull." Rinsler tangles the cord; Rinsler scrapes his knuckles on the wooden standards of the reel; Rinsler sucks his knuckles. Ken finally gets enough extension cord to plug in the trouble-lamp. Then he lowers himself onto the creeper and trundles under the Dodge with his trouble-lamp. "Your crankcase is torn up," he says. "And I don't know what else. It needs garage work."

"My friends have to leave this evening," says Rinsler.

"Not in this Dodge," says Ken. "The bottom will probably drop out. And the brake lines might have been cut. We dragged it over some big rocks."

"Can't you fix it?"

"Rinsler, I'm not a mechanic. I just know enough to know when you need to go to a mechanic."

Rinsler considers this betrayal, gnaws on it, is moved at last to ask: "Could you lend us your car?"

"For how long?"

"No more than a week."

"A week? No. It's not even my car."

"Two days, then."

"No. It's been promised, anyway, for this evening. You'll either have to rent one, or wait until the Dodge is fixed. I can put you up." He hands the keys of the station wagon to Albany Jackson.

"Thank you, Kenneth. We 'preciates it."

He wants to know what they are really going to do with the car, but he will not ask. "All right," he says, watching them climb in. Rinsler, D'Allesandro, and Ransome seem unwilling to leave the wounded Dodge. "We'll have to walk back to my place," Ken says, wondering if D'Allesandro knows how to walk. Ransome collects two duffel bags from the trunk of the Dodge and they commence to trudge.

At the side of the road near the culvert lies the winch that didn't work. He picks it up. He is disappointed in the winch; its failure seems a reflection on his willpower, the burning eye and the walking bone.

At the cottage, in silence, he prepares a fire, using pine cones and *The New York Review of Books* as kindling. He also prepares himself a drink, and gestures at the bottles if they want to join him. They do not.

Finally—what else is there to say to them?—he asks: "Would you mind telling me what's going on?"

Ten

RINSLER LOOKED AT HIS HANDS. From the winch: blisters forming. From the rack: knuckles bleeding. Coffin had done it deliberately. Somehow, instead of being a substitute for Rinsler's brother, Coffin had become a substitute for Rinsler's stepfather. He remembered being sent one summer, at age fourteen, into the San Bernardino Mountains, to a one-horse lumber camp run by friends of his stepfather. The idea had been to make a man by breaking a spirit. Rinsler was paid seventy-five cents an hour. Every morning it was freezing. Every afternoon it sweltered. Rinsler slept on a cot in a shack down the mountainside from the main cabin. The shack had a tin roof. The men in the main cabin woke him up at six-thirty each morning by throwing rocks which crashed on the tin roof and rolled over it, making the sky fall. He would put on pitch-stiff overalls, wash his face with cold water, try and fail to start a fire in the small stove, and go outside to piss. He would then climb to the main cabin for the invariable breakfast of pancakes the size of bicycle tires, syrup as thick as petroleum, dough that sat for hours in the stomach like swamp sludge. Down to the mill, where he stood between the saw and the furnace. The logs were sliced into planks. The bark and oddments were fed into the furnace. In the mornings Rinsler loaded the new, wet twelve-foot boards onto a truck. In the afternoons, he unloaded them up the road, stacked them in huge piles with sticks between each layer, running crosswise, to allow them to dry out. He wore gloves, but the gloves were ripped apart. His hands bled. Every Saturday morning it was his job to go with a crowbar into the furnace, to chip away at the refuse that had collected around the gas jet and threatened to choke it. The gas jet had, of course, been turned off. But the heat remained. It burned the pine pitch on his face and hands, seemed to glaze him beyond the redress of a hot shower, if indeed there would ever be hot water anywhere again. He wrote a letter to the child labor people in Sacramento. They never replied. He wrote a letter to his mother. She replied that it was only for another six weeks; stick it out. He wrote a letter to the local labor council in San Bernardino. They sent a man, an international rep, he called himself. The camp was nonunion. The international rep closed the camp by getting union men in trucks to block the road down the mountain. There was also one fire and one fistfight. Rinsler lost the fistfight; the foreman broke two of his teeth and sent him to the hospital in Redlands. During his week in the hospital he recalled with satisfaction having been on the line at the mill when the foreman sawed off one of his own fingers.

That was the beginning of his education. The international rep adopted him for the rest of the summer. Varstock was his name. He had somehow survived the purge of organized labor's left wing in the late 1940s. He had also somehow survived the bottle, and took pills to keep himself from going back to it. Rinsler accompanied him on his rounds of the union halls, those little stucco boxes full of folding chairs and wretchedly written magazines. Rinsler heard the younger men decline to agitate for pension benefits; refuse to agree on higher dues to help build a recreation hall for the older members, now emeritus, who had fought all the ancient strikes and secured the higher wages; talk about nothing but the second car or the second TV set they wanted—a sullenness so profound it amounted to moral fatigue, a suicidal selfishness. Rinsler disapproved. Varstock was heartsick. Varstock should have been outraged. When Rinsler returned home at the end of the summer, his stepfather had cleaned out the joint checking account and disappeared with the family car. Rinsler's hands healed. He promised never again to use them so savagely. They were for gripping pencils, turning the pages of books, dialing on the telephone, touching women.

Now Coffin was putting a record on the phonograph: Amalia Rodrigues singing Portuguese *fado*. Now Coffin wanted answers to his questions. Now Coffin, in his absurd fatigue jacket, with his clenched fist of a brain, his tumbler of rum, his Harvard education, his hot-house wife, the compunctions he handed out like calling cards, and the qualms he crapped wherever he sat—this Coffin would like to be told what was going on. Everything had always been going on; had Coffin expected everything to wait until he got around to wondering about it?

"Mark and Toby no longer want to be in the Army," said Rinsler.

Coffin considered this information. He was looking at the duffel bags. "Deserters?" he said.

"Political refugees," said Rinsler. "They were called up to go to Nam."

More consideration. "On their way to Canada?"

"They needed papers. Identification. Names and numbers."

"You."

"Me." It was important to make Coffin an accomplice. Rinsler pulled documents out of his briefcase and passed them along. Coffin read them.

"Why don't they stay and fight? Like you?" Coffin didn't know about Rinsler's heart murmur. No one knew, because Rinsler didn't have a wife who couldn't keep her mouth shut about matters Rinsler wanted to remain secrets.

"Are you in any position to encourage them to stay and fight?" said Rinsler.

"What do you mean by that?"

"I mean, you didn't exactly stay and fight when your turn came, did you?"

"If you mean leaving the institute, well—"

"I don't mean leaving the institute. I mean when it was your turn to go into the Army."

"Why don't you speak plainly, Rinsler?" His face was a potato going bad, growing mold.

"I mean that you were so afraid of the Army that you forced your wife to have a child that almost killed her, for the greater

189

glory of a draft exemption. Mark and Toby don't happen to be married. No wives and children to hide behind."

"Where do you get your information, Rinsler?"

"Why, from Marcy, of course. In detail. Did she lie to me?"

"When?"

"Last night. She was at the lighthouse."

"She was at the lighthouse. And what else did she tell you about me while she was at the lighthouse last night?"

"Let me think. She mentioned that you had written a pornographic historical potboiler about the siege of Londonderry, had it privately printed, and tried to palm it off as something a dead relative had done. She talked a lot about your feeling that the Mackenzies hadn't really done anything about slavery and racism in this country. That you were going to make up for it personally. That it was *evil*. Evil, I believe, was the exact word. That Wyke Regis was once upon a time part of the underground railroad from the South to Canada, and maybe the migrant workers were a way of doing it all over again, and this time doing it right. I must say, it sounded a little vainglorious. She said some other things, but I've forgotten."

"And how many people did she say them to?"

"Oh, just me. We were quite alone." Apply thumbs to pressure points; sweat the son of a bitch. "I told you: she's a liberated woman." Grin at him. "I got to thinking about the underground railroad, you know. I knew about Mark and Toby. Here you are, halfway to Canada. Boston isn't a comfortable place these days for certain kinds of transactions. We are watched. It seemed a natural solution. I knew you'd approve."

"Convenient," said Coffin. The fool seemed actually to be burning his hand in the fire. "All right. I'll call a garage and see about getting your Dodge fixed up."

Rinsler thought about the foreman's sawed-off finger, the *barbudo*'s submachine gun, a razor strop, his brother on the zodiac bedspread, Frosty the Snowman. Details of feelings. Like wow, man.

Eleven

Saturday

THERE WERE JARS ON THE KITCHEN SHELF, each lid the head of a nail, its member impaling an herb. The sunlight made eyes of the lids, which were blind, having denied spice. Seals tested, and found wanting. But it wasn't any ordinary sunlight. Its ordnance set fire to the shelf of jars, eyes, lids, nails. It scourged. Whatever the jars thought they were containing was transformed: into definitions/defamations; propositions/protestations; suppositions/suppositories; woulds that rot; won'ts that maybe; beastlinesses beyond the taming of namesakes; blamesakes absent without leave from the trees that grew out of the jars and boughed to her as though they were hammocks, catapults. My pelt, nailed to the shelf, admired for all the static electricity it absorbed/abhorred: ever so curlicute.

Sergeant Pepper had implored her to escape the cage. The cage consisted of nipples, veins, cavities, blood tides, kitchens, husbands, children. But Marcy did not consider Stephen a cage; he was a room in the house of her. Had she delivered eight perfect poems instead of Stephen at the hospital, she would not have been as pleased. She had not even bothered to tell the father that *each* time, no matter how bloody, was a miracle. He knew. Can you top this, buster?

Karen Constable had deplored the willingness of the sisters to be vandalized, to deform themselves according to a cookie mold that grew on masculine minds, stools of toads that had never been toilet-trained. But Marcy did not consider herself, nor did her husband consider her to be, any of Karen's stereotypes: statue on wheels; snow maiden stabbed by an icicle; shadow of her husband's substance, the key or the knife in his back; wild girl with blossom breasts waywardly combing through meadows of hair spray; pearl among stitches for trousers that were frayed from a muchness of tumescence; vengeful Amazon bearing rusty shears; nurse, witch, whore, buddy. Barely even a mother, and only that because she chose to bare and bear, having decided on the father.

Justine Dershowitz had deemed each act of heterosex an act of piracy, every surrender part socially conditioned reflex and part masochistic cyclothemia, a silver horn, a rending, a violation of daughter by father, Papa Bull in the bassinet. But Marcy hadn't married her father, hadn't even substituted for him, had in fact repudiated and transcended him. And what had happened at Pithiviers had not been piracy, nor surrender, unless giving your arms to each other was considered a surrender, which it wasn't: it was disarmament; followed by politics. And why, anyway, had she been born with all those eggs in her?

Rinsler had avowed a revolutionary dream, a Russian novel full of flags and destiny, the fire of the many lighting the nights of those who were alone, spacious hearts, free associations, collectivity, a wounding that was ultimately creative, an end to weeping in promises of steel. But at the Finland Station, in his lighthouse, Rinsler had been nude, a little boy wanting to play doctor, hung with a stethoscope instead of a sword. We have all of us always been the raw materials for somebody else's revolution; all revolutions are essentially personal; we are the energy that fuels them; we are colonized, exhausted, forgotten.

If she had driven up to Wyke Regis in the early morning, as she had tentatively decided to do last night, right now she would be preparing a basket for lunch at the pond: a skill she had perfected, and then abandoned, like threading needles or wiggling her ears. She would have chosen between hamburgers and hot dogs, relish and cheese, cucumbers and carrots, diet-cola and sherry, Charlotte Brontë and Doris Lessing. Hannah would be on the floor of the kitchen, trying to pull drawers open and dishes down. Stephen would be out in the orchard with his father, or following Butterfly around. She would see them, her husband and her son, approaching the cottage at noon on the grassy slope, Stephen absurdly small, a mimic of a man, self-important in his pretense, grave beside the Coffin. Her clue to be ready for their stomachs: the rings, the traps, of teeth; Saturday's half-day of apple-grasping over with; ridiculously, affectingly, proud of the ordinariness they had wrought, as she was of the marrying of one and the mothering of the other. *Mine.* An emotional equinox; all is even. As per custom, the picnic hamper deposited in the car; the three-quarter mile to the green gate on which Stephen would swing, having unpadlocked it; the descent into an interior more the heart of gentle artifice than of darkness; an apron of beach, flanked here by bathhouse, there by dock; Hannah, bare-assed, up to her ankles in copper-colored water; Marcy, with salt shaker and coffee can, looking for leeches; Stephen, with worms, pretending to fish from the dam for horn pout; the Coffin on the diving board, waiting for the wind to fill the pockets of his fatigue jacket and exalt him, awkward bird, his boots in the thistles, trying to clear the city of pines and flap his way to Pithiviers. He might even have offered to paddle her aluminum canoe. And she, remembering the mosquitoes, the twigs, the voices over the water like balloons that popped on touching them, years ago, at the confluence of Contoocook and Mackenzie, by the banks of bubbles of industrial detergent, remembering a giggly abashment at their nakedness—*is he a pointer? has he smelled a pussycat?*—remembering the leafprints on each side of her spine, the mark of the heliotrope, the bloodstone, on a buttock, mirrors moulting from the trees she saw, the crystal vault in which she spun, revolved, the sky that came down like a sail and wrapped them—*I like pirates*—even so, she might have, she would have, agreed. It mattered that much. The fatigue jacket might have been a pillow. The insects wouldn't have *dared.* . . .

On the other hand, which would have been on her anyway, thumbing her left nipple as though it were the switch that hums up the oil heater or grinds the rinds: she might have spent the morning on the phone with Mary or Polly Mackenzie, organizing a suckling pig for seventeen tartans; a tea for the wives of farm personnel; a scavenging among discards in musty barns for that perfect pair of andirons, ones with brass cowheads, ideal for the library at Thomas Hill; an appointment to pluck and shuck corn, ears with teeth—no, that time was past; eggplant, maybe?—a petition against gravel pits, housing tracts, motel developments, radio towers, industrial parks, snowmobiles; a fête for the superannuated, gray heads climbing out of fastback station wagons, sunstruck, with the prehistoric dignity of turtles, groping toward the garden and the white metal chairs and the hollyhocks and the dandelion wine, their anecdotes chains around their ankles; a funeral, for which music must be engineered; a birth, for which booties must be knit; hysteria, which needs exorcising; depression, which needs Styrofoam.

The third hand, like the third eye, was what you held and saw, smooth after the planing-off of mights and maybes. She hadn't gone to Wyke Regis because he told her it wasn't necessary. Why wasn't it necessary? It wasn't necessary because *she* wasn't necessary. If he had fallen in love with another woman, she could have coped: improvisations in food, in talk, in bed. But he had fallen in love with a whole family, before he had even bothered to vandalize her, and expected her to be their puppy, too, and how could she possibly compete with *that*, those thousand acres, the customs and ceremonies, the gabbling gaggle in her rising gorge, the galvanized iron ribbon of their solicitude? Why wasn't *I* enough for him?

Instead of driving to Wyke Regis, she had allowed Stephen to play with her typewriter. She had baked gingerbread men which were crumby. She had escorted her children to the MDC swimming pool, to find that it had closed after Labor Day and wouldn't open again until next July. She had been less than super at the market: canned food, canned music, canned people. Marcy hermetically sealed inside her seethe. Fruit-loops, rye bread, *TV Guide*, swordfish, olives, Green Stamps. Her tongue wrapped in cellophane. Every year in Wyke Regis the Mackenzies slaughtered a lamb, a steer, some geese, and an innocent outsider: to be dissected, stored in a locker, fetched when the stomach turned. Barbecued ribs of Marcypial; wearing her breasts like beanies as they chomped on her drumsticks. Unfair: they ate each other, too, and grew strong on the diet. They were devourers of ideas as well as people. Conversation counted. So did work, although it was usually the work of the men; the work of the women was to bring up the next generation of Mackenzies. She thought of Thomas Hill during the summer as a communications satellite, beaming memorandums, articles, and books from Wyke Regis to the world: the function and purpose of the land-grant college; the meaning of the green revolution in agriculture; notes toward a new method of teaching history in secondary schools; what happened to the idea of culture after the death of Matthew Arnold; science perceived as a way of reducing the number of things in life which can be blamed on God, thereby pinning the rap on *us*. No wonder they raised apples; it was a knowledge factory. It was *civilization*. And even when it decided to play for a while, it dictated memorandums, wrote articles and books on how to play. *Good* people, the kind of people I wanted to grow up to be. And now that I have grown up, I wonder if I have enough energy. They will take my son and teach him to use tools, to identify flora and fauna, to look up facts, to form and defend opinions, to launch projects, to ask the family for approval and to ride his sense of obligation like a skateboard into the corridors of power, a maker of policy. *Character*, which meant working harder than you had to and enjoying it. In fact, the sort of family that was supposed to have been abolished by Freud, old-age homes, the Pill, mother-in-law jokes, socialism, rigged quiz shows, and other manifestations of moral decline. You'll never see such a lively and confident anachronism again; come the revolution, we'll manacle every one of them to an ambiguity and drag them through the streets of qualm to dungeons of neurosis.

Hannah, trying to climb out of the passenger seat in the grocery cart, toppled onto the swordfish and curdled the anchovy paste with her screams.

Stephen had been solemnly collecting bags of potato chips. "My father," he said, "told me that potato chips are ears, clipped off the heads of bad people. Then *fried*. When you crunch them, the sounds are all the bad things the bad people heard and said while they were being bad. Is that right?"

"Probably. That's why potato chips give you pimples."

"What's a pimple?"

"A pimple is something that's too little to be a principle."

"What's a principle?"

"A principle is something you pretend is real, like the tooth fairy."

"If we planted pimples in the ground, would they grow up into potato chip bushes?"

"Ask your father."

And he would want to know, again, when his father was coming home. And, again, she would tell him. If only his father had *asked* his mother to come up, she would have been there, every weekend. Establish a policy: write an article about it.

In the afternoon, after Hannah's nap, they went to the river. Single sculls, oars like the wings of dragonflies, a Charles full of bottle caps and condoms. What did single scullsmen think about? The ax of the sun at the backs of their necks? The cords of veins in their forearms? What do goats think about? Tin cans and other goats? The green revolution? Her children were on strings from where she lay. As their paths crisscrossed, the strings were woven into a cord, a vein, a cable of blood. I should be reading. The white pages sucked at the black ink; columns of insect words were drowning; her mind was a palimpsest. Why did everything have to be so complicated?

Even taking a bath was complicated. Hannah, banished to the playpen; Stephen, furnished with a snack—a quiet obtained, and Marcy seized it, to bolt the bathroom door against her children. No sooner had she lowered herself into the tub and started thinking about Petronius when the howls began, and the small explosions. They had declared war in the living room. Stephen was pounding on her door. She was shouting at Stephen. Moans and sobs. I should have been a nun.

What did one wear to Cambridge parties this season? Saran Wrap? Sackcloth? Day-Glo paint and a pubic tassel? She decided against stockings. She decided in favor of a body shirt—eat your heart out, Beckwith—and pants. Sandals. Unpainted toenails. The tiniest bit of eye shadow. Not the tiniest bit of lipstick. Her hair crackled under the comb. She would leave it down, to the shoulders. She approved of her hair. Chestnut-colored, occasionally bursting into flames, although you needed a sunset behind you. She had always wanted to look like a Modigliani; certainly she felt like one.

A serape over the body shirt. Bundling up the children, their overnight camping equipment stuffed into Air France kit-bags. Swinging her fist of keys, all the locked doors of perception waiting for her. Tumblers will fall, like pigeons. The car was a barge, to bear her over the burning river.

Susan and Mike Culhane lived in a box. Everything was built

into the box except Susan and Mike, who merely rented it: book-cases, cabinets, closets, bed, even the lights. One felt that the box would go on humming and flushing whether anybody lived in it or not. If you opened the door to a kitchen cabinet, you couldn't open the door to the refrigerator, and vice versa. And yet Susan and Mike did not seem to require individuality of their appointments. They were in their second year of marriage; they played with each other like Yo-Yos; they could follow the spoor to their spores across the wall-to-wall carpeting to pillows propped up like tombstones, his and hers. Marcy envied them, because she had an excellent memory.

We never go out on Saturday nights, Susan told her. What, then, do you do on Saturday nights? We drink martinis, we eat roast beef, we watch as much television as we can stand, and then we go to bed, unless we happen to be in Wyke Regis, where we play bridge with my father and mother, and argue so viciously that we don't go to bed. They were proud of themselves; why shouldn't they be? Hannah sleeps through the night, said Marcy, and Stephen is exhausted. We've made up Mike's study for them, no problem, said Susan; you look *swell*. The box hummed. Hors d'oeuvres appeared from nowhere, cheeseboards, sausages on toothpicks, Syrian bread: as though the coffee table were a kind of huge electric toaster, popping up with goodies. Marcy declined a martini—not if she was going to Beckwith's party afterward—and had wine. They did not seem to find it odd that she was going alone to a party. Susan was of the opinion that her Coffin cousin was an idiot: they should mow down all the apple trees and raise peacocks instead. Mike sliced the rare roast beef so precisely that it fell upon their plates like tissues of a dissected brain, ready for mounting on slides for microscopic inspection. Marcy didn't really want to leave, but had to. You couldn't sit there all night watching them tickle each other's palms.

On arriving at Roger Beckwith's house near Fresh Pond, she turned off the motor and stayed at the wheel. She needed to decide on an attitude to take to the party. In what capacity was she showing up? As a systems break? A deviation hypothesis? An independent variable? Independent variable sounded good. Through the shrubbery, the house throbbed. She pulled at a ring on the door, and a squall of laughter greeted her. Roger had been playing with his tape recorders again.

She was let in by a girl wearing an MIT T-shirt and very little else. The girl had the face of something that had come up with the mushrooms, into which she was poking a Popsicle. She let Marcy in by leaving the door open and walking off with a switching of the ass that reminded Marcy of her ex-horse, Albertine. Marcy closed the door. The party was a kiln. All the attitudes and capacities were baking or cracking. Calcined deviation hypotheses. Friable Cantabrigians. The house had undergone a Canonical Variation since her last visit. Roger had pulled down a ceiling and knocked out a wall. The living room had been extended in two directions: two rooms long, two stories high, with a platform or balcony at the far end, on which motion-picture projectors had been mounted. They threw shadowy movies on the ceiling and walls, the seam between the two breaking the panels of the pictures, giving you dissociated chins and hips, feet and ears. Twin turntables and amplifying systems had obviously been hooked up in discotheque fashion, alternating loud rock musical groups. No one was dancing. From the balcony hung a steel star, formed by the Arabic numerals 1 through 5.

Roger appeared suddenly on the balcony, between the projectors. He was dressed entirely in purple, a turtleneck and tapered trousers ensemble, with a silver zipper slashing from his right shoulder across his chest to his left hipbone, then down the side of the pant leg to the bare foot. She thought of monitors patrolling the cross-walks at lunchtime in grammar school, their white belts, their lack of holsters. She waved at Roger. He waved back. Cupping her hands around her mouth, she shouted: "Where are the little people?" He grinned, indicated the bodies variously sprawled below him, motioned to her to stay put. He was fiddling with the projectors. The images altered: film footage of Nazi charnel houses, of blossoming bombs at Hiroshima, of napalmed Vietnamese children running in flames down roads away from tanks. Wagner on the stereo instead of rock.

On each side of the long living room benches had been yoked together. She tried to make sense of the objects arranged on the benches: eggs, serpents, pelicans, of metal, plaster, stone, glass, colored black, purple, silver, gold. Paintings and sketches of similar objects, and of crows, wolves, eagles. What looked like a chem lab in one corner: beakers, flasks, phials, basins, jugs, casseroles, candle-lamps, braziers, spatulas, hammers, ladles, shears, tongs, pestles and mortars. Dishes full of water, sand, and cloth, whose purpose it was impossible to guess. Situated among the couches and small tables in the center of the room were shapes of metal sculpture—cubes, icosahedrons, octahedrons, tetrahedrons—ranging in size from a domino to a pup tent. Roger sure knew how to throw up a party.

He presented himself to her like a marvelous and complicated gift. He kissed her hand. "I didn't think you'd come."

"Is there anything to drink?"

He led her to a stone crock and ladled something into a mug. "What is it?"

"Tequila and after-shave lotion," he said.

"After-shave lotion?"

"Marcy, you don't *remember*. Tetrahydrocannabinol. Delta 1."

"Ah, yes. The Being and Becoming racket. Programmed dreams." She peered into her mug as though it might bite her.

"A harmless high," he said. "Some salt will dehydrate you. The hang is over. Now over here I'm compounding something that will put ecstasy out of business." He picked up a pelican and dismembered it.

"What is it, Roger?"

"A kerotakis," he said.

"Let me ask the same question again. In a different way."

"Basically, it's a still. See: alembic, delivery spout, receiver, a tiny furnace. Like a Bunsen burner."

She was thirsty. She lapped at the mug, and enjoyed its scathing quality. "What are you compounding? A felony?"

"The Sophic Hydrolith," he said.

"Is it fattening?"

"The philosopher's stone," he explained. "You are not, perhaps, aware of the Enigma of Hermes. 'Unless you disembody the bodies and embody those without bodies, nothing which is expected will occur.' According to Geber, what we have here is not yet sufficiently decocted in the bowels of unclean."

"I should hope not. Roger, what is the meaning of that star? You *have* learned to count up to five at Insystec, haven't you?"

"There are five elements," said Roger. "Wood, fire, earth, metal, and water. There are five directions. North, east, west, south, and center. There are five eternal principles. The Creator, the soul, matter, time, and space."

"Five fingers to a clenched fist," said Marcy. "Five toes to an athlete's foot." Roger reminded her of Stephen.

"Yin," he said, "is feminine, watery, heavy, passive, earthy. Yang is masculine, fiery, light, positive, active. Let me quote Archelaus: 'Awaken from Hades! Arise from the tomb and rouse thyself from darkness! For thou has clothed thyself with spirituality and divinity, since the voice of the resurrection has sounded and the medicine of life has entered into thee.' Have some more after-shave lotion. It grows hair on your brain."

She refreshed herself at the crock. Ideograms had been scribbled all over the crock. Doubtless some Chinese blue joke. A crowd was gathering around Roger and his kerotakis, including the girl in the MIT T-shirt, whose nipples protruded like pretzel nuggets, and a number of pelicans whose eyes looked like ears to which Marcy wanted to apply Q-Tips. Where did Roger find these people?

"The investigation of perfection," said Roger. What, ho: one of the pelicans was Gerry LaForgue, who snorted at his section lady. Another, inevitably, was Segal, who grinned. Was Beckwith part of the *Crimson*'s executive competition? "This science," said Roger, "treats of the imperfect bodies of minerals, and teacheth how to perfect them; we therefore in the first place consider two things. Viz., *imperfection* and *perfection*. About these two our intention is occupied, and of them we propose to treat." LaForgue, outrageously, took Marcy's elbow; she made him give it back. "We compose this Book of Things, *perfecting* and *corrupting*, according as we have found by experience, because Contraries set near each other are the more manifest." Segal shook his head at LaForgue, still grinning, a manifest Contrary. Perfect, don't corrupt. Roger noticed Marcy's return. He parted the unseemliness of LaForgue and Segal, crossed her, cuffed an ear affectionately. "But perfect Bodies need not this preparation; yet they need such preparation as that, by which their Parts may be more Subtiliated, and they reduced from their *corporality* to a fixed *spirituality*. The intention of which is, of them to make a Spiritual fixed Body, that is, more attenuated and subtiliated than it was before." There was no one more attenuated than LaForgue, no one less subtiliated than Segal. Maybe Plimpton plays both sides of the street.

"Pre-emptive obfuscation," said Marcy. "What are you talking about?"

"Thomas Vaughan called it the torture of metals," said Roger, doing some strange things to his kerotakis. "Bonus observed: 'Nature generates frogs in the clouds, or by means of putrefaction in dust moistened with rain, by the ultimate disposition of kindred substances. Avicenna tells us that a calf was generated in the clouds, amid thunder, and reached the earth in a stupefied condition. The decomposition of a basilisk generates scorpions. In the dead body of a calf are generated bees, wasps in the carcass of an ass, beetles in the flesh of a horse, and locusts in that of a mule."

"Roger is into basilisks," said MIT.

"Basilisks deserve him," said Marcy. Rinsler was the frog; Roger was the scorpion; Coffin was the ass; LaForgue and Segal were beetles and locusts.

Roger took a strand of MIT's hair, and yanked on it. "*Aurum hispanicum*," he said. *Sea weedus*, thought Marcy. "Red copper, ashes of basilisks, human blood, and vinegar. Theophilus the Monk."

Marcy the bored. Segal took her mug and filled it. She accepted the mug, but not Segal, whose thoughts were headlines in eighty-point Bodoni, black acne. Clutching the mug, she risked the kitchen. It had been her experience that interesting people gathered in the kitchens of their hosts at parties, along with cockroaches and empty ice trays. Why was of no importance. Maybe they were into faucets. Anyway, they operated on the perpendicular. Perhaps their stamina made them more interesting. LaForgue followed her, his filament a worm, the brass buttons on his double-breasted sport coat trying to jump each other and king themselves. Marcy was conscious of the fact that LaForgue's sport coat was not the only double-breasted thing around. So was LaForgue. "Two thousand words," she said, "on Grottlesex as a substitute for handball." LaForgue, before deserting her, kissed the palm of her left hand; he had developed a bald spot the size of a Kennedy half-dollar; she was touched and didn't want to be. He walked away as though disdain were adhesive and stuck to the parquet floor. His soles squeaked.

In Roger's kitchen, five people had laced their arms and hands together to stitch a trampoline, a seat-suspension system such as one discovered under the upholstery of one's sagging car. A web, which they lowered to their knees and elevated until their elbows clicked. They dropped themselves into a well and hoisted buckets of air, invisible: with the earnestness of children trying out their first three-wheeler. "Love's Body," said the communicants, who were not interesting. De odor is rizing, thought Marcy. In Laforgueing the ribald one Rinslered love's body, Segals clausing, onto and into the breech.

Love's Body cauliflowered into fondling. Are we all so bored, full of holes, seeking stoppers? The kitchen trembled with a need to be kneaded: I dough nut what to you. Glazed today, gulped tomorrow. In the be-sinning was the verb, four French letters. Bull-full of stock exchange. Gland-full of trouble, bush in the bird. It was easier for strangers to talk with their glands; pubic speaking. She watched this thicket of exerting arms, ego-less huff 'n' puff. Don't they know their placenta? For the last time that night, she was not impressed.

She found a passageway leading to stairs that probably aspired to the balcony. There was a poster stapled up in the hall, hand-lettered, in colors all along the vomit spectrum:

THE EMERALD TABLE

(*Tabula Smaragdina*)

Ascribed to Hermes or the Egyptian Thoth,
God of Math & Science

True it is, without falsehood, certain and most true. That which is above is like to that which is below, and that which is below is like to that which is above, to accomplish the miracles of one thing.

As all things were by the contemplation of one, so all things arose from this one thing by a single act of adaptation.

The father thereof is the Sun, the mother the Moon.

The Wind carried it in its womb, the Earth is the nurse thereof. It is the father of all works of wonder throughout the world. The power thereof is perfect.

If it be cast on to Earth, it will separate the element of Earth from that of Fire, the subtle from the gross.

With great sagacity it doth ascend gently from Earth to Heaven.

Again it doth descend to Earth, and uniteth in itself the force from things superior and things inferior.

Thus wilt thou possess the glory of the brightness of the whole world, and all obscurity will fly far from thee.

This thing is the strong fortitude of all strength, for it overcometh every subtle thing and doth penetrate every solid substance.

Thus was the world created.

Hence there will be marvelous adaptations achieved, of which the manner is this.

For this reason I am called Hermes Trismegistus, because I hold three parts of the wisdom of the whole world.

That which I had to say about the operation of Sol is completed.

Hermes was obviously talking about a semiattached policy studies center.

"Touch me!" said a young man blocking her path in the hall. She could swear he had been knit together out of gold lamé; he looked like a banana popping its skin. "Touch me!"

"Where?"

"It doesn't matter where."

"It certainly does!"

"Then *here*."

"Certainly not."

"Seed of the dragon," he said, "Scythian water, water of the moon, milk of a black cow."

"Ravings of a demented mind," said Marcy. Had she conjured him out of her mug? She tried to drink him down.

"But what light do you shed," he said, "you doctors of Montpellier, Vienna, and Leipzig? About as much light as a Spanish fly in a dysentery stool!" He began to weep. She patted him on his metallic shoulder. He reached for, and was refused, a breast. Remarkably calm now, he said: "Do you know Digby's cure for a toothache? You scratch the gums near the aching tooth with an iron nail and then hammer the blood-covered nail into a wooden beam."

"Isn't it simpler," she said, "to go back seventeen trillion years and remember when Ron Hubbard planted his Gorilla Goal in you?"

"Ron Hubbard? Is he here tonight?"

"No. He had to check out a capping beam on Helatrobus."

"I've never been to Helatrobus. Do they accept travelers'checks?"

The conversation was deteriorating. So was her capacity to focus. She squeezed by him with a minimum of intimacy. He followed her. It seemed uphill to Roger, and the steel star was melting. The numbers were running away to find their prime. Roger was *primus inter pares*, because of his natural sense of logarithm. Whatever he was doing, it caused smoke, wisps of which made her want to sneeze. Yet the smell was sweet. It curled in the brain, then hooked it. Probably illegal.

Roger was wolf-faced: "Purge the original material of all that is thick, nebulous, opaque, and dark in it, by means of our Pontic water, which is sweet, beautiful, clear, limpid, brighter than gold, diamonds or carbuncles." He gave Marcy another draft of after-shave lotion. He was gloomy. "Purification, distillation, ablution, grinding, roasting, calcination, mortification, sublimation, proportion, incineration, decomposition, solidification, fixation, cleansing, liquefaction, projection."

Marcy sat down on the floor, scissoring her legs, a mendicant. Cup me. She felt she would topple, like Hannah, or as if she had been bending over and brushing her hair too long, down, blood sloshing in the skull cavity: how many strokes? The numbers kidnapped her. Banana-boy palmed her knee. Laforgue was back, and Segal, grinning stanchions.

"Then," said Roger, "the extracted body, soul, and spirit must be distilled and condensed together by their own proper salt." He muttered on about mercurial water, egg-shaped phials, amalgams. She whispered to banana he should split; she preferred black acne and brass buttons, the pedagogical imperative. ("Hi, Teach," said Segal. "You bet," said Marcy.) Roger, again: "Combination takes place slowly, one mingling with the other gently and imperceptibly as ice with warm water. This union is compared to that of a bride and bridegroom. When it is complete the remaining fifth of water is added a little at a time, in seven installments; the phial is then sealed, to prevent evaporation or loss of odor, and maintained at hatching temperature. The stages are these: raven's head, black as charcoal; granular bodies, like fishes' eyes; a circle around the substance, first reddish, then white, green, and yellow, like a peacock's tail; dazzling white; deep red. The fire rarefies soul and spirit, they combine into permanent, indissoluble Essence, of a beautiful purple which cures all imperfect bodies." The purple of Roger.

The music now was something harsh and Indian, a saw applied to the arteries. The pictures had become blobs, as though the walls had mouths and were trying with difficulty to breathe. Marcy identified a nostril. Roger transferred his proper salt from kerotakis to what looked like a water pipe. "A bodily substance," he said, "compounded of one, or by one, thing, and more precious by conjoining nearness and effect, and with the same natural connection converting naturally with better policies." His policies, for he sat down on her other side and lay his hand in her lap like a kitten. Wearily, he said: "I'm trying to put it all together. Egyptian magic, Greek philosophy, gnosticism, neo-Platonism, Babylonian astrology, Christian theology, pagan mythology. It's a pain in the anterior pituitary gland." She admired the kitten, which had a nostril on each finger, a bundle of sniffers. "Ye may not, according to Stephanos, overwhelm the moving things with much matter," said Roger. "Ye may not think about saffron of Cilicia and the plant of anagallis, and the Pontic rhubarb for themselves, and of other juices, gall of quadrupeds and certain beasts, of stones and destructive minerals, things that are dissimilar to the perfection-making, single, and one nature." The sniffers rubbed. They puffed at the water pipe. Flowers exploded in Marcy's head, their bloody petals settling like red snowflakes on her arterial scheme, flowing out through extension cords to the kitchen, the balcony, the five-numbered steel-starred clock that melted on the time it took to amalgamate nostrils, kittens, knees, bananas, flowers, serpents, carbuncles, pelicans, peacocks. It was unthinkable not to puff in the Cambridge of 1967, your thoughts heroic spiders, their legs needles, the walls of the mind a web, love's body dispersed on seas of film that blobbed and weaved, tides of let's-try-anything. "Ouroboros, the self-eating serpent," said Roger. "He never saw a Mobius Loop, alas." A lapping on shores of her; Arabic starfish; the lights going out all over Fresh Pond. "O moon," said Roger, "clad in white and vehemently shining abroad whiteness, let us learn what is the lunar radiance that we may not miss what is doubtful. For the same is the whitening snow, the brilliant eye of whiteness, the bridal procession-robe of the management of the process, the stainless chiton, the mind-constructed beauty of fair form, the whitest composition of the perfection, the coagulated milk of fulfillment, the moon-froth of the sea of dawn, the most worthy pearl, the flame-bearing moonstone, the most gold besprinkled chiton, the food of the liquor of gold, the chrysocosmic spark, the victorious warrior, the royal covering, the veritable purple, the most worthy garland, the sulphur without fire, the ruler of bodies, the entire yellow species, the hidden treasure, that which has the moon as couch." A puffing that put eyes on the needle legs of the spiders; they walked on diamond foam. "For it is white as seen, but yellow as apprehended, the bridegroom to the allotted moon, the golden drop falling from it, the glorious emanation from it, the unchangeable embrace, the indelible orbit, the God-given work, the marvelous making of gold." Of whom? She was the paddle, her body a canoe, the blobs diamonds, the spiders clocks, the moon an eye to which a kitten clung. "According to Tertullian," said Roger, "the magic arts were taught to mortal women by angels who fell in love with them. They laid bare the secrets of the metals, they made known the virtues of plants and the power of magical incantations and described those singular doctrines which extend to the science of the stars." You see how easy it is if only you are the edge, the cutting edge, the sharpness and not the blade, the idea of the sword and not the sword, the point and not the stress that yields the point, the light and not the crystal that contains the light, the fusing and not the elements that must be made to fuse, Ouroboros sans serpent. "Fission and fusion," said Roger. "Relativity. The conversion of mass into energy, energy into mass. Someone tipped them off. Democritus. Zosimos. Bonus. Magnus. Aquinas. Razi will save my Bacon. Thoth-control." To inhale was to become thirsty; to drink from the mug was to seek smoke as an adsorbent. Moonstones rattled like dice in her music box, a caromming among daggers that were electrified, on sore, bending walls, beneath which stamped circuitry transisted, states less than solid, shadows on flies' eyes, elision. Marcy's sandals were unstrapped by Segal. Banana-boy clutched himself at the pearl, fell forward head-first between the chicken wings of his gold lamé. The music was organs, Handel. Roger said: "I fell asleep and I saw standing before me at an altar shaped like a dome, a priest sacrificing. There were fifteen steps to mount to this altar. The priest stood there, and I heard a voice from above saying: *I have accomplished the act of descending the fifteen steps walking toward the darkness and the act of mounting the steps going toward the light. It is a sacrifice that renews me, eliminating the dense nature of the body. Thus by necessity consecrated, I become a spirit.* Having heard the voice of him who stood at the altar, I asked him who he was. In a shrill voice he answered in these words:

I am Ion, priest of the sanctuaries, and I undergo intolerable violence. Someone has come hastily in the morning and has done violence upon me, cleaving me asunder with a sword and dismembering me according to the rules of combination. He has removed the skin from my head with the sword which he held; he has mixed my bones with my flesh and has burned them with the fire of the treatment. It is thus I have learned of the transformation of the body to become a spirit. Such is this intolerable violence."
For his hand, Roger substituted his head in Marcy's lap. The pipe was their lollipop. "While he yet conversed with me, and I forced him to speak, his eyes became like blood and he vomited all his flesh and I saw him changed to a little imitation man, rend himself with his teeth and sink down. Filled with fear, I awoke and reflected—*Is this not the composition of the waters?* I was persuaded that I had rightly understood and I fell asleep again. I saw the same dome-shaped altar and at the upper part a water boiling and many people circulating continuously. And there was no one outside of the altar whom I could question. I then moved toward the altar to see this spectacle, and I perceived a little man, a barber, whitened with years, who asks me, *What dost thou look upon?* I answered that I was surprised to see the agitation of the water and of the men burned yet living. He answered in these words: *This spectacle that thou seest is the entrance, the departure, and the mutation.* I asked him, *What mutation?* and he replied, *This is the place of the operation called maceration, for the men who wish to obtain virtue enter here and become spirits after having escaped from the body.* Then said I, *Art thou a spirit?* and he answered, *Yes, a spirit and a guardian of spirits.*" She put her head on the floor, regarded bleeding shadows on the raftered ceiling, LaForgue's bald spot. Roger puffed, and with pouched cheeks kissed her, spinning on an elbow near her music box, poured smoky gold into her mouth, and coughed before continuing: "During our conversation, the boiling continuing to increase and the people uttering cries of lamentation, I saw a man of copper holding in his hand a tablet of lead. Looking at the tablet, he spoke the following words: *I command all those who have submitted to the punishment to be calm, to take one each a tablet of lead, to write with their own hands, to keep their eyes lifted, and their mouths open until their vintage be developed.*" Her basilisk was going to generate a lot of scorpions; she was, in

parallel bars, a dichotomy about to split, a spurt of scorpions, of worry beads. Nostrils in the armpits; a burning bush; banana-boy peeling. "The act followed the word, and the master of the house said to me, *Thou hast contemplated, thou hast stretched thy neck upward and seen what has been done.* I replied that I had seen, and he explained to me, *He whom thou seest is the man of copper, he is the master of the sacrifices and is the sacrificed. It is he who vomits his own flesh. Authority has been given him over this water and over the people here punished.* After this vision, I awoke again and said, *What is the meaning of this vision? Is not this water, white, yellow, and boiling, the water divine?* And I found that I had well comprehended. In the dome-shaped altar all things are blended, all are dissociated, all things unite, all things combine, all things are mixed and all are separated, all things are moistened and all are dried, all things flourish and all things wither. Indeed for each it is by method, by measure, by exact weight of the five elements that the mixing and separation of all things take place." She was the dome, concavity, convexity, burning glass, the lens on the eye that ignites, copper, altar, sacrifice. Vectors in geeselike V-formations attacked her pelvis, her rib cage; grabbed her throat; thumbed out the bulbs of her eyes on nerve wires charged, discharged, tremors along the fault lines of the egg about to hatch a copper-colored pelican. "In short, my friend, build a monolith temple as of white lead, as of alabaster, having neither commencement nor end in its construction. Let it have in its interior a spring of pure water, sparkling like the sun. Observe carefully on which side is the entrance to the temple, and taking in your hand a sword, seek then the entrance for the place is narrow where the opening is to be found. A serpent is lying at the entrance guarding the temple. Seize him, immolate him, flay him, and taking his flesh and his bones, separate his members. Then joining the members with the bones, make of them a step to the entrance of the temple, mount upon it, and enter. Thou wilt find what thou seekest. The priest, this man of copper, whom thou seest seated in the spring gathering to himself the color—do not consider him as a man of copper, for he has changed the color of his nature and has become a man of silver. If thou wishest, thou wilt soon have him a man of gold. Relying upon the clearness of these concepts of intelligence, transform the nature and consider manifold matter as being one. Never reveal clearly to anyone any such property, but be sufficient unto thyself for fear that in speaking thou bringest destruction on thyself." It was important to bring back her eyes. They rolled away like marbles. Like the universe, she had begun as a continuous mass of hot gas, and was expanding, dispersing, the ponderable matter of her fleeing from a still point in space, a frozen, timeless idea of herself. On the hi-fi system, they were torturing something, not metals: animals. Computer music that moaned through stone caverns to enter the vacancy she had created by her dispersal. She was afraid of dying. "Roger, I don't want to die. Roger, I am very sick." They were helping her to her feet. But she hadn't any feet. She had slipped through the net of her cells and was falling. Away. Their hands tried to save her. Too late. The hall, the stairs. "In a place in the far West," said Roger, "where tin is found, there is a spring which rises from the earth and gives rise to tin like water. When the inhabitants of this region see that it is about to spread beyond its source, they select a young girl remarkable for her beauty and place her entirely nude below it, in a hollow of the ground, in order that it shall be enamored by the beauty of the young girl. It springs at her with a bound seeking to seize her; but she escapes by running rapidly while the young people keep near her holding axes in their hands. As soon as they see it approach the young girl, they strike and cut it, and it comes of itself into the hollow and of itself solidifies and hardens. They cut it into bars and use it." They were on the balcony. They were at a door. They were through the door. She was looking at a window that was a wall. "Beautiful, isn't it?" said Roger. She was reduced to insect-consciousness. She registered, but she did not record, she could not analyze. The window was full of silent explosions of light. "Colored filters," said Roger. "I've wired the spectrum of light to the amplifier on the hi-fi. The sound band is attached to the spectrum. As the sound changes, so does the light. I'm making harmonies visible. It's like looking into your own body." "Roger—" "Here, drink some of this. You're among friends." The mug again, which her hands couldn't find, so the mug found her. Her friends helped her onto the bed. Her friends undid the buttons on her body shirt, slipped her arms out of the sleeves, unhooked the bra. So many friendly hands on her shoulders, her breasts. In the window: fleurs-de-lys. "The yellow lilies lie down with the snow-white lion," said Roger. "Thus the lion will be tamed, thus the yellow lilies will flourish." The pants came next. Of what use was this awareness? The naked girl, the spring of tin? They found her eye at last, between her legs, weeping. They soothed it. She had at least stopped falling; she floated, on wings spread from the eye. In front of the window: purple Roger, unzipping himself, emerging from himself like a barber pole, his red rings streaming to his feet. There were hands on her wings, tongues in her eye. "*Aurea progenies plumbo prognata parente*," said Roger. "A golden daughter born of a leaden parent." The making of gold, the making of silver, the making of gems, the making of purple, the making of Marcy. She already had one volunteer husband. There were so many volunteers. "Unless you disembody the bodies and embody those without bodies, nothing which is expected will occur," said Roger. Something inside her, a slipperiness. So simple, really. Gastrointestinal and urinary tract activity, at the start. Salivation is restrained or stopped. The secretion of gastric juices and the peristaltic movements of the intestines are inhibited. Digestion slows down. Malfunction of the colon and bladder. "Perfecting and corrupting," said Roger. "Contraries set near each other are the more manifest. Attenuated. Subtiliated. No more corporality." The weight was tolerable. Roger was insane. It was much simpler. Activity in the circulatory system. Constriction of the blood vessels of the gut. More blood flowing to brain and muscle. Increased heart rate, rising blood pressure. Parasympathetic compensatory reflexes are activated when the rise in blood pressure stimulates pressure-receptors in the carotid sinus. Pulse rate and blood pressure abruptly fall. Heart slows. Who is inside her? Which volunteer? "This thing is the strong fortitude of all strength," said Roger, "for it overcometh every subtle thing and doth penetrate every solid substance." Glandular activity. Adrenal medulla innervated by sympathetic system, discharging epinephrine and norepinephrine secretions into the blood. Stimulation of adrenal cortex and its hormones by adrenocorticotrophic hormone of the pituitary gland, which has been stimulated by hypothalamic activity. "Combination takes place slowly, one mingling with the other gently and imperceptibly as ice with warm water. Raven's head, fishes' eyes, peacock's tail. Seed of the dragon." Sweat glands secrete to dissipate heat generated by strenuous muscle activity and increased metabolism. Muscles at the base of hair follicles contract. Respiratory irregularities. Bronchioles dilation of the lungs, stepping up exchange of oxygen and carbon dioxide. Changes in the electrical resistance of the skin. "Moon-froth of the sea of dawn." Early phase of reaction: sacral portion of the parasympathetic system dominant . . . erectile tissues of genitalia innervated by sacral nerve group. "Most worthy pearl, the flame-bearing moonstone." Middle phase: short-term dominance of sympathetic system . . . ejaculation as sympathetic reflex activity. "Bridegroom to the allotted moon, the golden drop falling from it. Dome-shaped altar, entrance to the temple, sword." Late phase: secondary assertion of parasympathetic dominance associated with overcompensation, which is defined as *relief*, which is what we call pleasure. And then you start all over again. It's autonomic, really. I get laid with a little help from my friends. "The food of the liquor of gold," said Roger. And she couldn't breathe. She was choking. There was something alive in her mouth. The Ouroboros serpent. The whole writhing world was in her mouth, and her hatred of that world came up from the eye between her legs to meet it, to eat it alive. Her teeth were fangs. She sank them into it. She was going to bit off the head of the world, the serpent. She tasted blood. The screaming seemed to go on for hours.

Maybe it had gone on for hours. She became aware of no more weight. She could breathe. She couldn't see, but she could breathe. She touched her breasts with her hands. They were still there. She slid her hands down her body. It was still there. Sore, but there. She couldn't see because she hadn't opened her eyes. She opened them. All the colors had died, and the window was asleep. Roger was not asleep. He was on the floor under the window, in a fetal crouch, clutching himself, whimpering. She sat up on the bed. It felt like any army had trooped through her. How many of them had there been? She couldn't remember. Five would have been Roger's style. Five elements, five directions, five eternal principles, five bastards using her as a toilet bowl. She stood, and embraced herself to contain the trembling. Actually, she wasn't trembling as much as Roger. She walked over to him and pushed at his shoulder with her foot. He rolled over onto his back. His eyes were closed. His face was wet. He still covered himself with his hands. The hands were bloody. Fine. She hoped he hadn't gotten around to having a booster shot for tetanus. She hoped that her teeth were caked with bacteria. She kicked him in the face.

I have to go pee. She considered, and rejected, the idea of doing it in Roger's face. Her clothes were gone. Roger's purple zip-suit was there, but her clothes were not. I've got to get out of here. But she needed to find a bathroom even more, which was ridiculous. Everything has been destroyed, everything, and I have to go to the bathroom. She found a bathroom adjoining Roger's gym. She washed her mouth out with soap. She returned to the bedroom door and opened it a crack. The house was silent. She stepped out onto the balcony. Love's body had dismembered, devoured itself; the cannibals had all gone home. Naked, she ventured down the stairs and walked through the living room. She stopped to sniff at the kerotakis and the water pipe. She found the MIT T-shirt—I hope she had as much fun as I did—but not her clothes. She took some satisfaction in toppling all the eggs and pelicans off their perches and watching them shatter. There was nothing for it but to return to the bedroom. She paused on the balcony to throw the movie projectors over the railing into the living room below.

"I need a doctor," Roger said.

"Fuck you," she replied. She put on his purple suit and descended again. There was a phone on the wall in the kitchen. She called the police, reporting anonymously that all kinds of dangerous drugs could be found at a certain address in Fresh Pond, then hung up. Her purse with the car keys was at the front door where she had left it. She went out into what appeared to be dawn, on which she wasn't moon-froth. I wasn't even wearing a diaphragm, she thought.

On the whole, she would have preferred Rinsler.

Twelve

HE KNOWS AS LITTLE ABOUT WOMEN as he knows about Albany Jackson and Otis DeKalb, who did not return the station wagon last night. Photographs of his mother hadn't been of much help. During the war, he was raised by women in Wyke Regis, while the Mackenzie men went off to board rooms in Washington or on diplomatic missions to Latin America. Because Nicholas Coffin worried about U-boats in Boston harbor torpedoing the Massachusetts Bay Cordage Company, his son had been packed off to Thomas Hill, which was full of women. But the rooms of the house were masculine, even in the absence of men. Supper was served at the hour Wallace Mackenzie preferred it, whether or not he was there to eat it. No one smoked cigarettes in the library. The croquet court was mowed and rolled, although unused. There were maps on the walls of the billiard room—Europe, Africa, Asia —and flag pins which the women moved around to indicate who was fighting on what front. No Mackenzie died; their brains were more important than their bodies in the effort against the Axis powers. No Mackenzie ever seemed to die unnaturally, except his mother. Rooms full of purpose. A steamer trunk, stocked with the long gowns of women who had been married to the men in the portraits, a musky odor: the purposes of the hooks and sashes, the collapsible cages of cloth, the gatherings of silk into dimpled cushions, were unimaginable. He cannot recall having seen a pair of stockings drying on a shower rail, a brassiere in a hamper, panties on a clothesline.

It was not his father but his uncle, John Mackenzie, who explained the facts of life to him, as though it were a difficult problem in solid geometry. Perhaps his father hadn't known the facts. It was Susan Mackenzie, John's daughter, who had in the bathhouse at the pond, while they were changing into swimming suits, assured him on inspection that he was perfectly normal. He was eleven; they hadn't done anything about his normality but look at it. It was Cecile, James's daughter, who inadvertently supplied him with an example of perfection, later that summer: he was fishing for trout from the dam, alone and luckless, when she arrived on horseback, tethered the horse to a birch, went down to the dock, and removed her clothes. Unseen, he thought, he watched her walk to the end of the diving board and pause there for what seemed forever, white as the moon. He was astonished to discover the existence of nipples; and that she had pubic hair was like God telling you a secret. She jackknifed into the water and swam straight to the dam, where he stood paralyzed, a spike having been hammered through his skullcap, his stomach, the soles of his feet. "Hi, Kenny," she said. "The water's like a *bathtub*." She pulled herself up beside him to sun for a moment on the concrete abutment. "Catch anything?" The beads of water on her breasts might as well have been his tears. She swam back to the dock, put back on her clothes, got back on her horse, and trotted off. He hasn't forgotten her; he has even thought of her sometimes while making love to Marcy. She would marry a man who ran a fry shop in Brattleboro, Vermont, nineteen pieces of greasy chicken in a basket, no napkins.

It was, finally, Lucinda who showed him what to do with his normality. She was the oldest child of one of those itinerant families that seemed to arrive in Wyke Regis every summer when there was farm work to be done, in old trucks piled with bed-springs and rolls of linoleum. Her straw-colored hair had been home-cut to look like a broom. Her black eyes were too big for her small face, and didn't go with the hair. Her breasts, unlike Cecile's, were the size of teacups. Her rump was a pair of fists. She claimed to be part Indian, should have been in high school, wasn't. Their courtship was as formal as algebra, complete with special systems of notation, special systems of relationship, co-efficients, finite terms, and a closed field. The finite terms were three weeks. The closed field was the West Orchard, where they went to pick blueberries off bushes growing near what will now be called Rinsler's culvert, full of Dodges. First, they fed each other blueberries by hand; then by tongue; then tongues without blueberries, hands without stop. He persuaded her to unwind the bandage she called a blouse. She allowed as how she would rub him a little, but that was the limit. When he got below the waist, she bit his ear, until he learned to use his fingers for something besides scratching. When she at last agreed to let him see all of her at once, away from the culvert, under apple trees that seemed to him as safe as cathedrals, he soiled himself like a two-year-old. "It isn't the first time," she said. The next time, the next afternoon, he was, as she put it, permitted to sharpen his pencil in her machine. Someone has arranged things so that such initiations are as solemn as they are historic. He wrote poems for her. She vanished. One morning they were just gone, Lucinda, her family, the truck, the bedsprings, the linoleum. Whoever arranged things had used an eraser, and the equation was wiped off the blackboard. His Uncle John told him: "Two of the children in that family were Lucinda's." He hated everyone in the world but her; he didn't know what to do with his gratitude; he gave up writing poems.

Afterward, there had been what he supposed were the usual skirmishes: the girl in the camel's hair coat, who refused to take it off, before, during and after the football game; the folk singer from Simmons, who made a list of the unnatural acts she would not perform, most of which he hadn't even heard of, and they both signed it, and she was so bored by the time they got to bed that she fell asleep; a blind date so plain and so anxious to please that they wanted to kill each other for what he did to her; a researcher at *Scope* who was working her way up the masthead of the magazine, man by man; the young women in the blue bars of hotels, skyscraper lounges, frightened out of their wits by people on the street, by people on the next stool, by people in the corridor, behind the door, under the bed, inside the bottle, wrestling matches with death.

From these, he learned nothing useful about the way women

think, choose, settle for, desire; what their idea of the past, the future, the world, was. From *Lady Chatterly's Lover* he learned that he lacked ingenuity, but in his skirmishings he hadn't met a Lady Chatterly. Nor a Dostoyevskian Grushenka, for that matter. He found André Gide clear, but incomprehensible; the emotions made no sense. On the banks of, and the footbridges over, the Charles he saw evidence of a more meaningful dialectic: serious talk, secret laughter, profound silence, weightless mooning-about, love under a glass bell. (He would see it again in Paris; he would find it himself, he thought, in Pithiviers.) He longed for something like that: to be chosen, and to know why. A picnic hamper, the thigh of a bird, white wine in paper cups, discussions about Antigone, rain showers, discovering another self, a magnetic field, a sense of closure. Strength, serenity, children: the impossible clutter in the attic of the romantic imagination. In order not to hurt people, or to be hurt by them, you must know them. I do not know the person who matters most to me in a world that seems chiefly populated by maniacal toys, machines for doing damage.

What impressed him immediately about Marcy was her dignity, her composure. She had created herself. He approved of the job, the brown eyes that didn't blink, amber lights in the hair, her collarbone, the way she removed an earring when she was on the telephone, the way she allowed her hands to be silent when they touched something, especially him, the fact that she noticed more than he did, remarked on it more readily, judged. Even to watch her reading, or playing the piano, was to be seized with remorse that you were not the book, the keys, while at the same time to be filled with an inordinate satisfaction that you were being permitted to watch. To have behaved in a fashion so wholly uncharacteristic—to have embarrassed himself in the Paris bureau without caring, to have chased her halfway to Spain—seems even now both a proof of his love and the only good thing he has ever done. What else could he do? He returned to a hotel room that had been designed for misanthropes, and his thoughts were mice in the wainscoting. He went out onto a balcony that drooped like a lower lip from the gray hotel, and her face obscured a St. Sulpice he considered charming, her giggle muted the pigeons, a gendarme actually waved at him, he drank warm champagne, and for the only time in his life he believed in the existence of luck.

That ever since he has sought to be as uncharacteristic, as impetuous, as willing on a moment's notice to act, a volunteer instead of a witness, is not an embarrassment, it is another proof. Luck exacts its tithe.

In six years, you should learn something about the woman you love. He thought he had. She goes to sleep, and she wakes up, reluctantly. In between is work, which improves her temper. Her anger is offhand, easily dissipated by confronting it with some absurdity, some incongruity, a gift of a child or a husband who wants to be reassured that his crime isn't capital. She is, has always been, judgmental: the act counts; the ambiguities, the roiling motives, may be interesting but are not morally important. The things that matter most to her express themselves in brittle wit, pieces of glass that cut the fingers, if not the throat, but are nevertheless defensive: her feelings are as easily bruised as Hannah's skin; she does not want to suffer injury; she has only words—a demonstration of superior, disinterested intelligence—to protect her; irony disarms, disables. She is alone in her referents, metaphors, puns, priestess of a privacy one invades at enormous risk. One nevertheless invades it; it is a magical, generous room, very much like a glass bell, a place of trust. Invasions, surrenders, have to be negotiated, must be mutual, are always risky, depend on generosity, and yield whatever meaning there is to the history of private lives. It is not necessary in bed with her—it is not even desirable—to be a technician, a systems analyst of the nerve bundles and the hormone secretions, attempting to manipulate a bigger bomb for a smaller buck, everybody dying at the same time, just as the computer printout predicted. They come near each other, go away, return, defer, prolong. It is art, not science. It takes place in a cloud, not a Pentagon. It proposes no Hiroshimas calculated to the micro-second, a-bed and abroad. It requires listening. He believes that sex is the only sacrament with space for humor. He believes—

He believes lies. If Marcy has gone to Rinsler's lighthouse to pawn the confidences of their marriage for some sensational loose change, then her husband's articles of faith have been rewritten by a hack pornographer, a playboy after dark. Rinsler is a khaki-colored penguin. What would he do, fuck her with his beak? And afterward the printout from between her legs would be her husband's dossier? Would they wipe themselves with old love letters instead of Kleenex? It makes him sick, even trying to imagine it, because adultery is unimaginable to him. If his marriage is not a sanctuary, it is less than a business deal, a stock transfer, a dwindling margin. Not because they own each other's bodies, but because the history of their bodies together is an integral part of the history of their lives together: the integument and the ligature of all that they know about each other. The sanctuary is a space; their bodies are one of its dimensions; their minds are another; their sharing is a third. Remove one of the dimensions and what you have left is a cartoon, not a marriage. Unimaginable: and yet he is obliged to imagine it. *I would not have, I have not, done this to her.* And to choose Rinsler . . . it would be more than a betrayal, it would be an insult.

He is aware at six o'clock in the morning, slamming pans around in the kitchen to bang them out of sleep, leaving cigarettes to burn off the edges of the counters, queasy of stomach—he is aware of self-pity. Wounded pride. All right. But his self-esteem, his pride, are aspects of his marriage; they depend on it. If one of the legs he stands on has been lopped off, he is entitled to consider himself wounded. Rinsler's insinuations are undoubtedly lies. But if they are lies, how does Rinsler know about Stephen? *What is going on in her head?* And so he knows nothing about women, about his wife. And he had lectured Lavonia on the meaning of marriage. There is the shadow of a boot above his glass bell.

He carries the winch with him to the farm: perhaps he can use it to hang Rinsler, blame it on Israeli agents. The station wagon is not at the camp, either. Jackson and DeKalb have gone off to Canada with Marcy. A trade was arranged through James T. Worthless: Cindy Lou, and a gopher hole to be named later. Jackson has stolen my car; Rinsler has stolen my battery. He could ask at camp about the station wagon, but even if they knew, they would not tell. Jackson is the only one who tells him anything. He gets into the truck, the winch beside him on the seat. He rumbles the truck up to the cabin and sits there. He will not honk. He has no purpose to communicate. He is acquiring indifference. If they want to pick, they can haul-ass. If they want to watch television, they can jerk off into the electrical sockets. The underground railroad doesn't run on time; this one is over a hundred years late. Murdock is down in the pit, opening up the tractor hoods, counting batteries. Short is somewhere up on ramps,

Dennison beneath him on the creeper, with the trouble-lamp, looking at his busted crank-face. Stragglers emerge, half a dozen of them, Foy the only decent picker. Foy takes one look into the cab of the truck, decides Rollin has the downs, joins the others in the rear. He carries them into the orchard, and he does not go back for coffee.

She wanted to tell me about the others, the men before me; I didn't want to hear about it. It wasn't important. It was *before*. What was important was not to *compare*. She told me anyway, a little. The French instructor at Berkeley. I wanted to strangle him. He hurt her. No one has a right to hurt her. I would fly to California, find him, peel off his skin like a potato, use his spine to pole-vault back to her. Too much information clogs the computer, mangles the printout.

There is no talking or singing in the orchard this morning. No bitching, either. Foy has been watching the Nova Scotians pick; he handles his ladder like a sword, dispatching trees. I wonder if you can pierce ears with a paper punch; then the women could hang foreskins from rings on both sides of their heads, while drinking semen from C-cups and playing mah-dong. Rinsler is obviously lying. But why would Rinsler lie? What's in it for him? Who's it in Marcy?

Noon surprises him. He resents it. No more work. Motions fend off emotions. He carries them back again, and collects the checks from Abigail Murdock. Still no station wagon. He enters the cabin. No Jackson, no Richmond, no DeKalb. No Skinny Reid, Jimmy Lee Allen, their brothers, Gerald Walker, Spider-man Lavalle. The rest are waiting for him to take them down to town, since Leroy won't. To cash their checks at the one gas station, the one drugstore, the one diner, that will accept them. To walk then down the highway, a black platoon, a bunch of Martians, to the state liquor store, emerging with brown paper parcels, hiking then back up the hill toward the farm, to arrive there all hours of the afternoon, alone and in pairs, from the woods, from back roads, giggly and sullen, for an appointment with the dice. He takes them down. He always tries to do what's expected of him.

And later parks the truck at the cottage. Rinsler, D'Allesandro and Ransome are down in the grove, conferring over the millstone which has been tipped on its ear on an elm stump to make a cocktail table. The grove used to be the site of an outhouse, back in the days when Hannah Mackenzie was a child and still alive. Pines grew up around it; indoor plumbing made possible a playpen, whose ceiling soared as in a chapel, the sky dropping through a gear work of top branches. They do not belong there, but at least they are out of the house.

He opens a can of beer. He puts Bartók on the phonograph. He tries to call Marcy, and there is no answer. He goes upstairs and finds that the papers on his desk have been pawed over. He considers skewering Rinsler on a ski pole. He harks, through Bartók, a knocking on his door. It must be Madame Bovary. It is, instead, Foy with a wad of cash that would choke a Rinsler.

"I said I'd keep your check for you. But Jesus, *cash?* This isn't a bank. I don't even lock the house."

"I *needs* cash, Rollin. But the craps come over all ugly Saturday evenins. Stinkweed an' knives." He is listening to the Bartók. No, he is looking at the phonograph. "You jes' hide it in a hole some-wheres, 'til I ast you for it?"

He hides it in a hole behind the volume of the Encyclopaedia Britannica—fourteenth edition, 1937—that contains a notation on electrical engineering. "Foy, you don't happen to know where Jackson and DeKalb went with my station wagon, do you? I mean, I loaned it to them last night, and they aren't back yet."

Foy disengages his eyes from the phonograph. Calculates. White man much stupid. "No shit, Rollin, they took yo' *car?*"

"I loaned it. And it's not really mine. It belongs to the farm. I just hope it isn't broken down somewhere. They didn't say any-thing to you?"

"Rollin, that Otis, he got him a gun. I doan talk to guns. I got me enough moufs already, no extras needed in the back of the head. Wind'd blow through. Cold, *cold.*"

Rollin finds this routine, this little hanky-head word-shuffle, about as genuine as *Rose of Londonderry*. He is disappointed in Foy. "It doesn't matter." What does? Space and time. Marcy's hip.

"Rollin," says Foy, "I got me some James Brown albums. Ain't no record players in Leroy's shithouse. Maybe I could lissen over here?"

Rollin, who has never heard of James Brown unless Foy is talk-ing about the Cleveland fullback, considers this most recent vamping of his credulity. "Actually," he says, "there's a great stereo system at Thomas Hill. The big house. See it there." He points through the window; the valley is a lap; Thomas Hill is Papa Bear. "Let me know, and you can bring your albums over anytime. It's as big as a church."

"This evenins?" says Foy.

Does everything have to be always right now? "You're not playing craps tonight?"

"Brand-new albums," says Foy. "James Brown. Never heard 'em before."

"All right." Now. Everything. "Say seven o'clock. I'll be there."

"Thankyas, Rollin. You's straight."

Like a nail in my own Coffin. Maybe by seven o'clock I will have arrived in Boston by truck, have pulled down Rinsler's lighthouse with my winch. Foy replaces the screen door and gets threshed by the trees. Rinsler in the grove has upped the ante; the pines drop out; Rinsler bluffs. The millstone rolls down the hill toward Canada, crushing Donadio Ford and six apple bins, where Marcy is sleeping with Butterfly. Lucinda is in the irrigation ditch, letting Short grind his nose in her machine.

What does one do with an afternoon one doesn't want, looking toward a night full of nothing? It's the job of popular music to fill up such spaces in the head, the way it's the job of laughing gas to make you forget that your teeth are rotten. But he hates popular music, and isn't in a laughing mood. The gas is down in the outhouse, along with the turd. He descends to ask about their Dodge, and is told—these people couldn't conspire at mumblety-peg—that the Dodge has been towed away, is being straightened out, will be (gulp) crooked at least until Monday. What dusty faces! If they were in his cellar, he would give them away to the Merchant Marine. They are in his grove, his outhouse. The wheels of the tractors have made rings in the grass around them; the chapel is an aquarium, and they are guppies in it. *Rinsler!* Next time, Marcy, try a shmoo. Or a bowling pin.

One bows formally to the guppies, returns to one's cottage, tries and fails once more to telephone one's wife, fills a canteen with rum, mounts again into the cab of the truck, and hits the road in search of Jackson and DeKalb.

Not really. He won't find them. He hits the road merely to be hitting the road. One of the troubles with being an American these days is that there aren't many places to be alone except in a car. The woods are full of transistor radios. Climb up to the top of a mountain, and somebody is waiting there to sell you a lottery ticket or a used helicopter or his sister. Hitting the road, driving in circles, lengthening the radius of each circle. He passes through Harrisville, and stops to admire the functioning mill. This may be the only place in southern New Hampshire where they haven't turned their millstones into cocktail tables or lawn sculpture. It was owning a mill like this one that permitted his maternal antecedents to leave the farm for Exeter. Thirty feet of Mackenzie, they used to call them. Five boys, each six feet tall. And his paternal antecedents? Well, they had always made ropes, and there had always been private schools. Now they make winches as well. He confers with his canteen. Father makes winches; Rinsler makes wenches. There are no black faces in Harrisville.

I forgot to take Peace down to the doctor's office this morning. Peace may never walk again. Peace owes me money, though. We're even. Everybody else is in my debt.

It is early evening on his return to Wyke Regis, but too late to see the sun go down behind Monadnock from the terrace at Thomas Hill. On this terrace he presented Marcy to Wallace Mackenzie and his three sons six years ago. The sun was on my side that day, behind her, turning her hair to flames. She looked at the flagpole, the elms, the sheep, the forests that had once been plundered to make masts for King George's ships, the mountain, which wore a shawl of intricate clouds. Everybody else was looking at her. Her hair ignited the clouds as the sun sank. Fire in the steel-rimmed spectacles. Wallace Mackenzie inscribed and gave her his histories of the family and the town. While he showed her the library, after Ken had whispered a warning not to smoke there, John Mackenzie took his nephew aside and made approving growls. The family, said John Mackenzie, had always depended on strong women bringing new blood into tired veins. Wallace Mackenzie could hardly wait for a grandchild.

He tests the flagstones on the terrace. They seem good for another century or two. He tries the crank on the green awning. Needs oil, but there's no advantage to raising or lowering it. Night should not be allowed to fall so fast; it darkens the air between the ears; verbs begin to crawl. He abandons the terrace to its quadrille of things past. The mirrors in the hall play a game with him: eyes bleeding off the edges of perception, shadows without shape, rooms full of retrogradations and inversions, faces whose teeth comb manes of lies. Foy is late. So is James Brown.

One searches in the refrigerator for some cartilage to chew.

The doorbell. He is not prepared for what he opens on. Foy, yes. But with Foy is Cindy Lou. And behind them are half a dozen others: Bird-man, Root-man, Acton, Fisher, Peace, and the monkey of death himself, my Butterfly. Butterfly is his usual compost heap of sleeves and patches. Cindy Lou, barefoot, has sprayed on a red dress that leaves about as much to the imagination as fingerpainting on her would. The others are spruced up, having raided a secret box and found glad rags of a Saturday night, being boxed themselves in the broad stripes of sport shirts, tapered chinos, hooded looks. Under his arm, Foy carries enough record albums to start a radio station.

Check your knives at the door, please.

He receives the dark delegation. He wonders how many black people have ever been in Thomas Hill. A maid, perhaps? No, there had never been a black maid. Claudis Cantrell, maybe? No, Cantrell always bivouacked near the storage sheds, seldom emerged from his enormous Lincoln Continental, sent runners with messages and head counts. An African diplomat, probably: he seems to recall an Ibo in charge of a medical school, talking to James Mackenzie about foundation funding, to Sam Mackenzie about autopsies, to John Mackenzie about college administration.

"The stereo is upstairs, in the library," he says.

"Hey, Rollin," says Foy, "lookit what I won me in a crap game." And gives Cindy Lou a slap on the rump that moves the buffalo heads to wagging.

"She-it," says Bird-man, "the way that ass gets passed aroun', give a poor boy hope a-plenty. Jes' wait, say the poor boy, your turn gonna come."

"Shut your mouf, trash-man," says Cindy Lou. "You thinks wif your pants."

"What's in my pants is bigger than what's in my head, thas right."

"Ol' Bird-man," says Foy, "he got him a hummin' bird in his pants. Tweet, tweet."

He follows them up the stairs, noticing that in the back pocket of each pair of chinos is a pint-sized brown paper sack. Containing joy-juice. Like Cindy Lou. And he has left his canteen in the truck.

The library has no immediate comment on their invasion. The lamps are thinking about it. The books of sermons are trying not to think about it. The swords think only about throats. Butterfly sprawls in the Hepplewhite chair that used to be favored by Wallace Mackenzie: why do they tolerate Butterfly? Cindy Lou plays with the tongs: he is aware that Cindy Lou dislikes him: join the crowd: they are, or were, in a kind of competition for the men at camp. He is reminded of Lavonia.

The speakers are unnecessarily large, bigger than packing cases. On New Year's Eve, it takes three grown men to carry each of them downstairs. It is not New Year's Eve. He shows Foy the control panel, and how to work the changer. Bird-man and Root-man are already crouching on the oriental rug, opening their pints, leaving the bottles in the bags. It is time for him to find some joy-juice of his own.

He hasn't reached the bowels of Thomas Hill when the music starts. And the music penetrates even into the wine cellar. The music seems determined to shake the house down to its foundations, to wake up the rocks of New England. Is this what happened when they let sex into the Baptist Church? It certainly doesn't sound like the Unitarian Church. Unitarians sing as though they are embarrassed to be doing so.

He loads the dumbwaiter with a dozen bottles of champagne cider. He would have liked living here in the days when Thomas Hill was part of a working farm, instead of a manor house in which the family gathers only on vacations and holidays. Then this catacomb of cellars meant something, with hogsheads of cider and apple bins, the making of cheese and ice cream, the salting of butter in firkins, the tanning of foot leather, the spinning and weaving of flax and wool. A one-horse chaise in the carriage house, instead of a motorized lawn mower. But he lives here now; or visits, with James Brown instead of his wife. Thomas Hill consumes, instead of producing.

He ascends to the kitchen and hoists the dumbwaiter after him. There is a tray on which to pile the long green bottles; glasses and a corkscrew to secure; steps to be negotiated; a den of din to enter.

Foy and Cindy Lou are doing the sort of dancing we pretend to do on New Year's Eve. Foy has somehow removed the pins from his joints; he slides in and out of himself, as though his spine is a lathe whose rotation cuts and shapes his gestures. Cindy Lou is a leopard, a carnivore; her hands and feet are padded paws; her tail seems longer than three feet.

Root-man, Bird-man, and Fisher are on the floor, hugging their pints, watching Cindy Lou.

Butterfly's eyes are closed. He is talking. Ken has to apply his ear to Butterfly's mouth to hear what is being said: "Tweet, tweet, sweet, sweet, you bet, I get, tweet, tweet . . ."

Peace and Acton duel with the swords they have taken down from the mantle. The first light I've seen in Peace's eyes in three weeks—he's shouting something. Ken takes the swords away and sheathes them. Peace and Acton are not surprised. Peace bends to Ken's ear: "Hey, Rollin, where'd you get the fancy bread knives?"

Rollin shouts back: "Swords the Mackenzie substitutes brought back from the Civil War." The lights go out in Peace's eyes. "Substitutes!" screams Rollin. "When they got drafted, they paid people to go off in place of them. It was traditional!" Thinking: if Peace can duel, his back can't be that bad. So he owes me, too.

The record changes. Rollin waves one of the swords at Foy, then points at the stereo control panel. Foy turns it down. Rollin blesses the tray of bottles with his sword. "Try this," he says. "It's champagne, only made from apples instead of grapes. We make it here on the farm. From the apples you pick."

They are willing. The beads of sweat on the green bottles are not as big as the beads of sweat on Foy and Cindy Lou. How would Cindy Lou look on the diving board at the pond? Could you, from the dam's abutment, see her pubic hair? He unwires the Madeira corks, thumbs their prepuces. Done properly, you don't need a screw at all. The pressure builds, the cork pops, the spume would move Bernini to redesign his spigots.

Foy and Cindy Lou decide that they don't need glasses. They will swig from the same bottle. The others follow suit. Even Butterfly has been roused from his contemplation of the principles of rot, by the popping, and deserts Hepplewhite for the idea of foam. "Sweet, sweet," says Butterfly. It is probably not sweet enough for him. Rollin, of course, is obliged to drink from a bottle, too. Unheard of in Thomas Hill. Champagne from the apples of 1961, a very good year. Foy turns up the volume on the

225

stereo again. The music is this time slower, the Supremes. "The Motown sound," says Foy. He makes advances to Cindy Lou which she does not consider indecent. The books of sermons bite their lips and stop their ears with apocrypha.

Well, it is certainly complicated enough this time, even though he feels a fire is necessary and conspires with the hearth to spring one, poking at it with his sword.

They will finish the twelve bottles of champagne cider. Sometime in the course of finishing them, Foy will disappear with Cindy Lou. Rollin will imagine Cindy Lou spreadeagled on the billiard table. Foy will return, and Bird-man will leave. Bird-man will return, and Root-man will leave. Rollin will acknowledge the emptiness of the bottles and rise to rectify the situation. And find himself back in the wine cellar, his skull a drum, the music between his ears, uncorking a private bottle to nurse while cursing his wife, peering intently at the shelves for whatever would be perfectly appropriate.

He returns to the library at the same time that Fisher is returning and Acton is leaving. "Try this," he says, opening the bottle of *poire*. "It's brandy, only made from pears instead of grapes. Look, you can see the pear in the bottom of the bottle." A fetus.

They have resorted to their pints, but they are once more willing. The bottle is passed around. Acton returns. "Peace, now, you hear me, boy," says Foy, "doan do it in your pants before you gets there. Promise me now." Peace looks about to throw up. "Come on, Peace," says Bird-man. "Ain't your momma never tole you how? She tole ever'body else in town. An' tole 'em an' tole 'em and tole 'em, 'til they get it right."

Peace leaves.

And I saw as it were a sea of glass mingled with fire: and them that had gotten the victory over the beast, and over his image, and over his mark, and over the number of his name, stand on the sea of glass, having the harps of God.

Where is she, anyway? In John Mackenzie's bed? Foy is giggling. *And the first went, and poured out his vial upon the earth; and there fell a noisome and grievous sore upon the men which had the mark of the beast, and upon them which worshiped his image.* Bird-man and Root-man are like andirons on each side of the fire. *And the second angel poured out his vial upon the sea; and it became as the blood of a dead man: and every living soul died in the sea. And the third angel poured out his vial upon the rivers and fountains of water; and they became blood.* Fisher is at the window, looking down at a croquet court he can't see, the curtains on him like a toga; Acton sucks on the teat of pear. *And the fourth angel poured out his vial upon the sun; and power was given unto him to scorch men with fire . . . And the fifth angel poured out his vial upon the seat of the beast; and his kingdom was full of darkness; and they gnawed their tongues for pain. . . .* Peace returns. "Hey, Bird-man," says Peace, "she tole me she was your mother, man. Said she was got with you by a hummin' bird." *And the sixth angel poured out his vial upon the great river Euphrates; and the water thereof was dried up, that the way of the kings of the east might be prepared.* "No man," says Foy, "Bird-man's mother was got with Bird-man by a mongoose. Butterfly, Butterfly, lissen to me, Butterfly. Whatever you has that can flap, time's now to flap it. Pussy soft as cream of wheat, an' sad nobody want to eat it." Bird-man and Root-man lift Butterfly by his rope belt and haul him out of the library. "Sweet, sweet, cream of wheat," says Butterfly. Peace finishes off the *poire.* Rollin takes the bottle from him and smashes it in the fireplace, to liberate the pear. "This should taste good," he says. "It's collected the juice for years." In fact, it tastes like what it looks like: a fetus, an abortion brain. He passes it around. There are no biters. There is, instead, a scream.

Bird-man and Root-man come running back, howling with pleasure. "Look out, now, Foy-boy!" says Bird-man. "Pussy has her some *teeth!*" Foy grins, his back to the stereo.

"Woodrow Wilson Foy, you motherfucker, I won't *do* it! Not with that *cabbage!*" There is Cindy Lou, looking not much the worse for wear, and not wearing much of anything, just the red dress clutched in front of her.

"Come here," says Foy. As Cindy Lou moves forward, Bird-man and Root-man scoot around behind her to spy on the naked rolling. Foy picks up the other sword, reaches out with it to touch the red dress. "Let go of it," he says to Cindy Lou.

"No," says Cindy Lou.

"Let go of it, you bitch!"

She does; the dress hangs on the point of the scabbard; Foy flips it into the fire. "Now you turn roun' and stan' right here where my friends can take a look at you, you hear me?"

"Woodrow Wilson, I'm gonna cut your balls off, you bastard. I'm cold!"

She is also beautiful, although not quite so beautiful as Lavonia. "Now lissen here," says Foy, "you got a customer."

"I ain't gonna let that *diseased* ol' man touch my body," says Cindy Lou, doing her best to look dignified without any clothes on.

"You takes our moneys, we gets our choice," says Foy. "I'll ride you bare-assed on a bicycle all the way to Florida. I'll stop in ev'ry garage along the way an' 'low the dudes to fuck you up to your ears and outa your head. I'll give you to the elephants, baby."

"Woodrow, honey, that Butterfly, he'll give me a *disease*. Then what I got ain't no use to anybody. Woodrow?"

Woodrow considers the logic of this argument. Rollin moves to the other side of the hearth, raises his sword in his left hand, watches the dress burn. There you have it. I am Stamina. Cindy Lou is Virility. Foy is Fortitude. Two savages wreathed about the head and loins with, well, not laurel, but apples and pears; each holding in his exterior hand a baton or club erect. Cindy Lou is the mountain inflamed proper, even though her tail's no kin of mine.

Butterfly is crawling down the hall toward them.

"You takes our moneys," repeats Woodrow.

"Honey, *please*." She covers her breasts with her arms.

Foy relents. "All right, then. But then my frien' Rollin here, he got him a free ride, you hear. On the house."

Of course. There has to be a seventh angel.

Cindy Lou looks at Rollin without much ecstasy. She's weighing the alternatives, and they don't add up to much. "Okay," she says, "if you say so, Woodrow. But he's white and pukey."

"Foy," says Rollin, "I want to thank you very much. But I'm a married man." He wonders whether to explain the idea of sanctuary; decides against it.

"She-it, Rollin," says Foy, "I'm a married man, too, yessir, to three of the nicest girls in Florida. Now Cindy Lou, here, Miss Blue Ass, she got herself wedded and bedded ev'ry time she find a buck wif somethin' hard between his legs and five one-dollar bills in his han'."

"I appreciate it, Foy. I really do. But I don't think so."

And now Cindy Lou is mad. At *me*. "Well, if that ain't *shit*,"

she says. "You has yo'self some squirt-gun made of gold down there, boy? Too good for Cindy's mudpie. Stick that sword up yo' ass an' hop on it to hell, boy."

No matter how he looks at it, he doesn't think that screwing Cindy Lou will make him a good liberal. He shakes his head. "I have an idea," he says. "How would you all like to go canoeing?" Cindy Lou makes it impossible not to visualize Cecile. We've got to get out of this house. "Foy, you remember that pond we saw when we were digging rocks? There's a boathouse with a couple of canoes. Lots of paddles. How about it?"

Foy is about to say no. But, as in all farce, there are still some closets to be emptied. Some closets that are thumping up the stairs: Rinsler, who else? With Ransome and D'Allesandro as ballast. *And I saw three unclean spirits like frogs come out of the mouth of the dragon, and out of the mouth of the beast, and out of the mouth of the false prophet.*

"I'm sorry to have to interrupt your orgy," says Rinsler.

Behold, I come as a thief. Blessed is he that watcheth, and keepeth his garments, lest he walk naked, and they see his shame.

Rinsler says, "Ken, I've got to talk to you. It's important."

"You could have telephoned," says Rollin. "You could even have knocked on the door before barging in." Cindy Lou is on her knees in front of Foy, unbuckling his belt, loosening his chinos. *And the seventh angel poured out his vial into the air; and there came a great voice out of the temple of heaven, from the throne, saying, It is done.*

"I've been trying to get you on the phone for an hour. So has your uncle. And we pounded on the door for ten minutes. Those people you gave your station wagon to, they've been arrested. By the police."

Who else, but the police? *And every island fled away, and the mountains were not found.* "Arrested for what?"

"I didn't get it clear. Manchester? Does that sound right?"

"There *is* a Manchester, New Hampshire, yes. And a Manchester-by-the-sea in Massachusetts."

"New Hampshire, New Hampshire!" Rinsler is agitated. "They apparently drove last night to Manchester, your uncle thinks probably looking for women." He inspects Cindy Lou. "I don't know why." He is serious again. "They parked somewhere, and fell asleep, and a patrol car stopped and woke them up. Nobody had a driver's license. And somebody had a concealed weapon. A gun."

"Richmond was supposed to have the driver's license. Otis De-Kalb had the gun. Rinsler, when did this all happen?"

"Early this morning, your uncle said. He wants you to call the police in Manchester. I told him you loaned them the car. He says you've got to tell the police that. The police think it's stolen."

"But why didn't they call *me?* The police. Or DeKalb. Or Jackson. Jackson's got a brain. Why didn't he call me immediately?"

He doesn't expect an answer from Rinsler, but unfortunately he gets one: "John Mackenzie said that none of them knew your last name. So you couldn't be looked up in the phone book. They all just called you Kenneth, at the farm in Wyke Regis. The station wagon is registered to John Mackenzie, and the address is Thomas Hill. I guess there wasn't anybody here during the day. Answering the telephone, anyway. The Wyke Regis operator finally referred them on to your uncle at Berringer College. Everybody in Wyke Regis seems to know that the Mackenzies leave after Labor Day, and where they go."

He would like to make a bone-tap of Rinsler's head, drain whatever fluid there is from the marrow into a cider bottle, test it for deposits of irony. Is Rinsler even aware of the ironies involved? That the Coffin cousin who had spent so much time learning the last names of his crew members should be told that his crew members didn't know *his* last name is unspeakably symbolic of something or other equally unspeakable. Jackson, DeKalb, Richmond, Foy, Porter, Mason, Worthy, Fisher, Peace, Acton, Hudson, Lavalle, Reid, Walker, Wornum, Wilson, Talley . . . "Foy," he says. Foy is zipping up his pants. "Foy, do you know my last name?"

Foy switches off the stereo. The question has to be repeated. Then it has to be swept for mines. Finally it is answered. "No, Rollin, not rightly."

"Good. That means you're safe. Let's go canoeing."

Rinsler objects. "Aren't you going to call the police in Manchester?"

"If I know my Uncle John, he'll have told them what you told me. Tomorrow is time enough to worry about bail. Now we're going canoeing."

"Where?" demands Rinsler.

"What difference on earth does it make to you?"

Rinsler leads him into the hall. Ransome and D'Allesandro tag along. There is something unspeakably symbiotic about the association of the three of them. Rinsler also decides that the hall is bugged. Four people find themselves in the bathroom, behind a locked door, with an iron bathtub to lie down in, just in case the revelations get too heavy to bear standing up. Rinsler breathes on him:

"There was another telephone call. Just now." Rinsler is whispering. Who else would call at this time of night: Mad Tom? "Mark and Toby were followed," says Rinsler. "Army Intelligence." The mirror in the bathroom fogs itself. "The cops in Wyke Regis found the car in the garage. We gave your name this morning when they came to tow it. The cops called you. I pretended to be you. I said you didn't know anything about it, you'd found the car ditched on your road. They said they were coming up to talk to you about it. We left to come here."

How much hugger can a mugger stand? The bathtub seems a great place for taking it lying down. The woods are obviously full of Army Intelligence agents, Wyke Regis and Manchester policemen, Royal Canadian Mounties, the Stern Gang and the Green Berets, all of them transistorized. "We're going canoeing at the pond," he insists. "What good is that going to do you?"

"Is there a place we can stay there?" says Rinsler. "Just for the night?"

"There are a couple of islands. You wouldn't like the mosquitoes and the snakes, I suppose. There's the bathhouse. It has stalls. You'd have to sleep sitting up. It's possible, but not fun."

"None of this is *fun*, Coffin!"

On the contrary. It is so complicated as at last to have become fun. "Get into the truck," he says. "We'll all go canoeing."

And damned if they aren't all waiting, seven angels and a whore, in the library, ready to go to the pond. Don't these people have anything better to do? Cindy Lou is at a disadvantage, being nude. Coffin takes her by the hand, surprisingly yielded, up to the fourth floor of Thomas Hill. He opens the steamer trunk and pulls out the long dresses of the Mackenzie women. "One of them is bound to fit you."

She takes too much time pressing them against herself. A decision is made: something silk, with a bustle. She starts to put it on over her head, then pauses with it slung around her shoulders like a cape. "Rollin," she says, "you's straight. You can still have it if you want it." And she rubs herself with his hand. "No charge."

He wants it, but he's a married man. He kisses her on the forehead as, the first time, he kissed Marcy. "Not necessary," he says. "Maybe later." Jesus, if she doesn't make you cry, to look like this in a dress belonging to a woman who's been dead at least a century. Splinters in the eye. The difference between Lavonia and Cindy Lou is that Lavonia would not be so transparently pleased with such a dress, and glow so on wearing it, a rich, deep, wood color, the kind that collects twilights out of rains. It must be a class difference. Lavonia's father turned out to want to be middle-class. He wonders whether he can trust Cindy Lou in Rinsler's company on the way to the pond. He wonders if he can trust anybody in Rinsler's company. "Let's go."

He takes the sword with him. At the wheel of the truck, with the winch on one side of him and the sword on the other, and Cindy Lou and Foy next to him in the cab, he is ready for the Green Berets. What, in the rear, will Rinsler find to say to Butterfly?

The road from Thomas Hill to the pond runs right by the camp. Naturally, Foy has to whoop at the camp: "Hey, James T., you ol' piss-bag, where's yo' wife, James T.? Seen her in the woods with Mud-duck! Ol' Mud-duck, he use the fo'k lift on Cindy Lou Blue-Ass, James T.!"

"Woodrow," says Cindy Lou, "you's *bad*."

Heads appear in the windows of the cabin; a door slams; Coffin steps on the gas; maybe, going over a bump, Rinsler will fall out of the truck.

The green gate. He can't decide whether to take the sword or the winch with him. Leaves them both, climbing out, fumbling among keys. The lock gives, the gate swings. The headlights of the truck make bright the face of Settler's Rock. "See that," he says to Cindy Lou and Foy, back in the cab. "You know what that says?" He reads it aloud:

GEORGE MACKENZIE AND PERKINS SAWYER, AFTER THRIDDING THEIR WAY THROUGH THE UNFAMILIAR FOREST, CAME TO THIS PLACE SOME TIME BETWEEN 1736 AND 1740. AGAINST THIS ROCK THEY PITCHED A CAMP OF GREEN POLES AND HEM-

LOCK BOUGHS. WHEN, NEXT DAY, THE INDIANS STOLE EVERY MOUTHFUL OF THEIR EATABLES OF SALT PORK AND CORN MEAL, THEY WALKED BACK, HUNGRY, TO THE NEAREST SETTLEMENT.

"Heh," says Foy. "Indians. That's rich. What'd they do then, Rollin?"

"Oh, they came back two or three years later. George Mackenzie built a house right by, hard pine logs, ten inches square. Started a family and farm."

"But what about the Indians?"

"They gave the Indians syphilis."

"Heh. That's rich."

The truck is too big for this road. The cab is whipped by branches. There are shouts of alarm from the rear. But they achieve the beach. The moon is being nice to them. It paints a white avenue on the pond, from the dock to the float and beyond. Water is falling over the dam. Marcy hasn't brought a picnic hamper.

He unlocks the bathhouse, and tells the Symbiosis: "There it is. There's a door at the other end. It opens on a porch. You can watch us canoeing. Just let me get the paddles out." He removes the paddles, and circles around to the boathouse, unlocks that, too. He is followed by the angels.

"Rollin," says Foy, "I ain't much on water."

He pulls the two aluminum canoes from their shelves. He can't remember why he wanted to do this in the first place. "It's no more than four feet deep anywhere but the channel. The channel runs right down the middle of the pond to the dam, you see? The float is in the middle of the channel. A couple of yards either way, and you can stand up."

Foy is cheered by the fact that he can lift an aluminum canoe. "Iffen I go, you alls go, dig?" They dig, but it leaves holes in them.

"Watch, now. Cindy Lou, hold it steady for me." He gets in, moves carefully to the stern, sits down facing them. "I'll steer this one. Peace, hand me the long paddle." Peace does so. "Right. Now, Peace, you hold it steady while Cindy Lou gets in." Cindy Lou has too much long dress on for anything but clumsy movements. She makes it, but the canoe rocks. He wouldn't mind if she took off the dress, but feels that the suggestion is liable to misinterpretation. "Now, Fisher, you want to try it?" Fisher tries it. "Peace, you get in the bow. Up front. Back to me. Take a paddle. Somebody push us off." Bird-man pushes them off. They tip, sway, steady, and are water-borne.

"Bird-man," says Foy, "you hold this motherfucker steady, hear?" And he scrambles into the stern of the second canoe.

"Rollin," says Cindy Lou, "it's *cold* down here. Like Fisher, she is sitting on the bottom of the canoe.

"Yeah, the cold of the water comes right through the aluminum. Tuck up your legs. Sit on the bustle."

"Foy," says Acton, "I ain't gonna do no stupid-ass thing."

"Yeah you is, brother, les' I whup that stupid ass."

"Ain't. 'Sides, who gonna push *you* off?" Root-man is in Foy's canoe.

Bird-man says, "Come on, Butterfly."

"No, no," whispers Butterfly.

"No more than four to a canoe," says Rollin.

"An' I ain't one of 'em," says Acton.

"Lookit ol' Butterballs," says Foy. "He more a man than you, Bad Acton."

Bird-man is forcing Butterfly into Foy's canoe. Root-man gets a grip on him. Rinsler, Ransome, and D'Allesandro, the Symbiosis, appear on the porch of the bathhouse and take seats to watch.

"Yo' ass gets whupped when I's done paddlin'," says Foy. "Bird-man, you get in." Bird-man straddles the canoe with his back to Foy, shimmies down into the bow with his shoes in the water on each side of the nose. Acton pushes off Foy's canoe with his foot. "Whoo-ee," says Foy, looking like he wants to smash the water with his paddle. "Whadda I do now, Rollin?"

From the porch, Rinsler shouts: "Coffin, you're insane."

"Fuck you!" says Coffin. Now Foy knows his last name. "Foy, watch what I do with the paddle." He demonstrates. "Dig it deep in the water, straight down, keep it flat. Left arm stiff. Switch sides. Right arm stiff. That's it! You want to stop, you push the paddle *forward*. Right, right!"

Foy maneuvers. "Hiya, Cindy Lou Blue-Ass!"

"Hiya, Woodrow, honey."

"Stay away from the dam," says Coffin. And he paddles onto moon avenue, pleased with Foy.

"Whoo-ee!" says Foy. "Come on, Bird-man, les get some *speed*."

"Rollin," says Peace, "what's that?" Pointing into the white water, the shadow-grid of trees around them like approving uncles.

"Water snake," says Rollin. "Harmless. My son tried to catch
one this summer and couldn't. They don't know how to bite. They
just glide away."

"Rollin," says Peace, "them mother-snakes. Rollin, les head
back."

Rollin tries to scoop up the snake on his paddle, fails. They are
headed away from Foy, toward the creek. Giggles come across the
water. He looks over his shoulder. Foy has docked at the float.
Root-man and Bird-man are hoisting Butterfly onto the float.

"Hush-up, Peace," says Cindy Lou. "Piss in yo' pants if you
hafta."

"Hush-up yo'self, you bitch," says Peace. "You does all yo' thinking on yo' back, wif yo' pussy."

"Yo' finger doan mind my pussy so much, do it, Peace-piss? It
were yo' finger, weren't it? I declare, seemed like a finger to me.
Pinkie-finger."

Fisher says nothing. Neither does Rollin, who is looking for
frogs on lily pads, and finding none. They probably aren't out at
night. It's been fifteen years since he canoed at night. The moon
is now diced by the trees, the water is polka-dotted, the uncles inhale because Cindy Lou is tickling Rollin in the privacy of his
parts. Cindy Lou speaks only one language. Esperanto should be
so eloquent. Beware of dangling participles. If clause had his wits
about him, he would disqualify himself: by crossing his legs. Tickling is race war by other mean expressions. Emission is possible.

"Cindy Lou, *please*."

She giggles. "Later is maybe now."

Crossing one's legs is dangerous when one is steering a canoe.

"Rollin, *please*," says Peace.

Rollin reverses. His paddle works like a stork with flippers, pro-
pelling them toward the dock. The pines uncle. Indians are after
my salt pork. He instructs Peace on how to tether the canoe to
the dock. Peace and Fisher scramble up the ladder. Will Cindy
Lou still want to go on canoeing? Even a good liberal isn't perfect.

"Rollin, I'm *very* cold," she says.

"I've got rum in a canteen at the truck," he says, and grips the
ladder while she rises, her bustle an affront. Then follows the
bustle.

There is rot, as in Butterfly, in the wooden planks that are the steps that lead to a carpet of pine needles and the pile of cinder blocks that is the Mackenzie place for cooking out and the chancel of hemlocks that is the Mackenzie space for gnawing and large talk. Something to fix in the spring, after mud-time, before blackflies. Once he roasted a suckling pig here: there were little brown paper cups on its ears to keep them from singeing; its hooves were wired together and attached fore and aft to the spit to keep it from spinning; the wire pulled the hooves out and the suckling spun like a skewered child; the meat was delicious, but everybody refused to watch him cook it. Do Cindy Lou and Foy eat pig's feet?

Behind him, Foy shouts, "Snake! Snake!" There is a splash, then more giggles. Hemlocks want trimming. A whole summer has come and gone, and he hasn't been to the pond, missing even the picnic to honor the lifting of the Siege. Cindy Lou is lost in the shadows. He finds her again at the top of the beach. On the boat-house porch, Rinsler is smog. Rollin and Cindy Lou get into the cab of the truck and sip some rum. The beach is deserted, the water is deserted, the float is deserted. He looks again at the white float. No Butterfly.

"Excuse me," he says to Cindy Lou, and disembarks. At the water's edge, there's still no sign of Butterfly. "Rinsler!" he says. Rinsler does not reply. He runs up the bathhouse steps. Ransome and D'Allesandro sit silent beside each other in a stall, among old swimsuits on hooks, waiting for Army Intelligence. He pushes onto the porch, where Rinsler is smoking. "Did you see what happened to the man on the float?"

"I saw."

"Well, is it a secret?"

"The other canoe came by," says Rinsler. "Someone shouted *snake!* And threw a stick. The man on the float jumped off into the water."

"What happened then?"

"Nothing."

"What the hell do you mean, nothing?"

"Nothing. He just disappeared."

"The canoe didn't pick him up?"

"Not that I could see."

"And you didn't *do* anything? You just *sat* here like a turd?"

"You know I can't swim."

"You could have *shouted* to me!"

"It's your party, not mine. It's your responsibility, not mine. Besides, I don't see what you could have done. He probably sank like a stone."

"Butterfly! Hey, Butterfly?" No answer. "*Foy.* Where are you?"

"Yo, Rollin!" From the other side of the pond, near the marsh.

"Is Butterfly in your canoe?"

"No way, Rollin. Butterball's on that float."

"No, goddammit, he's not! Butterfly!"

There's an echo from the woods to his left: "Butterfly! Butterfly!" It occurs to him that there aren't supposed to be any echoes on the pond. "Where is you, Butterfly?" say the woods. We have visitors. "Pretty please, Butterfly!" He is being mocked. He hasn't time to worry about it. He clears the railing of the porch and jumps to the beach. Cindy Lou is not in the cab of the truck. He drives the truck down the beach to the water, and switches on the headlights: at the float. There is nothing to see. He backs up, turns, shines the lights toward the dam. At the intersection of truck beams and moon avenue, on the lip of the dam, there is something. Oh shit. Run, now, you son of a bitch, past the bathhouse, up the incline, to the abutment. Look at what the truck ran over, the moon fell down on: a bundle of old clothes in the water. Remove your shoes and socks, roll up your pants legs, tightrope-walk on the top of the dam, in ice cubes up to your ankles, the moon making eggs on your fatigue jacket, the pond a mouth. It would appear to be Butterfly, all right. You can't pull him up, he's water-heavy beyond the powers of your Enlightenment, you bastard. So run back again, bad news on white feet, twinkle-toes of death, student of character without a stomach, pedagogue propelled by the gas coming out of your ass. To your marvelous lamp-eyed farm truck and the equally marvelous winch your father made instead of rope. Gotcha. Reversing your field, then, back to the abutment: look at those entrechats! Join the club, feet! Stringing the winch on a gear ring that makes the dam gate go up and down like a guillotine while baring and shredding its teeth: clever, *clever.* Wading once more to your intersection: we need black moons to bloody our alabaster, all our bastards. Hooking the winch into Butterfly's sweatshirt: there should have been brown paper cups on his ears. Ratcheting back the body to the abutment, your pawl less than engaging, twenty-to-one gear ratios agree that drowning is bad for your teeth: let them eat Rinsler.

Artificial respiration doesn't work; kiss Butterfly good-by.

James T. Worthless is waiting on the beach, with Cindy Lou. My, how that girl gets around. James T. Worthless has a knife. Coffin, exceedingly clever, stops at the truck, opens the cab door, takes out the sword, starts up the beach toward them, brandishing it, inquires: "You want trouble, James T.?" He sees shapes in the chancel, hears rustling in the bustle bushes.

"The troubles I want ain't wif you, Rollin," says James T. Worthless. Porter appears at the confluence of hemlock and plank rot. Mason shows his draft card to the moon. There are others, but Coffin can't remember their last names.

"Butterfly's dead," says Coffin. "He drowned."

"Tough shit," says James T. Worthless.

Coffin gives James T. and Cindy Lou as wide a berth as the substitute sword will allow. He backs to the bathhouse steps, mounts them. "Here come the Vietcong!" he screams at Ransome and D'Allesandro, who are holding each other's hands in their stall. It's Rinsler he wants, the mother-toad. "Happy, now, are you, Rinsler? He's dead."

Rinsler has three eyes. One of them is the burning coal on the end of his cigarette. "I told you. It's your party."

"If you shouted, we might have gotten to him in time to pump some water out and some air in."

"Fun and games," says Rinsler.

Coffin slaps the side of Rinsler's face with his substitute sword.

"So now you're going to cut my throat," says Rinsler. "More fun and games."

"The scabbard's still on," says Coffin.

"It's your fault," says Rinsler.

"It's yours," says Coffin.

"Yours."

"Yours."

"Yours."

Coffin whams him again. Indeed, blood under the moon. "Leave my wife alone, or I'll kill you."

Rinsler has crossed his arms over his face, cupped his hands over the top of his skull, lowered his head into his lap, burned his prick with his cigarette. "You fucking fraud!" he says. "You and your pretty-boy guilt, you fucking boy scout! Save the world! *You* left your wife alone so you could be up here, sticking it into the camp whore!" *Thump!* "You blame me for taking advantage of what's available." *Swack!* "Maybe she *liked* it, better than boy scouts!" *Powie!* "Coward! Liar! Black meat, yum-yum!" *Biff, bam, ker-plunk.*

Coffin has approximated a death. He lowers the sword. Rinsler waits, spiders of blood on his hands. Silence.

Finally, Rinsler says: "Even so, Marcy was worth it."

And for the first time Coffin believes him.

Thirteen

UNDER THE STRIP OF MOSQUITO STICKUM on the bathhouse porch, above the bloody pool, the drowned moon, the closed eye, the dead body, Rinsler was pleased with himself. He wanted his neck rubbed. The crime was more than the punishment; the punishment was more than the crime; either way Rinsler won. He knew from experience that his hands would heal. His ears would survive. He had never, anyway, been a pretty-boy. But Coffin's healing would have to be inward and was therefore harder. An ulcer of the mind, not knowing what was true. Such not-knowing was leprous: nodules of doubt formed; the nerve lost its grip; the deficit, the victimization, was permanent. Amazing, really, how one brother was recapitulated by the next, as though our families and our lives were sonatas. Death had its own charm, enthralling children, the black hole in the camp whore, worm-fingered. Rinsler thought of deaths of the mind, cartwheels of the zodiac, brothers that had been bent and broken, pinned and disjointed, drummed and tumbreled, no brakes on their disk, butterflies whose motions were a tunnel and a fuse.

Coffin crouched on his pillbox near the dam, sheathed sword athwart his knees, guarding the corpse. Rinsler wished on Coffin tumbrels, nodules, worms. On Marcy, sonatas. On Mackenzies, mosquitoes. On Maoists, an incentive system. On Mark and Toby, each other. What night there was, black ribbons tangled in this moonlight, trembled. Ague, snakeroot. He intended to watch away the night by being one; to tick, a coiled witness, signifying.

Black siege of silver canoe: *why* didn't matter; *they*, on the land, were after *those*, in the canoe. Perhaps it was a friend of the land-lubbers who had drowned. They had stationed themselves at the beach, and at the pier where Coffin's canoe had been tied up, and at an inlet to the right of Rinsler where the bluff softened to a negotiable swell of ground. The canoe circled. Apparently, there was no place to make a safe landfall.

From the beach, someone screamed: "Foy, you piss-bag, come an' get yo' fo'k lift! Bird-man, Root-man, troubles I want ain't wif you. Kick that mother-Foy boy-ass outa yo' boat!"

From the silver canoe, laughing, came the reply: "Tell it to the rocks, James T. Worthless! I comes back wif my canoe fulla *snakes*. Snakes, James T.! Snakes up yo' ass an' out yo' ear!"

It was like going to the movies. No surrender! Rinsler was doubly pleased.

"James T.!" cried another voice from the canoe. "Foy-boy got him the loonies! James T., weren't *my* fault. I wants Florida come home an' chitlins. Please, James T. Ain't nobody's trouble but yourn an' loony!"

From the beach: "Hear that, Foy-boy?"

From the canoe: "Ol' Root-man, he can't swim an' he doan know how to paddle. He stay long's I do."

From the beach: "Foy-boy, you knows them pumps what pump up tires? We gonna fill them ol' pumps up wif grasshoppers. We gonna fin' yo' mother, we gonna stick that pump up yo' mother's pussy, we gonna *blast* her fulla grasshoppers, you hear me, Foy-boy? Then we gonna make you gobble alls the pieces, on co'nbread, hear?"

From the canoe: "James T., I allus knowed thas the onliest way you does yo' fucking, wif a tire pump. No way else, seein' how you's hung wif a grasshopper, ain't it?"

On the beach, there was frustration. The man called Worthless couldn't think of any way to get at the canoe. He kicked at the sand. Finally, he gave some instructions. Two others gathered stones. As the canoe swung round again, Foy laughing, the land-lubbers threw stones at it. The canoe retreated.

"Nice try, James T., no way. Throw yo' head, James T. Yo' head'd float on the water, James T."

"Gonna cut off yo' cock, Foy-boy, gonna fry it wif rice, gonna feed it to Cindy Lou whilst you watches."

"She-it, James T., Cindy Lou Blue-Ass, she already done ate it, no rice needed, whilst I watched."

There was now a scuffle on the beach. James T. had hold of the girl, had an arm twisted behind her back, a grip on her hair, and was forcing her into the water. "Foy-boy, you hear me?" He hit Cindy Lou in the stomach. When she doubled over, he knocked her to her knees. "I'm gonna hold her head under the water, Foy-boy, 'til you comes back. Hear me?" Cindy Lou began to scream.

And Coffin, from his pillbox, entered the conversation: "James T., that's a murder rap."

"Mind yo' own fuckin' business, Rollin."

"A murder rap, James T. With witnesses. The electric chair."

"Fried Worthless!" shouted Foy from the canoe. "Worthless grits!"

"Let her go, James T.," said Coffin.

A sound of motors in the trees, growing. James T. turned toward the sound. It was followed by lights: white lights, blue lights, flashing lights. James T. ran. The cavalry, the police, had at last arrived.

Except for the girl, the beach was deserted when two squad cars pulled up, followed by an unmarked sedan. The night was full of static and blue lights. Rinsler eased himself off the porch into the tall grass. Now if only Mark and Toby would stay put, they might—but Mark and Toby were not very bright. They came out the front door of the bathhouse with their hands up, surprising the police. The police probably weren't interested in Mark and Toby. Yet. Rinsler would have to cross the beach, and he wasn't feeling so terribly well. He used the truck as cover. The girl stared at him, then resumed brushing off her preposterous dress; it gathered in wet vegetable lumps around her feet, as though she'd married the moon. *As though.* Her lack of concern was dazzling. Rinsler's concerns were razors on his hog's hunched back; weapons. He had a plan. He limped the rest of the way to the trees, which received him with a sigh. He reached the pier. His bleeding hands on the ladder seemed ungrateful to him for all that he had done for them, the touchings of women he had monitored. Damn them. If he fell off the ladder—but he did not. And there was the other, the Coffin's canoe. Rinsler had never been in a canoe. There was always a first time. He lowered both feet, still strangling the ladder. The canoe rocked in a revolting manner, like a woman. Somebody had bobbled the moon. He squatted, liberating the ladder, gripping the cold hips of the canoe. *Hold . . . it!* She endured him, without gurgling. Now: if he untied the rope, if he used his hands as flippers and paddled quietly, quietly, into vulval shadows, away, somewhere dark and safe, to wait, they would all eventually go away, wouldn't they? The footsteps on his spinal staircase? They would. They would round up the unusual suspects, do something with the dead body. Ballpoint pens would bleed on official forms. Rinsler would survive.

But if the canoe capsized, he would drown. No boy scout. It posed a neat theoretical problem: how do you swim in the sea of the people if there aren't any people and you don't know how to swim?

He would not untie the rope. He would lie down, an umbilical figure, in the aluminum cunt and hope they wouldn't find him.

But, of course, they did.

Fourteen

Sunday

THE TELEPHONE RANG as she was getting out of the bathtub for the second time. "Aloha? Mrs. Kenneth Coffin? How aren't you? I am final. My name is Oona Lung, and I am your local representative for Fistic Cybroccoli. As you know, Fistic Cybroccoli strikes seven out of every ten consenting adults during an off-year election. I am calling here from our mission control at Pancreatic Hall in downtown Fresh Swamp to see if you would be willing, as I'm sure you always are, to subscribe to six hundred dollars' worth of magazines, ranging in élan from the *Worm-Runner's Digest* to *Popular Mechanix*, which subscriptions, to be delivered by negative reinforcement to a home of your choice, would send fourteen and a half deprived Camp Fire girls to leprosaria in surprising Mozambique. Mr. Cybroccoli is against the Vietnamese and needs your vote. May you be tabulated?"

"I'm sorrowful," said Mrs. Coffin, "but I speak a different anguish." And hung up. And stared at the wet footprints on her wall-to-wall pudenda.

Frémissements d'une feuille effacée. Shiverings of an effaced leaf. Valéry. And Marcy, after a shower and two baths. If nothing shows, then nothing counts. Wrong. Everything counts. There are always consequences. The body may be a wind, which washes itself. But the mind is closed, still, precise, a thing of shapes, having given form to what it knows, having systematized the feelings. The face will lie to him; behind it, there will be a nonhedonic calculus: of finite differences, of variations, of disgust. It seemed unfair that she should not have known that she had been, before now, reasonably happy. Compared to now, ecstatic. Being, now, alone with her own personality, which filled her head with forms and systems, which was a treachery. She estimated that men had been inside her almost a thousand times, not counting last night. Most of those men had been her husband. She could look forward to perhaps twice that many times in the future, if she were capable of looking forward, which she was not, after which the wind would wash itself, the leaf would be effaced, the shivering would continue in the mind, every word would be a lie, and the architecture of the lies would be a toilet the size of a cathedral constucted to contain the shiver.

I am turning over for a new thief.

Thinking this way was no help at all. One survived. There were trade-offs. The survival was part of the everything that counted. The trade-offs determined the quality of the survival. If she considered her marriage to be an indispensable part of her survival—and she did, emphatically: there were people who cared and people to be cared for—then the marriage must survive as well. If the marriage would not survive were her husband to know what happened last night—and it would not: his systems were monogamous to a fault, which was one, being Marcy—then her husband must not know what happened last night. She did not doubt his love; she did doubt his capacity to survive. Loving him, she was therefore obliged to protect him, as he had not protected her. He could not cope with a guilt that was free-floating, that did not attach itself to a crime. She could.

All crimes were personal. Societies, families, individuals, that didn't know this were rotten and would go on being rotten unto the last Fistic Cybroccoli.

She had better fetch the children from the Culhanes. She was already late. It was important that the world appear to be normal. The world is not normal, but what the world is not was insignificant compared to what it should appear to be. She went to fetch her children, by negative reinforcement.

Fifteen

POLICE STATIONS TEND TO LOOK ALIKE, whether in Wyke Regis or Manchester, having been organized along Freudian lines. Whether you're in for libidinal hanky-panky, potty problems, or the Primal Crime, it's the same nursery, the same crib. Desks are sergeants, fathers. Light bulbs are eyes. There are keys in the ears of the captain, who tunes his steel spring to a snappable fatigue: I've seen infantile traumata come and go, they're all alike, primate behavior, uterine regressions, oral, genital, you name it. My feet are flat because my archetypes are falling; my view is synoptic; my job is to prolong your expiation.

And yet, in Wyke Regis, their approach to Kenneth Mackenzie Coffin is positively Comtean. Just the facts, please; we haven't time for any of your ultimate causes. An innocent canoeing party, an argument over a girl. What about the sword? The sword is a family heirloom, at no time has it left the private property of the family, it remains safely in its sheath. What about Rinsler, Ransome, D'Allesandro? Rinsler is a colleague from Cambridge; he had not met, nor known of, Ransome and D'Allesandro until late Friday afternoon. What about this business in Manchester, a stolen car? A misunderstanding; a borrowed car; the lack of a driver's license, the existence of a concealed weapon—regrettable; he promises to go to Manchester. What about the corpse?

Poor Butterfly is judged by the coroner to have died an accidental death by drowning, although for reasons of their own they will later perform an autopsy on his body and find that his heart failed before his lungs filled: separation anxiety, away from the float.

Coffin is not judged, nor dissected. He is guilty only of being dumb, and that perhaps is forgivable, seeing as how he's a local boy, fine family, been in these parts two hundred years and more. What do they teach these kids at Harvard, anyway? How are the apples coming?

Manchester, to which Dennison accompanies him so that somebody can bring back the station wagon, is not very interesting. Otis DeKalb seems to have a police record down South; what with his gun, he's in trouble, and will be held. The station wagon has not been involved in an accident, or a moving violation. After an argument about which one of them was driving without a license, both Jackson and Richmond are fined and released. They return to the farm for their possessions; there isn't a camp any more, everybody having disappeared, Butterfly a portent. New Hampshire is bad luck. Jackson and Richmond will be leaving soon, too.

There are a couple of loose ends to be tied. Can the Nova Scotians finish the picking alone? They can, with bonus payments. Can Butterfly, what's left of him, be buried near Elizabeth Smythe Mackenzie's granite obelisk? He can't. The town won't allow it and neither will John Mackenzie.

Short is happy now.

I guess Terence Spider-man Lavalle got away.

Sixteen

RINSLER HAD BEEN MUCH AFFECTED ONCE, although he would deny it, by the story of the great temple at Benares, where, under the dome that was the center of the world, in front of the statue of Brahma, lay a brass plate with three diamond needles. At the creation, God placed sixty-four golden rings on one of the diamond needles, the largest ring at the bottom, the next largest on top of it, and so on up the needle to the sixty-fourth and smallest ring on top. It had been the task of the priests of the temple, day and night ever since, to transfer the rings from one needle to another, one ring at a time, never placing a larger ring on top of a smaller one. When all sixty-four rings had thus been transferred from God's needle to another one, the world would disappear. The trouble was, after you moved the first ring, the number of moves you needed to place each succeeding ring properly increased geometrically. According to the storyteller, if you made one move per second, it would require about fifty-eight thousand billion years to get the job done.

Everything takes time. Even the transfer of power.

Perhaps computers, or bombs, could speed up the transfer. But it would get done. Patience, work. Avoiding the excesses and self-aggrandizements of a Coffin. If Rinsler were to go to jail for aiding

and abetting deserters from the United States Army, then someone else, equally patient, would continue his work while he was
away. Staying power: professional revolutionaries, like priests
and the great turtles, had it. Perhaps he would finally get around
to reading Bruno Rizzi.

Mark and Toby were moves. The institute was a move. Coffin
was a move. Marcy had been a wrong move. He would not im-
plicate Coffin in the Canadian scheme. Personalities were one
thing; the police were another. There was a code covering that.
When they found out about the Suffolk County indictment, his
life would be more complicated, but not more troublesome.

In fact, it was liberating to be in a police station. In this police
station, anyway. Mississippi had been a different matter. But
here, in this serious little box, certain solemn rituals were assured.
He knew which questions would be asked, he knew the answers,
he knew he would not be clubbed, he experienced an electric
extension of himself, the switchboard of his staying power ablaze,
the thousands of circuits, the rings of events he contained, a
membrane of energy that blanketed the earth.

Energy: he *had* discovered an energizing principle equivalent
to Coffin's blackness. It was called envy.

One day the party would be over, for Coffin and the rest of
them. Wyke Regis would vanish. Indians would come out of the
woods and eat all the apples. The canoes would be birchbark
instead of aluminum. The house on the hill would burn down.
Smoke would rise from the valley as if from a hearth or an altar.
Every tree would be a spear, the baskets would be full of fish, the
hymns would rise like the smoke into a burnished sky, the membrane of Rinsler, a naked brotherhood would have returned to
a green land, the zodiac become a smashed pocket watch.

Moves. Rings. Needles. Turtles. Circuits. Marcy in Moccasins,
the moon a monod, Indian-givers. Move over, Coinneach Odhar!

"For the record," Rinsler told the Wyke Regis police, "Mr.
D'Allesandro, Mr. Ransome, and I are political prisoners."

They gave him a telephone, the way you give a child a cookie
to make him shut up.

First Epilogue

MARCY FOUND OUT SHE WAS PREGNANT after they had decided to move to New York. Ken had sought his old job back at *Scope*. *Scope* had not been surprised, but there was a better opportunity in its New York headquarters. Would he consider relocation? He would, providing that his wife could find a post in the city. She did, at Columbia, although she wouldn't start until the following fall. It gave them something to pretend to think about in the weeks immediately after his abrupt return from New Hampshire: silent, miserable weeks, during which they circled one another warily, wounded animals without enough energy to attempt a kill.

There was no doubt about *why* she was pregnant, and she dreamed of a serpent with Beckwith's face in its mouth, a hydra-headed beast, Siamese quintuplets. Terrified, she went to Sergeant Pepper, who was ready with an arsenal of advice. Names, prices, and a pitiless complacency. Marcy for two days wondered whether she might actually get away with it. But Ken noticed. It was almost as though he had been looking for the signs.

"Do you want the child?" he asked. On a morning when a spoon in a bowl seemed suddenly the rattling of a regiment of sabers.

"Do you?" she replied. The thought made her feel as bad as the situation.

"I don't want Rinsler's child, no."

And so she learned what her husband thought he knew about her, what Rinsler had told him. She had a choice. Which would hurt him more, Rinsler's lie, which at least implied volition, independence of will; or the helpless truth, strangers of an unknown number, victimization? How did men's minds work? Would the *number* of times she had been used count against her, even though her *mind* had not been raped? On the other hand, she was insulted that he believed she would have tolerated Rinsler. There was safety in numbers. Ideas—assassins, terrorists—divided by a desperate mitosis into cells that swarmed over her fantasies, rioting, anarchic, cancerous. The kerotakis and the water pipe, a permissible stupor, an accusation: You left me alone. There did not appear to be any advantage in not telling the truth.

She told the truth, and tears were easy. She should have cried long ago. She hid her face on his chest. "It was awful," she said. "Ken, I'm so sorry."

"Why, Mother?" said Stephen. "What have you done?"

"Nothing," said her husband. "Nothing." An empty face.

That night, having cried all day, astonished and grateful for his gentleness in their bed, she wanted to reward him. For his capacity to forgive. She would do it. She tried. She stopped, and switched on the light to see if his face was still empty. It was not, but whether it was full of pity or pride she couldn't tell. The face looked at her body. She decided that what the face was full of was morbid curiosity. She decided that the gentleness was a kind of pornographic imagining. She decided that the reward would be interpreted as something she had learned from someone else. She wondered whether, in fact, he even believed her. Her brain was a bivalve, lies and truths forever hinged. She turned off the light and, as usual, stared at the ceiling, which was the bivalve, which was Rinsler.

Two days later, she had whatever it was removed. It was expensive, but it hurt less than removing a splinter.

Second Epilogue

AND SO, WHATEVER IT WAS IN MARCY'S BODY, and regardless of who put it there with or without her permission, was sacrificed for our marriage. A substitution for my mother, for me, for Stephen, for Butterfly. That's what it's all about, isn't it? Substitutions, approximations, sacrifices, trade-offs, tourism.

We live now in a house in another city. I have a room of my own, full of books, and a silver bowl, full of sharp pencils, and a filing cabinet, full of the tear sheets of articles I have published. The room has one window, plugged with an air-conditioner, protected by an iron grille. On the street, directly in front of the window, is a light standard. New sodium-flare lamps were fixed to all the standards on our street yesterday, after months of discussion by the Block Committee. They make the night bright. Because it is late spring, there are leaves on the trees, filtering the light nicely. In wintertime, it will look like a prison camp. Neither writing a stern memo nor waving a credit card will alter the situation.

The children, Hannah and Stephen, also have rooms of their own and are upstairs asleep in them, among pots of paints and sleeves off phonograph records and random slips of Monopoly money. Marcy has gone to a meeting of the Parents Association, to talk about an open classroom in the public school. Last week it was my turn to go to a meeting of the Parents Association, where we talked about sex education. Marcy went, instead, to the meeting of the Block Committee, to cast our votes vainly against the new sodium-flare lamps.

Rinsler had a show trial in Boston, along with several other celebrated draft-resisters, attracting writers the way sweets attract flies. After two hung juries, he was released, when the Justice Department in an election year decided not to prosecute for a third time. Briefly, he was a folk-hero. Can Grendel be converted into a folk-hero? Obviously, yes. We saw him, on television, before the first trial, trying to levitate the Pentagon. We saw him, after the second trial, from our room in the Conrad Hilton in Chicago, managing not to be clubbed and gassed. Then, no more. He doesn't correspond.

We were invited to Lavonia's college graduation, and didn't go.

Roger Beckwith went to work for Henry Kissinger in Washington. Do the Southeast Asians know they are being gang-banged by games theorists?

The farm—Murdock, Dennison, Short, Staples, tractors, bins—has been leased to an apple imperium. I understand they rely these days on West Indian pickers.

Our last volunteer has departed for Buffalo, to canvass the Democrats. She and her group arrived at midnight on the Wednesday after the California primary, having been airlifted from Los Angeles to Kennedy; we gave them scrambled eggs and sleeping bags. They were nineteen years old, and they had worked in nine primaries. If they bothered to think about their hosts at all—why should they have?—they must have found us amusing, with our peace posters on the wall and our singing whales on the hi-fi, reading our radical magazines in lounge chairs on a sun deck overlooking a landscaped garden the size of a canoe. Would you like a martini?

I am playing with my typewriter, listening to the singing whales, consulting a snifter of brandy, smoking too much, and feeling as though someone had applied a magic scouring pad to my brain pan and scrubbed it clean and cold and blank. It heals, maybe. Only sometimes strangeness has seemed to run me through like a sword. It seems that the music is wrong, the drinks are wrong, the President of the United States never calls the locker room of a *losing* team—why should I consider *my* team to have lost?—and my wife is dying in the garden, under a magnolia bush as implausible as the President of the United States. I have rushed out. She will be weeding, planting, watering, reading. I count the children. I count myself. It doesn't add up. I should have gone with the volunteers. But after having volunteered most of my life, I've decided to stop doing harm. It's not political, it's personal.

In just six weeks, the children will go to New Hampshire, and Marcy and I will sail for France, where the only harm we can possibly do is to ourselves.